Foster ran open the mare's door and demonstrated how to put the nylon strapping in place so the horse was contained but still accessible. "You and the little one stay outside. No going in with the horses, no letting them out, and no feeding them fingers. They're herbivores."

"Got it." Shelby would've saluted the list of orders, but she was too surprised by the gesture. After yesterday, she would've expected scowls and grumbles from him, not access. "Thank you." Impulsively, she reached out and caught his forearm, gave it a squeeze. "I mean it. Seriously. Thank you."

He looked down at where her hand had landed, making her very aware of the solid feel of his muscles, the warmth of his body.

She pulled away and said, "Sorry," just as he said, "You're welcome," so the courtesies got muddled. Outside, a whole bunch of footsteps and voices were suddenly audible, and a chorus of "Rollin', rollin', rollin' . . ." broke out as the dudes migrated out of the dining hall and headed for the barn for their first day of riding.

Flushing, she stepped away. "I should go."

SUMMER *at* MUSTANG RIDGE

JESSE HAYWORTH

A SIGNET ECLIPSE BOOK

SIGNET ECLIPSE
Published by the Penguin Group
Penguin Group (USA) Inc., 375 Hudson Street,
New York, New York 10014, USA

USA | Canada | UK | Ireland | Australia | New Zealand | India | South Africa | China

Penguin Books Ltd., Registered Offices: 80 Strand, London WC2R 0RL,
England
For more information about the Penguin Group visit penguin.com.

First published by Signet Eclipse, an imprint of New American Library,
a division of Penguin Group (USA) Inc.

First Printing, June 2013

SIGNET ECLIPSE and logo are trademarks of Penguin Group (USA) Inc.

ISBN 978-0-451-23982-2

Printed in the United States of America
10   9   8   7   6   5   4   3   2   1

ALWAYS LEARNING   PEARSON

To my angel babies, BB and MR, with love.

Dear Reader,

Once upon a summer I met a handsome cowboy who winked at me and made me laugh, and after a while, made me think "what if?" What if I left my safe, familiar world for his? What would it be like to start over?

In the end I stayed in my life and he stayed in his, and when the summer ended he rode off into the sunset, as guys like him do. Still, I found myself wondering . . . what if? And after a while, I started writing down those questions, and those summertime dreams took on a life of their own, becoming the story of a woman who thinks she has it all figured out and a cowboy whose life doesn't look anything like hers.

Welcome to Mustang Ridge Ranch, and into the lives of the Skye family, their employees, and the guests who come to live out their dreams. Whether they're gathered around the campfire or riding out in search of the herd, the men and women of Mustang Ridge always find their way home. And sometimes they find each other.

I wish the same for you, dear reader, with all my heart. For now, though, I hope you'll turn the page and join Shelby and Foster on the ride of their lives.

Love,
Jesse H.

1

"Okay, no pressure. We're just here to have fun. Ready?" Shelby paused with her hand on a pair of saloon-style swinging doors to grin down at Lizzie, hoping her daughter couldn't see the nerves. "Me, neither, but let's do it anyway."

She pushed through into the dining hall of the ranch, which continued the Western theme from the log-style exterior, complete with rope accents, primitive furniture, and antler chandeliers. Thirty or so men and women wearing crunchy-new denim and unscuffed Western boots milled around long picnic tables with drinks in hand, creating a cocktail party's worth of noise, and a banner over the huge stone fireplace proclaimed HOWDY THERE, FILLIES AND STUDS. WELCOME TO SINGLES WEEK AT MUSTANG RIDGE!

The moment the doors banged shut behind Shelby, a dozen or so pairs of eyes zeroed in and gave her an up-and-down, making her very aware that her black pants, pin-striped jacket, and chunky boots probably said "straight from Boston" more than they did "we're stretchy and comfortable for a long car trip." Then the saloon doors swung again and her daughter came in behind her, and the eyes shifted away.

"Here!" A twenty-something blonde bounced up to them. She was wearing a green polo shirt embroidered with the Mustang Ridge logo on one side and her name—Tipper—on the other. She looked momentarily confused by Lizzie, but then shrugged and thrust two HOWDY, MY NAME IS _____! tags at them, along with a Sharpie. "You guys will want these!"

"But we're not—" Shelby began, but then broke off because Tipper was already bopping over to her next tagless victim, a curvy thirty-something brunette with an elfin haircut. Shrugging, Shelby offered Lizzie the stickers. "You want to fill them out for us? No? Okay, I'll do it." She wrote *Lizzie's mom* on one and *Shelby's kid* on the other, and stuck them in place. "That should take care of it, but stay close to me." Which was a given.

"Hello, ladies," said a voice from behind them, making Shelby do a turn-and-tuck so she was in front of Lizzie.

The guy gained points by holding a soda rather than a beer, but lost them by having added another exclamation point to his name so the tag on his purple rodeo shirt read HOWDY, MY NAME IS BRAD!! Having gotten her attention, he leaned in too close to say, "I've got a confession to make—it's my first time. How about you?" An eyebrow wiggle lost him another point.

Not that Shelby was interested enough to add up the pluses and minuses, but keeping score was an occupational hazard, as was the propensity to turn everything into a slogan. *Tired of being single? Try our new and im-*

proved Brad!! He comes complete with a one-bedroom condo, convertible, and new caps. Ex-wife sold separately.

She gave him a half-watt smile. "I've never been to a dude ranch before, if that's what you're asking. And I'm not really—"

"Everyone?" an amplified voice broke in. "If I could have your attention?" A pretty, late-twenties blonde climbed up on a low stage beneath the banner. She was wearing figure-hugging jeans and worn boots, and holding a wireless microphone that fuzzed out her voice a little. When the hubbub died down, she caroled, "Welcome to Mustang Ridge! We've got an incredible week of riding, roping, and mingling planned for you. First, though, I'd like to start by telling you a little bit about the ranch and how we do things out here in the great state of Wyoming. So please have a seat, any place where there's a booklet, and we'll get started!"

Shelby waited until the others had filtered to their seats, jockeying for primo positions next to their first-choice singles. Then she nodded to an empty table. "Let's sit near the back." Lizzie hesitated and shot a long look out the door, making Shelby grin. "Sorry, kiddo, orientation first. But as soon as we're done in here, I'll take you out to the barn."

It was why they were there, after all.

"Why, hello, aren't you a big one?" a woman's voice purred through the barn. "Then again, I heard that everything's bigger up here in Wyoming."

Foster finished squirting antibiotics into Loco's cracked heel and looked up to find a blonde standing just inside the double doors, with generous curves stacked inside brand-new Wranglers and a snap-studded pink shirt that looked like the top fastener could go at any moment, and might take out an eye when it did. He stifled a sigh—*play nice with the guests, you're part of the local flavor*—and said, "No, ma'am. I believe that's Texas."

He wasn't all that big, either—maybe six feet, one ninety. Nowhere near as massive as his assistant wrangler, Ty, who always looked like something straight out of the pro rodeo tour in fringed chaps, flat-screen-size belt buckle, felt Stetson, and gleaming ostrich boots. Foster, on the other hand, wore his usual "it's my day off" clothes: a battered black felt Stetson, plain T-shirt, faded jeans, and scarred ropers. As local flavor went, he wasn't much. But Ty wasn't there, Foster was, and the blonde was looking to bag a cowboy in her first five minutes off the airport shuttle.

She sidled in, skirted a pile of manure like it was a diamondback, and sashayed over to lean against the wall beside him. Which just went to show that she had zero horse sense, because that put her right in the line of fire if Loco leaped sideways or swung a kick.

Granted, Loco was anything but loco. But still.

She leaned in too close, giving Foster a good look at the local topography—a pair of nicely rounded breasts inside pink lace that would itch like crazy once she was out riding, with all the sweat and dust, and the bouncing around that beginners were prone to. Not that she would take any of the advice she'd be given over the next couple of days about wearing comfortable, low-chafe underclothes as they geared up for longer trail rides. No, she would wear lace top and bottom, and then complain. He'd bet money on it.

"What are you doing?" she asked prettily. "Is he hurt?"

He let Loco's hoof down and shifted the gelding away from her. "It's more preventative maintenance."

"Like a lube job?"

Ohh-kay. "You're going to miss orientation."

"How about you give me a private tour?"

Not even with someone else's privates. "Sorry, ma'am. Ranch policy." Not really, but it was a handy excuse.

Her eyes picked up a gleam. "I wouldn't tell."

"Go on, now, and join the party."

She pouted, but then blew him a kiss and flounced away, ruining her exit—or improving it, depending— by stepping squarely in the manure. She skidded and squeaked, but kept up her sexy wiggle all the way out of the barn.

Moments later, Foster heard a muttered curse and some scuffing noises outside, as she scraped her boots.

Chuckling, he moved around to Loco's other side, ran a hand down the mustang's shoulder, and touched the back of his fetlock. "How's this shoe doing? Sounded to me like it might be coming loose."

And that wasn't the only thing, from the looks of it.

Singles week. *Yeesh.*

After the herd in the dining hall had settled down to more or less pay attention, the blonde with the microphone announced: "My name is Krista Skye, and I'm one of the owners of Mustang Ridge."

Shelby stifled the urge to give her a resounding "Hi, Krista!" and opened the booklet in front of her.

The cover was emblazoned with the Mustang Ridge Dude Ranch logo, and the inner flap bore a glossy photo that she would've thought was Photoshopped if she hadn't seen the view on the drive in. The cloud-studded Wyoming sky was straight out of the *Simpsons* opening credits, the horizon was the poster child for "America the Beautiful"'s purple mountain majesty, sweeping fields ran along the ridgeline, and the ranch itself was nestled in a gentle valley beside a Crayola blue lake.

It was ridiculously gorgeous, assuming you liked the middle of nowhere.

"We're not going to go over everything in the book," Krista said, earning a few cheers from the hopped-up crowd. "Inside it you'll find daily schedules of our main events, along with alternatives if you need a day out of the saddle. The schedules and any updates will be posted here in the dining hall and out by the barn, so the main thing I'd like to go over right now is the rules of the ranch. We try not to go overboard, but you're in the Wild West, folks, and you're going to be dealing with livestock."

A big guy in the front row lifted a longneck in toast. "To fillies and studs!"

That got a sprinkle of laughter and a couple of eye rolls.

Krista grinned but stayed on task. "You've already read and signed the waivers, so you've got some idea of what I mean. We'll go over more safety precautions when we get to the actual riding part of things. For now, I'd appreciate it if you'd all look at page two and read along with me." Point by point, she went down a list of ten dos and don'ts that were mostly common sense, translated into dude-speak.

Don't kick dirt on the cook fire (pick up after yourself).

Don't take seconds until everyone's dished up their firsts (be courteous).

Leave every gate the way you found it (don't mess with the livestock).

Walk the first mile out and the last mile in (treat your horse well and he'll return the favor).

See to your horse before yourself (ditto).

When passing a cowboy, never turn and watch him ride away (trust your wranglers).

There's only one trail boss (follow orders).

When in doubt, tighten your cinch (always triple-check your equipment).

There's no such thing as a stupid question (never be afraid to ask a staff member).

And finally . . . cowboy up and have fun!

Giving Krista points for the presentation, Shelby tapped the page in front of her daughter and said in an undertone, "Read this. Know it. Love it. And I'm going to add number eleven: Don't go near the horses without a grown-up."

Ever since they had firmed up their plans to head west, Lizzie had been poring over her *Bridle Club* books until they were puffed up and practically disintegrating, and their Netflix account had given *My Friend Flicka* a good workout. But that didn't mean she knew what she was doing. Exactly the opposite, in fact, as she hadn't wanted to take lessons at a local riding school before coming out here.

"Basically," Krista continued, "we're asking you to follow the Cowboy Code by respecting your stock, your spread, your tack, and your fellow hands. In return, we'll feed you the best ranch grub you'll ever eat, bar none, and we'll teach you how to ride, rope, cut cattle, and square-dance. And because this is singles week, we'll also have a whole bunch of special getting-to-know-you events."

There was a shuffling in the crowd, and a stage whisper of "I'd like to get to know *you* better" from a woman in the front as she snuggled up next to Brad.

Shelby didn't get it but, hey, to each her own.

Krista continued. "Here in Wyoming, we're proud supporters of female empowerment. Since the eighteen fifties, Mustang Ridge Ranch has been bossed by Skye women four different times, seeing some of its most profitable decades and running thousands of cattle. These days the herds are smaller and our focus has shifted to giving you the best vacation of your lives, but the Skye ladies remain committed to this ranch and the people and animals on it."

She gestured to a nearby hallway, and an older version of her emerged from the shadows and came up to stand on the podium, shooting them a Mona Lisa smile. With fine white hair curled under at her shoulders, wearing jeans and a blue mock turtleneck, she looked to be in her sixties, maybe a bit older. At the sight of her, Shelby sat up a little straighter.

"This is Gran," Krista announced. "She and my grandfather, Big Skye, have been the heart of Mustang Ridge for more than half a century. She'll be cooking us some amazing, stick-to-our-ribs ranch food this week, served family-style, the way it has been for generations. My parents are also integral to the ranch operations, but they're off-property right now. As a proud member of the third generation of the current Skyes, I'm in charge of guest services, and I help with the riding. I'll be hanging out with you guys and making sure you have a fabulous week. Tipper here"—Krista indicated the girl with the "Howdy" stickers—"and her brother, Topper, will be your servers. Mary is our head of housekeeping and Joseph is our head groundskeeper. But if you have any problems with your cabins or whatnot, please don't hesitate to come find me, or leave me a message on the house phone." She paused, then grinned. "Okay, now for the good stuff . . . The riding is managed by our trail boss, Foster, along with his wranglers, Stace, Ty, and Junior. They're some of the best cowboys in the territory, and they're going to put you through paces you didn't even know you had."

"Mmm," said a woman in the front, "cowboys! Love me some cowboys."

The crowd buzz edged up a notch, and Krista held up a hand. "We'll get to the horses tomorrow, bright and early after breakfast. For now, remember how I said we're going to have some extra time to get to know each other and see if we can make some love connections? Well, in the spirit of Wyoming, we're going to have a few rounds of speed dating, ladies' choice. So, ladies, I'd like you to stand on this side of the room. Gentlemen, I'd like you to spread out, two or three to a table."

As the would-be speed daters started shuffling around under Krista's direction and with some nudges from Tipper and Gran, who were making sure nobody got left on the sidelines, Shelby whispered out of the corner of her mouth, "Lucky for us, we're not—" She broke off. "Lizzie?"

The bench beside her was empty.

Shelby's heart went *thudda-thudda* and adrenaline kicked through her in a mom's instinctive fight-not-flight response. But while she would've gone into berserker mode if she'd lost Lizzie back home, here she knew right where to look . . . and it was the most kid-like stunt her daughter had pulled in ages.

Grinning, she slipped out the back and headed for the barn.

2

"Aren't you a big one?" Foster mimicked, grinning as he led Brutus in from the geldings' pen, where a dozen or so mustangs were munching hay and snoozing in the sun.

The chestnut snaked his head around, feinting for a nip.

"Quit that." He nudged the horse out of his space, reminding him how the pecking order went. The mustang had been at the ranch since last fall's gather, and had been under saddle for nearly six months. He'd only been in the working string for a few weeks, though, and was still reserved for the wranglers' use because his better-than-average smarts were paired with an unpredictable streak wider than the stripe running down his nose. He wasn't dangerous, but Foster wouldn't exactly call him reliable yet, either. Given his quick mind, big feet and smooth gaits, though, Foster figured he was worth putting some time into.

Annoyed that his nap had been interrupted, the gelding rolled an eye back at him.

"Yeah, yeah, life's tough. You think this is hard

work, try being a real cow horse. Compared to them, you're just a glorified trail pony."

Then again, what did that make him? Head trail-pony wrangler? Executive greenhorn herder? Overlord of make-sure-the-dudes-don't-kill-themselves?

It made him employed, that was what. And saving for better days.

As his shaggy black-and-white dog, Vader, whuffed and darted into the barn, Foster clucked to Brutus. "Come on there, trail-pony-with-attitude. Let's fix that flat tire of yours and get you back in action."

As they came into early June, they were leaving a wet-dry-wet weather pattern that had turned the horses' hooves brittle, leading to a bonanza of quarter cracks and loose nails. Which meant that Foster—who was the ranch's farrier in addition to lead merry-go-round attendant—was busier on the horses' day off than he was just about any other day of the week.

He'd left Brutus 'til last because the gelding had pulled his shoe clean off yesterday up on the ridgeline and did some serious damage on the ride home, largely because Junior hadn't noticed. The young wrangler had gotten an earful, but it'd be up to Foster to bang a new blank into shape, clean up the hoof, and find some good horn to nail into.

"I'm onto you," Foster said, giving the gelding another nudge as they reached the barn, where the bright sun turned to murky shadows at the doorway and a nervous horse—or one with a questionable sense of humor—could spook. "Don't even think about it. This is supposed to be my day off, and I'm not in the mood to deal with your—"

Movement flashed in his peripheral vision as they stepped from light into dark, and Brutus gave a sudden elephant snort and exploded in a spook that was part pent-up energy, part "aieeeee, mountain lion!" The big gelding's shoes struck sparks on the cement as he tried to wheel and bolt, dragging Foster around with a thousand pounds of momentum and a cement-strong neck. Vader got in front of him and splayed all four feet, barking, trying to head off the runaway.

Foster hauled back on the lead. "Whoa, dang it! And, Vader, git!"

As the dog scurried out the back, Foster caught a flash of brown hair and wide, scared hazel eyes. He had only a split second to realize that the little girl was about to get flattened. Then Brutus swung his haunches around and bumped her hard, and she went flying across the aisle.

She hit the wall and went down in a pink-and-denim heap.

Foster's stomach headed for his boots, but his body kept reacting, using thirty-some years of experience to juggle the gelding away from the kid and down to the other end of the aisle.

"Knock it off!" he growled, getting right up near one of Brutus's white-rimmed eyes. Where normally he would've soothed, now he muscled the blockheaded chestnut under some semblance of control, then kicked open a nearby stall and sent him into it, still wearing his halter. "Don't you dare get tangled in that lead," he ordered, then ran the door shut and latched it tight.

He spun back, expecting to find the little girl still down. She wasn't, though. She was on her feet, plastered in the corner where the tack stall jutted out a few feet into the aisle. Her pink T-shirt and jeans were streaked with dust, her face sheet-white. All arms and legs, with a long torso and those big hazel eyes, she reminded him of a yearling in the middle of a growth spurt, when all the pieces didn't go together quite right.

She hadn't made a sound, wasn't crying now, just stood there, staring at him.

"You okay?" When she didn't say anything, he took a step toward her and reached out a hand. "Are you hurt?"

"*Lizzie!*"

Foster's head whipped around as a dark-haired woman in a ridiculous pantsuit raced into the barn wearing the same sort of look he'd seen before in a half-wild heifer's eyes when he made the mistake of getting between her and her newborn calf. The kind of look that said she didn't care what happened to her or anything around her as long as she got up close and personal with the little one, pronto.

He did what he should've done back then, saving himself a whole bunch of black-and-blues. He got the heck out of the way.

"Are you okay?" Shelby dropped to her knees, hitting so hard that the cement grated through her pants. Not seeing any blood, she whipped a look over her shoulder at the stranger. "What happened?"

"She spooked one of the horses, zigged when she should've zagged, and took a tumble. By the time I got Brutus in a stall, she was up and moving." He was straight out of central casting, filed under "cowboy, circa twenty-first century" in worn jeans, scarred brown boots, and a black felt hat that sat low on his forehead. Compared to the guys in the dining hall, he looked faded and authentic. And concerned. Points there.

Focusing on Lizzie, she brushed at the dirt smudges on her daughter's clothes and tried to remember how to breathe. *She's okay. It's okay.* But it wasn't, not when Lizzie could've gotten seriously hurt because her idiot mother had stopped paying attention for a few minutes. "Why did you leave the dining hall? I *told* you not to go near the horses without a grown-up!"

Lizzie didn't answer, didn't meet her eyes, didn't give her anything to indicate that she'd heard or understood.

"Is she okay?" He sounded dubious. "I don't think she hit her head, but she seems kind of out of it."

Shelby stood and faced him, tucking her daughter behind her. "She's fine."

"Maybe somebody should take a look at her. It's Stace's day off, but Gran has doctored more banged-up riders than your average E.R."

She's seen plenty of doctors. "We don't need anybody, thanks. And thanks for containing the situation." She had some idea of how fast things could get out of control when horses were involved, shuddered to think how much worse it could've been. "I'm very sorry she got underfoot. It won't happen again." She tightened her grip on Lizzie's shoulder. "That's a promise."

"But she's—"

"Perfectly okay just the way she is."

His eyes snapped up to hers, as if she'd just said more than that. "Oh. Sorry. I, ah . . . sorry."

"Don't be. I'm not." *Don't you dare pity us.*

He frowned at her, instead, and then looked at Lizzie. "What is she, seven? Eight? And you brought her to singles week? This isn't going to be our usual family vacation vibe, you know."

It wouldn't have irritated her so much if she hadn't already been thinking the same thing. "She's nine. Not that it matters, because we're not here for guest activities. I'll be working in the kitchen."

"You're . . ." He trailed off.

"The new assistant cook," she filled in.

"What happened to Bertie?"

"The doctor wants her on bed rest until she has her baby." Which was why Shelby and Lizzie had hit the road a week ahead of schedule, arriving in the middle of speed dates rather than next week's family reunion.

"You're a chef?"

"Nope. I'm in advertising, but a friend of mine knows Krista and the ranch. When she found out I wanted to get Lizzie away from the city for the summer, she set things up. The next thing I knew, I had a summer job and a place for us to stay." It was such a simple summary for what had been, in reality, a really tough choice involving dire warnings from both her boss and Lizzie's doctor, and the inner fear that they'd go into fall with Lizzie no better and Shelby's clients having forgotten who she was. In her line of work, you were only as good as your last campaign.

"A summer job." His face was deadpan.

"Yep. Now through Labor Day. Three months, give or take." She tipped her head. "Problem?"

He gave her an up-and-down just like the guys in the dining hall, only he didn't look nearly so appreciative of her round-toed shoes and clingy pants. "Nope. No problem at all. What Krista does up at the main house is her business. What happens in the barn is mine."

Shelby wasn't sure which annoyed her more, the way he'd zeroed right in on Lizzie's issues, the implication that she wouldn't be able to handle herself as a ranch cook . . . or how she was way too sensitive on both fronts.

Refusing to dwell on it—or on him—she snagged Lizzie around the neck in a fake choke hold they'd gotten from watching too much TV wrestling for a pitch that hadn't gone anywhere—*Women's Xtreme Wrestling. Fight like a girl!*—and tugged her toward the door. "Come on, kiddo, it's back to orientation for us. And consider yourself lucky if I don't tattoo a couple of those rules on the insides of your eyelids."

Foster watched them leave, telling himself it was because he wanted to be sure the little girl was moving okay. He wasn't sure whether she'd been shell-shocked or what, but it seemed that her mother had it covered. Still, he'd had a fall or two that he'd walked away from, only to feel it later.

"Kid's fine," he muttered, and it didn't take Brutus's snort to tell him that his eyes had wandered. Okay, so little Lizzie's mama had a fine rear view, with nice curves and a feminine wiggle. And the front view was just as good, all sleek and pretty.

So, that was Bertie's fill-in? Huh. Wouldn't have been his choice . . . but then again, it wasn't his choice, was it? And while Krista was whip smart, she had a soft heart and a penchant for good deeds. He should know; he'd been one of them a few years back. He only hoped she didn't get burned by this one.

"Ah, well. Not my problem." Besides, Gran might be a little nutty around the edges, but she was plenty sharp when it came to her kitchen, and she had Tipper, Topper, and Krista to back her up. They'd be okay, even if Ms. Fancy Pants flaked on them.

Whistling softly, he bent to pick up Brutus's chipped foot, determined to enjoy the rest of his so-called day off. Because starting tomorrow, he'd spend the next six days being the cowboy the guests wanted to see, the wrangler they'd ooh and aah over, the horseman they needed to have making sure they didn't kill themselves or any innocent bystanders. They would ride, laugh, drink, dance, pair off—some of them two or three times—and have a good time, thinking they were living the Wild West experience, when really they were getting the Disney version. In this case, the R-rated version. And then next week, Mustang Ridge would do it

all over again, starting fresh with a whole new cast of
characters and a different theme.

Rinse, repeat, and be grateful for the work, he thought,
casting another glance away from the barn. He wasn't
looking after the new assistant cook and her daughter,
though. No, this time his eyes went past them to the
horizon as he reminded himself that fancy females
were a distraction he couldn't afford when he had
plans of his own.

Shelby stuck her head through the dining hall doors
and winced. "Oops. Looks like we missed the rest of
orientation."

The cocktail party was back in full swing. Most of
the singles were clumped together in groups, with one
or two main players talking with wide gestures and
animated features while the others orbited like elec-
trons. A few pairs were hunkered together, heads close
in earnest conversation, and an intense foursome
looked headed for disaster, with a dark-haired guy trying to get the attention of a brunette, who was clearly
more interested in the salt-and-pepper gentleman next
to her, even though he was deep in conversation with
a strawberry blonde.

And so it goes.

Grateful not to be part of that particular dance,
Shelby started to back out, but then heard someone call
her name. The crowd eddied and Krista emerged, hands
outstretched. "You made it. I'm so glad you're here!"

"I'm, um . . . thanks?" Reminding herself she wasn't
on the East Coast anymore—the land of avoiding eye

contact in public—Shelby accepted a hug from a woman she knew only from Gertie's description, one phone call and a couple of e-mails. But that seemed to be enough for the owner of Mustang Ridge, who seemed like she hadn't ever met a stranger in her life.

Then again, that was probably a requirement in the business.

Up close, Krista was a thoroughly natural beauty, from the tips of her boots to her casual ponytail and makeup-free face. Shelby—a brunette whose lighter-toned eyebrows and lashes disappeared if left to their own devices—envied her the ability to pull it off.

With a Gwyneth Paltrow smile that lit her whole face, Krista looked down. "And this must be Miss Lizzie! Are you ready for an adventure?"

"She already had one," Shelby said drily, figuring it'd be better to fess up now than have it get back to the boss later.

"Uh-oh. That sounds ominous."

"Lizzie here snuck out of orientation and headed for the barn, where she spooked one of the horses and nearly got trampled."

"*What?*"

"She's fine," Shelby said quickly, "and so is the horse. Lucky for her, one of your men was there to do damage control." At Krista's raised eyebrow, she elaborated, "Jeans, T-shirt, black hat, and a scowl?"

"That's our trail boss, Foster." She grinned. "Did he give you the old 'barn's closed, get out of my space, it's my day off' routine?"

"That was the vibe, though he was pretty decent

given that he'd just had to pull my kid out from underneath one of his horses." Even saying it brought a shudder.

"Don't let him fool you. He keeps to himself, but he's a total sweetie once you get to know him."

Shelby wasn't sure that would ever be a word she'd use to describe the cowboy. The lines in his face had been set in a frown, his eyes cool. And there had been something about him. "I think I'll go with 'no comment' on that one."

"I knew I was going to like you. Come on. Let's go get you two settled into your cabin."

"I don't want to interrupt—"

"Please, interrupt. I'm begging you."

Shelby glanced back at the party. "Well, if you put it that way."

"Don't get me wrong—I love meeting all the new people on changeover day and making sure we get off to a great start. But this is different. You guys are here for the whole summer! I'm so happy to have you here. I'm a twin, did I tell you that? My sister, Jenny, is a videographer, and she's always off on all these cool assignments, which means I never get to see her anymore, not really." She slid Shelby a sidelong look. "No pressure intended."

"None taken." And no promises, either. But although Krista was proving to be something of a whirlwind, she was a happy one, bright and bubbling, like a soda fountain rather than a geyser.

"Do you have brothers and sisters?" she asked as she bopped them out the door and down a wide gravel path.

"A sister," Shelby said. "We don't speak anymore."

"I'm sorry."

I'm not. But in a way she was. Not that she and Mercy had stopped even pretending to have anything to say to each other, but that Lizzie had wound up with such a crappy extended family. "Life happens."

"That it does, leaving us to make the best of it." Krista linked an arm through hers, and tugged. "Speaking of which, let's check out your new digs!" She led the way along a gravel path that wound around the other side of the dining hall.

Now that she wasn't rushing to make it in time for orientation, Shelby could look around the ranch a little. She decided quickly that she liked what she saw, though she couldn't deny the sense of "we're not in Boston anymore, Toto."

The main house was a sprawling gray two-story structure with breezeways connecting it to the dining hall and another large wing, making it look like it had outgrown itself and octopused to the other spaces. Beyond it, the huge barn and several smaller shelters were all interconnected with a network of pipe corrals and split-rail fencing, where plump horses and pointy-hipped cattle munched from round bales and dozed in the sun. It would've looked like something out of *Blazing Saddles*, except that glossed atop the Old West was a newer, resort-type layer in the single-story log cabins that sat in clusters, maybe twenty or so of them marching down to the lake. At the shore, rowboats were tied to an L-shaped dock, a wooden pavilion held a dozen picnic tables and a huge fire pit, and an open area nearby was home to a herd of sawhorses wearing plastic cow heads for roping practice.

"Gorgeous, isn't it?" Krista said softly. "I always hated leaving, and loved coming home."

"Then why leave?"

"College. Growing-up time, that sort of thing."

"Ah. I'm familiar with the concept." Though in her case it had been a relief to leave, and she hadn't loved coming home.

Krista nodded. "Four years for a bachelor's and another two working at a chain hotel, because I'd seen the writing on the wall."

"That your family would have to turn this place into a dude ranch?"

"That we would have to do *something* if we wanted to survive." Her smile faded a little. "It wasn't a unanimous decision, by a long shot . . . but this is looking like our best summer yet, we're that busy. Too busy, in fact, for Gran to handle the kitchen on her own, which is another reason I'm psyched that you're here. I was just getting ready to start advertising for a fill-in cook when Gertie called me, and you know what they say!"

"Any port in a storm?"

"I was thinking of 'it was meant to be.'"

"Sorry. New Englanders are born pessimists."

"Bummer."

"Exactly." They shared a laugh.

"Well, we'll see if we can't turn that around in the next few months. Come on!" Krista led them past several clusters of pretty log cabins near the blue, blue lake, to another, slightly larger cabin at the far end of things.

When Shelby realized that was their destination, her footsteps faltered. "You're kidding me."

The cabin was like something out of a fairy tale, a little log playhouse down by the picturesque lake, with white curtains and purple flowers in the window boxes. It was the kind of scene she would've paid a photographer to capture and touch up so she could use it to promote something completely unrelated. Like mouthwash. *It leaves you feeling fresher than a summer breeze in the high country.*

Only this wasn't a picture or an ad campaign; it was the real deal. It couldn't be theirs. Could it?

"Of course I'm not kidding." Krista took the steps two at a time and opened the door.

Shaking her head, Shelby followed, with Lizzie right on her heels.

The inside of the cabin matched the rustic charm of the outside, with exposed logs and rough-hewn furniture that was finished with a smooth, splinter-free gloss. The single big room held two beds at one end, a double and a trundle, both covered with white-and-blue patchwork quilts done in a wedding-ring pattern. At the other end there was a love seat, a coffee table, and a bookcase that held a few paperbacks, along with a dorm-size microwave and fridge. A doorway led to a large bathroom and on the walls, framed photographs that looked like originals taken around the ranch—maybe done by Krista's twin?—were set opposite wide windows that looked out on a killer view of the blue lake, green fields, and whitecapped purple mountains.

Shelby stood there for a moment, trying not to gape.

Stomach knotting, she said, "I was expecting . . . I don't know. A tent or something."

"You don't like it?"

"Duh. But this place must rent for a fortune!"

Krista shrugged. "Only a small one."

"I can't possibly be working off this plus riding lessons—slash–day care for Lizzie."

"Close enough."

Shelby thought fast, tallying her summer budget against what it was costing to keep their apartment back home. "I can add some cash on top."

"Only if you want the tent, instead." Krista paused, expression softening. "Don't stress about it, please, Shelby. I'm happy with the arrangement if you are. To be honest, Gertie called right after I exhausted the local options for a fill-in cook. You have experience in a hotel kitchen, even if it was a while ago . . . and when I talked to you, I liked your vibe."

"Not to mention that I blathered at you." She had started the conversation determined to be professional, but had somehow wound up telling Krista about Lizzie, the therapists, and needing to get away. The knowledge made the churn in her belly worse.

"I didn't hear any blathering. I heard a mom who had done everything she could with the resources at hand, and was looking for some new ones. More, I heard about a family that needed someplace soft to land for a little while."

"So Lizzie and I are rescues?" It came out sharp, but that's how Shelby was feeling all of a sudden.

Krista shook her head. "I'm just offering you some

time away from real life . . . and getting my kitchen covered and helping out my gran in the process."

Dial it down, Shelby told herself. *None of this is her fault.* It wasn't anybody's really. Life happened, you took the knocks, and you moved on. She closed her eyes, forced herself to exhale. "I'm sorry. I don't mean to be a snot. I'm grateful, really."

"And you're road-lagged, worn out, and embarrassed that Lizzie pulled a disappearing act and ended up under one of the horses." Krista squeezed her arm. "You should see Jenny when she comes in off a long trip, or me after a tough group of guests leaves. You haven't even begun to scratch the surface of snotty."

Suddenly feeling every one of those miles—and the months leading up to the trip—Shelby exhaled. "Thanks. I . . . well, thanks. For everything. Seriously."

"You're welcome, and again, I'm very glad you're here. Both of you. Now get some rest, okay? I wish I could give you a few days to settle in, but Gran could use you bright and early tomorrow."

"I can pitch in tonight, if that'd help," Shelby offered, hoping she'd say no.

Krista's grin said she knew it. "No way—that'd be too cruel and unusual. Tomorrow morning, four o'clock, be there or be square. In the meantime, I'll have Tipper bring you guys some grub, picnic-style."

Which made Shelby feel even worse—about being tired, being snappish, losing her kid, not being sure this was such a good idea in the first place . . . "Don't put anybody out on our account. Please. I think we'll just grab our luggage out of the car, finish off our road food, and call it a night."

Krista hesitated, then nodded. "If that's what you want . . . but please remember that nobody here is keeping score. We're happy to have you."

But why? Shelby thought. She was trying not to be all New England, look-a-gift-horse-in-the-mouth about it, but in her experience, nothing came easy. When it did, there was usually a catch, or something just waiting to go wrong. The beds looked really soft, though, and home was a long way away. So she dredged up a smile. "Don't speak too soon . . . you haven't tasted my cooking yet."

3

A-tisket, a-tasket, a biscuit in your basket!

Shelby's alarm went off before dawn, and she lay there for a minute, disoriented by the quiet and the clean, fresh air that said she wasn't in their condo or a highway hotel.

Where am I? She was so fuzzy-headed that she almost followed it up with *Never mind that, who am I?* But Lizzie's breathing came from the other side of the room, reassuringly deep and regular, bringing things back into line. *We're at Mustang Ridge. We made it.* Shelby smiled into the darkness, a little ruefully as she realized she must've been tireder than she thought yesterday, to have snapped at her new boss. Granted, the snipe had been pretty low on a scale of one to bitchy, but still. *Oops.*

A night's sleep had done her good, though. It would take some time for her to get all the way used to the time difference and altitude, but she was up and moving, and ready to get started earning her and Lizzie's keep. Grabbing the small flashlight she'd left on the nightstand, she picked her way over to the dresser, where she pulled on her second-favorite pair of black pants, along with one of the logo'd polo shirts Krista had sent over, and a matching fleece jacket. Even in early June, the mountaintops wore snow and the pre-dawn air had a bite.

She found paper and a pen in the nightstand, and left a quick note: *Come find me in the kitchen when you're up, or else hang here until I get back. And don't forget Rule Eleven.*

Between the horses and the singles, she figured it'd be best to keep a close eye on Lizzie, though it wasn't like that was much of a chore. A glance at her phone showed that the booster was picking up the signal from the TinyGPS Tracker that Lizzie wore on her wrist, even though there wasn't much cell signal up here. It'd be enough, though. Besides, Lizzie tended to find a safe, quiet place to hole up with her iPad or phone to play games, read, or watch movies, always with the volume off or her earphones in. And after yesterday, Shelby wasn't too worried about her wandering again, at least not right away.

Pausing by the bed, she tugged up the quilt, tucked Mr. Pony closer to her daughter's cheek, and then dropped a kiss on her soft brow, whispering, "I love you, Dizzy Girl."

She inhaled the sweet scent of her kiddo, grateful that they were here, that they had survived the drive, the first day, all of it. And most of all that they were together. *We can do this,* she told herself, and headed off on a short hike of a commute that wasn't anything like her usual two-trains-and-a-smelly-bus routine.

Outside, the morning was cool, crisp, and sharp, and when she breathed in, the air filled her lungs with the scents of horses, grass, and open spaces. A few nerves prickled to life as she followed the pathway that led from the cabins up to the main house, which was a huge black shadow partway illuminated by the porch lamps and the light coming through the kitchen windows. *You can handle this, no sweat.* So what if she'd spent most of the past decade hyping ingredients rather than using them? Once upon a time she'd been a half-decent prep cook. It'd be like riding a bicycle— or, yanno, sex—the kind of thing a girl never forgets how to do.

She hoped.

Her boots thudded hollowly on the porch and the screen door squeaked like something out of a horror movie. The whole effect was creepyish, to the point that she expected to hear a wolf howl in the background. The minute she opened the heavier storm door and warm air spilled out, though, she stopped dead and inhaled a lungful that really should've come with a calorie count. *Hel-lo, come to Mama.*

The sweetness of brown sugar was overlain by the sharper smells of apples and cinnamon, in scent tendrils that practically wrapped around and pulled her through the door. She stepped into an open main room decorated in rustics and taxidermy, with a few color pops in pillows and curtains that added a feminine touch. At one end, couches and comfy chairs were clustered around a fireplace, with a flat-screen above. At the other end, a long dining table had a dozen chairs around it and a pretty flower arrangement in its center. In the middle, near where Shelby had come in, a reception desk held a computer station, a house phone, and a PRESS "1" FOR SERVICE sign on it.

It was a strange mix of home and hotel, but she thought it worked. More, she thought she could do something with it—something more than the bland *Your pleasure is our business*–style promos they were currently using.

"Which, come to think, might be a good way to pay Krista back," she mused, then filed the idea for future reference. She would need to get to know the place a little first, figure out what made it tick, what made it special compared to every other dude ranch with a pretty view and theme weeks.

And she was stalling, just a little.

Taking a deep breath of yummy air, she followed her nose by hanging a left past the reception desk and heading down a short hallway that had windows on one side and more gorgeous local photos on the other. At the end, she paused briefly and took a look at what would be, at least for the next few months, her home away from home. And she thought, *Oh, yeah.*

The kitchen was a long, relatively narrow room, where exposed beams and rustic finishes somehow managed not to clash with high-end commercial appliances and a long counter that was half stainless steel and half butcher block. Big mixers and processors sat in rows along the counter, and shiny chrome racks held bowls, dry goods, and smaller gadgets. Bunches of herbs and garlic hung from the rafters; a trio of doors led to a cold room, a walk-in freezer, and a pantry; and a wide arch opened into the hallway that led to the dining hall. The opposite wall held big double ovens, a commercial cooktop, and three big refrigerators. Two of the ovens had timers that were counting down, while dozens of perfectly browned muffins sat in cooling in racks near the stoves. And they smelled freaking awesome.

Krista's grandmother stood in front of one of the stoves, wearing a frilly blue apron over her jeans and mock turtle, and watching the numbers count down.

Shelby stepped into the kitchen. "Good morning, Mrs. Skye. I'm—"

"Shelby." She turned and smiled. "But you'll call me Gran. Everyone does." She glanced up the hallway, eyes twinkling. "You lose the little one again?"

Apparently, word traveled. "She's still in bed. She might come find me when she's up, if that's okay?"

"Of course. Or you're welcome to go fetch her."

"I don't want to take time away—"

"Poosh." Gran waved that off. "Kids take the time they take, and everyone else works around it, right? We all pitch in for each other here, because that's what family does."

Shelby exhaled. "That's not exactly how my family worked, but I get your point." And she was grateful for it. "Where do you want me to start?"

"Are you hungry?"

"Starving, but I can nibble and work."

That earned her an approving nod. "Then let's introduce you to Herman Skye."

Shelby looked around. "Is that your husband?" Yesterday she'd gotten the impression that it was just Krista and Gran running the ranch.

"Heavens, no. Arthur is off riding the fence line, probably won't be back until sundown." Gran went to the counter beside one of the big stoves, retrieved a big blue-and-white earthenware bowl covered with a red checkerboard kitchen towel, and carried it across to set it on the main counter. She paused for a second, as if waiting for a fanfare, and then whipped off the towel with a flourish. "Herman, I'd like you to meet Shelby. She's going to be helping out in the kitchen while Bertie is off having her baby. Shelby, this is Herman Skye."

The bowl contained an amorphous ball of beige dough that was about the size of Shelby's head, and smelled faintly of beer.

Staring down at it, she thought, *It is way too early for this.*

She was being *Punk'd*, right? There was a camera somewhere, watching to see how she handled it when her new boss formally introduced her to a blob of bread-to-be. "Um . . . hi, Herman. It's, uh, nice to meet you?"

"He's a valued member of the family." Gran gave the bowl a fond pat that jiggled the dough a little, then grinned. "Let me guess. You've never met a sourdough starter before?"

Is that what it is? "I've made sourdough a few times. Flour, water, a couple of those yellow yeast packets—"

The older woman covered the dough with both hands, as if blocking its nonexistent ears. "Herman, don't listen to her. It's not true!"

"Um."

"No Cookie would ever be caught dead with freeze-dried yeast. A good sourdough starter is the hallmark of a great ranch. Why, back in the day, during roundups the Cookie would sleep with his starter right there in his bedroll, making sure it didn't get too cold."

"He slept with his dough," Shelby repeated, resisting the urge to look for the hidden cameras.

"Not dough. *Starter*." Gran scooped up the air and breathed it in. "It's a living yeast culture. Every time I use part of Herman to bake with, I feed back the same amount of flour, water, and a few special ingredients to keep the culture alive." She bustled into the pantry, returning a moment later with a fat biscuit in one palm and a manic gleam in her eyes. She held it out. "Here. Taste this."

Shelby took the biscuit, which was admittedly a good-looking specimen, generously rounded on the bottom, rising through dozens of flaky layers to a slightly lopsided top. It was browned top and bottom, and the buttery smell made her mouth water. So she took a bite.

As she chewed, Gran enthused, "Herman has been alive for more than two hundred years, ever since Jonah Skye won his first five hundred head in a poker game, cashed in his gold to buy Mustang Ridge, and settled here with his wife, Mary. She started Herman with some yeast, flour, water, and a few potatoes, and he's been an important part of our kitchens ever since."

Shelby wasn't sure she wanted to know that any part

of her breakfast predated the Civil War. As biscuits went, though, it was good—fluffy, flaky, melt-in-her-mouth good. Amazingly, delectably good. So good that she was on the verge of a jingle, or at least a good tag line. *Starter Wars: a rebel alliance against little yellow packets!*

Okay, maybe not. And maybe the slogans were a knee-jerk response whenever she was out of her comfort zone. But how could she take this seriously?

"Well?" Gran demanded, eyes alight with biscuit fever.

"Best I've ever had." The cook might be whacked, but the biscuit was awesome.

"I *told* you! And that's a day-old Herman. Wait until you taste him fresh out of the oven!" She slipped a worn index card from the breast pocket of her apron and set it on the counter. "A triple batch should give us enough for lunch sandwiches and dinner rolls."

Okay, Shelby thought. This was something tangible she could work with. Snagging the card, she scanned the recipe, which was written in faded blue ink, with notes added in different colors and handwritings. She tried to imagine her newer-is-better sister keeping a family recipe like this, and failed. Her mother might have kept it, but she would've transferred the information to her computer, laminated a printout, and filed it in a color-coded plastic box.

"Here." A blue-and-white plate appeared at Shelby's elbow, holding a perfectly symmetrical muffin that still had a little curl of steam coming from its top. "Try this one."

Shelby still had most of a biscuit left, but she set it on

the edge of the plate and picked up the fat, perky apple-cinnamon muffin. After drinking in the scent, which would've been worth a fortune if they could've bottled it, she took a bite, savoring the sweet, buttery dough and plump raisins and doing her best to ignore her inner carb counter's gleeful *ka-ching, ka-ching, ka-ching!* "Mmm. This is amazing. You're a genius."

Gran's nod was smug. "Not me. Herman."

"This is sourdough? Get out."

"There's a dash of Herman in just about everything we make here. All the way from the salads and coleslaw to the batter for the chicken-fried steaks."

That struck Shelby as vaguely unsettling, but who was she to judge? It worked for them, and she was beginning to believe Krista's claim that Mustang Ridge served some of the best ranch fare in the territory. If this was the kind of quality the kitchen put out across the board, it would outperform many of her favorites back in Boston. Ranch-style, granted, but still.

She lifted her muffin. "Three cheers for Herman."

"Yes, indeed! Anyway, welcome to the kitchen. Fruits and veggies are in the walk-in, dairy's in the first fridge, and the rest is pretty well labeled. You should be able to find your way around. The last batch of muffins'll be out in a minute, and then we'll reset for bread."

Feeling like she had just passed a test of some sort— the Herman acceptance quota?—Shelby said, "I can see I'm going to have to get up before the roosters if I'm going to be useful."

"Poosh. I'm an early riser, that's all. There's plenty

for you to do, believe me. Bertie didn't usually get in until at least five thirty, so if you want an extra hour or so—"

"Nope. This is good." Shelby held up the card. "Want me to make some Hermans? It'll probably only take me twice as long as it would for you to do it."

Gran grinned. "I'll time you."

"But no pressure." Shelby returned the smile, starting to think that maybe this wasn't as weird as it had seemed at first. Eccentric, maybe, but not all the way over-the-top.

"Exactly." Gran bustled away, calling over her shoulder, "Give me a holler if you get stuck."

"Will do."

They worked together companionably for the next couple of hours, putting up not just a triple batch of Hermans, but also corn bread and chocolate chip cookies for later.

Once the baking was doing its thing in the ovens and cooling racks, they started two big slabs of pork slow-cooking in a broth that would later become green chili made from an old family recipe, and then tossed thick slabs of locally cured bacon and fat homemade sausage links on the wide commercial griddle. Shelby had a strong suspicion that Gran would've finished sooner on her own, but by the time Tipper and Topper—a darker-haired, slighter version of his big sister—arrived to wait tables and guests started appearing in the dining hall, the sideboards were loaded with a breakfast buffet that would've seemed like death-by-cholesterol back home, but fit right in with the mountain air and the thumps of Western boots on the bare floorboards.

Some of the guests dragged in solo and caffeine-starved, while others clumped together, talking animatedly. Shelby couldn't tell if they were continuing conversations from the day before, or if some of the couples had gone for the "early and often" theory of dating. *More power to them*, she thought. She might lean toward the "late and never" side of things, but that didn't mean she begrudged anyone else. If things had been different . . . but they weren't, and she was making things work for her and Lizzie. And that was what mattered most.

As the singles lined up and started digging into the heaps of food, Gran handed her a covered basket. "Some goodies for the little one. You're on break while the meat simmers. Be back around ten and we'll get the peppers roasted and skinned for the chili, and then pull together a simple cold lunch."

"Are you sure? I could stay and—"

"I'm sure." The older woman nudged her toward the door. "Trust me, you'll do more than a full day's work here. It's just broken up into chunks. Which means you should take your downtime when you can get it. Like now."

"But—"

Gran flipped a dish towel at her. "Shoo!"

Shelby shooed, grinning as she jogged down the steps.

"Morning!" Krista called from the gravel pathway. She was wearing the jeans and logo shirt that was apparently the ranch's working uniform, with the addition of a straw hat with a perky, flipped-up brim and a turquoise band. "How'd you sleep?"

"Don't remember. I slept through it."

"Ha-ha. Lizzie settle in okay?"

"Seems like it. I'm headed back to check on her now."

"Everything go okay with Gran this morning?"

"From my perspective, at least. I'm not sure how helpful I really was today, but I'll work on getting my speed up." Shelby paused. "Um, I met Herman."

"Oh?" Krista deadpanned it for a three-count, then chuckled. "I'm kidding. Don't worry about the Herman thing. It started as a way for her to mess with my mom—the two of them do *not* get along when it comes to sharing a kitchen—and it turned into a running joke that survived after my mom and dad bought an RV and took off for a grand tour a few years ago."

"So your gran doesn't really think her yeast culture is a member of the family?"

"He might as well be, after two hundred some–odd years. And did you taste him?"

Shelby wasn't sure she wanted to admit having tasted anything that went by "him," but she nodded. "Wicked awesome, as we say back in Boston."

"There you have it." Krista glanced at the basket. "Bringing some tidbits back to the nest?"

"Yeah. I can already tell I'm going to have to pimp the fruits and veggies, or we're both going to be rolling out of here like beach balls come September."

"Between the kitchen and the horses, I'm sure you'll

sweat it off. Speaking of which, I told Stace you'd stop by the barn this morning and talk about a plan for Lizzie."

Shelby hesitated. "I feel like I'm taking advantage—"

"Don't," Krista said firmly. "A deal's a deal, and our deal included guest privileges and riding lessons for your kiddo." She paused tellingly. "That was the point, wasn't it? To get her around the animals, let her relax, and see what happens?"

"Yes, but . . ." Shelby shook her head with a little laugh. "Why am I arguing?"

"Pride?"

"Something like that."

"So be proud of what you're doing for your daughter." Just like her grandmother had done a moment earlier, Krista made flapping motions. "Shoo! Go grab Stace before breakfast lets out, the guests stampede for the barn, and things get crazy in there."

"Okay, okay. I'm going!"

But when Shelby got to the barn, the only ones home were the horses.

The main barn consisted of two rows of stalls separated by a cement aisle, with rolling double doors at either end and a peaked roof made of corrugated plastic that provided shade but let some of the light through. The sweet smell of hay and fresh shavings had an undertone of ammonia and manure, reminding Shelby of the two years of riding lessons she'd had as a kid—a guilt present from her father and a bone of contention with her mother, who had hated all the dirt and hair.

Surprised to feel an echo of pleasure at the memory of those long-ago lessons, which had been a merry-go-round of fat ponies and instructors chanting, "Up-down-up-down," Shelby stepped into the cool interior. "Hello? Stace? Anyone?"

There wasn't any answer except for a whinny coming from a horse about halfway down the aisle. Shelby peeked into the stall, which held a pretty chestnut mare with a splotchy, heart-shaped star on her forehead, and an enormous belly. The nameplate on the door had her name spelled out in glued-on rope: SASSY.

"Hey, Sassy. Is that a baby in there, or are you just pudgy?" Shelby asked.

The mare pricked her ears and gave a hopeful *ho-ho-ho*.

"Sorry, girl, I don't have anything for you. I don't know if Hermuffins are safe for you to eat." Although technically they were mostly sugar and grain . . . and for all she knew, the Skyes had been mixing sourdough into their horses' rations for the past ten generations.

Sassy poked her head between the bars, and Shelby reached to stroke the soft nose, enjoying the tickle of whiskers, which was a new sensation. The barn she'd ridden at had kept the horses' muzzles clipped to smooth velvet, their manes pulled to perfect four-finger neatness, and their bridle paths and legs trimmed and sleek. "Guess I'm not in New England anymore, huh?"

The mare blew softly, as if in agreement, but then flattened her ears, backed away, and snapped around at one of her wide-load sides.

"I know, it sucks toward the end, doesn't it? Those

last few weeks, you don't know whether you want to be alone or not, don't know if you're hot or cold, hungry or pukey, happy or sad. And you don't even have a guy around to rub your feet and tell you it's all going to be okay." Which Patrick had done like a champ. It wasn't until later that things had gone south. Still, she smiled a little. "Trust me, it's totally worth all the pain and aggravation. And once you've brought your little one into the world, there isn't anything you wouldn't do to keep her safe."

A boot scuffed behind Shelby, and the mare's ears pricked. Blushing a little at having been caught deep in conversation with a horse—though as far as she was concerned, it was way better than talking to bread dough—she turned. "Stace? Oh. It's you."

Yesterday's cowboy stood a few feet away. Except unlike the day before when she'd been focused on Lizzie, now she saw only him. And, hello, how had she missed the fact that he was gorgeous?

He was wearing upgrades from the previous day's outfit—newer jeans, oiled boots, and a snap-studded shirt, and looked alike he could've stepped out of *The Horse Whisperer*, which was one of her own Netflix guilty pleasures. He was younger and taller than Redford, his face smoother, his hair darker, his jaw squarer, his hazel eyes more intense, but he had that same way of standing very still, very focused. A mid-thirties Ben Affleck does *Horse Whisperer II*, maybe. His shirt was tucked in, his jeans worn on their inner seams, no doubt where the saddle leather rubbed.

It took effort, but she pulled her eyes from the spot,

suddenly realizing that the whole singles week thing must've gone to her head. Because she wasn't the kind of girl to get dry-mouthed.

Blaming it on the pheromones, she cleared her throat. "You're Foster."

"And you're Shelby." He patted his chest. "Name tag."

She glanced down, then realized he was talking about yesterday. "Um, yeah. Right." Seeing his eyes go to the basket, she held it out. "Want a Hermuffin?"

"Ah. I see you've been assimilated."

She raised an eyebrow. "By the Biscuit Borg?" She took out a muffin, and darned if she didn't see a face in the raisins. "No, I think it's more overtly menacing than that. This is the Herminator. Only instead of 'I'll be back,' he says, 'You're toast.'"

She thought that one was pretty good, but he just gave her a level look. "Your Arnold impression needs some work."

Okay, maybe he hadn't been making a Trekkie joke, after all. At least he'd seen *Terminator*. "I'll put it on the list."

"You do that." He glanced at his watch. "Things are about to get busy in here, and I'm going to need Stace. I'll tell her you came by to . . . ?"

"Talk about Lizzie's lessons," she filled in.

"Sorry. We don't give private lessons."

"You do now. At least Stace does. Krista and my friend Gertie set it up."

That got his attention. "Gertie Roffler? The therapist?"

Shelby winced. Of course he knew Gertie, who stayed there every summer, and was talking to Krista about putting together a weeklong program for troubled teens. Which meant that he was undoubtedly doing the one-plus-one thing and connecting that to Stace being halfway through her certification as a therapeutic riding instructor, and Lizzie's odd behavior—at least it was odd to anyone who didn't know her—the day before.

Lizzie's condition wasn't supposed to be a secret; it was just that Shelby had gotten so used to not talking about it with her around, not wanting to reinforce the anxiety cycle. But Lizzie wasn't here, and it was probably better to get the story spread around now rather than later. "She has what's called 'selective mutism' or 'SM' for short. It's an extreme form of shyness, more or less."

His eyebrows climbed. "She can't talk?"

"She can." At least she used to. "For most kids, SM means they only talk to certain people under certain circumstances, like to their parents or siblings at home, but they freeze up with other people and in other places."

"But not for her?"

"She doesn't talk at all." It still brought an ache to say, even after all this time. And it still made her feel like a failure, even though it really shouldn't.

"Selective mutism," he repeated, frowning.

"It's not a very good name," she said, trying not to get all prickly over it. "That makes it sound like she's choosing not to speak when, really, she can't. She wants to—wouldn't you?—but the harder she tries, the more she locks up." She braced herself for awkward pity or, worse, the look that said, *Did something bad happen to her?*

But Foster just thought for a moment, then nodded slowly and tipped his head toward Sassy's stall. "You have any experience with them?"

"With . . . oh, the horses? Some. I took lessons for a couple of years as a kid."

"So you know enough not to feed them people food or get stepped on?"

Okay, so that was a "no" on the muffins. "Um. Yes to the first, and I can only do my best on the second." Where was this going?

"Sassy's getting close to her due date, so she'll be in either her stall or the attached run-in twenty-four-seven. Peppermint here"—he pointed across the aisle to a stall that on first glance looked empty, but on a second look proved to have a pair of furry ears just visible over the four-foot wall—"is too small for singles week—lucky him—so he'll be here during the day, too. Feel free to bring Lizzie in when things die down, and introduce her."

"Wow. Thanks. That's really—"

"Not a problem. Hook up the web stall guard." He ran open Sassy's door and demonstrated how to put the nylon strapping in place so the horse was contained but still accessible. "And you and the little one stay outside. No going in with the horses, no letting them out, and no feeding them fingers. They're herbivores."

"Got it." She would've saluted the list of orders, but

she was too surprised by the gesture. After yesterday, she would've expected scowls and grumbles from him, not access. "Thank you." Impulsively, she reached out and caught his forearm, gave it a squeeze. "I mean it. Seriously. Thank you."

He looked down at where her hand had landed, making her very aware of the solid feel of his muscles, the warmth of his body.

She pulled away and said, "Sorry," just as he said, "You're welcome," so the courtesies got muddled. Outside, a whole bunch of footsteps and voices were suddenly audible, and a chorus of "Rollin', rollin', rollin' . . ." broke out as the guests migrated out of the dining hall and headed for the barn for their first day of riding.

Flushing, she stepped away. "I should go."

"Good idea," he said, so levelly that she couldn't tell whether he meant she should get out ahead of the singles, or she should get away from him while the getting was good. Either way, she turned tail and slipped out the back, clutching her basket of muffins and feeling like she'd made a narrow escape. Because whether he was a sweetie or a grump didn't change the fact that she was at Mustang Ridge for a very specific purpose, and it wasn't to hook up. *Okay, let's institute Rule Number Twelve*, she thought. *No summer fling, not even with a hot cowboy.*

Hopefully, she would do a better job of following Rule Twelve than Lizzie had done with Rule Eleven.

4

By Thursday afternoon, Shelby had more or less settled into the routine—up at four to help with the
day's baking and breakfast, a few hours with Lizzie,
back to the kitchen for lunch, and then a couple of hours
free before the dinner rush. Gran had been right about
it being a full day, but it still worked out to fewer hours
than her regular job plus commuting and cooking, and
gave her more time with Lizzie. Add in the scenery and
the ranch atmosphere, and it felt like a vacation more
than a job.

So when Gran told her to take off midday on Thursday, she hesitated. "Are you sure? We can go on Saturday, instead." Most of the staffers had changeover day
to themselves.

"And miss having Lizzie all prepared for tomorrow?
Shame on you."

"But you said yourself that the riders are going to be
starving when they get back." The wranglers and
dudes had carried picnic lunches with them for the
daylong ride up to the high pasture. Shelby and Lizzie
had waved them off just after breakfast, wearing rain-

coats against a chilly drizzle that had turned everything gray and misty. Krista and the wranglers had worked the crowd until thirty-six horse and rider pairs and three rangy farm dogs were strung out along the trail leading up to the ridgeline, disappearing into the mist. Shelby had "oohed" and "aahed" and taken pictures, but the little images on her phone hadn't come close to capturing the moment, which had instantly won a place on her internal top-twenty list.

Learning to appreciate the Wild West thing didn't mean she was ready to give up Starbucks and manicures permanently, though, which was part of why she was feeling guilty about playing hooky to drive into town. Rumor had it there was a coffee shop that made a half-decent latte.

"We'll be fine," Gran assured her. "Herman and I will hold down the fort until you get back. We can always holler for the Terrible Ts if we fall behind."

Shelby grinned. Tipper and Topper weren't exactly terrible, but they were pretty low in the initiative department and tended to hang out and gossip with anyone in earshot unless given direct orders. And those orders needed to be simple and explicit, as she'd found out the hard way after asking Tipper to watch a white sauce, only to have her closely scrutinize it as it boiled over onto the stove.

"We've got dinner handled," Gran said firmly. "Go do Mom stuff."

Shelby went, but all during the half-hour drive into town, she kept second-guessing herself, feeling guilty about taking the time off when Krista and Gran were giving them so much already. Until, that is, she pulled into Bootsie's Saddlery, and Lizzie's eyes lit. All week, she'd been practically a ghost, either hanging out in the cabin or sitting in a corner of the kitchen, jacked into her gadgets, playing or reading in silence. Now, though, she sat up straight and reached for the door handle before they were even parked.

Seven days driving cross-country: hundreds of dollars. One summer sabbatical: thousands. Your child's expression when she sees a two-story-tall plastic boot out in front of a log cabin? Priceless. Shelby didn't care, though. She would totally take what she could get.

"Okay, kiddo. You ready to get some riding gear so you're all ready for your lesson tomorrow?" Shelby waited a ten-count, trying to balance the awkwardness of the pause—and the anxiety it would provoke in Lizzie—against the hope that the tack store might be enough incentive to get her the "yes" nod that was one of the last real ways that her daughter communicated, and then only rarely these days.

Some SM kids chattered away using notes and texts, while others developed a vocabulary of gestures and body language. Ninety-nine point nine-nine-something percent of them interacted nonverbally with their family members and even outsiders. Lizzie, though, was one of the tiny fraction that didn't. She wasn't autistic, wasn't learning disabled. She was just . . . silent. And the treatments that usually worked with SM kids hadn't made a dent.

Refusing to let her grin falter when her daughter just kept staring out the window, Shelby undid her seat belt and opened the door. "Come on, then. I bet they've got a pair of boots and a helmet with your name on them!"

The interior was just as wonderfully kitschy as the outside, with spinning racks of silver-accented belts, glass cases of huge, blinged-out buckles, rows of gleaming leather boots, and a paint-chip wall of hats at the back. Racks held peacock-hued shirts with snap studs, matching his and hers, and four-sided shelves offered every version of Wrangler jean known to mankind. Short staircases on either side led to rooms full of tooled saddles, horse blankets, and grooming accessories, and the air smelled of leather and new clothes.

Shelby stopped just inside the door and took a deep breath. It wasn't exactly her normal territory, but shopping was shopping, and she knew how to do that with some serious style. And with a latte buzzing through her system, she was good to go. "So, kiddo, where do you want to start?"

Lizzie stood frozen in the doorway, overwhelmed.

A dark-haired twenty-something came toward them, wearing crisp blue Wranglers, a snap-studded blue shirt, and the same kind of "I know what I'm doing" swagger worn by the wranglers up at Mustang Ridge. She dimpled at them. "Can I help you ladies?"

"Did the deer-in-headlights paralysis give us away as newbies?"

The dimples got deeper. "That, and Stace asked me to keep an eye out for you. Shelby and Lizzie, right?"

"Yep," Shelby said. *And we're a long way from home.* Back in Boston she barely knew the people in the apartments on either side of her and rarely saw the same employee twice at the big stores they frequented. Telling herself it was sweet, not creepy, that Lizzie's new instructor-to-be had called ahead, she added, "Lizzie here is starting her riding lessons tomorrow, and Stace gave me a list of basics she'd like us to get—helmet, heeled boots, a few grooming supplies, that sort of thing."

Shelby had met briefly with the ranch's only full-time female wrangler—who called herself a cowboy, claiming that the word "cowgirl" was only for sissies these days—and had liked her immediately. Plump and pretty, with dark hair and an easy smile, Stace had offered some good theories about a lesson plan for Lizzie, and ways to tie it into the more traditional SM therapies. For starters, she had suggested getting Lizzie some of her own equipment so she'd have a sense of ownership and something specific to take care of in the barn. That had made good sense to Shelby . . . and she was forced to admit that she needed some new clothes for herself as well. Three pairs of stretchy black pants and city boots weren't going to cut it at Mustang Ridge for much longer. She had brought other clothes, but they were even fussier. And as the days got pretty hot—even hotter in the kitchen—not appropriate for day-to-day life at the ranch.

"Right this way." The clerk turned and headed deeper into the store, gesturing for them to follow. Over her shoulder, she said, "I'm Torie, by the way. How about we start with a brain bucket?"

"A . . . right. Helmet. Lead on."

Torie brought them to a side room that had crash

helmets displayed on the walls, with boxes stacked beneath. They ranged from the velvet-covered kind Shelby remembered from her childhood, all the way to shiny composite versions that looked more like mountain biking gear. "So helmets aren't uncool out here in the Wild West? I haven't seen anybody wearing them at the ranch."

The younger woman started pulling boxes off the stacks. "Then there must not be any other kids there this week."

"No. It's singles week."

"Oy."

"You're telling me." Though to be fair, aside from the public decompression of a hot-and-heavy, forty-eight-hour-old "relationship" late Monday and a hair-pulling squabble over who had won a romantic private dinner for two on Wednesday, things had been relatively quiet on the guest front. Shelby had ducked a couple of invitations, soothed some hurt feelings, and mostly stayed out of the way.

"Well," Torie said, "helmets are required at Mustang Ridge if you're under eighteen or riding in a speed event, which is more than a lot of ranches do. But if you ask me, anybody who throws a leg over a horse's back should wear an approved helmet like this one, one hundred percent of the time." She pulled one of the bike-type helmets out of a box, brushed Lizzie's hair back from her face, and settled it gently in place. "Hm. That's not the right shape for you, is it, Lizzie? Looks like you're not really an oval kind of gal. We'll try a manufacturer who swings round."

She didn't seem curious about Lizzie's lack of response, suggesting that Stace had filled her in. For a change, Shelby was grateful. Back home, the gossip got them sidelong looks, pity, and people who talked slow and loud. Here, it got Lizzie the space and lack of pressure she needed.

"How about this one?" Torie asked, pulling out another contender and tucking Lizzie into it. The helmet was a big, round shell in a blah beige color, like an overturned salad bowl. There was no visor or anything, just an adjustable nylon harness that fastened under her chin and a wheel at the back that snugged it onto her head.

Torie fiddled with the adjustments and the webbed harness, buckled Lizzie securely into the contraption, and turned her to face Shelby. "What does Mom think?"

Mom thinks it makes her look like a roll-on deodorant. "Is it super safe?"

"Crash-tested and approved with all the alphabet soup agencies." The younger woman winked, apparently reading her mind, or close to it. "Don't worry, finding the perfect helmet cover is the fun part. We're just getting the fit right first. Once you've got a shell, you can put everything from a Western hat to a jockey's polka dots on it. Better yet, you can switch out different styles when you get bored."

"Oh, well, in that case, I love it." Kneeling down in front of Lizzie and getting nice and close to her, so she'd be blocking out the overwhelming peripherals, Shelby said, "How does it feel, kiddo? Is it comfortable?"

Because it was important, she made herself wait out the response this time, zipping the urge to fill the silence with background babble. Finally, after what seemed like forever, Lizzie gave an almost imperceptible nod.

Relief washed through Shelby, and she felt giddier than the moment deserved, maybe, but still. "Do you want to pick out a cover for it?"

And, wonder of wonders, she got another nod, this one faster and more definite. And for a second, she saw a hint of the old Lizzie in those big brown eyes.

Forcing herself not to overreact and scare her kid back into hiding, she kissed her cheek. "Good job. Let's see what Miss Torie has for us."

A fun fifteen minutes later, they settled on two helmet covers: a straw hat like the ones the wranglers wore, and a stretchy pink nylon cover that made the helmet look like a horse's head, with pricked ears, a yarn mane, big cartoon eyes, and nostrils painted on the visor. The whole effect was one of a slightly startled *My Pretty Pony*, or maybe *Puff the Magic Dragon*. Which was still way better than a roll-on.

"Boots next," Torie declared, "then grooming supplies. And then how about something for you, Mom?"

"Jeans and a few shirts, definitely, then maybe a pair of boots."

"Style or comfort first?"

"Both?"

"Ariat," Torie decided. "Justin or Abilene might work for you, too, but let's start with the Ariats, as they have killer arch support."

"Got anything on sale?"

"Ah, a woman after my own heart. We'll get you hooked up."

Torie was as good as her word, supplying them both with cowboy clothes and all the trimmings, to the point that it was getting on to dinner by the time Shelby and Lizzie emerged from Bootsie's, hauling bags and feeling all Westerny.

Lizzie would've done the Easter Bunny proud in a sparkly pink belt, purple kid-size boots that Torie assured them would be great for riding, and a straw hat with a bright pink band. Shelby, on the other hand, had kept it pretty subdued on the theory that she was already a poser for wearing cowboy clothes, and adding bling would make it worse. But although she was outside her comfort zone, she had to admit it . . . her new boots felt *good*. Pointy toes aside, there was something about walking along with her heels doing a little *click-thud*, and the way they made her wiggle more than she normally would. Or maybe that was the jeans. Torie had stuffed her into a pair of stretchy Wranglers that were seemingly imbued with five percent spandex and five percent magic, because that was the only way her butt could possibly look like that.

"When in Wyoming," she said, and grinned down at Lizzie.

Her daughter stopped dead and grabbed her hand so suddenly that she looked around, wondering what had scared her. It took a moment for her to realize that she was tugging for her mom to lean down.

Shelby squatted. "What is it, baby?"

Lizzie leaned in and kissed her cheek.

*   *   *

Friday morning dawned gray and drizzly, getting some grumbles from the guests and making Shelby worry that Lizzie's evening lesson would wind up canceled. By lunchtime, though, the sun broke through in a glorious double rainbow that had to be a sign of good things to come.

At six thirty that evening, with the end-of-the-week barbecue well under way and Tipper and Topper minding the picnic tables down by the lakeshore, Gran pointed at Shelby, who was washing pots. "You're done for the week. No arguments. It's lesson time. Stace is waiting for you and Lizzie."

"I—"

"What did I say about arguments?"

Shelby laughed and held up her sudsy hands in surrender. "Wasn't going to argue, I swear. I was going to say, 'Thank you, Gran. You're the best.'" After a week together, they had fallen into an easy rapport, which pretty much consisted of Gran urging Shelby to take extra time with Lizzie when the schedule permitted, and Shelby pretending that Herman was a member of the staff.

Gran offered her a big smile. "Have fun, the two of you. And don't forget there's a bonfire later. Music, drinks, s'mores, the whole nine yards."

"We'll see you then," Shelby assured her.

When she got back to the cabin, she found Lizzie parked in her corner, glued to one of her near-disintegrating *Bridle Club* books. But while it looked like she hadn't moved since Shelby brought her back after an early dinner, she had changed into her new jeans and boots, and right next to her feet sat her horse-headed helmet and the little plastic bucket filled with brushes and other grooming gear. Everything was carefully labeled with her name, as if being bubblegum pink wasn't enough of a clue.

"Hey, kiddo. It's lesson time!"

Lizzie's head came up, and Shelby saw her daughter's battened-down excitement as she grabbed the grooming kit and her helmet and came over. They had visited the barn every day that week, but although the webbed stall guard had let Lizzie poke her fingers through to meet Sassy and Peppermint, it wasn't anything like actually riding them. Shelby thought it had been good, though, giving Lizzie time to get comfortable with the big animals.

Now, though, it was time to take the next step.

As they came up the path to the barn, Stace emerged with a wave, calling, "Hey, Lizzie. Are you ready to ride?" The freckled young woman had her reddish hair braided underneath a blue-and-white baseball cap and was wearing a matching baseball jersey with a running-horse emblem on the chest and her name on the sleeve.

"I thought we were riding, not playing baseball," Shelby said.

"Riding lesson now, softball league at eight." Stace grinned. "You should come. We could use a catcher."

"No, thanks. I'm not great with hand-eye coordination." Or letting strangers throw things at her. Besides, she was planning on helping out with the bonfire later. It wasn't officially part of her duties, but she had a feeling that Krista and Gran could use another set of hands. "I appreciate the invite, though."

"Maybe next week." Stace winked. "There are a few single guys there I bet would love to meet you."

No, thanks. I'm sticking to Rule Twelve. "How about we meet some ponies, instead?"

"The good news is that horses and men aren't mutually exclusive. At least not out here in cowboy country." Stace led the way into the barn, gesturing for Shelby and Lizzie to follow. Once inside, she held out a hand to Lizzie. "So, what do you say? You want to learn how to halter Peppermint and lead him out of his stall?"

Lizzie hesitated, but at an encouraging nudge from Shelby, crossed the short distance to Stace's side. She glanced back a couple of times.

"I'll be right here," Shelby assured her.

"I love your helmet," Stace said, getting Lizzie's attention. "How about you put it on? It's a good idea to wear one all the time when you're around horses, not just when you're riding them."

Shelby started forward to help, but Stace held up a hand to stop her. "No. No offense, but she needs to do this on her own." To Lizzie, she said, "I get that you've got SM, and I won't pester you about talking. But I do need to know that you can follow my instructions, because that's how you're going to learn how to ride. More, you're going to have to communicate here—not with me, but with Peppermint. You need to tell him when to stop, when to go, when to turn, and what direction to go . . . not with words, but with your reins and your legs. So . . . do you think you can do that for me?"

Shelby held her breath. She didn't remember the last time Lizzie had "talked" to a stranger, even just with yes and no. But maybe—hopefully—the horses would be the key.

After a pause, Lizzie put down her brushes, put on her helmet, and fumbled to click the chin strap into place.

Stace grinned and rapped her knuckles on the top of the helmet. "That'll do, Lizzie. That'll do just fine. Okay, let's get Peppermint out of his stall. Please hand me the halter and lead over there, hanging on his door."

Shelby hadn't realized she was holding her breath until it came out in a whoosh, along with the relief of realizing that Gertie was right. Stace was as good as any of the aides who had worked with Lizzie back home. Maybe better, at least in this context. That should've been a given, because Gertie was awesome, but still, Shelby had been harboring doubts.

Now, finally feeling like things were getting under way, she leaned back against the wall, a little surprised to find herself right beside Sassy's stall. Attracted by the conversation, or maybe the hope of a treat, the chestnut poked her nose through the bars. Shelby stroked the soft nose, feeling the long whiskers tickle her fingers, and said conversationally, "How are you doing, Mama? About ready for that baby to be born, I'm guessing."

"Any time now," Stace put in. "She's at three hundred and twenty days. The average is three forty, but it's a pretty big range. It's more about development than actual timing with horses, as foals cook until they're done, and then they come out. I've seen some mares go over the year mark."

"Ouch."

"They didn't look too happy about it, that's for sure. And a couple of those babies were huge." Turning back to Lizzie, Stace showed her how to hold the halter. "Okay, now we're going to open the stall door, and you're going to put the halter on his head. Ready? Here we go." She opened the stall door fully to reveal Peppermint. Just as he had every time they patted him through the stall guard, the fat roan pony stood like a statue, ears pricked forward as if to say, "Ooh. I like little girls!"

But suddenly, Lizzie's face went rigid and her knuckles whitened on the halter.

Shelby's stomach gave an *uh-oh* clench. *Come on, baby. You can do it.*

"That's it," Stace said brightly. "Just put the loop part around his nose, pull it up, and buckle the strap behind his ears." She waited it out, but after a minute Peppermint snorted, dropped his head, and started picking at the wispy remnants of his afternoon hay, losing interest in the little person who stood frozen at his door.

Which was one of the challenges of using animals in therapy. They had minds of their own and attention spans that were often far shorter than those of the people involved in the process. More, they were less predictable when they were bored and looking for entertainment.

"How about if I put him on the cross ties for you, and we can use your new brushes?" Stace asked, shifting gears. She eased Lizzie off to the side and haltered the pony. "He's not too muddy, so we're going to start with the curry. That's the oval-shaped rubber one that fits in your hand. You're going to make big circles with it, rubbing him all over his body to bring the dirt and loose hair to the surface of his coat. Please go grab that for me while I get him out of his stall."

Lizzie did as she was told, moving so fast it was almost jerky, as if she was trying to prove that she could follow directions if they didn't involve going into the stall with the pony.

Shelby's stomach was doing nervous flip-flops, but when Lizzie looked over at her, she found a smile. "You're doing great, Dizzy Lizzie. One step at a time, kiddo. Just listen to Stace and she'll talk you through everything."

Peppermint's unshod hooves thudded on the cement, rasping as he turned his pudgy little body into the center of the aisle, where Stace clipped him onto a pair of long ropes that came down from high on the wall. "See how this keeps him in the middle so it's safe to work around him? There's other stuff we can do to stay safe, too. Whenever you're working around a horse, you want to let him know you're there by touching him, first where he can see you"—she demonstrated by stroking the pony's shoulder—"then working your way around the back. You want to keep talking and touching him the whole time so he knows where you are. You don't ever want to startle a horse or come up right behind him without letting him know you're there, or else you might get kicked." She moved back to the pony's head. "Can you come over here and give him a pat on his shoulder so he knows you're here?"

Lizzie stood pressed against the wall, clutching the pink currycomb in one white-knuckled fist. She didn't nod, didn't shake her head, didn't do anything.

She couldn't. And that was the hell of her condition.

Unable to bear it any longer—and not sure she was helping by staying out of the way—Shelby headed for the pony. "Hey, Peppermint! I'm Lizzie's mom. Aren't you a good boy?" She squatted near Peppermint's shoulder, giving him a couple of pats the way Stace had demonstrated. "See, kiddo? He's a good guy. Want to come give him some scritches?"

Nothing happened.

After a minute, Stace said, "Can you come over here and hand me the curry? I'll give it to your mom so she can brush him for us."

The currycomb dropped to the floor, bounced twice, and lay still. Lizzie's eyes filmed with tears, and she was suddenly breathing hard and fast, huge gulping gasps that rattled in her chest.

Heart sinking, Shelby stood. "Hey, kiddo. No pressure, remember? We're here to have fun. If this isn't fun—"

Lizzie burst into tears, not silently, but with a wail of rage and pain, followed by raw sobs that were shocking after all the silence. Like a stutterer who could sing, she could cry at top volume.

Only when pushed to the edge, though. Only when it got to be too much.

"Oh, baby." Shelby went to her knees and gathered her shaking daughter against her in a full-body hug that, no matter how hard she tried, still wasn't enough to fix things. "It's okay. You're okay. There's nothing scary here, and nobody's mad at you."

That was the best she'd been able to figure, that the meltdowns came when Lizzie felt pressured—to speak, to be normal, to be herself. Before, the pressure had come from her teachers, friends and family. Now it was coming from inside.

She so wanted to love the horses, but they terrified her. Maybe because of what had happened that first day, maybe just because they were bigger and stronger than her. It didn't matter, really. It only mattered that she was clinging to Shelby, sobbing her heart out with wails that sounded like they were coming from an animal, a baby, something incapable of speech.

"What can I do?" Stace had gone pale, her eyes wide and dark.

"Nothing," Shelby told her. "Not right now, anyway. And don't stress, it's not your fault. It's nobody's fault. We're just going to have to call it a day for now." Maybe for good. This was more than anxiety, more than a healthy pushing of the limits.

Heart twisting, she picked up her daughter and straightened. Lizzie clung, wrapping long arms and legs around her and burrowing in, helmet and all. Shelby's back pinged a protest, but she ignored it to sway back and forth, whispering, "Shh. It's okay. You're okay."

"Do you want me to get someone—"

"No. I've got her." She tightened her grip, and said, softer, "I've got you. I promise."

Lizzie didn't hear, though. She was sobbing, shuddering, gulping for breath, with her face hidden away from the outside world as she fought the scary world inside her.

Knowing what her daughter needed—what they both needed—Shelby carried her all the way back to their cabin. Her legs burned and her back was howling by the time she got to the three short steps leading up, but she made it, all the way up and inside. She shut the door behind them so it was just the two of them against the world. And then she sat on the love seat, held her daughter close, and fought to hold back tears of her own.

5

Later that night, after Lizzie finally sniffled herself to sleep, Shelby put on one of her fancy new shirts and a pair of the butt-hugging jeans and headed toward the lake, where the noise and the flicker of firelight left no question as to where the party was going down. She really wasn't in the mood, but figured she had to put in an appearance, both because she had promised Gran, and because the gossip would've made the rounds already—and she'd rather face the whispers and sympathetic looks now, without Lizzie.

She knew the drill.

When she got to the lake, though, she couldn't make herself turn toward the bonfire, where Ty was playing something slow and bluesy on the guitar and several couples were slow-dancing, silhouetted against the fire with enough romance to make her cranky.

Instead, she headed the other way, toward the boathouse, where it was darker and quieter. *Just need a minute. Then I'll go eat, drink, and pretend to be merry.*

The dock running out into the lake gave beneath her feet, and her boots echoed, sounding very loud. So loud, in fact, that she shucked them off, along with her socks, and carried them to where the boards ended. The float swayed beneath her feet and gave gently when she sat, with a rocking motion that took away some of the tension.

Yes, this was what she needed. Not being in the thick of the party, but being able to watch it across the lake, seeing the firelight and hearing the laughter and music. Blowing out a long, slow breath, she swung her feet around and into the water. And nearly yanked them right back out again. "Holy . . . brr!"

"It's a little early in the year for swimming," a man's voice said from the darkness behind her.

Jolting, she almost landed right in the icy water. "Yeek!" She twisted around. "Foster? Is that you?"

She hadn't seen much of the head wrangler over the course of the week, as he kept to himself and mostly stuck to the barn. She'd seen him from a distance, though, riding a tall bay gelding, with his shaggy black-and-white border collie always within whistling distance. She had seen how he led on the way out, then trailed behind the riders on the way home, making sure all the stragglers made it back safely. And she had noticed that even when Ty and the others scattered for the day, Foster stayed behind to finish up whatever needed finishing, often burning the lights in the barn long after sunset.

She hadn't been looking for him, not really, but she had been aware of him all week, just as she was very aware of him now. The moon was waning, the firelight too faint to show her any details, but she could just make out the denim jacket he'd pulled on against the chill, and the curve of the black hat he wore low on his brow.

"Sorry. Didn't mean to startle you." He moved closer so he was standing over her, the dock dipping farther beneath his weight. "Not in the mood for a party?"

"Not so much." She clicked on her little flashlight, gave him an up-and-down, and hid the thudding of her heart by frowning at his boots. "How did you sneak up on me in those things? I sounded like a Budweiser Clydesdale."

"Practice." He squatted down beside her. "Nice night. Smells like rain, though."

If you say so. "You didn't follow me out here to talk about the weather." She paused. "Stace told you what happened." There was no reason to be embarrassed, she reminded herself, no reason to wish she and Lizzie could've met him at their best. And no reason to want to take a deep breath, much as she did every morning when she came into the kitchen, only this time inhaling his scent rather than the smell of Gran's baking.

He stared out over the water. "I owe you an apology. If it hadn't been for Brutus spooking—"

"Don't, please. The if-onlys will make you crazy." She grimaced, though she doubted he could see it in the darkness, even if he'd been looking. "Ask me how I know."

"Maybe she'll come around, given some time and patience. Stace said she really wants it, and the horse-crazy thing can be a powerful motivator." He paused. "I've had kids start out terrified of even the dogs, and been riding by the end of the week. Lizzie is good with the other animals, and you've got time to work on it. She'll come around."

"Maybe." Across the lake, the partiers were line dancing around the fire, arms linked, legs kicking like they were trying out for the Rockettes. "Let's just say that I haven't had a lot of luck waiting her out. That's part of why we're here."

"How long has this been going on?"

"Two years." Her throat ached on the words. It had been two years since she heard her daughter's voice. Two years of therapists, cognitive behavior modification, stress reduction, and strict routines, none of which had really changed anything. And now . . . "I told myself not to get my hopes up for a quick fix, but I never would've guessed it'd go like this. I thought the horses would be perfect. Everything I read about therapeutic riding . . . well, I guess it all assumes that the patient isn't terrified of the horses."

"They're big animals, she's already taken a fall, and she's nervous."

"It was more than nerves. It was . . ." She shook her head. "The mutism is rooted in anxiety, so adding more stress into the mix isn't going to help, not the way Gertie had hoped."

"So where does that leave you?"

"Cooking ranch food for the summer while my daughter hangs out in the cabin and reads? I don't know. Maybe she'd like to learn how to fish. Or, heck, maybe I should just take her home." She shook her head. "No, scratch that. I couldn't leave Krista and Gran in the lurch. Which means I'm back to 'I don't know.'" She glanced over at him. "Tell me you're here because you've got a suggestion." Maybe he and Stace had put their heads together.

"As a matter of fact, I do."

She stared at his profile. "Really?"

"I think you should take a few lessons yourself."

"I . . . what?" Her stomach gave a queer little twist.

"The therapies are all about modeling behavior, right? When kids can talk to their families at home, but not anyone outside, you either bring a teacher or therapist into the home or send the parents to school, set up a safe environment, and work on making the kids feel comfortable enough to talk. Once they've got that down, you gradually introduce new people or places, adding a little bit at a time and showing them they can do it." At her startled look, he shrugged. "After Stace told me what happened, I did some poking around. Google is my friend."

"Seriously?"

"Just because parts of cowboying go back to the eighteen hundreds doesn't mean it all does. I've even got an iPhone. Er, somewhere."

"Well, then." Really, though, it wasn't the computer she was questioning. It was him. Why was he doing this? Krista was a softie, Gran needed her help, and Stace wanted a case study for extra credit. And they were all warm, kind, and friendly. Foster, though . . . she didn't know where he was coming from. He was an undeniable presence at the ranch, but he wasn't a joiner, didn't seem like he wanted a friend. Yet he'd looked up SM therapies online, and he'd sought her out to talk about them.

"The way I see it, you're doing the same sort of modeling, except it's harder because she's completely silent, so you're down to encouraging any interaction at all. Stace said you tried all the by-the-books stuff back home, with no luck, so Gertie suggested coming here."

Her throat threatened to clog with the emotions that were way too close to the surface, threatening the "everything's okay" attitude she did her best to maintain. Lizzie needed to see her being calm and in control, needed to feel like there wasn't anything to fear, no pressure, no anxiety. But that was such a crock. Shelby wanted to shout on a daily basis, wanted to scream, wanted to pitch a fit and demand to know why this had happened to Lizzie, to them—only there wasn't anyone to ask, nobody to answer, leaving them both locked in silence. It was maddening, heartbreaking, exhausting.

Oh, so exhausting.

Foster didn't need to know any of that, though. He was offering to help, and didn't need her spewing at him the way she'd blathered at Krista. So she breathed past the surge of tears and kept herself together. As she always did. *Deep breath.* Voice low and steady, she said, "She's always liked animals. We thought . . . *I* thought that learning to ride would make her feel brave. Maybe even that the horses would be something she could talk to."

"It could still work that way, which is why I think you should do some riding. You're not at home anymore, not around familiar things. SM kids are all about being in a safe place, right? So maybe you need to be her safe place, even when it comes to riding."

"But the horses are her thing, not mine. I wanted her

to do it . . ." She shook her head, frustrated. "I wanted her to be brave and do it alone. Which just made things worse, didn't it?"

"Not every training moment is going to be a good one. Trust me on that one."

She bristled. "She's not a horse."

"No offense intended, Mama Bear. That's just how my brain is wired." He tapped his temple. "Cowboy, you know."

Deciding to let it go, she looked at him sidelong. "Mama Bear?"

"A grizzly protects her cubs no matter what, and she's fierce at it." The crinkles at the corners of his eyes deepened. "You should've seen yourself coming into the barn to rescue her that first day."

"I looked like a grizzly?"

"Not exactly, but let's go with it."

"Hm. So Lizzie is, what, a high-strung horse that needs to be sacked out?" Maybe it wasn't the worst comparison. In the absence of words, they were stuck reading her body language and guessing at the cues.

His eyes glinted. "Ridden some greenies, have you?"

"I'm not sure two years of doing donuts at the local riding school counts as the kind of riding you're talking about." And neither did the horse-crazy phase when she read every horse book she could get her hands on, and watched *The Black Stallion* over and over again on the VCR, crying a little when Alec and the Black galloped along the deserted island and slept together near the fire, neither of them alone anymore.

Kid stuff, she thought, and didn't let herself yearn.

"Everything counts," Foster said firmly. "And I don't think she needs sacking out—that'd just scare her worse. No, this would be more like when we use an experienced horse to help settle a timid greenie. Baby horses can't exactly hold their mama's hand, but they get reassurance from physical contact, by bumping up against bigger, stronger horses. They also take cues on whether stuff is scary or not, watching to see what their older herd mates do. So when I'm training a nervous young horse, I'll ride out with someone else on a veteran and let mine get in real close if he needs to. In the early stages it's not about a youngster learning how to be brave on his own. It's about getting him out there and doing the job. Then, later, you can wean him off the buddy system and get him working alone."

Ranch-isms aside, it resonated. "So, from a training perspective, you think I should be the old gray mare? Is that better or worse than a grizzly?" She shifted, wondering if he could sense her discomfort, wondering what he thought about it.

"I think you should be right there for your daughter to lean on while she tries something new, just like you've always been."

She swallowed to ease her suddenly tight throat. "By riding with her rather than watching from the sidelines."

"When you're training a greenie, especially one that's prone to getting twitchy, it's important to stay flexible. There are hundreds of different ways to train a horse, some with big names and advertising budgets, others that fall under the headings of gut feel or 'because that's the way my grandpappy did it.' No one theory is going to work on every horse, and with some horses you wind up going through a whole lot of theories before you hit on one that gets the job done."

"So, how do you know which one will work?"

"Most of the time, you don't. Not right off, anyway. You give something a really good shot, and if it doesn't work, you try something else." He paused. "Question is, are you ready to try something else?"

She wavered. "I can't expect Krista to fund lessons for both of us."

"Krista's in charge of the main house, but when it comes to the barn, I'm the man."

Yes, you are. She might've thought it before, but now it was confirmed—he wasn't just a cowboy; he was a smart, well-spoken guy who knew himself and knew his stuff, and she liked that. And despite their rocky start, she was beginning to like him, and not just in an "ooh, pretty" way. She respected the way his mind worked. Plus, she appreciated that he'd apologized for Lizzie getting scared, even if it wasn't his fault, and . . . Well, she liked *him*. A lot.

When she'd been getting ready to leave for the summer, a couple of friends at the office had ribbed her about having a hot affair while she was out West. She had laughed them off—*not in the market, spending the summer with my kid*—but now parts of her that had been quiet for a Very Long Time were starting to wake up. Fortunately, though—or unfortunately, depending on whether she was letting her head or her heart do the voting—Foster didn't seem to be interested in her, not that way. He was sitting right beside her, not making any sort of move except to talk about Lizzie. Which was good, because it put them on the same team—and she'd keep telling herself that until it sank in.

Focusing on that—and ready to admit that his suggestion was a decent one—she said, "At least let me pay for my lessons."

"Not happening. You'll be doing me a favor."

"How do you figure?"

"I've got an older gelding who could use some work outside of the dude string."

"Let me guess. Another one of Krista's rescues?" It hadn't taken her long to see that the ranch was sprinkled with three-legged cats and geriatric cows. A retired horse or two wouldn't surprise her in the slightest. It also wouldn't shock her to find that it was missing an ear or something, which in a way made her feel better about the whole thing. They would be a couple of charity cases helping each other out.

"Is that a yes?"

Still not sure how to take him, or his interest in Lizzie, she nodded. "Yeah. Okay. And, Foster, seriously. Thank you."

"No biggie."

"It's a biggie to me." If he'd been Krista or one of the others, she would've reached out for a handclasp or one-armed hug of thanks. As it was, she gripped the edge of the dock. "You don't know me or Lizzie except in passing, but you've given this more thought than most of my friends back home ever have, you came up with a new suggestion that nobody else had thought of, and you came out here to talk to me about it. That's . . . it's not what I'm used to. So thank you."

He shrugged. "Things work different out here."

"I guess they do." Different from the people she knew in Boston, different from her family, different from everything she was used to.

"So . . . come to the barn around ten tomorrow morning, after the airport shuttle heads out and things get quiet. And bring Lizzie."

A smile tugged. Apparently, he'd been confident enough in his plan that he'd already set things up for Stace to come in on her day off. Mentally promising to pay the instructor for the lesson, she nodded. "Okay, ten tomorrow. And again, thanks."

He just nodded and stood. "I'll leave you to your alone time."

"Actually, I think I've had about enough. My feet are freezing." In fact, they were full-on numb, as if her legs ended at the ankle. "I think I'll pull myself together and hobble over to the bonfire. You headed that way?"

"Not tonight. Enjoy yourself, though." He melted back into the darkness, until all that was left of him was a low whistle and a call of "Come on, Vader."

A patter of paws on the pebbly shore was the only sign that his constant shadow had been waiting patiently for him. And then they were both gone, disappearing as quietly as they had come.

Shelby stared after them for a long moment, then shook her head. "Gift horse. Mouth. Don't do it." She'd be grateful, instead, and find some way to repay the head wrangler for his kindness, whether he liked it or not.

Retrieving her iceberg tootsies from the water, she rubbed some warmth back into them with her socks, then put her boots back on. A look across the lake said that the dancers had given up on the line and were doing the boogie-woogie, though the numbers had thinned. Ty was still strumming his guitar, though, and the fire was still going strong.

An hour ago, she had been tempted to head for the hills. Now she headed for the party.

"Shelby!" Krista waved her into the firelight. "I wasn't sure you were going to make it!"

The bonfire, which had started the night as a huge pile of logs and pallets, was halfway burned down, and threw off enough heat that most of the plastic chairs had been pulled back to a safe distance. Twenty or so people were left, some guests, some employees. Ty had just set aside his guitar in favor of a beer, and the others were sitting around in twos and threes, rocking conversation and marshmallows with equal enthusiasm.

Krista and Gran were sitting a little apart from the others, near a folding table that was loaded with bags of marshmallows and Hershey's bars. Herman's bowl sat at Gran's feet. Apparently, when she'd said, "Everyone who's anyone comes to the bonfire," she meant it.

Krista dragged an empty chair over and wedged it between her and Gran, then patted the seat. "Plant it, sister."

Shelby planted it and poked her feet toward the fire. "Sorry I'm so late. What'd I miss?"

"You're only late if the fire is out. However, you

missed the last round of speed dating." Krista gave her a shoulder bump. "I waited for you as long as I could, but I finally gave in."

"I'm crushed."

"Thought you would be. How's Lizzie?"

"Sleeping off a doozy of a cry hangover."

Krista's eyes filled with sympathy. "I heard. I'm sorry."

"Thanks, but hopefully it's just a bump in the road." Not wanting to dwell on it anymore tonight—especially now that she had a new plan—Shelby looked around, counting heads. "So . . . what's the final tally for singles week?"

"Tracy Lee and Dwayne have been inseparable since day two, and they only live a couple of hours apart, so that seems promising. A few other couples are maybes, and everybody seems to have had a really great time, even if they didn't pair off."

"S'more?" Gran held out a toasting fork, handle first.

"Absolutely." Shelby leaned over to take it. To the bowl, she said, "Hey, Herman. Enjoying the heat?"

Gran laughed. "That's the graham crackers."

"What was I thinking?" Shelby asked, and got an elbow from Krista, who smothered a laugh.

"Silly girl." Gran pulled the towel back, selected two specimens that apparently passed her quality control standards, and held them out, along with a Hershey's bar. "You know the drill, right?"

"Five years in Girl Scouts, thank you very much." She accepted the ingredients and loaded a couple of marshmallows onto the fork. "So, did everybody make it down to the party?"

"Everyone but Gramps," Krista said matter-of-factly.

Shelby winced. "Sorry." She'd meant to fish a little on Foster, not hit a sore spot. She hadn't even officially met Gran's husband of more than four decades, but she'd seen Big Skye from a distance a few times, and had caught a reassuring glimpse of him and Gran sitting on their front-porch rockers, holding hands and watching the sunset.

"Don't tiptoe around it on my account," Gran said, nibbling on the corner of a cracker. "I love my Arthur dearly, but Lord, he is *stubborn*. It's not that he wants to go back to running cattle, but he can't bring himself to accept the dudes, either. He just wants to ride around the upper pastures, pretending that nothing's changed and he's not getting older."

Krista pulled her in for a hug and kissed her cheek. "You're not getting older, you're getting better, both of you." After a moment, she said, "Speaking of family members you'd occasionally like to strangle, I talked to Mom today."

Gran rolled her eyes. "And how are things on the *Rambling Rose*?"

"That's my parents' RV," Krista told Shelby. "My mom's name is Rose, and they're rambling, for sure. Right now they're in Niagara Falls, on the Canadian side."

Gran frowned. "I thought they were headed for Virginia Beach."

"I guess they took a detour? Some famous chef or

another is doing a guest stint in Niagara, and Mom just had to be there."

"What is it this time," Gran grumbled. "French? Indian?"

"Pastries."

The older woman made a sound that could only be described as a growl.

"Anyway," Krista hurried on, "Dad sounded like he was having a good time. He talked his way into one of the hydroelectric plants and got a behind-the-scenes tour."

"I bet he loved that." To Shelby, Gran said, "My Eddie was only a cattleman because this is a family ranch, but he's really an engineer at heart. When he was little, he used to take things apart to see how they worked. Most of the time he even put them back together properly."

Shelby smiled. "He sounds like a neat guy. I'd like to meet him." Not the least because Gran had confided that her son had stuttered as a child, and had gone virtually silent for a time.

"They mentioned maybe heading this way for Christmas," Krista said, "but I have a feeling they'll wind up going south rather than trying to get through the weather."

Shelby and her slowly thawing feet wouldn't blame them. Summer in Wyoming was gorgeous, but she didn't want to be here come winter. Pretty was one thing. Snowed in for six months with a limited number of people and spotty FedEx was another.

"Pastries, huh?" Gran muttered.

Krista nodded. "Yep. And they're having a tacky contest."

"A what?"

"Tacky contest. I guess parts of Niagara are wall-to-wall souvenir shops, so they decided to see which one of them could find the worst souvenir. Last I heard, the front runner was a ceramic tea set with a pair of breasts as the cream and sugar dishes, with nips on the lids to use as handles. I'm betting you can guess what the teapot is shaped like."

"Krista Jane!" Gran said.

Shelby snicker-winced. "Ew. Seriously?"

"Seriously."

"That's tacky."

"Yep."

"Well, look at it this way. It'll make a heck of a regift for a Yankee swap somewhere down the line."

"There's that."

They fell silent as Shelby pulled her toasting fork away from the heat and built her s'more. She tried to remember the last time she and her mom and her sister had hung out like this, chatting, and had to go way further back than she wanted to remember. And even then, there hadn't been the same sort of amused affection, the kind that said family loved family, even when they made each other a little crazy. Maybe, as Foster had said, things were just different out here.

Sure enough, a moment later, Gran said, "So, what else made the tacky list?"

6

At ten o'clock the next morning, Shelby and Lizzie set out for the barn. The little purple boots slowed as they neared the barn, though, and Shelby could see her daughter's anxiety notching up.

She hesitated, not sure what to do. Push it? Back off? Was this the battle she wanted to pick today? *Probably not.* So she stopped and knelt down in front of Lizzie so they were eye-to-eye. "Do you want to sit on the bench outside and read?"

That got an immediate nod.

Reminding herself that a few days ago that quick a response would've been cause for a major celebration, she stifled the spurt of disappointment. "Okay, but stay right there. Stace or I will come get you when it's time to go to the arena."

Lizzie headed for the bench without a backward glance.

Sighing, Shelby straightened and slapped some of the dust off her jeans, hoping she was doing the right thing this time and not just setting them both up for another fall.

The barn was cool and empty, save for a few horses in their stalls. Peering around, she called, "Stace?"

"She's not here," said a familiar deep voice, and Sassy's door rolled open. A long, lean figure stepped out, wearing a black Stetson and making a silhouette that could've been labeled *cowboy*.

Shelby stopped dead in the middle of the aisle, hoping he couldn't see her flush. "Oh. Hey, Foster."

He studied her for a moment, then nodded. "Hey yourself. Change of plans."

Her stomach shimmied. "No lesson?"

"Different trainer."

"You?" The word headed for squeak territory.

"That okay?"

The short answer was "Heck, yeah." The long one was . . . well, she didn't know what it was. All she knew was that her palms were suddenly sweaty. "Sure. It's fine. Um . . . thanks. I really appreciate it."

He nodded and looked past her. "Where's Lizzie?"

"Out front. She didn't want to come in, and I didn't push it."

He nodded. "A good trainer learns to pick her battles."

"She's not a pet," she said, her voice sharper than she'd intended. Blowing out a breath and forcing herself to level off, she added, "Sorry. I'm frustrated with her, which isn't fair. And maybe I'm a little nervous about riding. It's been a long time."

"I haven't lost a beginner yet, and I don't intend to start with Gran's new favorite assistant." He gave her an up-and-down. "What are you, maybe a fourteen, fourteen and a half saddle?"

"I rode in a sixteen as a kid."

"English and Western measure different."

"Right. Then whatever you think is best." She followed him into the tack room. "I want a helmet."

"Good call, role model and all. Besides, it's just smart riding."

"You don't wear one."

"I do when I'm starting colts or riding hard and fast, but I'll admit I get lazy when I'm on dude-herding duty." He dug out one of the bicycle-type helmets and handed it over. "Adjusts in the back. See if that works." He pulled a saddle off a wall rack, slung a thick saddle pad and another pad over the top of it, and then added a dark leather bridle that gleamed with silver accents and looked far more expensive than the rest. As he headed through the door, he glanced back to say, "Oh, and lose the belt."

She followed him out. "Excuse me?"

He set the saddle down on its horn and patted one lean hip, indicating his empty belt loops. "A real back-country cowboy stays away from anything that could get caught."

"On what?"

"Branches. Saddles. Cow horns."

She shuddered. "I thought I was just doing arena laps today."

"The safer you start, the safer you stay. When you're riding, it's best not to wear anything that won't break loose." He plucked at his shirt. "Snap studs give. Buttons don't."

She suddenly found herself staring at the smooth,

tanned skin at his throat, and the way it moved when he swallowed. Her flush had faded, but now it came back with a vengeance and settled in her lower belly, reminding her just how long it had been since she'd done any riding of the more intimate kind, or even seriously wanted to.

A really, really long time.

What were they talking about again? Oh, right. Safety. "What about Ty? He wears button shirts and a big, shiny belt."

He arched an eyebrow. "You want to be a real cowboy or a TV rodeo wannabe?"

"Neither." But she undid her belt and hung it on the wall, stifling a *boom-chicka-wa-wa* she didn't think either of them could handle. Then she held out her hands and gave a showy twirl. "All set, boss?"

He didn't even crack a smile. Just nodded. "All set. Let's introduce you to your horse and get this show on the road."

As Foster led the way to Loco's stall, he knew he was in big trouble. Heck, he'd known it since this morning, when she was the first thing he thought of. Not Vader, who'd had his paws on the bed and a breakfast-hopeful look in his doggy eyes, or all the stuff he had piling up on his not-really-a-day-off list. Nope, he'd been thinking about a fancy piece of city woman who might be getting along okay at Mustang Ridge, but didn't belong at a ranch long-term. No way, no how.

"Down here," he said over his shoulder. "You're going to be riding this guy." He rolled open Loco's door to reveal the chiseled bay gelding, whose coat had an extra bloom thanks to an early morning groom.

Her eyes widened. "He's a rescue?"

He chuckled. "No. He's Loco."

"Really?"

"Nope. He's lazy as a slug." Actually, the gelding had plenty of get-up-and-go, but he knew how to take it down a few notches for a less experienced rider. Foster could've pulled almost any of the horses out of the dude string for the job, but there wasn't another horse he trusted like he did this one, and he didn't want anything to go wrong. Granted, you couldn't guarantee anything when it came to horses, but Loco was as close to a guarantee as he could get. "Here." He produced the butt end of a carrot and handed it to her. "Go ahead and make friends."

"Thanks. Hey, Loco. Hi, Loco." She held out the treat on her flattened palm, and the horse reached out, touched her with his nose, and whuffled for the carrot. When he took it, transferred it to his back molars, and started crunching away, she grinned up at Foster. "He's a real gentleman, isn't he?"

Something funny happened in the pit of his stomach. "Yeah. He's a good guy." *And so are you, so hold yourself together. You're not going to make any moves on her.* She was there for her daughter, not to bag a cowboy, and didn't need him panting after her. "You want to put him on the cross ties and get him tacked up?"

"Aye, Captain."

He stood back and let her go through the motions, seeing how much she remembered, and not letting himself spend too much time dwelling on the *W*s stitched on the back pockets of her jeans. Loco enjoyed his second thorough grooming of the day, closing his eyes and practically snoozing in the aisle as she slicked off the dust he'd accumulated in a couple of hours in a fresh stall. Then she used a hoof pick to clean out his feet, handling herself with enough confidence to make Foster think she'd had more horse experience than she let on, or just had a real natural feel.

When she got to the tack, she made it through the saddle pads and saddle, but then faltered and looked over at him. "Um . . . help?"

"What's wrong?"

She held out the rope girth. "Not enough buckles."

"English is for sissies," he said mildly, but took the girth and showed her how to feed the cinch straps through, around, and back through again, so they would tighten without binding. "Bridle?"

"That, I've got." She fitted the fat snaffle bit into the gap behind the gelding's front set of teeth, slipped the one-ear headstall in place, and buckled the throatlatch with plenty of room. She ran the reins through her hands. "This is nice leather."

"It's an oldie, but goodie." He didn't mention that he'd won it, along with his saddle, a truck, and a whole lot of other stuff. All part of a past he didn't need to look back on.

When she had everything in place, she looked over at him. "Good to go?" At his nod, she held out the reins. "Will you hold him for me while I go get Lizzie?"

"I'll get her. Meet us out in the arena."

She looked startled, but after an almost imperceptible pause, nodded. "Okay, thanks."

He was a little surprised, too. He didn't have anything against kids—his nieces were cute little things,
his nephews satisfyingly destructive, and some of the
kids who came to the ranch turned out to be crack little
riders—but for the most part, he kept his distance.
Now, though, he headed out to the front of the barn
with the sort of curiosity and low-grade anticipation
that he usually felt when he was facing off opposite a
new greenie—a combination of hoping that things
wouldn't get too rough and wondering how things
were going to turn out.

Granted, Lizzie's mom had a point; she wasn't a
greenie or a house pet. Still, he thought that maybe he
could help. If nothing else, he was darn good at reading
body language.

The little girl was sitting on the bench out front,
kicking her legs and staring at her computer pad with
what looked like total absorption. But when he came
out of the barn, her shoulders hunched in a little, letting him know she'd seen him. Kind of like a mustang
avoiding eye contact but flicking back an ear to say, *I
know you're watching me.*

"Lizzie?"

She hesitated, then looked up at him with the sort of
semiinsulting blankness he associated with teenage
greenhorns and was usually followed by "Yeah?
What's it to you?" or the ever-annoying "Whatever."

He didn't think she meant it that way, though. Not when her shoulders hunched in even farther and her fingers tightened on the computer tablet.

"Your mom is taking Loco out to the arena. Come with me, and I'll show you where you can sit and get the best view." He made it an order, not a question.

She hesitated, then stood slowly, never taking her eyes off him. He didn't stare back—that was predator behavior, and while she wasn't prey, she sure acted like it.

Which got him thinking, and not in a good direction. Was she afraid of him? Afraid of men? Afraid of new things in general? More importantly, why? Her mother made it sound like it was just one of those things, a phase that some kids went through, especially ones who were shy to begin with. And the reading he'd done backed that up . . . but it also said that very rarely, cases of SM were brought on by trauma, and when they were, the cases were severe.

He glanced back to make sure she was following— she was, though from a distance—and led her through the barn instead of walking around. That didn't seem to bother her, and she even glanced into Sassy's stall on the way by.

Good sign, he thought, and headed for the arena, where he put her in the covered judges' stand they used for rodeoing and timed events. Then he turned his attention to her mother.

The city fancy—*Shelby*, he thought, not liking the nickname now that he'd gotten to know her a little, and gotten to respect what she was dealing with—stood near the mounting block talking softly to Loco, who had his head pressed flat against her chest while she stroked his face and fondled his ears.

For a second there, Foster seriously envied his horse.

Aware of Lizzie's eyes suddenly locking on him, as if she had caught some of the vibe, he cleared his throat and said to Shelby, "You ready to ride?"

Shelby grinned. "I think I put him to sleep."

"Looks like. Let's wake him up and get some work out of him."

He spent the next while coaching her through the process of checking her unfamiliar tack, then mounting up and guiding Loco through the series of exercises he usually used to evaluate the guests who claimed to already know how to ride. Unlike most of the guests he dealt with eight months of the year—where the beginners tended to grossly exaggerate their abilities and the experienced riders tended to underplay theirs for fear of being stuck with a bronc—Shelby was right about where he would've expected for someone who was getting back into the saddle after a couple of years of good lessons as a kid. And yeah, as he'd thought, she had a pretty good natural feel.

Hopefully that wouldn't backfire, making Lizzie jealous rather than giving her courage. They'd have to play it by ear.

Once Shelby got a little accustomed to the idea of neck reining and stopped trying to sit like an English rider on the more chair-seated Western saddle, she did a fair job of guiding Loco through a simple pattern of walk, jog, and lope, with some halts that Foster threw in to show her how good the gelding's emergency brakes could be. Not that she needed them, as Loco was being an angel—which was why, once upon a time, he'd made the big bucks.

Foster didn't let himself admire her natural posture or soft seat except as a means to an end—*hello, keep it professional*—and kept an equal eye on Lizzie, too, because that was the point of the whole exercise. Sitting up in the judges' box, she seemed intent on her e-reader, lips pursed, fingers working to change pages at regular intervals. But her body was angled toward the arena, and once or twice he caught her looking over at Loco, following her mom's ride.

Shelby must've seen the same thing, because after she finished walking the gelding dry from his light sweat, she rode over to the judges' stand and reined to a halt. "Lizzie, how about you come down here and meet Loco?"

After a pause, the girl put down her e-reader and drifted to the front of the judges' box. But she stalled at the edge of the platform.

"Come on down," Shelby urged brightly. "He's fine. You're fine."

Instead, the kid sat next to the stairs, dangling her legs over the edge and looking anywhere but at her mother.

"How about if I bring him over to you?"

Whatever-faced, Lizzie kicked back against the supporting beams, both feet together, hitting with dull, echoing thuds that had Loco flicking his ears.

"Lizzie. Please stop that." Shelby's snap brought the gelding's head up, but didn't have much effect on the kid. If anything the drumming got louder. Shelby flushed a little, and Foster could see her doing a ten-count in her head. And now, like last night, he caught a flash of how hard she worked to keep herself level when it came to her child.

Before things escalated to the point of things-we'll-regret-later, he stepped in between them. "Hey, Lizzie, I'm going to need your help this week, if you're up for it."

Shelby frowned. "What did you have in mind?"

"I need her to babysit you."

The foot banging stopped.

Talking to Lizzie now, he said, "Your mom did a great job with Loco, don't you think? So she's going to help me out by riding him during the week while I'm out with the guests. But as good as she did today, I don't think it's safe for her to ride completely alone, so I'd like you to come out here with her every day and keep an eye on her for me. Can you do that?"

She didn't nod, but he felt as if she was really looking at him for the first time, really seeing him, like when a newly gathered mustang finally made its first eye contact, starting to think that maybe humans weren't that bad after all.

"I'm not trying to scare you," he continued. "I trust Loco and I trust your mom. But sometimes things just happen, and it's not anybody's fault, but people get hurt." She blinked, though he didn't know if he was getting through. "That's why I want you to keep an eye on her and Loco." He paused. "Do you have a way to call for help if you get in trouble?"

Shelby drew breath to answer, but when he shot her a warning look, she bit her lower lip and subsided.

Pretending he was waiting for a greenie to approach him and take a carrot butt from his hand, Foster just stood there, staying chilled out, not staring at her or anything. Just hanging out, waiting. *No agenda, nothing to see here, all the time in the world.* He enjoyed the way the sun warmed his hat, smelled the char from last night's bonfire, felt the good press of his boots in the Wyoming soil. And, when his head started getting too hot, he thought it was just about time to swap out his black felt hat for summer white. In the high country, black and white hats didn't signify villains and good guys, but rather whether a cowboy was trying to warm his head or keep it cool.

So he let his thoughts wander underneath that too-hot hat . . . And after a few minutes, the little girl slowly reached into her pocket and pulled out a bright pink whistle.

Shelby made a noise in the back of her throat.

He kept his expression neutral. "That's a good-looking whistle." Not wanting to push it one step further and take ten steps back, instead—which was always the risk with this sort of thing—he looked over at Shelby. "She willing to use it?"

"Doubtful. She doesn't like to make noise. But she's got her phone, too. The signal is spotty in places, but I got boosters for both of us. She's got the ranch's main landline under emergency contacts and an SOS tone she can transmit. Krista and Gran know it means to come find her, and how to do it using her TinyGPS."

She was staring at her daughter, expression unreadable.

"It's a start." To Lizzie, he said, "Okay, how about this? If you think your mom needs help and you can't get through on the phone or with the whistle, I want you to slowly climb down out of the stands—slowly, okay? You don't want to spook Loco by moving too fast—and then, when you're out of his sight, I want you to book it to the barn first and then up to the house. Grab some grown-ups and drag them back here. Got it?"

He waited. *No agenda. Just watching the grass grow.* He knew better than to let his mind latch on to all the stuff he needed to get done today. Animals could smell that kind of pressure, and invariably chose the worst possible moment to misbehave or hurt themselves. And kids—at least according to his sister—had the same radar. Better, even.

After a long-feeling while, Lizzie nodded.

"Cool." Not making a big deal out of it, he glanced over at Shelby. "You ready to hop off and let Loco head back out to the corral with his friends?"

"Sounds like a plan," she said, and if she seemed a little toned down, he figured she was tired, or wilted from working in the sun for a solid hour on the first really warm day of the summer.

Lizzie trailed them from a distance and plonked back down on the bench with her reader. Foster would've liked it if she had come in with them, but he didn't push it. Pleased enough with the day's progress, he was whistling as he came into the barn, where

Shelby already had Loco on the cross ties. He came up beside her as she struggled with the cinch.

Instead of helping her—she'd learn faster figuring it out on her own—he hitched his thumbs in his pockets and said, "I thought that went well."

She whirled on him, her expression fierce. "Next time, *talk* to me first before you make a decision like that about my daughter." She wasn't loud, but her whisper packed as much of a punch as the finger she drilled into his chest.

Uh-oh. Angry mama bear alert. He backpedaled. "Wait a sec. I didn't mean—"

"I don't have any doubt that your intentions were good, but that's not the point. The point is that she's my kid. I know her—and her condition—better than you ever could."

"But I—"

"Should've asked me first whether I want to ride during the week." She took a furious breath. "Not to mention that—"

He did the only thing he could think of: he put a hand over her mouth and said firmly, "My turn." His body was already jangling, and it just got worse when he touched her, but what mattered was that she was right. "I get it. I'm the boss of the barn, and I'm not real used to running my decisions past anyone. But I overstepped just now, and I'm sorry."

She stepped back, away from his touch, eyes suddenly wary. But she didn't launch any more salvos. Instead, she took a deep breath and looked down, concentrating as she swiped her hands on her jeans, completely oblivious of the smudge of dirt on her cheek.

It was an extremely cute smudge, he couldn't help noticing.

Finally, she sighed and looked back up at him. "Okay, then. Thanks for understanding. And . . . well, maybe I'm overreacting. Probably. Sorry about that."

"No problem. Comes with the territory, I expect."

"You can say that again."

"Want to make it up to me?"

Her eyes narrowed. "How so?"

"Nothing funny, so you can stop giving me that look." It made him grin, though, and wonder whether maybe she wasn't as immune to him as he'd been thinking. "I'm serious about wanting you to ride Loco for me during the week. He likes you, he could use the work, and it'd be something you and Lizzie could do together, especially if you ask her to watch your back. I'm not a parent, and I don't play one on TV, but it seems to me that the sense of responsibility might do her good, help her get more involved with the horses, give her some power. You know the drill."

She hesitated, then slowly nodded. "Yeah. Sure. That sounds good."

"All righty, then. It's a plan."

He turned away as she grabbed a brush and got to work on Loco's sweat-salted coat. But although he should've felt good about how they'd gotten out of that one without any bloodshed—and better yet, they were back on common ground, and had a training plan in place—he couldn't settle. Because as he headed into the tack room, he could still feel the softness of her skin against his palm, and he knew darn well he was lying to himself, or at least trying to.

This wasn't just about him helping Lizzie get over being afraid of the horses, not anymore. It was about the little girl's mama, too, and the way she made him feel. And what the heck was he going to do about that?

7

A kiss is just a kiss,
but Mint-Os fresh breath is an all-day affair.

By late that night, after the new crop of guests—arriving for a three-generation family reunion, heavy on the Irish—had been welcomed, oriented, and fed, and had scattered to their cabins, Shelby was flat-out, bone-deep exhausted. So tired that, not long after Lizzie crashed for the night, she flopped down on her own bed.

Where she lay staring out the window as the stars came out.

"Go to sleep, dang it," she muttered, and tried to follow her own orders.

A while later, a coyote—or maybe even a wolf?—howled in the distance, shivering the back of her neck. A couple of others answered, even farther away. The room cooled. Her thoughts spun, refusing to quiet, or even settle enough so she could deal with them. Not that there was anything to deal with, really. Things were fine. One day at a time. Rome wasn't built overnight. Have a Coke and a smile.

"Okay. This isn't working." Shoving out of bed, she yanked on a pair of yoga pants and flip-flops, zipped a fleece over her sleep shirt, and headed for the kitchen. Five minutes later, as she pushed through the kitchen's back door into air loaded with the yeasty scent of rising bread, she muttered, "Some nights, a girl just needs ice cream, damn it."

"Amen, sister."

Shelby stopped dead. "Oh!"

Krista sat at the end of the stainless steel counter with a distinctive pint in front of her. She held up her spoon. "Phish Food?"

"I thought Ben and Jerry were forbidden." Gran had a near-pathological aversion to Deadheads and ice cream with crunchy stuff in it, which meant that the B&J boys were verboten.

"Ergo, we must destroy the evidence," Krista said. "I could use your help."

"Something tells me you're doing fine on your own. I'll just grab some cake and get scarce."

"Don't be dumb." Krista kicked out a stool. "Grab a spoon, instead."

Giving in, Shelby snagged a bowl and spoon and rummaged in one of the big commercial fridges for a half-full bowl of whipped cream left over from dessert. Behind that was a wrapped chunk of day-old devil's food cake, which she also pulled out.

"Ooh, gimme." Krista beckoned. "I didn't know that was in there. See? I'm already glad you're here. Hey, are there any cherries and hot fudge? We can make some killer brownie sundaes."

"We shouldn't."

"Why the heck not? It's Saturday night."

Unable to argue with that logic, Shelby found the cherries and sauce, along with a Ziploc bag of chopped walnuts. They spent a few minutes assembling a day's worth of calories—maybe more—in two big bowls, and then Krista said, "Come on. I've got an idea."

"Not more food."

"Nope. Follow me."

Krista led the way up a wide staircase and along a hallway with bedroom doors leading off on either side, to the window at the end. She ran it open, letting in the night. "I hope you're not afraid of heights." Not waiting for Shelby's answer, she ducked through the window and disappeared into the darkness. A moment later, her voice floated back. "Oh, jeez. Cabin Five left their shades up. Come on, we'll go around to the other side."

Forewarned, Shelby kept her eyes off the glow of the cabin windows as she edged one leg and her ice cream out, and then balanced on the sill while her vision adjusted to the moonlight. "Krista?"

"Over here. You want a hand?"

"No, I'm good." She could see her now, leaning back against a dormer halfway down the peaked ridge of the dining hall roof. Grateful that she was wearing flip-flops rather than her still-slippery boots, Shelby picked her way over and sank down beside her with a sigh. "Nice. This is nice. Good idea." Then she dug up a bite of sloppy sundae, popped the spoon in her mouth, and nearly groaned. "Even better idea."

"Tough day?" Krista's voice held a thread of amusement.

"I'm not the one who was sitting in the kitchen on a midnight date with our boys B and J."

"You would've been if I came down fifteen minutes later."

"Good point." Shelby looked up at the sky. The moon was on its downswing, the stars more prominent than before. "You were there first, though. Everything okay?"

Krista dug into her sundae. "Yeah, I was just . . . I don't know, thinking things through."

"Ranch things?"

"Ranch things. Family things. Guy things."

"You've got a guy? Why didn't I know that?"

"Because he's not my guy anymore."

"Ah. Sorry."

"Don't be. I'm not." But she dug into her bowl with a vengeance. Then she exhaled and set her spoon aside. "Okay, maybe I'm sorry, but more that I put so much of myself into something that I should've known wasn't going anywhere. Things worked so well between us in college that I thought . . . I don't know. That it would work in real life, too. Only it turned out that our ideas of 'real life' were too far apart." She shook her head. "It's so obvious now, I don't know why I didn't see it sooner."

"Don't." Shelby wanted to reach out to her, but wasn't sure exactly how, so she took a bite of ice cream, instead. Then, as her temples throbbed with impending brain freeze, she said, "Trust me, it's not worth doing the hindsight-is-twenty-twenty thing. Or only a little, to try and take the lessons learned, and then move on."

Krista shifted to look at her in the darkness. "Is that what you've done?"

"More or less."

They sat in companionable silence for a moment, spooning up calories and appreciating the dark, quiet night, before Krista said, "So, tit for tat. What brings you out for therapeutic ice cream this evening?"

Shelby hesitated. "I don't know. I'm just feeling . . . unsettled, I guess."

Krista glanced at her. "Homesick?"

"No, it's not that. At least I don't think so." Home was just . . . home. She didn't miss it, didn't really think about it. Which should have surprised her more than it did.

"Are you worried about Lizzie?"

"Always." But she sighed. "It wasn't her today, at least not directly. It was me. I got irritated with her and took it out on Foster."

"Foster? I thought Stace was teaching you."

"She had something to do, so he filled in." She was guessing there, but it seemed the most likely explanation. "I guess I owe you a 'you were right and I was wrong' on Foster. He really is sweet, deep down inside. He sure put up with my Cranky McBitchy Pants routine like a trouper."

"What did I tell you? He's the best. He's been working here six, maybe seven years now, since the first summer we went dude. I've never seen anyone better with the horses and cattle, and the guests love the strong, silent routine."

It took an effort, but Shelby squelched the urge to

ask anything more about him, partly because she wasn't a big fan of gossip, and partly because she didn't want to give Krista any ideas about her and Foster. "Anyway, he handled himself really well, even when I tried to bite his head off after the lesson."

"How was the ride up to that point?"

"Fun. Loco is an absolute doll."

"Duh."

"I know, right?" Shelby could finally laugh at herself a little. "Here's poor Foster, trying to help me out by putting all this thought into how we can get Lizzie comfortable with the horses. He lets me ride a lovely babysitter of a horse and does his best to make me look like a star in front of my kid, and how do I thank him? I snarl at him for doing exactly what we'd agreed, which was to get Lizzie involved in my riding."

"Aw, Foster's tough. He can take it."

Shelby thought about that V of skin at his throat beneath his snap-studded shirt, and how he wore the shirt because it would peel off easy if he got in trouble. Which got her thinking about the noise those snaps would make, the feel of them giving way beneath her fingers . . . *And he's doing you a favor. Don't complicate things any more than you already have.* "He shouldn't have to take anything like that from me," she insisted. "I need to do better. Lizzie needs to know she's safe, no matter what."

"What about you?"

"Excuse me?"

"When do you get to feel safe? Or, heck, when do you get to do something for yourself?"

Though sorely tempted to take a monumental bite of her melting sundae, Shelby sighed and let the spoon clink against the side of her bowl. "I do plenty for myself back home. Lunches out. Pedicures. The occasional chocolate binge."

"Dates? Vacations?"

"Hello, pot? This is the kettle."

"We're not talking about me anymore."

"I vote we backtrack."

"Overruled." Krista grinned. "Look, I know you're here for Lizzie's sake, and this probably wouldn't be your first choice for an extended summer vaca."

Shelby fidgeted with her spoon. "I like it here."

"Glad to hear it, but that doesn't change my point. Even though this summer is about Lizzie, it can be a little about you, too. In fact, it might be better that way. It can't be easy for her, knowing you took the whole summer off from your job and came all the way out here just so she can be around the horses. That's its own sort of pressure, don't you think?"

"She doesn't have a clue that's what's going on."

"Are you sure? Kids understand more than you think sometimes."

Shelby almost said, "Talk to me when you're a mom," but she held it in. "If she knows that much, then she knows there's no pressure."

"Sometimes there's a difference between knowing something and believing it, deep down inside."

Shelby frowned. "You're assuming she knows how much of this summer is aimed at her. I never put it that way, never even hinted at it."

"She's a thinker."

"She's nine." But how much did she really know about how her daughter's mind worked? The last time they'd had a real, back-and-forth conversation, Lizzie was seven and Mr. Pony was brand-new. The knowledge ached like a pulled muscle.

"All I'm saying is that it can't be easy being the focus of all this attention, even if it's subtle."

That resonated, and not in a good way. "So I should . . . what? Ignore her half the time?"

"Now you're being snippy." But Krista didn't sound offended. "I'm just saying it might be good for her to see you doing something for yourself here, too. You know, having a little fun, getting out, enjoying yourself."

"Riding was fun." Surprisingly so.

"But not your choice to start with. Try again."

"Softball with Stace?"

Krista laughed. "Not if it makes you sound like you're suggesting a recreational root canal. Look, you don't have to come up with anything right now. This isn't a test and you're not being graded. I'm just saying you should think about getting out a little, having a little fun." She nudged her with an elbow. "Being a little naughty."

"Watch it, or you're going to get me in trouble with Rule Twelve."

"What?"

"Never mind."

Between work, riding, a trip into town, and exploring the ranch's activities with Lizzie, the week flew by so fast that Shelby was startled to hit the kitchen for her afternoon shift and see wings, burgers, pulled pork, and corn bread listed on the master wipe board.

There was no sign of Gran, but the familiar blue-and-white bowl sat on the steel counter, covered with its saucy red-checked towel, so she said, "Hey, Herman, what gives? I thought barbecue night was on Fridays."

"It is," answered a deep, booming voice.

Shelby jolted, then laughed back over her shoulder. "For a second I thought I was going over to the dark side."

Gran stepped in from the hallway and said in her normal voice, "Talking to the sourdough, you mean?"

"I don't mind that part. It's him talking back that worries me."

"Give it time. We all go a little crazy out here—it just takes different forms, depending on how you look at the world. I chat with my bread, Arthur pretends it's still the 'seventies—minus the shag rug and all his hair—Eddie married Rose, and Krista has her rescues. Who knows how it'll show up in you?"

"Fortunately—or unfortunately, I suppose, depending on how you look at it—Lizzie and I won't be here long enough to contract full-blown ranch-itis." Though she had a feeling the place would stick with them long after Labor Day. Maybe not the way she had hoped in terms of the horses—over the past week, Lizzie hadn't done much more than sit on the bleachers with her whistle, playing on her iPad while Shelby rode—but they'd had some other fun mom-daughter adventures, storing up experiences they never could've gotten in the city.

"Poosh." Gran waved that off. "Look at Eddie and Rose. Last I heard, they were taking drag racing lessons—drag racing!—at some track in Ohio. And Jenny is down in Belize, living in a tent and eating bugs or something while filming one of those reality TV shows. We're not normal, I tell you." She grinned evilly at Shelby. "You're already losing track of the days. That's the first symptom of ranch-itis, and once you start the slide, there's no turning back."

"Is it really Friday?"

"All day."

"Jeez. Guess I must be having fun." And she was, really, but just not in the way she'd expected. She liked riding Loco, liked having the huge outdoors to wander with Lizzie, seeing everything from purple flower-filled fields to the neighboring ranch's buffalo and ostrich, and the occasional tantalizing glimpse of the free-ranging horses that gave the ranch its name. She hadn't seen any predators yet, but Krista had mentioned finding mountain lion prints the other day. In a weird way, though, it didn't feel all that different from the city. Shelby carried her pepper spray, stayed aware of her and Lizzie's surroundings, and made sure someone back at the main house knew where they had gone on their rambles. And even though Lizzie hadn't made the big breakthrough they both wanted, Shelby thought she was making more eye contact, smiling more.

Maybe. Hopefully.

"So," she said to Herman. "I guess that means it's barbecue day?"

"Yes, ma'am," Gran said in her Herman voice.

Thinking it sounded like Cookie Monster after he'd been kicked in the nuts, Shelby stifled a grin. "Want me to get started on the wings?"

"Sounds good. We'll work on the corn bread." Gran tucked Herman under her arm. "And don't forget the bonfire later tonight. Marshmallows and gossip, be there or be square."

"I wouldn't miss it for all the s'mores in the world. We'll be there."

But by the time the stars came out and the bonfire was under way, Lizzie was tired and withdrawn, and after a brief debate with herself, Shelby left her daughter with her phone close at hand and a horse movie on her iPad, and went down to the party alone for the second week in a row.

And, for the second week in a row, she found herself hesitating at the edge of the lake. This time, though, it wasn't because she was ducking Krista and the others. It was because she wanted to see someone else more.

She wasn't sure if Foster had been avoiding her, or if he'd just been busy with his normal duties and hadn't had the time to find her and say hi. Not that he would've had any real reason to come find her. Unless he'd wanted to, in which case he would have.

Right?

"Note to self," she said. "Get a grip." She wasn't the silly sixteen-year-old version of herself who'd fallen stupid in love with the captain of the football team two towns over, only to find out too late that he had girlfriends in three different high schools. And she wasn't the starry-eyed romantic she'd been at twenty, when she'd fallen for Patrick because he'd been everything her father wasn't, or so she'd thought. No, she was a grown-up and a mom who had learned that her hormones had some seriously bad judgment in the guy department. Or maybe they had wised up, too, because there was no arguing that Foster was a good man. He was quietly thoughtful, good with animals and kids, and responsible as the day was long. But even if she was interested in more than a "what if" sort of way, she didn't have any reason to think he felt the same sort of *va-voom* she did. He'd been nothing but professional.

Which made him a safe crush, come to think.

Hello, head case.

Laughing at herself, she headed for the dock, shucked off her boots, and stuck her feet into the water, shivering as the cold bit in. It felt more refreshing than painful this week. Did that mean it was getting warmer, or was she cowboying up?

"Ready for a swim?" Foster asked from close behind her.

This time she managed not to jump out of her skin, barely. Hoping he couldn't see her blush, she twisted back to grin up at him. "Not unless this pond comes with a heater. I like my creature comforts."

Don't babble, she told herself, and stifled an inner laugh. When was the last time she'd gotten flustered talking to a guy? She worked with men all the time, from the hot UPS guy all the girls in the office drooled over to the high-rolling creative directors of huge companies, and they didn't get to her one bit. This guy, though—this cowboy—had her tripping over her words.

It's the atmosphere, she told herself, *and the fact that there's a limited pool of Y chromosomes here.* If she had met him in the city, he would've blended into the crowd.

Okay, maybe not.

The silence had stretched out long enough to get a little awkward, so she added, "I didn't hear you this time, either."

"I invoked my supersecret ninja mode." He gestured down.

There was the humor she'd suspected, thought she'd seen, only to have him hide it, as if he didn't want her to notice. "Ah," she said, following his gesture, "no boots. Ninja, indeed." And darned if she didn't get a little charge out of seeing his bare feet and rolled-up jeans. One of his big toes was crooked, and his ankles and the tops of his feet were lightly dusted with short, wiry hairs and a few surprising freckles, just visible in the muted moonlight. "I, um, guess that means you're ready for a swim?"

"Not so much, but if a city girl can hack it, so can I." He sat down and swung his feet around to drop them into the water with a sigh. "Ah. Balmy."

"My thoughts exactly." Sort of, only she wasn't feeling the lake's chill anymore. He'd left a good distance between them, so it didn't make any sense that she could feel the heat from his body. Or that when he shifted to brace one hand between them at the edge of the dock, it was as if he'd touched her, even though he was still several inches away.

Hello? A grip. Get one. It wasn't even like he'd come to see her, not really. Like any good trainer, he was checking in on the week's progress.

"I should thank you again for letting me ride Loco. He's been incredibly patient with me. I've gotten to where I can just about complete the pattern at the trot—um, I mean 'jog'—and I can sort of fumble through it at the lope, though it's not pretty."

Foster just nodded. "And Lizzie?"

She squelched the ingrained instinct to give him the standard *she's fine, everything's fine.* "Not much progress to report, I'm afraid. She'll sit outside the stalls all day with the guards up, feeding wisps of hay one at a time, but she won't set foot inside the barn if there's a horse on the cross ties."

"It'll come."

She wished she had his confidence, but while he knew horses, she knew her kid. "Stace has been great—she's swapped over to unmounted lessons, teaching her about the parts of the horse and all the equipment, and explaining some of the theory of riding, and especially how to read their body language and stay safe around them." And Lizzie, in her own way, was eating up the lessons. She stayed focused and quiet, even nodding to herself from time to time. But when Shelby brought up the idea of her riding, or even helping brush the saintly Loco, she shut right back down.

"Stace knows her stuff. And she knows when to push, when to lay off. You've got plenty of time yet, Mama Bear. Don't let it get you down."

She blew out a breath, trying to stem the prickles of irritation. "I know you're right, and that's what I keep telling myself. Only it's what I've been telling myself for the past two years." Longer, really, because before

Lizzie's problems, things had been going from bad to worse with Patrick, with her waiting it out and telling herself to be patient, that things would get better. Only they hadn't, not on either front. "I just wish—" She broke off, suddenly aware that her pulse was too quick, her fingers wrapped around the edge of the dock hard enough to hurt. "I wish it could be different, that's all."

"Getting frustrated'll just make things worse."

The blush got a thousand times worse. "You think I don't know that?"

"I'm just saying."

"You're—" She bit it off and made herself count to ten, concentrating on the chill of the water . . . and, after a moment, the knowledge that she was only annoyed because he was right. This wasn't about Patrick or the past two years. She needed to focus on today, and the knowledge that Lizzie had made some progress since they'd come here. "Darn it. I'm not mad at her. It's just . . ." She sighed. "I'm not. I love her like crazy, no matter what."

Had she said that enough recently?

He nudged her with his arm. "Don't beat yourself up. We all have those days. It's not about never getting frustrated, whether it's with a kid, yourself, a horse, a job, or whatever. It's about holding it together until you get someplace where you can blow off some steam without it setting things back."

She looked over, expecting to see his profile as he stared across the lake to the fire, where Ty strummed his guitar and several couples were swaying in a slow dance.

Instead, he was staring straight at her.

The flush came back with a vengeance, this time starting in her chest and warming her there for a second before it spread up her throat to her face. "Um."

"How do you blow off steam, Shelby?"

Had he called her by name before? Maybe once or twice, but never before while looking at her as if she was his entire focus. No horses, no Lizzie, just her. Heat prickled along her nerve endings and gathered in her belly, and she had a sudden crazy image of reaching for him, touching him. His denim jacket would be faintly rough, the leather-lined collar smooth, and then his skin would go from soft to raspy where beard stubble roughened the skin, making textures in the reflected firelight. He wasn't wearing his hat—was that in the Ninja Code?—and his hair swept back from his forehead in thick, inviting waves that made her itch to touch, to explore.

Don't do it, she told herself. Either things would get real awkward real fast, or else they wouldn't, and she'd be going down a path that didn't make any sense. Sex—or any sort of romantic entanglement, really—wasn't recreational for her. It was . . . well, she didn't know what it was, but it wasn't recreational.

"Seriously," he pressed. "What do you do to decompress?"

"I, um . . ." She scrambled to reassemble her thoughts, wondering if Krista had said something to him, or if everyone looked at her and wondered what she did for fun, if anything. Did she have an invisible *I Seriously Need to Get a Life* tattoo on her forehead? "I don't know. I just hold it together, I guess." Most of the time, anyway. And when things built up to the point that she couldn't hack it anymore, she waited until Lizzie was asleep, shut herself in the bathroom, and had a good shower cry. And she so wasn't telling him that.

"Better to give yourself an outlet. Take it from someone who knows. Things can build up without you realizing it, and then you'll make mistakes that can echo on for longer than you think."

It was the closest he'd come to saying anything personal to her, and the regret in his voice was palpable. A little shimmer went through her, a tightening of the heat inside. "Like what kind of mistakes?"

"Not the kind you'd make with your little one, not in a million years."

In other words, MYOB. She frowned, but didn't let herself push. "Okay, so what do you do to blow off steam?" That shouldn't have felt like a cheesy pickup line, not when they were talking about her daughter. Except they weren't exactly talking about Lizzie anymore, and it was starting to feel more like getting-to-know-you conversation than planning strategy.

Maybe. Possibly.

He shrugged. "These days, I play the guitar a little, ride out by myself a lot, watch a movie now and then. When I was younger, I would've gone up into the high country and wasted some bullets. Maybe gotten drunk and picked a fight. Didn't take me too long to figure out that didn't fix anything, and I didn't much enjoy it, so I went in another direction."

She looked away, to where the dancers had made a ring around the bonfire, and seemed to be doing the chicken dance. "Yeah. I get how that is."

Silence descended. It didn't feel awkward this time, but it wasn't quite comfortable, either. More like they were both waiting for something. After a moment, he said, "You want to tell me about when she went quiet?"

And there it was, the question everybody wanted to ask, but few ever did except the doctors. It wasn't hard to answer, though—not when she'd been over it a million times in her head, trying to find the missing piece, the "aha" moment that would fix everything. Except there wasn't an "aha," wasn't any magic cure.

"It started when she was six and a half, in first grade," she said, staring out over the water. "Her teacher let me know she was having trouble reading, and getting flustered about it. We worked on it, and she was getting better, but there was this bully . . ." She shrugged. "Anyway, SM usually grows out of a combination of things—perfectionism, shyness, sensitivity, sometimes a learning disability and the shame that comes with it . . . It all goes into robbing a kid of her voice, a little bit at a time, until one day she's not talking at all, not even at home."

"And her father?"

"That was part of it. Patrick and I had been struggling for a while, holding it together for Lizzie's sake, and because we kept hoping it would get better." At least she had kept hoping it would, telling herself that all he needed was a couple of new jobs for his company, a little less pressure from his boss, fewer boozy nights out with his coworkers. "When she started having trouble, he . . . checked out, I guess you could say. He didn't want to deal with a learning-disabled kid on top of everything else."

"She seems plenty bright to me." Foster's expression stayed mild, but his voice gained an edge.

"Having a hiccup in the learning process doesn't mean a kid isn't bright, even brilliant, or that she can't catch up. For some of them, it just means they need a little extra help to get over a hump here and there. That's how it was for Lizzie, at least when it came to reading." She paused, wondering how it was possible that those chaotic, upsetting months could boil down to a couple of sentences. "By that time, though, the SM had kicked in and Patrick had moved out. We kept the divorce as amicable as possible, and he promised to be good about visiting, but when she went all the way quiet, he disappeared. I haven't heard from him in more than a year."

Foster made an annoyed sound at the back of his throat.

"It wasn't his fault, at least the SM part. It wasn't anybody's fault. It just . . . happens sometimes." She looked up at the stars and the pretty blue half-moon overhead. "I did everything I could, read everything I could get my hands on, tried all the therapies, but nothing helped. She slipped away, into her own head, getting quieter and quieter. After a while she even turned off the volume on all her games . . . and I got in the habit of leaving the radio on all the time, or the TV, just so there was some noise in the condo." She glanced back at him. "Not here, though. Here, the quiet doesn't bother me nearly so much."

He stayed silent for a moment, then exhaled a pent-up-sounding breath. "I wish I knew what string to pull here, what button to push that could help her."

Pressure lumped beneath her heart. "You've already done more than I can ever repay."

Another harsh noise. "You don't owe me anything."

"Lizzie, then. You've been incredibly helpful, and since she's not going to tell you she's grateful, I will."

"That's not what this is about." He turned to face her fully, voice dropping, almost as if he was talking to himself when he said, "Maybe it started that way, but even then I was fooling myself."

Her pulse thudded in her ears. Did he mean . . . ? No way. *Down, girl.* "I don't understand."

His rusty chuckle seemed even more out of practice than the lopsided smile that curved his lips, making him suddenly look younger and easier, and maybe even a little mischievous. "Then I'm even worse at this than I thought."

The *thudda-thudda* of her pulse suddenly went to a *boom-chicka-wa-wa* and the heated prickles in her belly flared outward, becoming an all-body flush. Still not sure she was reading him right, she said, "Worse at what?"

"This." He moved in and kissed her with unerring aim in the moonlit darkness.

8

When Foster had finally given in to the urge he'd been battling all week and gone to find Shelby, he'd meant to ask about Lizzie and Loco, and talk to her about riding plans for both of them. He'd told himself "hands off" so many times it'd become a Yoda-esque mantra: *Stay professional, you will. Hands off, you'll keep.*

Yeah, he thought as he tasted her. *Not.*

This might be the worst move he'd pulled recently, but it sure as heck felt like one of the best. Maybe *the* best. Her lips were soft and lush, and they parted beneath his with a surprised noise that invited him in. He took that invitation, sliding closer on the dock and slipping an arm around behind her to deepen the kiss.

And hello, fireworks.

He didn't remember the last time he'd kissed a woman—okay, he did, and it was way too long ago—but he sure didn't remember this sort of sizzle. If there had been, he wouldn't have waited so long. Because, damn.

The curve of her breast brushed against him as his

arm settled naturally at the dip of her waist, bracketing her against him. The dock rocked beneath them as his tongue touched hers—or maybe that was the whole dang world moving as her flavor lit him up and made the icy water feel warm around his ankles. It was the kind of moment that cowboys had written songs about for more than two centuries, the kind of kiss that could end old feuds and start new ones. And make a smart man make a big mistake . . . like getting in too deep with a woman like her.

But where before that had rung true, now the vibe was faintly off, because even though she was from the city, and fancy as all get-out—even in curvy Wranglers and snap-studded shirts that should've made her look like a local—there was more to her than just that. She was Lizzie's mom, Krista's friend, Gran's backup, Loco's new human. She liked it here, and the people and animals at Mustang Ridge liked her back.

Which meant . . . heck, he didn't know what it meant, or if it should mean anything at all. Especially when she made a sexy noise at the back of her throat and cuddled up against him, making his skin feel like it was stretched tight. He ran a hand over her thick, glossy hair and drew her closer as he added a nibble, a nip, a heated breath against her throat. He wanted to ease her down to the dock that swayed beneath them and lie beside her, wanted to take her, make her his own.

Instead, slowly and with piles of regret coming straight from the tight places inside him, he ended the kiss and pressed his lips to her forehead.

Then, after a moment that wasn't nearly long enough, he shifted away, still with an arm around her in case she was anywhere near as wobbly as him.

Shelby blinked up at him and pressed her lips together in a move that sent a lightning burn of heat straight to his gut. "Oh," she said, her voice soft, husky, and surprised. "I thought . . . I kept telling myself . . ."

"What?"

"That this was all about Lizzie. That she's a project to you, like one of your mustangs."

"You said she wasn't a horse."

"She isn't. But, Foster . . . you and me . . ." She shook her head even as she lifted a hand and touched his jaw with a soft caress that heated his blood. "I'm not sure this is a good idea."

He didn't have any answers for her, didn't even have them for himself. "Can we just leave it that it's a pretty night and you're under my skin, and we're both going to think about that kiss after I leave?"

As cowboy poetry went, that pretty much sucked. But she smiled a little, anyway, and ducked her head to exhale a soft breath. "Okay. Yeah, okay."

He climbed to his feet, careful not to touch her again, because he wasn't sure he'd be able to stop things this time if they started up again. "Meet me in the barn tomorrow morning. I'll take you riding."

She looked up and met his eyes. "It's a date." She hesitated. "Um, unless it's not. In which case, it's just a ride. Either way, I'll be there."

It's a ride, he thought, but his mouth mutinied and said, "It's a date."

*   *   *

The next morning, Shelby headed to the barn alone, mentally running through what she needed to say to Foster. The key points she needed to remember were things like "only here for the summer" and "need to focus on my daughter" with detours through "flattered" and "if things were different, I'd love to ride you like a trick pony."

Okay, so not that last part. But still. That kiss.

Wow.

Within a nanosecond, her cowboy crush had gone from being hands-off to being extremely hands-on, and wonderfully so. She didn't even remember the specifics of who did what—the details had gotten lost somewhere between *ohmigod* shock and *mmmmm* while her hormones sat up and sang a medley of soda commercials, heavy on the "What a feeling!" refrains.

After, though, she'd seen his face and heard the little voice in her head, and knew there were big reasons why she shouldn't go there. *Not in the market, just here for the summer, focusing on my daughter*. Know it. Love it.

But as she reached the parking area in front of the barn, her boots were dragging and the voice inside her head had stopped being all logical, and instead sounded way more like Krista, telling her, "*You need to do something for yourself now and then.*" Granted she hadn't said, "You need to do Foster"—she'd been thinking more along the lines of a hobby. Karaoke, maybe, or trout fishing. And Shelby didn't think Foster had been thinking about sex when he'd suggested she find a way to burn off her frustrations rather than letting them build up.

Then again, maybe he *had* been thinking about sex, because apparently still waters ran pretty deep in that department, and the attraction she'd been fighting was a mutual one. Ever since their kiss, she'd been seriously thinking about things like summer flings and temporary hookups for the first time in . . . well, ever.

And she should really stop it, man up, and be a grown-up about this. She needed to be a mom right now, nothing else.

Choco-delights, a small voice caroled in her head. *Because being a grown-up is overrated.*

"Oh, shut up," she muttered. The ads—showing women busting out of their offices and whooping it up at amusement parks, motocross, and other events— had been one of her more successful campaigns, sure, and she had a feeling the Choco-delights account had been the deciding factor in her boss's giving her a summer sabbatical rather than an ultimatum. Still, she didn't really need the Choco-chicks weighing in right now.

The barn doors were closed despite the early warmth of the day, which was unusual. Frowning, she rolled one of them aside, and called, "Hello?"

"Hey, Shelby," Stace called back. "Come on in!"

An initial pang of disappointment turned to confusion as her eyes adjusted and she saw a small crowd gathered at the far end of the aisle. Krista and Gran were there, along with Stace, looking expectant. Nearby, male voices rumbled from inside an open stall.

"Oh," Shelby breathed as comprehension dawned. "Sassy!"

Krista's grin lit her face. "We're having a baby! Come see. Or, wait, do you want to go get Lizzie?"

She only hesitated for a second before deciding that the experience would be good for her kiddo, even if it sparked a more in-depth version of the birds-and-bees conversation than the basics they had already been over. "I'll be back in a flash."

It was more like five minutes by the time she and a breathless Lizzie made it to the barn. Krista beckoned them in, eyes alight. "It's a boy, and he's almost all black, just like his daddy!"

Lizzie dogged Shelby's heels into the barn, pressing close as they joined the little knot of people outside the stall door, and looked in.

"Oh," Shelby said, her breath catching.

The double-size broodmare stall was thickly bedded with straw rather than the usual shavings, and the bedding rustled as Sassy reached down to nudge at a dark, damp foal that lay sprawled in the stall, its little ribs heaving with each labored breath.

Foster stood at the mare's shoulder, his face lit with such quiet pleasure that the stains on his shirt and jeans didn't seem that awful, and the earthy aroma of the stall was almost pleasant. His eyes went to Shelby the moment she came into view, and she met his gaze, too caught up in the moment to worry about what she was supposed to say to him, how she was supposed to act. Instead, laughter bubbled up. "Don't you look like a proud papa?"

He grinned and patted Sassy's sweat-dampened neck. "She did all the work."

"You don't need a vet?" Shelby suddenly realized that she and Gran were the only ones there who'd given birth, and there was a good chance that Gran had done something ranch-approved, like popping her son out in the back bedroom with a midwife and no drugs. *Shudder*.

Foster shrugged. "If things go wrong, it usually happens too fast for outside help to arrive, so it's best for a rancher to be ready for anything."

"He's being modest," Stace said. "Our Foster is a miracle when it comes to births. Foals, calves, puppies, kittens, you name it." She shot a fond look in Krista's direction. "Granted, it's not too often that we keep a riding horse stalled up with a Foal-Alert stitched in and a closed-circuit camera hung in the corner. Usually, we just keep an eye on them when it gets close to their time."

Krista just grinned. "The stud fee wasn't cheap, and Sassy is special. And like Stace said, I knew I had one of the best in my corner. Foster here has dealt with pretty much every possible delivery problem a horse or cow can have, and has a damn good track record of pulling everybody through safely."

He shrugged, looking a little "aw, shucks" about the whole thing. "I just do what makes sense."

"And read everything you can get your hands on, plus do the occasional ride along with Doc Lopes to the university's repro barn." To Shelby, she said, "He tries to say it's all about feel and listening to the critters, but he studies his butt off, too. Not one to leave things to chance, our Foster."

He cleared his throat. "Moving on, Doc will be here in a bit to make sure everything's good with Mama and pull blood on this little guy. Hopefully by then he'll be up and at 'em, and will have gotten his first bellyful of milk."

"Speaking of which," Krista said, winking at Shelby as she took pity and let him change the subject, "do you think we should help him up? He should be about ready to get vertical and nurse."

They all turned to study the little foal. Everyone but Shelby, that is. She took the moment to study the man of the hour.

Foster stood hip-shot at the mare's side, totally at ease with himself and the animals who relied on him. With a wisp of straw in his mouth and his hat tipped back on his head, he should've looked like the print ads for the ill-fated *Farmer Wants a Wife*, or, better yet, *Cowboy U.* But he wasn't one of those cowboys, at least not the way the target demographic thought of them. He wasn't outdated, wasn't so focused on the land that he ignored technology.

She didn't know what he was, except that he wasn't anything like what she'd expected to find when she and Lizzie had headed off on their big Wyoming adventure. None of it was how she'd expected, really. Especially him.

As if he'd felt her eyes on him, he glanced over and winked.

Flushing a little—and since when did she blush so easy?—she looked down at Lizzie, who stood pressed against her side, staring raptly at the foal.

The creature was the general size and shape of a Great Dane, with a dished face and bunny-lop ears. He was all black, or maybe dark brown—it was hard to tell with his hair still curled in damp rings—with one white hind leg and a star on his forehead. His wispy mane, stumpy tail, and pale, soft-looking hooves reminded her of Lizzie's trusty Mr. Pony, but he was no stuffed animal. He breathed rhythmically now, and when Sassy looked away, he made a soft "wheee" sound that brought the mare's head back around.

That was about it, though, and Shelby saw Gran and Krista looking more and more worried as the foal's eyelids drifted open and then closed again, and his breath stirred the straw. He stayed lying flat out, not making any real effort to stand.

"Let's give him another minute," Gran suggested. "He's just tuckered out from all the excitement."

Krista made a humming noise. "He needs to eat."

Lizzie looked up, and Shelby gave her shoulder a reassuring squeeze. "He'll be up in a minute. You'll see."

But one minute dragged on to five, and then ten, until finally Foster said, "Stace, how about you come on in here and give me a hand?"

Working together, they folded the foal's legs underneath him and rolled him up onto his chest, into a more natural-looking position. But he seemed content to stay there, head nodding as if he was falling back to sleep.

Foster rocked back on his heels, considering. "Not much fight in him."

"He knows you're helping him out," Gran said, but her expression was troubled.

"Come on, little guy," Krista urged. "Your mama's waiting for you. The dairy bar is ready for business."

The little horse didn't lie back down. But he didn't try to stand, either.

Shelby rubbed her chest, where anxious knots pulled tight. Had she made a mistake, bringing Lizzie out to see the newborn? "How long before you get really worried?"

"It can take a while for them to find their legs." But Krista was pensive.

"Let's get him up," Foster decided. "Krista, grab Sassy for me."

While Krista stood at the mare's head, holding on to her halter to keep her from following the foal around and turning things into an awkward game of Ring Around the Rosie, Foster and Stace dug into the straw to link their hands around the foal's chest and rump.

Stace counted down, "One, two . . ." And on "three" they lifted, boosting the foal onto his limp, Gumby-bending legs.

"Come on, little guy," Stace crooned. "Don't make us do all the work." But it sure seemed as though they were bearing most of the weight as they carried him over to Sassy and got his head underneath her, in the vicinity of her two-teated udder. "Here you go, buddy. Breakfast!"

There was some fumbling and soft instructions traded back and forth. All Shelby could really see was Stace's and Foster's backs, and the worried expression on Krista's face. After a few minutes, Stace and Foster lowered the foal back onto the straw and Krista let the mare go so she could circle around and sniff her baby, making sure all was well.

Only it wasn't.

"He doesn't have a suck reflex." Foster shook his head. "I'd say he's a dummy."

Krista made a low, broken sound of dismay.

"What does that mean for—" Shelby broke off as a solid, denim-wearing rocket launched itself from her side and flew into the stall. Sassy's head whipped up and her eyes went wide. "Lizzie!" Shelby started to grab for her, but hesitated, not wanting to spook the mare further.

"Whoa there!" Foster scooped up Lizzie on the fly, only to find himself holding off an attack as she slapped at him open-handed, as if wanting to claw but afraid to do damage.

"Easy." Krista grabbed Sassy's halter as the mare tried to whirl. "Easy, girl, she won't hurt your baby." To Foster, she snapped, "Get her out of here."

But Foster swung around and hoisted Lizzie up onto Sassy's corner feeder, instead. "Hey there. Hey." He shook her gently to get her attention, then caught her chin and held it steady until her blazing eyes focused on him. "What's this? I'm not hurting the little guy."

Lizzie's mouth worked and a fat tear ran down her cheek.

He looked over at Shelby. "What gives?"

"I don't . . ." She made a soft noise as it clicked. "Dummy. Some bullies at her old school used to call her that. You know, dumb rather than mute?" Her heart twisted at the memory of that cruelty, the scars it had left. Now, as then, she wanted to go back and take away every one of those taunts and insults, buff away the tears. She couldn't, though. She could only try to make today better, but how? Should she go in the stall? Stay put? She hesitated, because Lizzie didn't seem to be headed for critical mass. If anything, she was on the way down, sagging back against the wall, her mouth working in silence as tears flowed down her face.

Foster caught her arms. "Look at me, Lizzie. Hey. Hey there. It's not the same thing. A dummy foal is one who can't figure out how to nurse on his own right away, and maybe has trouble standing, probably because he didn't get enough oxygen during the birth process. It's not an insult, it's just a name. A condition. And it's something we can help him with, okay?"

Shelby started to go in, but Gran held her back. "Wait. He's got it."

It was harder than she would've imagined to make herself stay put, but she did it, watching as Foster found a clean spot on his own sleeve and mopped Lizzie's face, and then said matter-of-factly, "We're not giving up on him, if that's what you're worried about. All this means is that he's going to need some extra help. Right now we might have to bottle-feed him, or do other things until he figures it out. But we're going to do what he needs, and we're going to help him get better. Understand?"

And, bless him, even with all the other stuff going on around him, he stood there, waiting. Until, finally, she nodded.

Shelby swallowed hard, seeing her daughter's body uncoil and the color come back into her face. And even though she had always made a point that it wasn't up to the rest of the world to work around what Lizzie needed, that it was up to her to make a safe place and keep things on an even keel, she knew that she couldn't have handled this, not the way he just had.

What was more, he had pulled Lizzie into the stall, not out of it. Even in the midst of chaos, he'd been thinking about getting her near the horses rather than farther away.

"Go on, then." Foster boosted Lizzie down and gave her a nudge. "We've got a bit more work to do in here. You can watch from the door."

"Halloo," a new, age-cracked voice called from outside. "Anyone home?"

"Hey, Doc." Gran waved him in. "Glad you're here. This little guy could use some help."

The veterinarian proved to be a stooped old man about Gran's age who walked with a cane and grumbled about his aches and pains all the way down the aisle. The moment he got inside the stall, though, he set the cane aside and focused utterly on his patient, first making sure the foal wasn't in immediate distress, and then moving to check on Sassy.

Foster eased out of the stall to give them room, winding up as if by accident leaning on the wall beside Shelby. She went hot and cold, and got a funny shimmy in her stomach as she remembered what she'd been planning on telling him—*flattered, need to spend time with Lizzie, etc., etc.*—wanting to pull back from the temptation after last night. But how could she say "thanks but no, thanks" to a guy who wasn't just great in general, he was great with her kid, too?

Admit it, you don't want to.

Okay, fine. She didn't want to. All the logic in the world didn't change the way all her senses hummed just from standing right next to him, and the added warmth that came from knowing the attraction went both ways.

"Sorry about the dummy thing," he said in an undertone.

"Don't be. You handled it great. Seriously." She hesitated. "Is he really going to be okay? Oxygen deprivation is serious business in people."

"Less so in horses, though we'll need to keep our fingers crossed and our feet moving on this one. Dummies usually turn around okay, anywhere from a few hours to a couple of weeks after they're born. Once they're up and nursing on their own, they generally don't look back." He still looked worried, though.

"What's next?" she asked as Krista and the vet bent over the foal.

"We'll see. Sometimes they just need some help remembering that they're hungry, and how to get up on those long legs of theirs. In the meantime . . ." He glanced around, looking for Lizzie and finding her just outside the stall, watching intently as the vet took a blood sample from the foal.

"In the meantime, what?" Shelby pressed.

"If it's okay with you, I'd like to ask her to babysit the foal."

Her lips curved as she imagined Lizzie's reaction to

the request, and having it come from him. "The same way she's been babysitting me?"

"Same theory, but on her own. Just a couple of hours at a time, in between bottle feedings if we need them."

"Make-work, Foster?"

He shrugged. "Not exactly. I just thought it would be good for everybody concerned."

And he'd remembered to talk to her about it first. "I think it's a great idea. Have at it. And thanks. Again."

"You're welcome. Again." He turned to meet the vet as he stumped out of Sassy's stall. "So, Doc, what's the verdict?"

"You know the drill as well as I do. We'll watch and wait, and see if he figures it out on his own. If he doesn't, you'll have to give him a hand." The vet lifted the foal's blood sample. "I'll get back to you with his numbers, and we'll decide where to go from there in terms of immune support. In the meantime, get some food into him, watch his bowels, and keep a sharp eye on Mama to make sure all of her systems are go. All of which you already knew."

"Never hurts to hear it again."

"Ayuh. Anyway, I'll be going. Unless you need anything else from me?"

"Couple of tubes of Banamine?"

"You got it."

Krista, Stace, and Gran headed out with the vet, alternately pressing him for reassurance, asking for additional meds, and offering him muffins. As they moved off, Foster nodded back to Sassy's stall and said to Shelby, "Well, will you look there?"

Lizzie was just inside the door. She was squatting down on her heels the way Stace had shown her, so she'd be able to move quickly if she needed to. The stall guard wasn't up, and Sassy was only a few feet away, stretching out her neck to see if the little person had brought her a treat. And instead of retreating to safety, Lizzie reached out and stroked her nose.

The words—of gratitude, of joy, of relief—backed up in Shelby's throat, jamming together and leaving her speechless. So instead, she took Foster's hand and gave it a squeeze. To her surprise, he threaded his fingers through hers and squeezed back.

As they stood there, holding hands, it suddenly seemed like an out-of-body experience to Shelby, like something happening to another woman, one who'd lived a different life, made different choices.

After a moment, he tightened his grip and then pulled away, moving to stand farther up the aisle, away from Sassy's stall. Then he called, "Lizzie? Come over here for a minute, please."

She looked at him, hesitated, and then rose and shuffled over, moving slowly but surely, like she had gotten caught in his gravitational pull.

Shelby knew just how that felt.

He dropped down onto his heels, putting them close to eye level. "I've got another job for you . . . but I need you to do something for me, to show me you're ready for this job, because it's very important. So first . . . do you have your whistle with you?"

It took a minute, but she not only nodded; she pulled it out and let it dangle.

"Blow it for me."

Lizzie froze.

"Foster . . . ," Shelby said softly, then pressed her lips together.

"Here's the deal," he said matter-of-factly. "I want you to take a couple of shifts per day, watching over Sassy and her foal. I'm going to need to know whether the little guy stood up by himself, and whether he ate anything, so I'm going to need a way to communicate with you. And I need to be a hundred percent certain that you can call for help immediately if there's a problem."

Her big brown eyes had gotten bigger and bigger as he spoke, and a new sort of tension vibrated through her, not quite anxiety anymore. The sight sent nerves thrumming through Shelby. Was it time? Was this going to be the thing that finally broke through?

Please. Oh, please.

"This isn't about you talking," Foster said calmly, like he was doing a "whoa there, easy there" to one of the horses. "And this isn't some kind of therapy or a game—it's what this little guy needs from you, right here and now. So I want you to blow the whistle and prove to me that you can make some noise in an emergency."

Shelby held her breath as Lizzie stared at Foster and slowly—ever so slowly—lifted the whistle to her lips. And blew a quiet *fweep*.

It wasn't much as noises went, but to Shelby it was a trumpet fanfare, a *ta-daaa* of epic proportions. She wanted to holler and Snoopy-dance, but held herself in check, vibrating with suppressed excitement that she didn't dare let loose right now. Inwardly, though, she was channeling *vroom-vroom* car commercials and "come party with us" restaurant ditties.

Foster was his usual calm self. The only thing that suggested this was anything out of the ordinary was an added gleam in his eyes. "Okay, that's good. Now I need you to blow once for yes and twice for no. Understand?"

She hesitated, then gave another short *fweep*, a little louder.

"Right. And do you think that's loud enough to call for help?"

That got a slow head shake.

"What was that? I couldn't hear you."

Lizzie scowled, but blew twice. *Fweep-fweep*.

Shelby had to wipe her sweaty palms on her jeans. This was happening. It was really happening. Her daughter was making noise.

"Okay, so now give me a good blast, one that'll let us know there's a problem."

After only the briefest hesitation, and with a sudden glint in her eyes, Lizzie took a big breath and blew as hard as she could: *FWEEEEEEEET!*

There were startled exclamations from outside, and Gran and Krista came through the doors, moving fast, full of "What's wrong?" and "Do you need us to grab Doc before he leaves?"

Foster laughed aloud—an open, carefree sound that took away Shelby's sudden desire to weep with relief and put her back in Snoopy-dance territory, instead.

"You'll do," he said, reaching over to ruffle Lizzie's hair.

And so would he, Shelby thought, swallowing past a catch in her throat at the sight of the two of them together. So would he.

Later that night, Foster went down to the dock, even though it wasn't Friday. And Shelby was sitting there, waiting for him. Even though it wasn't Friday.

He let his boots thud on the dock this time, which brought her head around and put a smile on her face. "You did that on purpose."

"Yep. Not in the mood to go in after you tonight if you spooked and fell in."

"I can swim."

"Let's not test it."

"Hmph." But she was still smiling at him as he sat down beside her, shucked off his boots, and dipped his toes. "You just do night check?" she asked.

The ranch-ism sounded strange coming from her, but he nodded. "Yep. Sassy's doing well, and we got most of a bottle into the little guy. He's still not making any effort to nurse, though, or get up on his own."

"How long are you going to keep calling him 'little guy'?"

"Until we're sure he's going to make it," he said bluntly, then felt bad when she let out a soft sound of distress. "I'm sure Krista's already thinking up some handles for him. Maybe Lizzie could help."

"Voting by whistle?"

"Something like that. How's she doing?"

"I think she would've slept in the barn if I hadn't hauled her in for the night."

"Straw's not the worst mattress." And he'd spent dozens of all-nighters in the barn by Lizzie's age, watching pregnant stock and doing bottle-baby duty. *Different worlds,* he thought, reminding himself that it mattered. "You get any action with the whistle?"

"She took it to bed with her." Her smile was pure joy. "Better yet, she told me—one for yes and two for no—that she wanted chocolate ice cream, not strawberry."

"Bet that felt good."

"You have no idea. It's the first time in . . . God, I don't even want to think how long it's been since I had a real two-way conversation with her that didn't feel like I was pulling teeth for a few nods. Even just *tweet* and *tweet-tweet* are a huge step forward. And her expressions! Did you see her face when she was looking at the foal? That was brilliant of you, really. I've tried to get her to use sounds like that before—whistles, bells, clickers, you name it, I've tried it. But you made it work."

He shifted, not comfortable being anyone's brilliant. "The horse thing started with you and Gertie. I just came at it from another angle, that's all."

She glanced over. "You don't want me to be grateful?"

"I . . ." *Yes. No. I don't know.* This was why he did better on the range. Horses and cattle spoke with their faces and bodies, simple conversations like "Give me that" or "Scratch me here" and the species-transcending "Go away, she's mine." Basic emotions, basic concepts.

Problem was, humans expected more than that. At least they did once you got past talking about the simple things, like horses and the weather. And it wasn't so easy for a guy to say, "I want you" or, "Touch me here." Things like that came with strings, expectations, pressure, and he wasn't up to any of that. Been there, failed that.

Which he probably should've kept in mind last night.

Chest tight with the pressure of wanting to get this right, he said, "Look, I don't want you to take this the wrong way, but I'm not . . . I don't want you to think I'm paying attention to Lizzie to get in with you, or to be part of, you know."

Her smile vanished. "An instant family?" she filled in for him.

"Yeah. That. You should know I'm not looking to start something serious, or step into the daddy role, or anything like that."

"You think that's what I want?" Had he heard her voice this cool before? He didn't think so.

He tugged at his collar, even though it was already undone by a couple of snaps. "I believe I mentioned how much I suck at this."

That got a quiet laugh out of her, and then—even better—the kind of sigh that said she was breathing rather than staying tensed up. The kind that, when he was working with a greenie, said he was okay to move on, there wasn't an explosion brewing.

After a moment, she said, "Yeah, you did mention it, which is why I'm going to let you off whatever hook you've put yourself on. Because here's the thing—I was going to tell you something along the same lines this morning."

His gut gave an odd lurch. "You were?"

She lifted a hand. "Scout's honor. See, here's the thing. I had it all worked out in my head: I was going to say that, as fun as it was kissing you last night—and, hello, 'fun' is an understatement—we probably shouldn't get involved. We're coming from two different worlds here, and I'm going back at the end of the summer. Besides, Lizzie is my priority, period, full stop, do not pass Go."

He shifted to face her. "You *were* going to say that. Past tense?"

"Caught that, did you? Okay, yeah. After this morning . . . Let's just say I had a change of heart. Not because of gratitude or the whistle breakthrough, or even because you were so darn cute with the foal, but because I saw what Krista told me the very first day I got here."

"Which is?"

"You're a sweetie."

Whatever he'd been expecting, it wasn't that. He knew what folks said about him, that he was distant, cynical, closed off, better with horses than people. Or, if they were members of his family, they called him overprotective, even when they should've been blaming him for how things had gone down. But a *sweetie*? No way. "Excuse me?"

"In your own gruff sort of way, yeah, you're a

sweetie. With the horses, with Lizzie, and yes, even with me."

He must've swallowed a disbelieving laugh wrong, because there was a funny pressure in his chest. "Which means . . . ?"

"That I like you, in a warm, fuzzy, and friendly sort of way . . . and that I'd like you to kiss me again, with a bunch of feelings that aren't at all fuzzy or friendly." She hesitated, then said, "And now I've gone and shocked you."

And then some. But he shook his head. "It's not that. Well, maybe it is, kind of, but not in a bad way. I just can't remember ever talking to another woman like this."

"Like what?"

"Not having to guess what she's thinking, and losing points when I get it wrong."

She lifted a shoulder. "I guess it's a city girl thing."

Not in my experience. "It's a you thing, and I appreciate it. In fact, I appreciate a whole lot of things about you, from the way you are with Lizzie, to the way you look in the moonlight." He touched her cheek, using his knuckles rather than his work-roughened fingertips. "And especially the way you say what you mean rather than expecting me to read your mind."

Her lips curved. "I thought you said you were bad at this."

Seeing the invitation in her eyes, he leaned in. "I am."

"Not the way I see it."

"Then I'm a lucky guy," he said, and closed the last

small distance separating them, and kissed her before she could rethink things.

And, man, what a kiss.

Her skin started off cool but quickly warmed against his as the kiss went from warm to hot to supernova in the space of a breath. His skin tightened, his body hardened, and all of the aches of a long day fled in the face of desire. He skimmed a hand over her hair, down to where it ended in curls at the middle of her back, the softness echoing through him as if he were stroking her bare skin.

She smiled against his lips. "Sayonara Rule Twelve."

"What?"

"Nothing. Do that again."

He brushed his lips across hers, but then shifted away and rose, collecting both their boots and holding out a hand. "Come with me?"

She didn't ask where they were going, just let him lift her and lead her along the dock, which dipped beneath them, making him feel like the ground wasn't at all solid under his feet.

Or maybe that was her. He wasn't sure anymore.

With the very few guys she'd dated since her divorce, Shelby would've asked where they were going, or braced herself for the "no, we're not going back to your place now" conversation. But with Foster, she simply followed him down the dock and onto the sandy lakeshore, thinking it was strange how much she trusted him, how much she felt as though she knew him, even when she didn't, not really.

They didn't go far, just a short distance up the slope leading away from the lake, where he stopped and tugged her down. There, she settled beside him in a soft dip that caught the contours of her body, a natural lounge chair of ground that urged them together. The wispy grass was cool against her hands but warm against her chilled feet, where grains of sand stuck to her wet skin. The rest of her was warmer still, heated where their bodies pressed together.

"Here." He curved an arm around her, pillowing her head against his shoulder and urging her close.

It was natural to turn in to him, natural to meet his lips with her own. And oh, so wonderful to feel the heat that poured into her bloodstream, the tingles as once-familiar nerves reawakened, sending her messages of pleasure and *yes, oh, yes*.

They kissed urgently, endlessly, tasting and touching. He gripped her waist, skimmed his free hand up her body to her shoulder and back down again to trace her waistband. She was tempted to tug her shirt loose, wanting his hands on her breasts, her belly against his, their bodies pressed skin to skin.

But at the urge, nerves zinged through her, bringing the sudden knowledge that this was too much, too fast—and yet a big part of her didn't care. Should she pull back now? Keep going? She didn't want to stop, didn't want to tease, didn't want to get in deeper than she'd intended. And she was definitely on the verge of "deeper."

As if he had sensed her sudden anxiety—and maybe he had, he was that well tuned to her body language—

he eased the kiss and settled back, tucking her close to his side. He didn't say anything, didn't need to. He just held her as both of their breathings slowed and the world came back into focus around them.

After a moment, she said, "It's lovely out here." She didn't know if she meant their little niche, the lake-front, the ranch, or the entire high country. All of it, really.

"I like to come out here sometimes, just me and Vader, and look up at the sky."

Cuddled up against him with her heart thudding against her ribs, she followed his eyes up to the shimmering curtain of stars overhead, and couldn't decide whether it made her feel very small and insignificant, or somehow larger than herself. And whether she could feel both at the same time. "Do you have a favorite constellation?"

She felt him look at her, as if surprised by the question, but then he shifted to tug her closer, so their heads were right next to each other as he pointed. "See that bright star there? Then a few degrees to the right, five more that make almost a right angle?"

Squinting up, she said, "Um. Maybe?"

He chuckled. "Tonight's not perfect for it—they're pretty faint, especially with half a moon. But that's the Cowboy's Boot constellation. You can see how it makes the outline of a boot, complete with a big spur hanging off the heel." He sketched it with a finger, bringing it alive.

"Oh, I see it!" She grinned up at the night sky.

"And those three next to it are called the Arrow. Behind it is the Little Horse, and they're chasing Vulpecula, the Little Fox." He drew finger pictures as he spoke, drawing out a line of pursuit. "But since they're all at fixed positions relative to each other, it goes on forever, without the arrow or the horse ever catching Mr. Fox."

"What's the connection between the boot and the fox?"

"Besides proximity? I'm not sure there is one." There was a smile in his voice. "The boot just is what it is. Though if you follow where the toe is pointing, you can find the Dumbbell Nebula. If you've got a dark night and a decent telescope, that is. The nebula has all these cool colors in it, and looks three-D, like you could just reach out and touch it." He paused. "I'd ask if you wanted to come see my telescope, but I'm afraid it would sound like a bad pickup line."

"It's better than asking if I wanted to see your etchings," she said lightly. Astronomy. Who would have thought? "Were the constellations used for navigating across the open country?"

"Not that I've heard tell."

"Then what are they good for?"

A laugh rumbled in his chest. "Being a decent story, I guess. Or maybe making a man feel less alone when he's wrapped up in his bedroll next to a banked fire, hearing the wolves in the distance and knowing there isn't another human being for miles and miles."

She thought about that for a moment, tried to picture it, and found that it was impossible, even lying out in the open with him, under the big night sky. "We really do come from different worlds, don't we?"

His shrug shifted her closer. "That's one of the nice things about Mustang Ridge. While you're here, you're part of this world, living by the code, more or less."

Which sounded good, but there was a big difference between dude-ified trail rides, comfy beds, and buffet meals and the kind of life he was describing. Which seemed very lonely to her, very cold. She shivered.

"You getting chilly?"

Not really, but she also wasn't sure it was a good idea to stay where they were and keep doing what they had been doing—or were on the verge of doing. "I should go," she said, only part of her meaning it.

He didn't argue or try to talk her out of it, just climbed to his feet, drew her up, and then pulled her into his arms for a long, thorough kiss that chased away all vestiges of chills and loneliness, and brought back the excitement. It reminded her not just that she wanted to stay right where she was, but also why it was a really good idea for her to leave.

Too much, too soon. And very tempting.

When they parted, he leaned his forehead against hers, breathing deeply. There was a rasp in his voice when he said, "Seems to me I still owe you a trail ride."

Pleasure bubbled up inside her. "Is that the cowboy equivalent of a coffee date?"

"Something like that. I'm leaving tomorrow for the summer mustang gather, though. I'll be gone a week, maybe ten days."

She wouldn't let herself be disappointed. "Then I guess I'll see you when you get back."

"That's a promise. And, Shelby?"

She smiled up at him, relieved that it could be this easy when two people were on the same page—no fuss, no drama, just a man and a woman sneaking up on the idea of enjoying each other's company. "Mm?"

"It wouldn't hurt if you thought of me a time or two. Because you can bet your shiny new boots that I'll be thinking about you."

9

Beans, beans, they're good for your heart . . .

Toward the middle of the following week, on day four of Foster's being off at the gather—not that Shelby was counting or anything—there was a stir at the side door leading to the kitchen, and Junior clumped in, carrying a salt-cured something or other that very much resembled half a pig.

"I've never seen so much bacon before in my life," Shelby announced, staring in horrified fascination as he carried it into the cold room. "I think my arteries just hardened. Atherosclerosis by osmosis, with a side of a sodium spike in my blood pressure."

"Stuff like that doesn't count on a roundup," Gran said complacently. "It's a clinically proven fact."

"Baloney."

"Nope, bacon."

The rest of the statement caught up with Shelby and she let the cold-room door thump shut. "Wait, did you say roundup?"

"I sure did!" Gran scooped Herman's bowl off the

counter and did a little twirl that made her ruffled blue apron flare out. "We're taking this show on the road next week, baby!"

"But I thought the roundup was . . ." Oh, wow. The Fourth of July. Where the heck had the rest of June gone?

Gran dimpled at her. "Days and weeks aren't that big a deal out here, at least not the way they are for some people. We're more worried about seasons."

"But Lizzie and I aren't even close to being ready for the roundup." When she'd first talked to Krista about the summer schedule, it had seemed that the timing would be perfect for roundup week—they would've been there for almost a month, plenty of time to get Lizzie ready to ride out with the group, while Shelby would ride in the chuck truck with Gran, driving ahead to each overnight camp so they could have a hot meal waiting.

A month, check. Ready to ride, not so much.

"There's room for three in the chuck truck," Gran assured her.

Not that it was open for discussion, really. If Gran was going, then so was Shelby, and by extension, Lizzie. "Okay. Right. Roundup week. Thus, the half a pig."

"There's also a fifty-pounder of beans and two big bags of flour in the pantry, and most of a cow in the freezer."

"What, no butchering on the trail?"

"Health codes," Gran said, looking mildly disgusted. "That, and we've found that the guests prefer not to know where their meals come from."

Trying not to let on that she fell in that category, Shelby said, "Okay. Flour, bacon, beans, beef. What can I do to help get things ready to roll?"

"Nothing right yet. It'll be business as usual until midday Saturday, when we pack up the wagon and ride out."

"No orientation?"

"The roundup is for returning riders, by special invitation only." Pride shone in her face. "Krista and Foster have turned this into such an event that there's a waiting list."

"Nice." Shelby didn't try to ignore the warm shimmies that came at hearing Foster's name; she enjoyed them, instead. After all, wasn't that the point of them having agreed to a summer fling—or at least a summer flirtation? "He'll be back from the gather in time?"

"Last I heard. If not, he'll catch up with us. Krista and the wranglers can handle the ride out to the high pastures, and the first couple of gathers. It's the way home that can get tricky, once all the cattle are lumped together and not convinced they want to be going where we want to put them."

"I'm not sure I blame them."

"We're not bringing them all in. Mostly the wranglers will just be microchipping the latest arrivals and snipping the new crop of bulls. That can happen up in the high country."

"Like I said." Shelby grinned. "Anyway. There's got to be something I can do to help between now and then."

Gran waved her off. "Go ride your horse."

"Loco?"

"Yes, Loco. He'll sulk if he gets left behind, and it's never pleasant to see a handsome man sulk."

"Hello, anthropomorphism."

"Fine, don't practice. Then see how you feel when you fall off in front of the guests."

Forget the guests, she didn't want to fall off in front of Foster. The idea of riding with him, though, out on a roundup, no less . . . Okay, that was seriously cool. "But I'm not going to be riding with the group. There's no way I'm abandoning you to cook while I play green-horn."

"We'll figure something out." Gran slid a pan of brownies onto the cooling rack. "Right now it's our turn to get Lucky."

Shelby didn't bother trying to work out if that was meant as a joke; she just went with it. Krista had christened Sassy's foal "Lucky Bugg," combining his sire's name, Ima Bugg, with her own optimism. Thus, the little guy had become "Lucky" by default, and also as something for him to live up to. That hope was starting to wear thin, though, as days passed and the little guy still couldn't get up or figure out how to nurse on his own. Every time, they used their fingers to push his tongue into the curved shape needed for suckling . . . and every time, he just stood there, letting the milk run down the back of his throat.

Still, he had gained some weight. Enough that Shelby was starting to feel the strain of lifting him onto his feet and supporting him while he nursed. And if she was feeling it . . . "I could go find Tipper—"

"And rob me of my chance to get my hands on all that squishable baby cuteness? You wouldn't dare."

Having learned not to argue when Gran got that look in her eye, Shelby held up her hands in surrender. "Just a thought. Come on, then. Let's go get Lucky."

"Now you're talking."

The barnyard was quiet, but as they approached the main doors, Shelby slowed and cocked her head. "Do you hear that?"

Gran cocked her head at the pinging noise. "Someone's phone, maybe? Or it could be birds. They like to nest in the eaves, and the hatchlings peep like crazy."

But when Shelby got inside, she saw instantly that it wasn't either of those things. *It's not a bird, it's not a phone, it's . . . Lizzie!*

Wearing pink play clothes, with her flyaway brown hair tamed back in a matching scrunchie, she sat on an overturned bucket. The stall door was open, the web guard at half-mast because Lucky wasn't about to escape and Sassy wasn't going anywhere without him. Bent over her iPad, gaming away, Lizzie didn't seem to be paying any attention to the horses . . . except she'd turned on the volume. More, she had turned it up all the way, so the chirpy *pings*, *pongs*, and *sproinngggs* of whatever she was playing reverberated through the barn.

"Look at them," Gran said softly.

"I see." Lucky lay on his chest in the soft shavings that had replaced the birthing straw. He was curled up with his long legs folded under him, as he so often was these days—which was an improvement over lying flat out, but still not normal for a five-day-old foal. But where Shelby was used to seeing him with his nose buried in the shavings, propping him while he snoozed with his eyes mostly closed, now his head was up and his little radar-dish ears gave little twitches with each digital noise. Sassy seemed intrigued, too, and stood over Lizzie as if watching the game.

Progress, Shelby thought, feeling a wide smile split her face. "Hey, Tizzy Lizzie!" Her voice nearly broke on the words, but she forced herself to hold it together, keep it casual. "Is Mr. Lucky ready for his threesies?"

She didn't get a yes or no, but Lizzie got up, moved her bucket aside, and unclipped the stall guard the rest of the way, then held it open with a Vanna flourish.

"Thank you, young lady." Gran sailed through, smiling widely when little Lucky gave a soft whicker. "And you, too, young man. Isn't that a nice, hungry sound? What do you say we do something about that empty tummy of yours?"

She and Shelby got on opposite sides of the foal, linked hands, and gave him a "One, two, three, *hup!*" And even though Shelby tried to take most of the weight as they stood, she saw the strain in Gran's face and felt a few protesting twinges in her own back.

"Come on," she urged, juggling the foal a little in the hopes that he'd get a clue and lock his legs for stability. "You can do it." But it was like trying to prop up a sawhorse on pool noodles.

"Over we go," Gran said, shuffling in the shavings so Lucky was pointed toward his mama.

"Tipper could—"

"March!"

Shelby marched, and together they got the little guy lined up with the taps. He still wouldn't take the teat himself, so Shelby kept him propped up while Gran held his head and squirted milk in his mouth, more or less. Unlike the first few days, though, when he'd hung limp, now he tried to crane around and take a nip at his mother, or look back at Shelby with adorable eyes that made her say, "Awwww," even when she wanted to noogie him for having the attention span of a flea.

"Stop wearing it and start drinking it," Gran said with some asperity. "Better yet, stop lying around like a man, waiting for someone to bring you your yummies. I thought you said you were hungry."

"Sing it, sister." Shelby was a little out of breath. "Ouch. Get off my toe. Seriously, if you can be this squirmy, you should be able to do this yourself."

Lizzie hovered in the doorway, looking more like an overprotective mama than Sassy, who stood quietly, having gotten used to the fuss.

"That's it!" Gran said suddenly as he made a grab for her fingers and found Sassy's udder, instead. "That's where it's coming from. Just latch on and—good boy!" Her crow was soft, so as not to startle the little foal, but her eyes shone. "What a fine fellow!"

Shelby grinned over at Lizzie. "He's nursing!"

Okay, maybe that was a bit of an overstatement, as he only made it a few gulps before he lost his grip—or his train of thought—and they had to get him organized all over again. And he didn't make any real effort to hold himself up while he nursed. But baby steps counted, and the mood was high by the time they lowered him back down to a soft nest of clean shavings.

"I'm going back to the kitchen to play with my potatoes," Gran announced, but then pointed at Shelby. "And I don't want to see you in there any earlier than five tonight, got it? Everything's under control and you've been doing more of your share this week."

"Hello, pot? This is the kettle speaking."

"Well, the pot is the boss, and she says five." With that, Gran swept out, head high, but moving slower than before.

Shelby looked back at the little foal. "How about you cut her some slack and start finding your eats on your own?" Either way, she was going to have to talk to Krista about getting Gran even more relief in the kitchen, not just assistance but actual shifts off, days off. She had been delaying, not wanting to tattle, but enough was enough.

With that decided, she had a couple of hours free, and a roundup on the horizon. Glancing at Lizzie, she said casually, "I'm going to take Loco out for a loop around the ranch. You okay keeping an eye on these two?"

Not only did she get a nod, but Lizzie stayed put on her bucket while Shelby put Loco on the cross ties not ten feet away. *Progress, indeed.*

Shelby was just finishing up her ride—it was so nice out that one loop around the ranch had turned into three—when Loco's head came up and his ears whipped forward, his attention fixing on the main trail coming down off the ridgeline.

"Not today," she said, taking in a little rein, just in case. "We're sticking close to home. No getting crazy until next week's roundup, okay? And preferably not then, either." She still couldn't quite believe this was her life, and that she would be riding out in the backcountry—maybe even herding some cows—and cooking bacon-flavored beans over an open fire. It seemed like it should've been something she heard about secondhand over extra-foam-please lattes, the kind of story that made her promise herself a vacation that would soon be forgotten in the face of three frantic clients and a call from one of Lizzie's teachers.

Loco's head stayed up and he took a dancing step to one side. "Easy, buddy," she crooned, tightening the reins further but making sure the rest of her stayed relaxed. "Easy, there." But then dust stirred at the top of the ridge and a horse and rider came into view, walking flat-footed. The blaze-faced horse whinnied, and Shelby relaxed the reins. Loco had just been trying to tell her there was company coming. "Okay, you win. Let's go see what's up."

When they got close enough, the woman waved and called, "Hey there! Hi! You're Shelby, right?"

"That's right." She was a little surprised at being recognized, but then again, this week's guests—a large group of women who knew each other through an online equestrian message board and had met up annually at Mustang Ridge for the past five years—knew their way around the ranch, its people, and the horses.

"I'm Dana. Cabin Six."

"You're back early. Everything okay?"

"Justice here threw a shoe, and without Foster to do his fix-a-flat routine up in the high country, I decided to come back down rather than risking a bruise."

"Bummer," Shelby sympathized. "It's a beautiful day for a ride. Come on, we'll walk you in. I was headed that way myself."

"Thanks." She glanced over as Shelby reined around to fall in beside her, and did a sudden double take. "Is that Loco?" She gave a low whistle. "Wow, girl, you rank."

"Why, is he the barn favorite?" She had guessed something of the sort based on his buttery soft bridle and memory foam saddle pad.

Dana gave her a funny look. "No, he's Foster's."

Shelby's stomach gave a shimmy. "One of his projects, you mean."

The other woman shook her head. "Nope. His own personal horse."

"But he has others. Like, a string."

"Just one. I once heard him say that Loco and his saddle were the only two things he brought with him when he came here, the only two things that mattered." She smiled, not unkindly. "I take it you didn't know."

"He told me . . ." Shelby cleared her throat. "Um, no. He didn't mention it."

In fact, he'd let her believe Loco was one of Krista's rescues. Her pulse stepped it up a notch at the realization that she was riding his horse, using his equipment. And he'd handed it all over before they got involved. But why?

Head spinning, she patted the glossy bay's neck and

fought to steady her voice, keep it light. "You've been holding out on me, huh, Loco? I'm guessing you've got a few stories to tell."

"I'd say. He was the RRC's horse of the year three years running." At Shelby's blank look, Dana elaborated, "It's a circuit of ranch rodeos—they're rougher and more hard core than the professional rodeos, strictly for working cowboys." She looked around and lowered her voice, though they were very alone. "Foster doesn't know that a few of us recognized him. We figured if he doesn't want to make a big deal of it, then we won't, either. Back in the day, though, he and Loco were the best of the best."

I'm not a gossip. I'm not a gossip. "How long ago was the day?"

"Eight, maybe ten years ago?"

Before he had come to Mustang Ridge, then. Shelby patted Loco's neck again. *I wish you could talk.* Did it count as gossiping to ask a cowboy's horse about him?

Dana had followed the gesture. "So . . . what's he like to ride?"

"Very kind and smooth. Soft-mouthed, too."

Dana's smile went a little wicked. "We're talking about the horse, right?"

"Yes," she said too quickly. "Absolutely. Foster . . . he's just helping me out with my daughter." And giving her his personal, prized horse to ride, pretending she was doing him a favor. Her body buzzed with pleasant tingles, even as she reminded herself not to take any of this too seriously. For all she knew, it was the Wyoming equivalent of him having the waiter bring her one of whatever she was drinking.

"Your daughter's the one who's been sitting with Lucky?"

"That's my Lizzie."

"Cute kid." Dana shot her a sidelong look. "Seems to me, a man who's good with animals has daddy potential. Always wondered why Foster didn't have a family."

"It's not like that." And even if it was maybe just a little "like that," she didn't want to talk about it, not with Dana, not with anyone. He was too much of a presence. Krista relied on him, Gran baked him chocolate chip cookies with extra nuts even though she didn't think nuts belonged in cookies, and Stace worshipped him as a big-brother-slash-mentor and started every other sentence with "Foster says." And then there were the guests. Some of the men tried to outcowboy him, while others tried to be him, and more than half of the women Shelby had seen so far, from eight to eighty, batted their eyelashes and sighed after him when he passed. They all wanted his attention, his approval, and she didn't want to be part of the herd. It was like seeing a picture of Clive Owen in a coworker's cube and being annoyed because Clive was her celebrity crush and she didn't want to share, only so much worse, because Foster was real. More, she didn't want to upset the balance that worked so well at Mustang Ridge.

Then again, Krista knew he'd lent her Loco, and she

hadn't said anything. Why? Did she approve? Disapprove? Or was Dana wrong that it was so unusual for him to lend out his horse?

As they reined up in front of the barn, the other woman shot her a dubious look. "Should I have kept my mouth shut? I didn't mean to make you uncomfortable."

"You didn't. I'm not." Shelby wasn't sure what she was, but it wasn't uncomfortable. "At least now I know that Loco's an old pro."

"You couldn't be in better hands, horse or man."

There it was again, that sense of familiarity. And a spurt of jealousy that made Shelby want to bare her teeth at the other woman. Which wasn't cool, considering that she and Foster were just having fun.

"Well, it was nice chatting with you," Shelby said as she swung off Loco. "I hope Justice—" *FWEEEEET! FWEEEEET!* The shrill whistle cut her off and sent her stomach plunging. "*Lizzie!*"

"I'll take care of Loco." Dana held out a hand. "Go!"

Shelby didn't argue. She tossed the reins and bolted for the barn.

Lizzie stood at the back, just outside Sassy's stall, waving her arms in a *come on, come on, come on* gesture. Shelby flew to her side, heart pounding. "What is it? What's wrong?"

But the moment she saw her daughter's bright, happy face and looked over the web gate, she saw that it wasn't something wrong, so much as something very right.

Lucky was standing on his own, with his head under Sassy's belly and his little broom-wisp tail flipping back and forth as he nursed.

"Oh!" Shelby breathed. "Look at him!"

He only took a few more gulps before losing interest, but even then he stayed on his feet, wandering around and poking at the corner feeder and shaking his head now and then as if to say, "Okay, it took a few extra days, but I'm ready to go now."

As her adrenaline started to drain, Shelby hugged Lizzie closer. "Oh, sweetheart, you just about gave me a heart attack." She didn't care, though. Not when it looked like Lucky was going to be lucky after all. And not when her daughter had called her to come and see.

10

If Shelby hadn't been involved in packing for the roundup, she never would've believed that so much of Mustang Ridge could go mobile, and look good doing it.

Bright and early Saturday morning, the twenty-eight riders—eight from the ranch and the twenty invited guests—were mounted and waiting in the parking area. The chuck truck was parked off to the side; the converted military transport was stuffed full with food for man and beast, along with bedding, cookware, camping gear, first aid, and entertainment, in a stripped-down version of the usual dude experience. They'd be camping in boo-yah luxury compared to how it would've been back in the day, when everything that couldn't be packed on a cowboy's saddle would've been jammed into the mule-drawn chuck wagon, or left behind. Still, Shelby was feeling very pioneerish as she settled into the crawler, riding shotgun beside Gran, with Lizzie strapped into a rumble seat behind them.

They didn't have airbags, AC, or, she suspected, any real suspension. Yep, pioneering in the twenty-first century.

Gran glanced back. "You two comfortable back there?"

Lizzie nodded. Herman, who had been moved to a tall, insulated Tupperware container with holes punched in the lid, was Bungee'd into the rumble seat next to her, wearing his red-and-white-checkered towel at a rakish angle.

"They look good to go," Shelby said, shooting Lizzie a "roll with it" wink and getting back a small smile that warmed the heck out of her heart.

It wasn't the big breakthrough she'd been hoping for, the one all the experts had warned her not to expect, where Lizzie would wake up one morning singing the Toastee Krunch jingle, but she didn't have to wait long for the nods or head shakes now, and the iPad's volume had stayed on. Lizzie had tucked the whistle back away, but Shelby wasn't letting that bother her. Not when she was getting the occasional look, wink, or smile, those small interactions that had been missing between them for so long.

Gran leaned out the truck's giant window side and called, "What do you say, boss?"

Krista, sitting astride a lean, mottled gray gelding with one blue eye and one brown, shook her head. "No boss here. I'm just the temp."

Foster hadn't made it back yet, but nobody seemed to be worried. Krista said that the gather could drag on if the weather wasn't right, or he might stay an extra day or two if there were some particularly promising horses in the group. Shelby kept reminding herself that he hadn't promised to call, didn't have her number, and might not even know where his phone was. So there was no point in feeling as if he'd been gone for a really long time. Still, she'd kept an eye out for his truck, hoping he would make it back for the roundup. She wanted to tell him about Lizzie and the whistle, wanted to tell him how much Lucky had improved, wanted to ask more about Loco's history, wanted to know more about *him*.

He'd told her to think about him, and she was sure doing that.

She only hoped he had done the same.

"He'll be along," Gran said, and Shelby thought it was aimed at her.

Krista stood in her stirrups, took off her hat and waved it in a wide, sweeping motion. "Okay, gang, listen up! Foster wouldn't want us to waste such a gorgeous day waiting on him, so I declare this Fourth of July roundup officially on! We ride out in five . . . four . . . three . . . two . . ."

Everybody yelled, "One!" And, laughing, they headed out of the parking area, following Krista's lead through the gate and onto the dirt road leading up the ridgeline. The crowd bottlenecked at the opening, so some of the horses stood for a minute, excited but obedient as they waited their turns. Then they, too, picked up a slow trot and started off on the journey.

"Not exactly the Snowy River cavalry charge I was expecting," Shelby said drily.

"Walk the first mile out and the last one back," Gran said piously. "Unless, of course, you're driving." She patted the cracked dashboard.

Shelby gave the aged dials a dubious look, but didn't argue. She figured that, worst case, they would break down and the riders would circle back around to find them. In the meantime, they certainly wouldn't starve, as they were the ones with all the food. Besides, it was too beautiful a day to worry, and with Lucky out of the woods and the kitchen gone mobile, it felt like they were ditching school, skipping work, and heading out on an adventure.

She was going to roll with it.

So as the horses and riders streamed up the road, turning dust-hazed and indistinct, she fished in her foot-well for the soft-sided cooler she'd loaded with leftovers. "Catch," she said, and tossed Lizzie a biscuit, then offered Gran the bag. "Want one?"

"Don't mind if I do. There's no better road food."

Despite brief nostalgia for McMuffins and Starbucks chai, Shelby held up her biscuit. "To Herman!"

"To Herman!"

They did a three-way biscuit clink and laughed as Gran hit the gas and sent them rumbling off in a different direction from the one the riders had taken. They would go around the hill and strike out cross-country, shortcutting the day's ride so there would be plenty of time to rustle up dinner before the riders reached camp.

It took six hours of bumpy driving to reach the first campsite, and by the time Shelby staggered down from the high cab, she felt like her ovaries had been scrambled. She perked up, though, as she filled her lungs with clean, thin air and took a look around at a colorful three-sixty landscape that looked like it'd been painted on a backdrop, like some artist's rendition of the Wild West.

"Well, this doesn't stink." Which was the understatement of the week, because it was flipping gorgeous.

The shallow, grassy bowl had a stream running through its middle that separated the stock pens from the campsite, while a double line of trees on the banks provided a windbreak against the gentle breeze. The stock side was enclosed by slipboard fencing that could be easily switched around to juggle horses and cattle, as needed. Some of the sections were down, giving it a weathered feel that was picked up by the open fire pits on the other side of the stream, with all of it surrounded by a panorama of purple-veined, snowcapped mountains rising to the cloud-scudded blue sky.

Flowers dotted the grassland with splashes of purple and white, and a bird trilled in the middle distance. The noise startled Shelby, as if her city senses were still trying to say, "This is a movie or something—it can't possibly be real." But the tick of the chuck truck's hot engine block was very real, as was the sight of Lizzie reaching for a butterfly, then watching as it fluttered up and away.

"I've got a job for you," Shelby called. When Lizzie looked over, she nodded down the hill. "Splash on over there and put up as many of those boards as you can, please. I bet Krista and the others would love to get here and find the fencing already tightened up. Oh, and while you're down there, grab some sticks and deadwood. Carefully! Don't pull anything down on top of you. We'll use it for the fire." She glanced at Gran and said in an undertone, "It's safe for her to run around, right?"

"Compared to playing in traffic or walking through Central Park at night? Definitely."

"Not helping. And I've bet you've never set foot in Central Park."

"No, but I watch *Law and Order*. All three of them."

"'Nuff said." Raising her voice as Lizzie started down the hill, Shelby called, "Keep your eyes peeled, your ears open, and your whistle with you. If you see something you don't like, freeze and call one of us."

"Don't worry." Gran patted her hand. "I've got a rifle and a sawed-off in the truck."

"Oh, that makes me feel loads better." Oddly enough, though, it did make her feel better, as did seeing Lizzie looking down at the ground, watching for snakes.

"She's got good instincts," Gran said, then glanced at Shelby. "And so do you."

"When it comes to predators?"

"When it comes to lots of things." She faced the chuck truck and put her hands on her hips. "Okay, first things first. Let's get the fires going and the beans on the boil. They'll take the longest, and if there's not much better than a perfectly slow-cooked bean, there's not much worse than a badly done one." She wrinkled her nose. "Except maybe the aftermath of a bad batch."

"Oh-kay. Fire and good beans. Let's get on it!"

After a word from Shelby, Krista had talked to Gran

about taking it easier and letting other people do the heavy lifting. Which might've been past due, but meant that Shelby got to lug the heavy Dutch ovens from the truck to the fire pits. Gran followed her, tsking, though Shelby couldn't tell if she was worried about the ovens or her assistant cook. Probably the ovens, because without them, there wouldn't be any biscuits. And what was a roundup without biscuits?

By the time the sun kissed the mountains and the sky got a little purple around the edges, the beans were well on their way—not good yet, but not bad, either— and she and Gran were pulling biscuits out of the ovens. They weren't as uniform as the ones that came out of the kitchen on a daily basis, but when Shelby bit in . . . "Mmmm. These are . . . what are they? Something's different."

"It's the ovens. They give it a special roundup flavor."

"They sure do." It was tempting, but Shelby held off on a second, hearing the carbs do a *ka-ching, ka-ching* in the back of her head. Forget the freshman fifteen, she'd put on the sous chef sixty if she didn't watch herself.

"Let's get the next batch going, and get the jacket potatoes wrapped up and buried in the coals. Then we should have time to take a breath, as the riders won't be here for a—"

Fweeet!

Shelby whipped around at the whistle, and found Lizzie down by the stream. There wasn't a bear or mountain lion in sight, but she pointed off into the distance, where ant-specks were just visible against the green, ribboning in their direction. "Correction," Shelby said with a laugh, "the riders are already here."

"So they are."

Things whipped into high gear then, and they dragooned Lizzie into wrapping the potatoes while Gran seasoned the beans and Shelby turned the steaks in their marinade.

Krista led the way into camp twenty or so minutes later, with a group of very happy riders in tow. Ty, Stace, and the other wranglers brought up the rear. Relaxed chatter filled the campsite as the guests broke off into groups, some to see to the horses, others to set up camp using the tents and the rest of the equipment filling the back of the chuck truck. After passing off her horse to Stace, Krista crossed the stream and came up to the fire pits.

"Any problems on the ride?" Gran asked.

"Zero, zip, zilch, nada." Krista snagged a cooling biscuit and bit in. "Mmmm. Roundup Hermans rock."

"There's an ad campaign in there somewhere," Shelby said. "Maybe." She hadn't forgotten her plan to craft a slogan—and maybe even a campaign—for Mustang Ridge, to thank Krista and Gran for helping her out. She just hadn't connected with exactly the right idea yet.

It would come, though.

Gran poked a couple of the potatoes, turning them in the coals. "Did you see any cows?"

"A few pockets here and there. We moo-ved them around a little—get it, moo-ved?" Krista paused, but only got eye rolls, and shrugged good-naturedly. "Anyway, we gave the dudes a refresher on working cattle, bunched up a dozen or so of them—cows, I mean, not guests—in a good-looking valley, and left them there, figuring we'd pick them up on the way back. No reason to run the flesh off them." She paused, then nudged Shelby and pointed downhill. "That's got to feel good."

Lizzie was headed from the corral to a growing pile of tack with bridles draped over her shoulder, a saddle cradled in her arms, and a Tigger bounce in her step. She still wouldn't handle the horses, but she had apparently appointed herself the head tack schlepper.

"So, ranch therapy is working?" Krista asked.

"Seems that way."

"You're not sure?"

Darn it. Shelby squeezed her eyes shut, annoyed with herself for letting the cracks show, especially in such a gorgeous spot, with them surrounded by some seriously yummy smells. "No, it's working. Of course it is. Look at her!"

"Preaching to the choir." Krista paused. "But you're worried that she's still not talking."

Shelby wanted to say, "No, I'm sure she'll get there," but she squelched the fib, hesitated, and said, "I'm trying to hold it together . . . but yeah, I'm worried. It's been two years, and she was older than most SM kids to begin with. In a few years, she'll be a teenager, and—" She clamped her lips together. "And I need to stop it. I'm putting too much pressure on both of us, whether I mean to or not. I'm just not very good at taking myself out of the equation."

Krista gave her a funny look. "Why would you want to do that?"

"It's my job to stay positive and not add more stress to the mix." She rolled her eyes. "Sounds easy when you say it that way, doesn't it?"

"Not so much. That's basically like saying you need to love your daughter—because of course, you do—but at the same time, be unemotional when dealing with her. Which is pretty much impossible, because you love her."

"Welcome to my world." But Shelby felt her smile wobble.

"What else do the 'experts'"—Krista put the word in finger quotes—"say you should be doing?"

"Encouraging her to interact with me as much as possible. Using positive reinforcement. Setting her up to succeed and then praising the heck out of her. Pretty much the same stuff you and the others do every day, with both the horses and the guests." She paused, grimacing. "I hate to admit it, but I don't think I'd make a very good horse trainer. I get impatient waiting for results, and when something isn't working, I never know whether to keep trying or switch to another theory entirely. I just don't have the right instincts."

"Poosh," Gran said. "Nobody does the first few times around, even with help. That's the difference between being a horse trainer and being a mother. A trainer gets dozens, maybe hundreds of go-arounds to figure it out and streamline things. A mom has to make it up on the fly."

"Gee, thanks."

"I'm serious. Foster's been training mustangs off and on for most of his life, and even he'd tell you that he gets it wrong now and then."

"Speak of the devil," Krista said. "Rider ho."

Shelby's heartbeat kicked it up several notches as she turned to see a tall, lean cowboy riding toward the camp on a rangy chestnut with a wide blaze. Forcing her voice casual, she said, "I thought it was 'land ho.'"

Krista shrugged. "When you're on the ocean, you care about land. Out here, we care about our riders."

It was that simple, Shelby realized with a smile. And in a way, so was the warm flush of anticipation that washed through her when she saw Foster riding her way. She didn't know what was going to happen next between them, but she was looking forward to finding out.

Gran nudged her toward the corrals. "Go ahead. You'll want to tell him how well Lizzie's been doing."

"But I should—"

"Take five. We'll start the steaks when you get back."

Foster didn't remember the last time he'd ridden so hard to catch up. Maybe back when he was a boy and the older cowboys left for the roundup before school got out. Or maybe never, because his father and grandfather had drilled it in early and often: *A true cowboy doesn't do anything in a hurry, especially when he's dealing with his stock.* The slower the cattle herded, the more flesh they kept on their bones, and the easier a man went on his horse and dog, the more they'd have left in the tanks when he needed it.

But Vader had kept up without flagging and Brutus clearly hadn't minded the pace. If anything, the gallop had done the high-spirited chestnut some good, because he was riding smooth, minding his manners, and putting one foot in front of another like a real riding horse. Granted, a good night's sleep should take care of that, Foster thought as they started down into the shallow bowl that held the camp. But still.

"You made it." Ty dropped a couple of split rails to let him into the corral. "Made good time, too."

"Fast horse."

"Only when he goes straight. How was the gather?"

"Too many machines." He hated the helicopters and ATVs, would rather have gone pure old school when it came to pulling feral mustangs off the preserves and culling them for sale.

Ty made a disgusted noise, then held out a hand. "Take him for you?"

"You don't have to." A man saw to his own horse before himself, always.

"Offered, didn't I? We got in early, and camp's in good shape. And I'm betting you're behind on sleep or food, or both."

Speaking of food. "Cookie all set up?" Tradition said that the camp's cook was always Cookie, whether it was a hairy old coot with a schnapps habit—ah, fond memories—or a trio of lovely ladies.

"Yeah, Shelby and her mini-me are here."

"That wasn't what I asked."

"You didn't have to. A man gives away his horse to a woman, that says it for him."

"Brutus needed a few come-to-Jesus rides, and Loco is enjoying the break."

"If you say so." Ty grinned, then nodded past him. "Anyway, she's right behind you."

Giving it fifty-fifty that Ty was yanking his chain, Foster turned around. And saw her.

With her dark hair braided back, wearing a logo'd snap shirt, jeans, and a mysterious smile, Shelby looked like a rodeo queen who'd gotten roped into the cook shack for the day. If he'd never met her before, he might've thought she was a local and wondered why he'd never seen her before. As it was, he could see the city polish in the way she'd tied her bandana in a jaunty, off-center knot at her throat, and the wink of a glittery bracelet on her wrist.

All too aware of Ty standing behind him, probably smirking, he caught her hand and led her back up toward the stream, where the double row of trees provided some cover, some privacy. They were surrounded, with people on one side, horses on the other, but once he tugged her through into a thicker stand of brush, it was like they were all alone, standing on the pebbly edge of the stream while the water rushed by, drowning out the other sounds.

He wanted to tell her how he'd ridden hard to see her, how he'd missed her, thought about her, almost borrowed a phone to call her, but didn't because hearing her voice would've made things worse, not better.

But the words crammed in his throat, sticking there as she moved into his arms. He didn't know if he'd pulled her close or if she had made the move; all he knew was that she was up against him, her body warm and curvy, her eyes bright with anticipation. And the only rational thing to do was kiss her.

He reached down as she came up on her toes, and their mouths met seamlessly, perfectly. Her flavor was new and fresh, yet deeply familiar, as if thinking about her all week had reset his neurons to recognize her taste.

The kiss stretched out, wet and warm, and so welcoming that he wasn't sure where his body left off anymore and hers began, except where he was hard and aching, and wanted more. But this wasn't about getting more, not right now. It was about having a good time and getting to know her, and it was about letting her know he was glad to see her, and damn glad she felt the same way. So he told his body to cool it down and he eased the kiss, keeping his hands gentle and making himself step back when he wanted to dive in.

Despite all that, it took him a moment to find his voice. And when he finally did manage to unmute, all he could do was grin down at her and say, "Hey there."

He'd spent the past week looking forward to seeing her again, and that was the best he could come up with? Man, he was lame.

But she smiled back. "Hey, yourself."

"How's it going?" He sucked. Seriously. Part of him wished they could've just kept on kissing and skipped the other stuff. Except that he liked talking to her, too.

Life would just be better if she handled the conversation, especially right now.

"It's going good. Really, really good." Her smile lit. "Lucky is up and nursing on his own, and Doc says all systems are go. Lizzie was there the first time he stood up on his own, and called me using her whistle. I'm afraid to jinx myself by saying she seems better, but she does, knock on wood." Her words came fast, as if she'd been storing up things to tell him. "I've ridden Loco every day . . . and the cat's out of the bag on him being your prize possession. I know gratitude makes you squirm, so I'll just say thank you for trusting me with him." She grinned, looking lighter and more carefree than he'd ever seen her before, as if during the week he'd been gone, she had unlocked parts of herself that she'd been keeping hidden away. "Oh, and dinner's almost ready."

He couldn't stop smiling, probably looked like a fool. He didn't care, though. What mattered was that she was there, she'd had a good week, and he was so dang happy to see her he could burst. Finding his voice and a few of his brain cells, he finally managed to string together more than a couple of words. "You . . . wow. How long was I gone again?"

"It felt like forever."

"I know what you mean. Looks like I've got some major catching up to do. Maybe you could help me out with that?"

Her grin went wicked. "Absolutely, cowboy." But then she shot a guilty look in the direction of the campsite, which was barely visible through the trees. "I should get back and help Gran put the steaks on, though. She was good about letting me sneak off to say hi, but I don't want to leave her in the lurch."

How could he not adore her? "Meet me later, after dinner. We'll take the horses out."

"A moonlit ride?" She sighed happily. "That sounds wonderful."

"Good. Meet me back here once things settle down around the camp."

"I will." She stepped in, reached up, and brushed her lips across his. "I need to go."

He caught her waist, held her close, and turned the kiss real, reawakening all the urges he'd started to tamp down, and welcoming the sharp ache. "I'll see you later. And, Shelby?"

Her cheeks were flushed, her eyes bright. "Yes?"

"For the record, I most definitely thought about you."

11

Dinner wasn't like anything Shelby had ever experienced before, and not just because she and Gran were cooking over open fires. Sure, it put her back in that "is this really my life?" place to flip the meat with long-handled tongs and hear the juices sizzle onto the coals below, then slap steaks onto tin pans with ladlefuls of beans and a biscuit on the top, and hand the whole yummy-smelling mess to someone wearing a cowboy hat and a layer of trail dust. And the snorts and occasional whinnies coming from the other side of the stream, along with the smell of horses and wood smoke, made it all that much more intense.

But it was more than that.

It was Foster.

Every cell of her body was aware of him, tuned to him. She knew where he was without looking, but she kept looking anyway, needing to convince herself that of all the stuff that didn't quite feel real, this part was. He was here, and they had a date for later tonight.

Riding in the moonlight. Wow.

"Medium-well, please."

The order brought her back down to earth. *Hello? Got a job to do here.*

"Medium-well it is." She loaded a steak and the trimmings, handed it over to the guest—a big guy in his forties with a barrel chest, almost no butt, and a pair of bright red suspenders holding up his jeans. "Enjoy, and don't forget to come back for seconds! Next?" She grinned at a dirty, happy-looking Lizzie. "Let me guess. Well done to the point of burned, plus A-1 sauce?"

Beside her, Gran faked a shudder. "Oh, the horror."

"Yeah, but she'll take an extra biscuit." The two littlest ones, to go with her small steak and half a potato.

Gran beamed. "Well, that makes all the difference, then. Enjoy."

As her daughter turned away, though, Shelby, said, "Ahem?"

Lizzie turned back.

"Do me a favor and wash something before you eat. Your hands would be a good place to start." And darned if she didn't get an eye roll. A really, really small one, but still. Grinning, she turned back to the chuck line. "Next?"

"Chef's choice," said a deep, smooth voice.

Shelby's heart thudded double time as Foster stepped into position opposite her, but she found a grin that she hoped covered some of the too-intense sizzle. "Just a plain potato, then?"

"There's nothing plain about you." His slow, sexy smile made her belly tighten as she handed over his food. "Thank you kindly." He tipped his hat. Then he glanced around, lowered his voice, and said, "I'll see you later, Shelby."

"For seconds?"

He winked. "If you like."

After that, the rest of the line was pretty much a blur. Unlike back at the ranch, everyone was responsible for washing his or her own pan and utensils—another cowboy rule, apparently—which meant that cleanup was a snap. Dessert was a Tupperware of brownies and cookies, and the leftovers went in a couple of coolers at the end of the chuck truck, to tide folks over as the night went dark and the cook fire farthest away from the tents became a marshmallow toaster.

As things wound down, Shelby said, "Do you want me to help—"

"Nope," Gran interrupted. "You're done. Go sit by the fire or something."

"I vote for 'or something,'" Krista said as she came around the truck. Her eyes gleamed. "I just happened to see Foster on the other side of the stream, saddling Loco."

Shelby was grateful for the darkness. "Must be taking him for a ride. It's his horse, after all."

"Figured that out, did you? And no, he's not taking Loco, at least not alone. Brutus is already tacked. Looks like he's headed out for a night ride, and is expecting some company." She paused, then tipped her head toward the corrals. "Go on. Gran and I will hang out with Lizzie, put her to bed when she fades."

Shelby hesitated, throat closing. "You haven't asked. Neither of you has asked."

"We figured you'd tell us when you were ready."

"I'm not ready." She pressed her palms to her burning cheeks. "For any of it. And Foster . . ."

"Is a big boy," Gran filled in for her. "He's been making his own decisions—and ours, at least when it comes to the horses—for a long time."

"Okay." She exhaled. "Right. He's done this before. It's not a big deal. Just two grown-ups having a little fun, that's all. Nothing to see here."

"Um . . ." Krista looked at her gran. "Not to freak you out, but no."

"Never?"

"As far as I know, you're the first woman who's caught his eye since he's been here." Krista grinned evilly. "But no pressure."

Yikes. Shelby swallowed hard. "It's not . . . we're just . . ." Jeez, what was it about him that reduced her to stammering?

Krista gave her a little shove. "Go. See what happens. If you ask me, you guys might be good for each other."

Relief washed through her, cool and cleansing. She hadn't realized how much she'd wanted their approval until she had it. Loner or not, Foster had been theirs for a long time. "I . . ." At a loss—for words, for logic—she hugged Krista hard. "Thank you."

"Any time. Don't worry about Lizzie. We'll take good care of her."

"I'll go tell her." At least that she'd be going out for a ride and would be back later. As for the other stuff . . . well, they would have to see.

Heart starting to thud against her ribs, Shelby headed for where Stace and Lizzie sat near the fire, toasting marshmallows.

"Wait," Gran called. When Shelby turned back, she held out a Ziploc. "Want a biscuit for luck?"

She was stuffed, but it didn't matter. "Absolutely." When it came to men—and especially this man—she could use all the luck she could get.

She was coming, Foster told himself. Of course she was coming. He'd seen her excitement earlier, and he'd felt the spark between them in the chuck line. A woman didn't look at a man like that and then stand him up.

Right?

Loco nudged him, then shook his head until his bit jingled. Beside him, Brutus stood quietly, still relatively tame from the hard riding they'd done to reach the camp.

"She'll be here," he said, giving Loco a fond pat. "Stace said she's been doing a good job with you, has a nice feel." And from one horseman to another, that was high praise.

Suddenly, Brutus's head came up, and he elephant-snorted into the darkness.

"Don't you dare," he growled.

"Oh," said a voice from the shadows. "Should I leave?"

"No! I wasn't talking to you." His pulse picked up as Shelby materialized out of the darkness. "You can totally dare."

"To do what?"

"Whatever you want, within reason." He held out Loco's reins. "How about we start with a ride?"

She didn't quite meet his eyes. "Thanks for getting him ready."

"You were busy. Great meal, by the way. It really hit the spot." He winced. Give it another minute and he'd be talking about the weather. Darn it, he'd been doing better there in the dinner line, had even managed to flirt some. But now it was back to feeling strange, like this was too important, even though they agreed this was just a summer thing, some fun between a couple of adults who didn't get much in the way of fun, at least not like this. "Ah, can I give you a leg up?"

She hesitated, then nodded. "Okay."

No doubt she could've gotten on from the ground, but she went ahead and faced Loco with one hand on the saddle horn, the other on the cantle, and crooked her leg. He caught her knee and boosted her up with little effort, then waited while she found her stirrups.

A light buoyancy pressed at the back of his throat, making him want to rub his chest as he snugged up on Brutus's reins and climbed aboard, settling easily into the rubbed-smooth saddle. It was a little like the feeling he got on a perfect morning, or when a stubborn greenie finally got it and started working with him, not against him. Only right now it was coming from her, from being with her in the darkness. And from something inside him.

He nudged Brutus over next to Loco, who stood with his head up and his ears pricked happily. "You two ready?"

Her eyes shone in the moonlight as she nodded. "I know this is all in a day's work for you, but it's an adventure for me."

"I love a good adventure. Let's go!"

He led the way up the hill, along the stream, and away from camp, grateful when a small, wispy cloud scudded across the moon, giving them a bit of darkness for their escape. No doubt Ty, Krista, and a few of the others would be watching the horses leave—and would keep an eye out for their safe return—but he'd rather not be on public display, at least not in this.

Been there, done that.

"Ride on up next to me," he said, waving her forward as they reached the crest of the hill. "I'd like it, and so would Brutus. He hasn't done much night riding yet, and would appreciate the company."

She nudged Loco up and the horses jostled together in the darkness, with Brutus taking reassurance from the older, steadier horse, bumping Foster's and Shelby's legs in the process. She filled her lungs and tipped her head back to look up as the moon broke free of the cloud, bathing the world silver and blue, the light so bright that it threw their shadows on the ground. "I never would've guessed you could ride by moonlight." Her voice was full of wonder.

"Horses have pretty good night vision." *Come on, you can do better than this.* "I, ah, ride out lots during the full moon. Never brought anyone else along before, though."

She was silent for a moment, the only sounds the creaks and jingles of their tack and the clink of horseshoes against the occasional rock. Then she said, "So . . . is this the local equivalent of buying me a drink, or is this first date territory?"

It wasn't until he exhaled that he realized he'd been holding his breath. "I'm taking you someplace special. At least I think it's special."

"First date," she decided, and sent him a little smile. "It's been a while."

"Bet I've got you beat," he said, determined to stay in the not-talking-about-the-weather zone if it killed him.

"Try me."

"It's been a few years since I skinny-dipped."

"Is that a metaphor, or are we talking real nudie swimming?"

"The latter. And that's the second date, cowboy-style."

She grinned. "Then what's going steady?"

"That's when he lets you ride his favorite horse," he said, then winced, afraid he was accidentally getting in too deep already. Where did banter stop and expectations begin?

"I . . . um . . ." She stared at Loco's ears. "One of the guests last week told me he was yours. Dana. She said Loco was a celebrity. You, too."

"That was a long time ago. But yeah, Loco and I are a team. Where I go, he goes." He chuckled. "Don't freak, though. Letting you use him was for my own peace of mind. I knew he'd keep you safe and teach you right, and wouldn't do anything to set things back with Lizzie. Besides, Brutus here needed some saddle time with someone who wasn't going to put up with his back talk." He gave the mustang gelding a pat. "We seem to have reached an understanding."

"You're good at that. Understanding things, I mean. Horses. People."

"Don't give me too much credit. I'm much better with animals."

"Lizzie would disagree. So would I."

And wasn't that a bloody miracle? "She's a special case. As for you . . ."

"Ye-e-s?" She drew out the word.

"Bear with me. I'm about as rusty as a guy can get, and I wasn't very good at this stuff to begin with." Hadn't had much practice.

Her lips curved. "You're doing okay from where I'm sitting. You know. On your favorite horse."

He laughed, finally starting to believe that he wasn't imagining things, and they were actually on the same page here. "You're okay, Shelby. You're very okay. Come on. Let's ride."

They rode for maybe an hour, catching glimpses of the stream as they wound along ridges and valleys, and picked their way across some loose rocks. They dismounted once to lead the horses across one of the rocky sections, then remounted on the other side and continued on. After that first spurt of conversation, they rode mostly in silence, settling into the rhythm of the horses and the night. Shelby decided that she liked how he didn't feel the need to fill the air with chatter. Sure, it meant she didn't know all that much about him, but how much did that really matter? They were just having fun.

And she was having fun. She really, really was.

As they entered a small stand of trees, he reined Brutus to a halt and said, "Listen. Can you hear it?"

Loco had already stopped, as if reading her mind. She cocked her head, lips curving when she realized that what she'd initially thought was a breeze ruffling the leaves was the rush of water. "Rapids?"

"Even better." He clucked Brutus forward, and within moments they were pushing out of the trees, to where the moonlight splashed silver on a wide pool of water churned up by a twenty-foot waterfall.

"Oh!" she breathed. "It's beautiful!" The water fell down from a sheer, rocky cliff, split around a promontory, and plummeted to the pool, which roiled and spun and then fed out in a narrow river that headed back the way they had come.

While she gaped, Foster swung down from Brutus and rummaged in one of his saddlebags. "Hop down. I've got halters and hobbles, and Loco will make sure Blockhead here doesn't get it in his head to leave us high and dry."

"We could always hike back."

His teeth flashed. "Ty would never let me live it down."

She looked at him for a moment, realizing that he was smiling more than she'd seen from him before, and looked much more relaxed. Was it being out in the backcountry or being with her? Probably both, she decided, and grinned. "What else have you got in those bags? Bathing suits, maybe? I have it on good authority that skinny-dipping is reserved for the second date."

His chuckle sounded rusty. "How about some Twizzlers?"

She put a hand to her heart. "Don't tease me."

"No tease. Twizzlers."

"Gimme."

"Nope. See to your horse first."

She watched what he did with the halter and hobbles, and tried to copy his expert motions. Within a few minutes the horses were contentedly grazing and Foster had the saddlebags slung over his shoulder. "This way. There's a very cool picnic spot up on the ledge."

He billy-goated his way straight up the rocks beside the waterfall, leaving her standing at the bottom, staring up at him. "You're kidding. That's not a path."

"Sorry. I'll come back and show you."

"No, never mind. I can handle it." Determined not to get herself busted back to city-girl status, she dug her pointy-toed boots into the space between a couple of rocks and started to climb.

It was only maybe ten or twelve feet up the low cliff he'd scaled, but the slippery stone surface made it feel as if she'd gone twice that far before her fingers found the edge of a gritty ledge.

A strong hand closed on her wrist, warm and sure despite the moisture. "I've got you."

She clambered up with his help, very aware of his hands gripping hers and then his arm around her waist as she teetered momentarily on the edge, about to do a Humpty Dumpty, but not really scared because he was there for her to lean on. Their bodies brushed and bumped as she righted herself, the friction turning the night suddenly warmer than it had been moments before.

Kisses were all well and good, but her body wanted more. And she wasn't sure whether it was getting ahead of her or not.

"There's a dry spot over here." He led her to where a big boulder offered some shelter from the spray and formed a lawn-chair-like depression. He sat down and leaned back, patting the smooth stone beside him. "Come on. It's more comfortable than it looks."

He was right, she found as she settled in beside him, leaning back against the smooth stone backrest, with their arms brushing and their legs just shy of touching where they stretched out along the ledge. They were about a third of the way up the falls, near where the water split. That spray, and the mist rising from the churning pool below, made the air dance silver in the moonlight. The trees made the little grotto seem very private, and the distant mountains made the world around them seem limitless. The sound and shimmering rush of water were hypnotic, the rocks still held some warmth from the day, and she found herself settling into the rocky niche, relaxed yet still very aware of him.

"So, do you come here often?" she asked, then laughed. "Oops. Minus two points for the lame pickup line."

"Jeez, hope we're not keeping score here, or I'm doomed."

"A moonlit ride, a waterfall, and processed sugar? I

don't think so." She kept her answer light and teasing, but his offhand comment hit home all of a sudden, giving her an inner "oh, wow" as she realized she'd mostly gotten out of the habit over the past few weeks. Always before—with her family, her career, her day-to-day life—there was a scorecard.

Not here, though. Not with him, and not with Krista or Gran. They offered to help because they wanted to, not because they were keeping track.

Unaware of her *hello* moment, he answered her original question. "I get out here a few times a year. Sometimes I just stop off on my way by. Other times I'll stay and camp a day or two. I've seen some amazing sunsets." He pointed off in the distance, where a gap between two mountains made a perfect triangle. "In the late fall, when the sun lines up just right, it looks like something out of a dream, deep blue up in the sky, going down to red and orange, all these layers going down behind the mountains."

"It sounds gorgeous," she said, and felt a little pang knowing that she wouldn't be here come autumn.

"So is this, in a different way." He looked at her for a long moment, letting her know he liked what he saw. Then, grinning, he flipped open one of the saddlebags and rummaged inside, and held out a couple of Twizzlers. "I believe I promised you dessert?"

"Oh, baby, come to Mama." She took one and held it for a moment, absorbing the sweet, rubbery smell.

He chuckled. "Wouldn't have pegged you for a junk foodie."

"I've got a stash of Cheetos and Swedish fish in my

cabin. I snuck them in from town and hid them in my dresser."

"A woman after my own heart."

The darkness hid her flush. "The way I see it, what Gran doesn't know won't hurt her . . . and when you've lived on preservatives for as long as I have, it's not easy going cold turkey."

"Understood." He held out his own Twizzler. "To moonlight rides, waterfalls, and processed sugar."

Amused to have two food toasts in one day—first biscuits in the chuck truck, and now this—she Twizz-clinked. "To first dates, roundups, and new adventures."

"Amen."

She took a ceremonial bite when he did, and gave a big "Mmmm." But then she warned, "Don't tell Gran about this, or I'll take you down with me for Twizzler pimping."

He chuckled. "Twizzler pimp. I like that. Might have to put it on my card."

"You don't have a card. Or if you do, it's with your phone, lost somewhere in your . . . what? Apartment? House? Trailer?"

"I live in a bunkhouse."

"Of course. Silly me."

"When Mustang Ridge went dude, the Skyes decided the bunkhouse was too far away from the main ranch to work for the guests, so they renovated it and made housing part of the head wrangler's pay. When I took the job, Ed—that's Krista's dad—helped me set it up with solar panels and a cistern, and I've upgraded the gadgets along the way, tightening things up so I'm pretty self-sufficient without being nutso about it."

"An ecofriendly bunkhouse. I like it." It was another layer, one that fit with the astronomer. How many more did he have? How long would it take to get to know all of him?

Longer than she had, she knew, and stifled the pang.

"It suits me for now." He paused. "Anyone back at the ranch would've told you that, if you'd asked."

Pulling her brain back where it belonged—enjoying the moment rather than worrying about the future—she shrugged. "I didn't ask. I've made a point not to gossip, with a couple of slips here and there. It seemed too high school, I guess, pumping the other kids for info on you, and whether they thought you liked me, or like-liked me."

That got a grin. "I'd say it's not just high school. That sort of stuff translates worldwide, possibly even to other planets."

She shifted as a pointy rock dug into the base of her spine. "I can see it now, the jock gray aliens passing notes in the back of class, while the little green ones—their version of band geeks, don't you know—travel in packs, even on dates."

"Something like that. Here." He put his arm around her and drew her against his side. "I make a better pillow than that rock."

Yes, you do. His body was warm beneath the tough cotton of his shirt, and musky with trail dust and sweat. She leaned into him, suffused with the strangeness of letting herself lean on a man, even as parts of her remembered exactly how this was supposed to go, how it was supposed to feel.

Like riding a bike, she thought, and felt a wash of heat.

"Anyway, no, I didn't ask Krista and the others about you. I figured that this—whatever it is, whatever it becomes—should stay more or less between the two of us. Not a secret, but not a village affair, either."

"I couldn't agree more. Well, then . . ." He tightened his arm around her. "I guess the next question is, what do you want to know about me? Because it's been a while, but I'm pretty sure that a first date should include some form of twenty questions, maybe more."

The questions swam in her head, but she also wanted to keep in mind that this wasn't a first date between two strangers, trying to get a sense of each other or figure out how they synched up—or not—in relationship terms. So she said, "Whatever you feel like telling me, I'd enjoy hearing. Or you can ask me something. Or we can just sit here and cuddle. No twenty questions, no scoring, just the two of us together because we want to be."

She felt him look down at her. "You're not much like other women, are you?"

"I guess that depends on the other women. And no, I'm not asking about them. We're here and now, just enjoying each other's company."

"No," he said softly.

"No?" She looked up at him in surprise. "We don't enjoy each other's company?"

"No, you're not like other women at all. Period. And

I enjoy the heck out of your company. What's more, it seems I'm going to kiss you now."

If she'd thought before that her pulse was racing, now she realized that had just been a prelude to the real thing. "It seems I'm going to let you kiss me. I might even kiss you back."

"Oh, yeah." His smile was slow and devastating as he bent toward her, urging her up with his arms. "You sure will."

Their lips met and clung, fanning the banked heat to a strong, sure glow. He took it soft and slow, sweeping his tongue between her lips, first a taste, then a caress. She softened against him and reached up to touch his neck, his jaw, and rub her thumb along the unfamiliar beard-bristle that said he'd been away from a razor for some time.

To her surprise, she liked the raspy feel of it, just as she liked knowing that he'd come straight from the gather, riding hard because he'd wanted to see her.

She broke the soft, drugging kisses to whisper against his lips. "I heard it's in the Cowboy Code that you're not supposed to touch a man's hat."

He chuckled. "If you're another man, then yeah, it's liable to get you in a fight. But if you're a woman, it falls somewhere between skinny-dipping and borrowing his horse." He reached up, removed his hat, and set it on her head, tipped back so he could catch her neck and draw her close once more.

His hat was warm and musky, his lips insistent, his body a contrast of hard and soft against hers. *Ah,* she thought, *this.* This was what she had given up, walked

away from, deprioritized. This was what she sometimes missed at night, the ache that never quite went
away. The kisses, and the feeling of a man's body
against hers, inside hers.

Yes, this.

But as their kisses grew deeper and darker, it
stopped being familiar, and started growing new,
strange, and urgent. She moved restlessly against him,
caught his groan in her mouth, and slipped a hand into
the open throat of his shirt to touch the wiry hair and
warm skin beneath. They kissed, caught, held, shuddered, and slid a little lower on the stone, until they
weren't so much sitting anymore as lying together,
wrapped up in each other. And even as the heat and
hormones were all for sliding lower, part of her was
thinking that it was too much, too fast.

She murmured and flattened her hand against him,
and he eased back with a muttered oath, one that was
more wondering than unhappy.

Keeping his arms around her, he pulled them back
up to where they started, leaning back against the rock
in a safer, more upright position. His ribs were heaving
and his voice wasn't quite steady as he said, "Whoa,
there. Slowing it down now, before we skip a few steps
and wish we hadn't."

"Okay," she said, trying to slow her breathing.
"Yeah, okay. That'd probably be best."

He gathered her close and kissed her brow, her
cheek. "I'm not saying I'd regret anything we might do
together. But I want us both to enjoy the ride."

"Walk the first mile out and the last one in?"

"Something like that." But his eyes were intense on hers. "Okay?"

"Okay." She blew out a pent-up breath. "Yeah, more than okay."

"Want another Twizzler?"

"Is that a metaphor?"

"Nope, it's a Twizzler."

She laughed, accepted the faux licorice, and settled in against him, enjoying the feel of his too-big hat tipping down over her brow and the sound of his heartbeat, sure and strong, and still quick from their kisses. They ate the Twizzlers, opened another pack, shared a quick, sticky kiss, and watched the waterfall.

After a while, she said, "How about you tell me Loco's story? A horse like that, there's got to be a story."

"Ah."

She could hear his smile.

"Yes, indeed. There's always a story when it comes to a horse like Loco." He eased a little lower on the rock and urged her closer to his chest, so his voice rumbled beneath her cheek as he said, "I grew up on a ranch that was a lot like Mustang Ridge would've been, before it went dude. It was smaller, though, strictly a family operation. The Double-Bar H. My ma and pa did most of the work, though my grandpa ran the place, at least in name. He'd lost my gramma to cancer, and never really got past it, but he was good with me and my sister, Tish. And he had a way with horses like nobody else I've ever met."

When he paused, she wasn't sure what to say. She'd asked about the horse and got the story of the man, in a way she probably wouldn't have if she'd asked about his family or childhood.

Maybe she was starting to figure out this cowboy thing. Sort of.

Nestling in closer, she said, "I guess you take after him."

"I'd like to think so, and that's where Loco comes in. Growing up on the Double-Bar H, Tish and I were riding pretty much as soon as we could walk, and we helped bring on the young stock all along, doing different parts of the training as we grew up. It was family tradition, though, that on our sixteenth birthdays, we got to pick a foal or yearling for our own, and do all the training from the ground up. Tish—she's a year older than me—picked a spitfire of a mare that she named Beauty, because she was. And the next year, I picked out Loco."

"Why the name? Was he crazy?"

"Actually, I named him Luke. The Loco part came later, when it came time to start him under saddle."

She felt him shrug.

"We worked it out over the years, and nowadays there isn't anyone else, man or beast, that I trust more."

Shelby laughed softly. "Gran was saying to me earlier how it's harder being a parent than a horse trainer, because a parent has to get it right the first time."

"I won't argue with that."

"But you got it right."

"I got lucky. He's a hell of a horse."

And you're a hell of a man, she thought, but didn't say. So instead, she said, "So, he's what, twenty now?"

"Twenty-two and still going strong, though he'll show his age now and then in the winter."

"Don't we all?"

He laughed and hugged her close. "Don't you believe it, Mama Bear. You and Stace could be sisters."

"Hardly. I'm thirty-three." Which made him five years older, yet it sort of felt like those numbers should be reversed. She was the one with the nine-year-old and the mortgage, while he had a horse, a saddle, and a beat-up old truck. That was the nice thing about what they were doing, though. All that mattered was today, tomorrow, maybe the next day. So she would take it one day at a time and enjoy the ride.

"I'm liking thirty-something," he said. "It's old enough to have learned a few things about impulse control and patience, but still young enough that I can tell myself I've got time yet to figure out what I want to be when I grow up."

"Ah, yes, that one. I'm familiar with the concept."

"Not sure you want to stay in advertising?"

"Not sure I want to work for someone else for the rest of my life doing it."

"And here I first thought we didn't have much in common." He paused. "Don't get me wrong, Krista is the best. But it's not my own place, you know?"

She held up her Twizzler. "To being your own boss."

He clinked. "Amen."

He chuckled and held her close, and they stayed like that in comfortable silence for a bit, watching the water fall and the mist rise, and the patterns they made in the moonlight. Before long, though, he squeezed her tight and said into her hair, "We should be heading back. If we stay out much longer, they're liable to send the dogs out after us."

"I know." And the last thing she wanted to do was worry Lizzie or any of the others. "Speaking of dogs, where's Vader?"

"He was tired from the long run earlier, so I asked Lizzie to watch him for me."

Her heart took a slow roll in her chest. "Oh. I didn't see him when I talked to her."

"He's learned his lesson about getting too close to fire pits. But he's there, keeping an eye on her, and vice versa."

"Thank you."

"No biggie."

She caught his hand and squeezed it. "It's a biggie to me, and to Lizzie. She hasn't had much in the way of positive male attention in the last few years, and I think . . ." She hesitated, hating to put it into words, but unable to call it a coincidence. "Please don't think I'm trying to put you in the daddy role, because I'm really not. But at the same time, I'm not sure she would have gotten as far as she has without you. Not just because you're a man, but because of everything you've done for her. For us."

"She would've gotten there." When she started to shake her head, he caught her face in his hands. "Hey. She would have. Maybe not this fast, or this same way, but she would've gotten there, thanks to you."

Shelby closed her eyes. "You're good for me, Foster. I wish I could give you back some of what you've given me."

"No keeping score, remember?" He kissed her lightly on the lips. "When can I see you again?"

She laughed, because they'd be camping within yards of each other, she with Lizzie, while he doubled up with Ty. Who, Gran had warned, snored like a jackhammer. But she knew what he meant, and the question gave her a glow. "I'd give you my number, but rumor has it you don't have your phone glued to you twenty-four-seven."

"Not so much." He kissed her nose. "So let's make our date right now. Tomorrow night, after things die down. Meet me by the horses, like you did tonight. I'll bring the junk food and show you something special."

"Skinny-dipping?"

His grin went lopsided. "You'll have to wait and see."

12

The next few days were a blur to Shelby, but in a very good way. The roundup was an unqualified success, with a ten percent increase in the number of calves that were microchipped, immunized, and—in the case of the young males—snipped, and a fat two hundred being brought down to the ranch to be sold, ensuring that the herd didn't get too big. The days hadn't been blazing hot, there weren't any real accidents or injuries, and the horses and riders were holding up great under the work. The chuck truck was chugging along, rolling along easier now that it was lighter by five days' worth of provisions, and Shelby and Gran had been roundly praised each night for the camp meals. But if the days blurred, the nights stood still.

Shelby and Foster didn't go skinny-dipping after all, as the water was even colder up closer to the mountains. Instead, on the second night—it was Sunday, though not like any Sunday she'd ever had before— they rode out to a cliff where, sheltered in a shallow cave high up above ground level, some long-ago artist had chiseled a pattern of spirals and stars, and barrel-chested stick figures hunting with arrows and spears.

With the hobbled horses picking at grass down below, snorting now and then, Shelby leaned into Foster and dangled her legs over the edge, enjoying the flutter that came with the height . . . and the man. She let out a sigh. "It's a fabulous night."

"We get lots of great nights out here." He stretched an arm around her and drew her closer. "But the company makes this one perfect."

She grinned up at his strong profile, silhouetted against the blush of sunset. "Your sweet talk is getting better. You been practicing?"

"Brutus gets a kick out of it." He reached into the saddlebag he'd brought up with him, and held out a bottle. "Drink?"

"Orange soda?"

A chuckle rumbled in his chest. "Gran always says my palate stopped developing at age twelve. Besides, I wasn't sure what went with Nutter Butters."

"What doesn't go with Nutter Butters? Gimme."

He proffered the packaged cookies with a flourish. "Asparagus?"

"Excuse me?

"Asparagus doesn't go with Nutter Butters."

She bit in, considered. "I could make it work. Maybe tie them together with a white sauce, or some Brie." Though that might be stretching it.

He faked a shudder. "Real cowboys don't eat funky cheese."

"Is that part of the code?"

"If it's not, it should be."

"Okay, then, no asparagus with our Nutter Butters."

"Or brussels sprouts, broccoli, or lima beans."

"You got something against vegetables?"

"Not if it's lettuce or carrots. Peas are okay in limited doses."

"Ah." She nodded knowingly. "You're a bag-o'-salad guy."

"A what?"

"Tell me there hasn't been a bag o' salad in your fridge recently." At his expression, she grinned. "Typical bachelor fare."

"Oh? And you've never succumbed to the temptation of American blend or spring mix?"

"I didn't say that. Hey, it's an accepted single mom shortcut. I figure I get points because Lizzie eats her veggies . . . as long as I don't try to feed her asparagus, broccoli, brussels sprouts, or lima beans."

"Just one more reason for me to like your kid."

The offhand comment tightened her throat, made her want to reach out to him. *He doesn't mean it that way,* she reminded herself. *We're just having fun here.* And they did, eating their cookies under the stars and sharing peanut-flavored kisses that teetered on the edge of more.

More heat, more touches, more desire.

On Monday night, after a long day of collecting cattle on his part and cooking on hers, they snuck away again and rode out to a bubbling spring that held the sweetest water she'd ever tasted, and a mossy carpet where they cuddled and looked up at the stars. They were both bone tired and didn't talk much, but where silence so often made her feel like she should jump in and fill it with something, now she relaxed and enjoyed the quiet, the night. The man.

They breathed. They touched. They kissed. And when the air cooled, the horses grew restless, and they headed back to the campsite, she was utterly, bonelessly relaxed. They would have tomorrow, the day after that, and the day after that.

I'm on vacation, she thought, and tried not to grin like a fool.

On Tuesday he got Stace to cover the dinner service, and brought Shelby to another waterfall while the sun still hung in the sky. This waterfall was taller and narrower than the first, a long, thin cascade that bounced off rock after rock, turning almost entirely to mist by the time it hit bottom. There, a pebbled shore stretched up past where the mist turned everything wet, offering a perfect spot for the picnic he drew from an oversize saddlebag. After spreading a wool blanket and guiding her down, he dug into the provisions and produced a bottle of wine, pale and slender, and gleaming yellow in the sun. "I filched a nice Chardonnay from the truck, if you're in the mood."

She almost hid the split-second hesitation. "Ah . . . sure."

"Or not," he said easily. "I brought lemonade, too, in case alcohol's not your thing."

"No," she said softly. "I'd like the wine."

He paid too much attention to pouring. "I take it that you're not exactly a party animal? City girl like you?"

"City girls aren't all the same," she said with some

asperity. "That's like saying everyone who lives in Wyoming is a cowboy."

"Bite your tongue."

"Like I said. But you're right, I don't party much. I like a little wine now and then, though, with ... friends."

This time the look was longer, and didn't slide away. "With someone you trust, you mean. Someone you know won't go overboard?"

She wasn't sure she liked how easily he read her. She enjoyed being the focus of his attention, but some things didn't have any place in a romantic picnic under the wide-open sky, with a handsome cowboy who made her feel special. She wasn't ashamed of this part of her life, though, at least not anymore. So she nodded and said, "Something like that. Which means that yes, I'd like some wine, thanks." Leaning back, hoping that would be the end of it, she looked up at the waterfall. "Is that a cave up there?"

He handed her a plastic cup. "Yep. About fifteen feet deep, though it gets pretty low in the back. A big mama cat used it a few years back, though there hasn't been any sign of her in a while."

Her heart shimmied. "You actually climbed up there to see?"

"Once or twice a year." He grinned. "It's part of my job to keep track of the local predators, make sure they don't get too many cows. Or dudes, for that matter."

"I'm going to file that under 'things I don't want to think about,' thank you very much." Just like she didn't want to think about him playing Spider-Man up on the wet rocks and sticking his head in a mountain lion's den.

"So . . . I take it your ex was a drinker?"

Apparently, that wasn't the end of it after all. She made a face, but said as easily as she could, "My ex, my father. I'm a flipping generational cliché, though I tried hard not to be." Patrick had seemed like all the things her father wasn't—ambitious, upwardly mobile, family-focused. It wasn't until later that she'd seen the familiar patterns, the frustrations and missed opportunities, and how every setback was always somebody else's fault. The boss, the supervisor, her. She shrugged. "Wounds healed, lessons learned, blah, blah. And it's way too pretty a night to dredge that stuff up. Let's just drink our wine, have our picnic."

"Of course." Foster took a swallow and looked out over the falls. In the fading sunlight, the mist made shimmering rainbows that seemed suddenly magical, as if the evening had taken on another dimension. "I just wondered . . ."

Darn it. "Go on."

He hesitated, choosing his words. "Sometimes people send me retraining projects, horses that have gotten labeled rogues or broncs, or just bad actors for one reason or another. With some of them, they've got holes in their educations, steps that got skipped along the way, and I just have to backtrack and fill in the gaps. Other times, though, there's something in their history, some bad experience that's made them stop trusting humans. Not always, mind you, but enough so I have to ask."

"Oh." Her fingers tightened, denting the flimsy cup.

"Right. No, it's nothing like that." She had done her best to shield Lizzie from how bad things were getting toward the end of the marriage. And in his own way, so had Patrick.

"Still. I'd like to hear the story if you wouldn't mind telling it."

She didn't want to bring the past into this pretty place, didn't want it to intrude on their time together. But he was asking for Lizzie's sake. "There's not much of a story, really. There wasn't any violence, no drunken rages or big, spectacular fights. I didn't even realize how bad the drinking had gotten until after Patrick left, when I was clearing out the old house and found all these stashed bottles and crossed-out receipts, like hiding it from me had been some sort of game."

"Maybe he was hiding it from himself, too."

She turned up her palms. "It's a disease, and it's nothing I could've fixed even if I had known how far it had gone. Trust me, I get that. But it doesn't stop me from feeling stupid that I didn't catch the signs." More, she hated that she hadn't been the one to walk away, which was just dumb.

"It's usually easier to see the trail you've already ridden than the one in front of you."

Reminding herself that she had needed to get through it to be where she was today, and that for all the heartbreak at the end, Patrick had given her Lizzie, she found a grin. "Seriously, I could do a year's worth of advertising just using the Cowboy Code."

"Your average minivan doesn't need to be walked the first and last mile of every trip."

"I could work with it." She dropped her voice to announcer level. "Buy Velveeta for your little buckaroo . . . because real cowboys don't eat funky cheese."

"You might have something there."

"Or not." She shrugged, relaxing some, because Foster was easy to talk to, even about this. "Anyway, there wasn't a big triggering incident for Lizzie's SM, although I have no doubt the divorce factors into her confidence problems. There's nothing I can see that we haven't dealt with as best we could. And trust me, I've been over it a million times." In her head, with Lizzie, with the therapists.

"I don't doubt it for a second," he said firmly. "And if it came across as an accusation, or like I thought you'd missed something, I'm sorry. That wasn't how I meant it."

"No, not really. I guess I'm still touchy about it, even after all this time." Then again, it hadn't been that long, really. Only a couple of years since Patrick walked out, a year or so since she had found her way back to being her real self, someone she was proud of. But at the same time it seemed like forever ago, as if parts of her marriage had happened to someone else.

"You've got the right to be touchy there," he said with a faint nod. "And like I said, I didn't mean anything bad by asking. I'm just feeling my way." He paused, then asked, "Does Lizzie see much of her grandparents?"

It took her a second to catch up to the subject change, another to squelch the frustration. It was a beautiful sunset, with wine and a picnic, and she didn't want to talk about this anymore. Which made her feel selfish, and as if she was in danger of losing some serious mom points. But hadn't Krista—and even Foster himself—told her she needed to take some time for herself? Although in all honesty, Lizzie had her worried today. She'd seemed happy enough the first couple of days, helping set up the corrals, toting tack and water for the riders, and pitching in with the cooking. But yesterday the glow had notched down and today she'd been moody and withdrawn, mostly sitting by herself and thumbing through a worn book.

She's just tired, she told herself, as that had been Gran's diagnosis, too, as the folding cots and thin tents made for some uneasy nights even in the safety of camp. Not to mention that Lizzie's electronics were out of juice, which was guaranteed to get a scowl from just about any modern-day kid.

But at the same time, it was hard not to wonder whether some—or all—of the issue was that her mom was kind of dating. Lizzie had waved it off when she asked—*no big deal, whatever*—but still.

"Shelby? You okay?"

She focused on Foster and wondered if she was making a mistake. "Yes, I'm sorry." What had he asked again? Oh, yes. "We don't have any contact with my parents. Like I said, my father was a drinker."

"Was. He quit?"

"He died," she said flatly. "Eight years ago. Heart problems, liver failure, you name it, he had it by the end." Six decades of abuse, and his body had finally given out.

"Any other family?"

"My mother and sister. We're not close." Hello, understatement. "Or, rather, they're close to each other, but not to me or Lizzie. She only met them a couple of times when she was very little, and I haven't seen either of them since the funeral. Honestly it's better that way."

That got her a long look, but he said only, "What about her grandparents on the other side?"

She let out a breath. "Sally and Paul. They're good people, and first on my 'in case of emergency' list. They live outside Seattle, though, and aren't in the best of health, which makes it hard to stay close. I take Lizzie out to see them at least once year, but it never feels like enough."

"I bet it's not easy to keep up a long-distance relationship without talking on the phone, or at least e-mailing."

"We try. I put their calls on speaker, and the three of us chat about what we've been doing while Lizzie listens in, and I e-mail them photos at least once a month, but . . ." She shrugged. "It's okay. All we can do is our best."

"Sounds lonely."

"She's got some friends at school, a couple in our building. I make sure she gets out and interacts even though she'd rather stay in by herself and read or play games. She likes gymnastics, though, and dance." She tried not to sound defensive.

"That's good, but I wasn't talking about just Lizzie." When Shelby stiffened, he shifted over and wrapped an arm around her, so they were sitting side by side, staring through the mist. Which made it easier to hear the husky sympathy in his voice when he said, "Shelby, darling, it sounds to me like you do a whole lot for everyone around you—especially that sweet little girl of yours. But who's going to do nice things for you?"

She didn't let herself pull away, but her voice gained an edge. "I don't need anybody. We're fine, just Lizzie and me. We can take care of ourselves."

"No argument here. I just hope that if you take anything away from Mustang Ridge for yourself, it's that you need to have some fun of your own now and then. You've been down a hard road and come out the other end in one piece." He tightened his arm. "Be good to yourself. You've got a great life, a great kid. Make sure you enjoy them."

The reminder of that life—and the fact that they wouldn't always be sitting together, out here in the middle of nowhere—brought a quiver. "I . . ." She blew out a breath, made herself relax. "I'm trying. I'm out here with you, aren't I?"

"Yes. That you are."

"And I'm doing things like this."

He arched a brow. "Like what?"

Determined to dispel the gloom that had come with talking too much about the past and future rather than the glorious now, she turned and rose on her knees beside him. "This."

For the first time she initiated a kiss, leaning into him to press her lips to his, hard and ardent. His mouth opened beneath hers and she delved in, aroused by the hint of wine and the clutch of his hands on her arms, her waist. She pressed against him, feeling wanted, feeling powerful. Maybe she was on her own in the real world, but right here and now, she was with him.

When she pulled away, heart pounding, he tightened his fingers and let out a low growl. "Do that again."

She wanted to—wow, did she want to!—but didn't dare. Not now, after a conversation that had left her feeling a little off balance and more than a little vulnerable. "Maybe later." Smiling, she retrieved her wine and sipped, enjoying the flavor and the faint tingle against her tongue. "Tell me you have chocolate to go with this."

"Dessert before dinner?"

"Or for dinner. Don't tell me you've never dined on chocolate chip cookies and root beer?"

Grinning, he reached for the saddlebag. "Chocolate cupcakes do it for you?"

"Always," she said, and settled in beside. By unspoken consent, they stayed away from serious things while they watched the sun go down. Instead, they munched on junk food and talked about small, silly things long after the rainbows blazed red and gold, then faded to night. And it was perfect.

The following evening it rained, not just a soaker, but ominous thunderstorms that rolled through, blackened the sky, and sent wind whipping across the campsite. There wasn't any question of Shelby and Foster sneaking away—she stayed put with Lizzie in their tent, playing gin rummy by camp lantern and working not to flinch when lightning flashed and thunder rolled. Lizzie's eyes stayed wide and worried, though, and Shelby sometimes had to prompt her when it was her turn.

The thunder moved on after an hour or so, but the rain and wind stayed put, as did the scared expression on Lizzie's face. When the third gust hit their tent in as many minutes, making the canvas boom around them, Shelby threw up her hands. "Enough! Uncle!" As Lizzie stared, she gathered up their sleeping bags and pillows. "Come on, kiddo. Grab Mr. Pony and let's go. We're sleeping in the truck tonight." It was late enough in the roundup that most of the back was clear of provisions. There would be plenty of room for them to stretch out, unless too many other people had come to the same decision.

A little to her surprise, they were the only ones to take shelter in the truck. And yeah, maybe bailing out of the tent confirmed that she was a city girl despite the boots and jeans, but when Lizzie crawled into her arms and curled up in her lap, Shelby decided she didn't care. For tonight, the most important thing was being a safe place for her daughter.

On Thursday night, their last night on the trail, things cleared up again much to everyone's relief, and Shelby and Foster slipped away for some more alone time. It was late but the moon was bright, letting the horses pick their footing up a steep, rocky hill to a grassy plateau, where he left the hobbled horses to graze, then led her over to the edge and down a narrow trail that took them partway down into a moonlit valley.

"We'll sit here." He guided her to a wide, flat ledge, where rocks encircled a scorched spot and a split log made a bench. Sitting beside her, he dug into his saddlebag and pulled out a sloshing canteen and their evening snacks. "Pixy Stix and Kool-Aid?"

She laughed. "I'm so going to have to detox after this week."

"Is that a 'no'?"

"I didn't say that. Hand them over." She looked around, not really sure why there was an evidently well-trafficked viewing spot right here. The valley was soft and rolling, the distant mountains were pitch-black against the moon-blue night, and the stars spread around them like a canopy. But all that could be said for tonight's campsite, too. "What are we— *Oh*," she breathed, "mustangs!"

The horses appeared out of the darkness like ghosts, floating across the valley floor, their hoofbeats inaudible from the humans' vantage point. There were twenty of them, maybe more, three of them mares with foals tagging more or less at their heels. Or, rather, scampering from side to side with little hopping bucks, like the ones Lucky had started to throw in when he and Sassy went out in their paddock.

"See the dark one out front, keeping an eye on everything? That's the alpha mare." Foster kept his voice low, his mouth close to her ear, making the moment even more intimate, more special. "She bosses the herd, leads them, keeps them safe. She's chased off all of the bachelor stallions except for that guy over there—the stocky fellow with the high whites on his rear legs, bringing up the rear of the group and keeping them safe."

"They're beautiful," she breathed. "And so different! I thought that they would look like the ranch horses. And they do . . . but they don't."

"Nope," he agreed. "The wild ones have an extra something to them. An air of freedom, maybe, or an extra layer of cautiousness. Whatever it is, it gets inside you and stirs the blood. At least it does me."

"Me, too."

He cocked his head, a small smile tugging at his lips. "You like it here?"

"I love it. Thank you for bringing me." She leaned in and brushed her lips across his. "I can't think of a better way to spend the last night of the roundup."

"Watching wild horses with my lady? I can't, either."

Even as the thrill of his words shot through her at the pleasure of being his lady, if only temporarily, he returned the kiss, deepened it, and amped up the sizzle a hundredfold. A thousand. She murmured and crowded closer, loving the feel of his arms around her, his body hard against hers. His lady. Yes. She'd take that.

From below, one of the mustangs whinnied. From above, one of the saddle horses answered.

She broke the kiss. "Are they okay?"

His lips curved. "Loco will keep Brutus in line, and the wild ones are too smart to waste the effort investigating. So I think we should—" His face blanked suddenly, his eyes fixing past her shoulder.

"What—" She started to turn.

"No. Stay where you are. Don't. Move. Just let me—" He shot an arm past her, grabbed something and yanked, dragging a piece of what looked and felt like black rubber garden hose over her shoulder and down her arm. Except that then it moved, curling up and around his arm.

Snake!

"Ohmigod!" She scrambled to her feet and flew back, slamming into the solid rock behind them. She would've screamed, but all the oxygen had suddenly vacated her lungs.

"Breathe," he told her with a chuckle in his voice. "He didn't mean any harm." The snake's head protruded from his fist, fanged and gaping, and the rest of it—four feet, maybe more—was looped over his forearm, making her think of boas and pythons and every *Animal Planet* show she'd ever seen.

Air trickled back in, making her head spin. "No . . . harm?" She would've scooted farther away if it hadn't meant free-falling. "It's a snake!"

"Just a harmless one. He eats rodents, not ranch cooks." He held out the creature, which stared at her with beady eyes the size of chocolate chips.

She plastered herself against the stone. "Get him out of here!"

"Sorry, buddy," he said, rising and carrying the snake to the far side of the ledge, where the downslope was heavily overgrown. "Three's a crowd, especially with this crowd." He released the creature, then used the toe of his boot to keep it aimed away. "Go on. Bet there's a nice, fat mouse in there for you."

Not helping, Shelby thought, and tried to quell the shudder.

He sat back down on the bench and gave it a pat. "All gone."

"You're sure? Look again." Did snakes travel in packs?

Smothering a chuckle, he pulled out a flashlight and scanned the area. "We're snake free, honest."

Swallowing hard, she tried to find some humor in the moment, because he sure as heck looked amused. "What are you, a snake whisperer?"

"Nah, just not a city slicker." He cocked a brow. "Want me to grab him back and show you how to wrangle?"

"Not on your life." She wielded her sugar stick like a light saber, holding him off. "Don't even think about it."

"Oh, I'm thinking about it." He wiggled an eyebrow. "Trust me, it wouldn't be the first time one of the wranglers threatened—quietly, and in private—to tuck a creepy crawly into an annoying guest's bunk. Since you're one of the gang, not a guest, seems to me I can do more than threaten."

She gave him a narrow stare, but started to relax as the fight-or-flight adrenaline drained from her. "Let me guess. You tortured your sister—Tish, is it?—mercilessly when you were kids."

"Isn't that a little brother's job?" He stretched, wrapped an arm around her, and drew her down to rest against his side, her cheek pillowed on his chest. His voice rumbled against her as he said, "Besides, she gave as good as she got, sometimes better."

"Oh, really?"

He chuckled. "Yes, really. I think her shining moment—one she reminds me of to this day—was sneaking into my room one night while I was sacked out asleep, exhausted from roundup prep, and giving me a sissy manicure, complete with pink polish."

She smiled, imagining it. "And you, of course, hadn't done anything to deserve it."

"I might've put a black snake—one not unlike our friend over there—under her pillow."

She slanted him a look. "I thought only city girls squealed over that sort of thing."

His eyes warmed, gained a glint. "She was having a sleepover that night with a few friends from town. Trust me, they squealed plenty."

A laugh bubbled up. "Thus, the nail polish. Let me guess—she hid the remover."

"She didn't need to. I woke up late and had to scramble to get outside before the roundup left. I howled plenty when I saw the polish but didn't have time to do anything about it, so I just grabbed a pair of gloves and ran." He held out a hand, looking at it as if he could still see hot pink. "She was already mounted up, laughing her butt off." He laughed, too. "It was a five-day roundup like this one, and danged if I didn't keep those gloves on the whole time. No way I was letting the others see. I never would've lived it down, not with the guys we had back then, plus my pa and grandpa."

Warmth moved through her, mellower than attraction, deeper than friendship. "It sounds like a nice way to grow up."

"It was. I hate that Tish's kids won't get the same chance we had."

"Why not?"

"The Double-Bar H belongs to someone else now."

She winced, remembering that so many local ranches—most of them, in fact—had gone under in recent years, or been forced, like Mustang Ridge, to diversify. "I'm sorry."

"Me, too. Sucks knowing it's not there for us anymore, and that the guy who has it has let it go to hell. The buildings are falling down, the fencing's a mess, the fields have gone to seed . . ."

The rawness of his voice tugged at her, but she didn't know what to say.

He shifted, looking off over that horizon and no doubt seeing the place where he'd been raised. "I miss knowing it's in the family. We're all scattered now—my parents to Flagstaff, Tish and her family to California. One of these days . . ." He broke off, shook his head. "Probably won't ever happen."

To her surprise, where usually he was the one reading her, now she could see into him. "You want to buy it back." Or maybe she wasn't seeing anything, maybe it was a lucky guess based on knowing how much he appreciated tradition without being stuck in the past.

He nodded slowly. "Yeah. I'd like to get the Double-Bar H back in the family. Someday."

She gripped his hand where it rested on her hip, squeezed his fingers. "You'll do it, Foster. As far as I can tell, you can do anything you put your mind to."

He chuckled. "I sucked at trig."

She found a smile, though her heart still hurt for him. "Real cowboys don't need tangents?"

"More like there was a pretty brunette sitting right next to me in class, making it hard to concentrate. Kind of like right now."

"You're definitely getting better at the sweet-talking." Content to let him change the subject, pleased that she'd learned something new about him, even if it was something sad, she snuggled against him. Then she smiled as one of the foals spun an exuberant donut around his mother, who put her ears back and ignored him. Which made her think about Lucky, about being back at the ranch, which was bittersweet. "It's hard to believe this is our last night."

He tightened his arm around her. "It's only the last night of the roundup, sweet Shelby. The way I see it, the summer's just getting started."

13

On Friday morning, though, as the riders mounted up for the last leg of the trip home, Shelby was pensive. Despite their moonlight dates and the things Foster had confided in her last night, she couldn't help wondering how their vacation-within-a-vacation romance was going to change once they were back at the ranch. Gran and Krista had been great about hanging out with Lizzie, but that wasn't a big deal when everyone was camping together. Once they all headed for their respective homes and cabins, it wouldn't be so simple. And then . . .

No, she wasn't thinking about the "and thens." Not yet.

Still, she sighed deeply as she watched the riders getting ready, and saw Foster confer with Stace, who would be riding flank.

"Go on," Gran said from behind her. "Saddle up and ride in with the herd. You've earned it."

She shook her head. "I'd rather hang out with you and Lizzie in the truck."

"Baloney." She nudged Lizzie, who stood beside her. "Tell your mom to run and hop on Loco."

Lizzie didn't give her a yes or no, didn't really do anything. She just stared at the milling horses and their riders as they sorted themselves out around the cattle, preparing to start the drive.

"I'll be fine in the truck," Shelby assured them both, knowing this wasn't the time to push Lizzie on her worsening moodiness.

Not here, not now. But soon.

"If you're sure . . ." Gran didn't look convinced.

"Positive. You want me to load up the coolers?"

"Sure, thanks." At that, she headed around the back of the chuck truck, but quickly looked up when hoof-beats sounded nearby and a tall, lean shadow blotted out the sun. Her pulse thudded. "Morning, cowboy."

Sitting astride Brutus, Foster looked taller in the light of day. Or maybe it was because she was on the ground looking up. But then the crinkles deepened at the corner of his eyes in a not-quite smile, and he looked like himself again. "Good morning. Sleep well?"

Not in five days. Not since her body had fully wak-ened to the fact that she still had girl parts, they were still in fine working order, and they hadn't been used in a long time. Oh, and there was a likely candidate—a very likely candidate—only a few tents away. "Well enough."

He searched her eyes. "I'll see you back at the ranch?"

"I'll be there."

"Good, because I've got a surprise for you."

Something loosened inside her, and she grinned. "One of these days, I'm going to have to surprise you."

"Count on it. Tonight, though, it's still my turn."

"Skinny-dipping?"

He laughed. "Wait and see." Then he touched the brim of his hat, reined Brutus in a smart one eighty, and jogged off, calling, "Okay, cowboys. Move 'em out!"

Shelby was humming as she slung the coolers in the back of the chuck truck. Suddenly, the end of the roundup didn't seem like that big a deal anymore.

Back at the ranch, everything was pretty much the same as it had been when they left, which Shelby found oddly disconcerting. The parking area looked the same, the barn hadn't changed, and the skeleton crew that had stayed behind didn't have anything to report. How could that be, when it felt like they'd been gone for weeks, maybe longer?

Then again, that was the sign of a good vacation, wasn't it?

In the barn, it was quickly apparent that Lucky was bigger and stronger than he'd been. When Shelby and Lizzie came in, the black foal whickered and started doing exuberant laps around Sassy, who looked like she'd about had it with her offspring, shooting him flat-eared, annoyed looks that only another mother could fully appreciate.

Turning to her own offspring, Shelby said, "You want to hang out with these two for a bit?"

Not looking at her, Lizzie marched over to her bucket, righted it, and plonked down on it with her back to her mother and her stiff shoulders telegraphing "go away."

Shelby stifled a twinge of hurt, followed by a pointless sigh. *We'll get through this. We always do.* Most of all, she hoped it didn't signal the start of a backslide of all the progress Lizzie had made this summer. "I'll be in the kitchen if you need me."

Lizzie's shrug was a loud and clear *I won't*. She didn't mean it, though; she was just being a kid. And if Shelby kept telling herself that, maybe she would lose the urge to hit the tub of leftover brownies in the back of the chuck truck.

Shaking her head, she turned for the kitchen, instead. It felt strange being back inside the main house, with running water, refrigeration, and soft chairs, but it didn't take her long to get into the swing of things, and she felt more or less settled by the time she and Gran had finished unloading the truck with Tipper's and Topper's help.

After that, they pulled together cold salads to go with a quick-and-dirty dinner of hot dogs and hamburgers, with cupcakes for dessert. They were just putting the last batch of cupcakes into the oven when Topper shouted, "Riders ho! They're back!"

"Come on." Gran caught her hand. "Let's wave them in!"

"What—" Shelby found herself whisked outside to the front porch of the main house, where Gran grabbed a piece of rebar from the corner, and used it to jangle the dangling triangle that hung near the door. The loud *jing-a-ling-a-ling* pealed through the air as the lead rider came over the ridgeline, followed by a stream of cattle that swelled and grew, until the roadway was full of movement—the hump of dusty brown backs, the churn of legs, the swing of heads and tails, and the rocking-chair lope of the outriders curving around the herd, sending them home.

There was movement down in the ranch yard, too. Drawn by the dinner bell, the ranch employees came out of the buildings where they'd been working, to stand on the porches or out on the dusty road and cheer for the returning riders.

"Yahoo!" Gran shouted, and waved her arms over her head, and the call was picked up by the cleaning staff, landscapers, and spare barn workers. Shelby laughed and joined in until the last rider in—a tall, lean man wearing a black Stetson and riding a big blazed-face chestnut—paused at the top of the ridge, took off his hat, and waved it in answer.

She let herself think he was waving at her.

As the commotion died down and the others went back to work, she said, "That's lovely. Everybody comes out to wave when the riders bring the cattle in?"

Gran glanced over at her own house, in the middle distance. "Everybody but Arthur. As far as he's concerned, it's not a real roundup."

Not sure what to say to that, Shelby gave her a one-armed hug and then stood there, with an arm slung around the older woman's waist, as the drag riders nudged the herd down the hill and the flankers raced around to push the animals into the holding pen.

Her eyes stayed locked on Foster, her mouth drying

at the sight of him, sure and supple in the saddle as he and Brutus cantered a wide loop around the corral. The cattle streamed in, shaking their heads and bellowing, then diving on the piles of hay and chop that the barn workers had put out for them. After that, Foster and Stace disappeared behind the barn, no doubt to see to their horses before helping the others. Shelby watched him go, and then let herself watch a moment more, enjoying the warm anticipation that said she'd be seeing him later.

Once the cattle were secure in the pipe corral, the rest of the riders trickled into the parking area and started dismounting with a chorus of groans and good-natured taunts being tossed back and forth, and, when they saw Shelby, a couple of shouts of "What's for dinner?"

She laughed and called, "Burgers, dogs, and all the fixings," and got a cheer in response. Realizing that Gran had already slipped off to the kitchen, she turned and headed up the steps.

Behind her, though, somebody called, "Shelby? Hey, Shelby!"

She turned to find Stace headed her way, with Lizzie dogging her heels so close she was practically stepping on the back of Stace's boots. Grinning, Shelby said, "You bellowed?"

"Yes, ma'am. I was wondering if you'd let me borrow your kid for the night."

"You . . . what?" She looked down at Lizzie. Her eyes were suddenly clear and bright, and she nodded a vigorous *yes, yes, yes* that Shelby mentally translated as "Please, Mom, can I go? I'll be good, I promise."

Where had that come from?

"Princess is close to foaling," Stace said. "Her milk has come in, her teats have waxed up, and . . . well, sparing you the details, she's close. Which means I'll be on foal watch tonight, sleeping out on a cot, and I could use the company."

More nods. *Yes, yes, yes.*

Who are you and what have you done to my kid? Shelby thought. But on the heels of that, she heard boot steps behind her, felt a flush on the back of her neck, and knew who it was. She just *knew*. And she got what was going on, with the invitation if not with her daughter.

Lizzie dug into her pocket, pulled out her whistle, and gave a soft chirp that went up at the end like a question mark. *Please?*

And how could Shelby say no to that? "Yes. Okay, yes. If you're sure you don't mind?" she asked Stace.

"Absolutely. She's been so good with Lucky that I'd love for her to see the whole process. Princess is an old pro at this, so hopefully there won't be any problems this time. And who knows?" She slung an arm around Lizzie's neck. "Maybe we've got a new vet in the making. Doc's got to retire one of these years, you know."

The sight of them together and the look on Lizzie's face put a boulder-size lump in Shelby's throat. "Dress warm, okay? Bring your bedroll and an extra blanket, and—" She laughed. "And you won't be miles from home, so you can grab stuff whenever you need it. Okay, fine. It's fine."

"Thanks!" Stace said brightly. To Lizzie, she said, "Come on, let's get our camp set up."

As they headed off, with Lizzie skipping at Stace's heels, Shelby turned around, planted her hands on her hips, and faked a scowl. "You arranged that, didn't you?"

Foster rocked back on his heels. "That depends. Are you mad?"

"I should be." And yet she wasn't. She wanted to think it was because that was the first smile she'd seen from her kid in a couple of days, but knew that wasn't the whole reason. Which lost her some serious mom points. "I'm not, though, mostly because Lizzie looked so happy. She's been really down."

"Seemed okay just now."

"Thus my lack of irritation." Sort of.

He sent a look in the direction Stace and Lizzie had gone. "Is she upset that you've been going off with me at night?"

That was the question, wasn't it? "I asked her, and she said she was fine with it." She'd asked several different times and ways, in fact, until the "yes" nod had become an "aw, Mom, come off it" eye roll. "But still."

"Yeah. Still." He hesitated. "You want me to talk to her?"

With any other guy, she would've "I'm the mom"'d him and turned him down, but Foster and Lizzie had their own deal outside of her. Which she thought might be part of the problem—that Lizzie wasn't so much jealous of the time she was spending with Foster, but vice versa. She shook her head, though. "Not yet. I'm going to let it go for a day or two and see if she rebounds now that we're back in familiar territory. For all

I know, she was suffering from iPad withdrawal. Regardless, it seems like I've suddenly got the evening free, thanks to you and Stace. And Princess, of course." Her lips curved as the blood hummed in her veins. "So . . . did you have anything in mind, or is it my turn to pick a mystery destination?"

He frowned. "I don't want to cause trouble."

"You won't. You're not." And if he was, she would deal with it. "In a weird way, it feels good to be hashing about something like this. Sure, the SM complicates things by making a conversation into a guessing game, but at least this is normal kid stuff."

"Normal kid stuff," he repeated. "You mean like her mom dating?"

"That would be the one." Her heart gave a *thudda-thudda*. "Which brings us back to the whole 'I've suddenly got the evening free' thing." And the night, too, though she wasn't going there. "I believe you were going to ask me something?"

"Pushy little filly, aren't you? Okay, fine. I'll ask . . . Shelby, will you come to the bunkhouse later for dessert?" He grinned. "And no, that's not a metaphor. I was thinking popcorn and a movie, if you're into it. Or—"

"A movie? On a real TV?" She nearly moaned it.

"A big one, with surround sound, even. And I'll let you pick the movie."

"I'll watch a guy flick if it gets me a couch and a snuggle. *Apocalypse Now* or *Enter the Dragon* or something. I'd even grit through *The Three Stooges* or *Jackass*, if that's what it takes."

He chuckled. "Okay, I guess it's movie night, then. Say seven? Will that give you enough time after the dinner rush? Or would you rather do it later so you can hang out in the barn for a bit with the girls first?"

That loosened a tension she hadn't really been aware of. "Yeah, I would. Especially if my darling daughter is coming out of her snark fest."

"Stay as long as you want, or until they kick you out, whichever comes first. I'll wait as long as it takes."

And that, she thought, was what made him the real deal.

Foster told himself he wasn't going to clean up the bunkhouse—not looking to change, begin as you mean to go on, that sort of thing. Then he cleaned up anyway.

Eh, the place needed it.

He transferred the mountain of to-be-fixed tack from the love seat to the spare bedroom that only really got used when Tish and her kids visited, then sorted the slippery piles of magazines and comics into a "keep" pile that followed the tack into the spare room, and a "recycle" pile that quickly overflowed the recycling bin. The sofa cushions got banged out on the front porch, and his gramma's afghan went over the back of the sofa, covering the destruction done by the last litter of rogue foster kittens Krista had foisted off on him.

He could've sworn he'd done the dishes before he left for the gather, but somehow there were still a few in the sink, wearing crusties he didn't want to think about. They went in the dishwasher with an extra soap pod, and he wiped down the counters with bleachysmelling cleaner. Finally, he soaked a couple of paper towels with Endust and swiped at the end tables, TV, and video racks, not so much dusting as making it smell as though he'd dusted.

Vader watched the proceedings with a look of canine mistrust, then slunk off when the vacuum came out.

"You're lucky I don't have enough time to give you a B-A-T-H," Foster called after him, then decided that since he needed a shower anyway, they could get in a two-fer.

So after running the vacuum around the living room and swiping the kitchen and downstairs bath with one of those mop pad thingies, he rousted Vader out from underneath his bed and dumped them both in the upstairs shower to scrub off two weeks' worth of trail grime, hard riding, and—at least in his case—mirror-free shaves. Six soggy towels and a puddle on the bathroom floor later, they both smelled better, but suddenly, Vader was shedding like crazy, coating Foster in a Shake 'N Bake layer of black and white hair that itched like crazy.

"Well, at least they're clean hairs," he said, and doubled up some duct tape to play lint brush before pulling on clean jeans and a favorite T-shirt.

Back downstairs, he looked around and decided that he and the main room both looked pretty good. A quick trip into the kitchen, a head poke into the fridge followed by the eviction of some hairy dairy, and he was good to go in there, too. But when he headed back into the main room, he stopped dead and groaned.

It smelled like Endust and wet dog.

"You need a blow-dryer or something," he said. "Maybe some Febreze."

Vader shot him a *Seriously, dude?* look and jumped up on the couch.

"Oh, no, you don't. Down. Now. Go sleep in your own bed for a change."

The border collie heaved a sigh and complied, leaving Foster standing in the middle of the main room with escapee dog hairs on his jeans and a definite funk in the air just as headlights came over the hill and shone in his front windows.

"Oh, crap. She's here." The kick of excitement was tempered with dismay. He should've met her somewhere, picked her up, taken her riding—anything that would keep them in the dude ranch space they knew worked for them, with him in full-on cowboy mode. Because what if she didn't like Foster the guy as much as Foster the wrangler?

It was too late now, though, because boot steps thunked on the porch, there was a pause—yeah, he so didn't have a doorbell—and she knocked.

Vader whuffed, shooting him a *You gonna get that?* look.

"Oh, shut up." Resisting the urge to swipe at his jeans or straighten his shirt, Foster took a deep breath and opened the door.

And there she was.

The gut punch one-two'd him as it had each time he'd seen her over the past week, a sort of *there you are* followed by a deep possessiveness that left him feeling twitchy and heated. She was wearing a pair of black, clingy pants and a soft blue shirt that dipped low in the front, serving to reinforce that they weren't out in the backcountry anymore. It was strange, seeing her on his porch wearing fancyish clothes. But strange in a very, very nice way. The kind of way that had him wanting to reach out and haul her in for a deep kiss. But he knew he wouldn't want to stop at a kiss—not tonight, not with too many soft, horizontal surfaces within range—so he kept his hands to himself, and chuckled down at the bright orange bag she held clutched in front of her. "You brought Cheetos."

A subtle tension eased out of her face. "It was that or the Swedish fish, and it's impossible to look at all attractive while eating Swedish fish."

"Cheetos make your fingers DayGlo orange."

Her smile went wicked. "True, but then you get to lick them off."

"Hel-lo." Heat kicked into his bloodstream, though it wasn't like he needed more of a buzz. If his system got revving any faster, he was going to go caveman, grab her, and drag her upstairs. And that was the exact opposite of the whole "take it slow and don't skip any steps" theory they had agreed to. It had seemed like a good idea at the time, when he'd at least partly been figuring that some one-on-one would convince them both that this was a bad idea. Only it hadn't done that. Exactly the opposite, in fact, and now the anticipation was killing him. Every kiss, every touch, every wicked look and sassy comment just made him want her more.

"Nice." She tapped his T-shirt, with its "May the Schwartz be with you" on the front in cartoon letters.

She had probably missed the reference and was just being nice, making conversation, but he liked that she hadn't made a face at the spaceship. "You drove over?" he asked, and then winced. Brilliant. Um, yeah, that was her car in the driveway. Duh.

"I thought about hiking over from the main house, but after a week on the trail I'm feeling lazy." She paused and tipped her head. "That's okay, right? If you don't want people seeing my car—"

"No! No, it's fine." Better than fine, though he wasn't quite steady with the sudden surge of *hell, yeah* that raced through him, the one that wanted everyone else to know she was there, with him. "Ah, are things okay with Lizzie?"

"I guess so. She seemed fine, and her mood didn't change when I said I'd be out with you instead of back at the cabin."

"Stace will call here if she needs to."

"That's what she said." She paused, took a breath. "So . . . this is a little weird, isn't it? No horses to focus on, no riding to do. Just the two of us, a bag of Cheetos, and a movie. It's . . . it feels more official somehow. But in a good way."

"We could go out if you'd rather."

"No way." She dimpled. "Unless you don't want me to see your den of iniquity."

"Better sooner than later, I guess, though I'm afraid I'll have to disappoint you on the iniquity." He stepped back. "Come on in. Make yourself at home, though I have a feeling your home probably doesn't look like this."

She came in, glanced around at the framed movie posters and rodeo memorabilia, and laughed. "Not so much. But it suits you. And you weren't kidding about the flat-screen, were you? It's huge."

"One of my hidden vices."

"Oh? What are some of the others?"

"Junk food, which you already knew about. Comic books. The occasional convention, though I swear I don't wear a costume."

"Aw, and here I was, imagining you as Wolverine." She crouched briefly to pat Vader.

"Wait. He's—"

"Wet. And shedding." She grinned up at him. "But clean." She gave the wiggling dog a good scratch, shook off the loose hair, and didn't seem at all put out when some of it clung.

Pressure fisted in his chest, even stronger than he'd felt the last few days, reminding him suddenly of the feeling of riding along an eyebrow trail with a hard surface on one side, a steep fall on the other.

Standing, she headed for the double rack of discs on the wall. "You've got quite a collection here. And you know what they say about all the things you can tell about a man from his videos."

He didn't know what they said, and decided it was better that way. Like his vices, the movies probably screamed "stalled in adolescence" even though he was pretty sure he hadn't. He just liked to unwind after a long day of dude-ing it, and had long ago learned that movies were better for him than some of the alternatives his buddies had leaned toward. He didn't try to explain, though. He just said, "Ladies' choice, either there or online."

"Hmmm . . . what to watch, what to watch . . ." She went along the rack, making a humming noise. "*Star Wars*? Tempting, but I'd want to see all three in a row and we'd be here 'til morning. Props for not having the newer ones. They were just tragic. *Blade Runner*, *Dune*, a couple of seasons of *MST3000*—you're dating yourself. But here's *Wall-E*, three *Transformers*, and all the latest superheroes. Chris Nolan only on the Batmans, I see, none of the cheesy older ones." She flashed a smile over her shoulder. "You've got good taste, cowboy."

He was also having trouble catching his breath. "You like sci-fi?"

"What's not to like?" She kept browsing. "All of the new *Battlestar Galacticas*—again, very cool, but not looking for a film festival. Besides, the finale annoyed me. *Fifth Element*, one of my favorites." She paused and tapped two discs off to the side. "*Princess Bride* and *Ladyhawke*?"

"My sister gave 'em to me. Good movies, though. Want to watch one of them? Or I've got a dish, we could get an on-demand." He'd even watch something with "Wedding" in the title if it made her happy. Except it seemed that he wouldn't have to. He never would've guessed her for a sci-fi wonk. And oh, boy, he was in even more trouble than he'd thought.

It was one thing to share some killer kisses and

moonlit conversations, another to find an unexpected piece of common ground.

"Only if there's something you're jonesing to see," she said. "Otherwise, how about this one?" She held up his copy of *Cowboys and Aliens*. "Or is that too much like your day job to be fun?"

Finding a smile, he said, "Can't say Loco and I have ever had to fend off an aerial attack, except maybe a buzzard now and then. You want to put the movie in while I wrangle some popcorn?"

She eyed his entertainment system, which wasn't brand-new, but had more buttons than the average cockpit. "Brave man. You're not afraid I'll click on something you'd rather I not see?"

"Nope. But if you're worried about it, I'd stay away from the computer cache."

Her chuckle warmed him. "Oh, Pandora, don't open that box." But then she flipped him a sassy salute. "Aye-aye, trail boss. I'll subdue the movie, you herd the snacks, and we'll rendezvous at the couch in five."

"You want ice cream?"

"You got anything with chunks in it?"

"Always. If not, we can mix in the Cheetos for some texture."

She laughed. "Then yes, ice cream, please. Hold the Cheetos for right now."

"You got it." Unable to resist—and not fighting the urge too hard—he caught her by the back of the neck and drew her in for a kiss that started out quick but just as fast mellowed to something longer and lingering.

When it ended, he was breathing hard as he pressed his forehead to hers. "I'm really glad you're here." Then he let her go and stepped back. "Five minutes. Couch. Be there or be square." And he headed for the kitchen, knowing he'd better get moving before he gave in and skipped some steps.

She blinked after him, looking as warm and befuddled from the kiss as he was. Because as he dug in the freezer for the Chunky Monkey, his head was spinning and he couldn't feel the floor beneath his feet. And for a guy who usually had his boots planted firmly on the ground, that was a heck of a thing.

14

*New at MagicMatch.com: twenty points of compatibility,
and how to know he's the one for you!*

The movie was a solid B-plus, the snacks a satisfying hodgepodge, and the company an A all the way. And as the credits rolled, Shelby snuggled closer against Foster's side, unwilling to move, even to turn off the DVD.

They had drifted low on the chaise end of the soft couch so they were pretty close to horizontal, tangled together in a comfortable curl of bodies. Her boots were off, her feet linked around the backs of his calves, and she was lined up with him everywhere else, her head pillowed on his chest. With an age-softened afghan thrown over them and Vader snoring softly nearby, she was utterly content.

"Like it?" he asked, his voice rumbling beneath her cheek.

She shifted to look up at him, and her heart got all warm and fuzzy at the sight of him, drowsy-eyed and relaxed. Even though she knew he'd been asking about the movie, she said, "There isn't anything I don't like about it."

His eyes sharpened and heated, and the hand he'd been stroking down her back paused and urged her up against him, instead, so their lips met.

They had kissed during the movie—quick pecks and longer explorations—but none of those kisses had been anything like this one. Now he rolled against her and held her close so they were pressed together at every point as they kissed and kissed again. He touched; she tugged clothing free; he kissed her throat, her lips; she skimmed her fingers along his ribs and the lean play of muscles. Breathing went ragged—his, hers—and she shuddered against him, unable to think much beyond *I want* and *yes, there.*

He eased the kiss but didn't pull away. Instead, he touched his lips to her cheek, her temple, pressed his face in her hair. "I promised we weren't going to skip any steps."

The huge flat-screen had defaulted to the DVD's menu page, offering "Home," "Play" or "Extras," which made her want to laugh. *Just press Play, please.* She hadn't expected to find someone, hadn't even been looking, really, but here he was, in living color, a man who was somehow exactly right for the woman she'd become here at Mustang Ridge. A man she wanted to be with, here and now. "Would we be skipping steps?" she asked.

He gave a raspy chuckle. "We still haven't swum naked together."

"If I go jump in the lake now, will you take me upstairs?"

He caught his breath, then shook his head, but not like he was saying no. More like he was trying to clear it. "Are you sure?"

"Aren't you?"

In answer, he stood. And then, before she could rise to join him, he'd scooped her up against his chest and lifted her as easily as she'd seen him muscle hay bales into place. "Foster!"

He headed for a hallway. "Hm?"

"Put me down!"

"Second thoughts?"

"Only for your back. I'm—"

"Lighter than a weanling," he said easily. "No squirming, though. I'd hate to drop you." He faked losing his grip, then caught her again.

She collapsed against him, wrapping her arms around his neck and laughing helplessly. "Cowboy goes caveman. Oh, help." Inside, though, was a glowing warmth that said *this is real*.

"That's better. I like saving a damsel in distress. It's part of the code."

The hallway was wide and high, with bark-on logs for beams and white plaster on the walls. They passed a couple of closed doorways, then reached an open arch at the end of the hall. He stepped through, but then stopped with a muffled noise that was part laughter, part dismay.

Turning back, he set her on her feet, angling so his body was blocking the view. "I, ah, didn't pick up in here. Sorry."

Feeling unutterably tender—with the man and the

sheepish look on his face—she ducked to look under his arm. It wasn't bad, really, just cluttered, with more clothes folded on the bureau than hanging in the open closet, and an unmade bed piled high with a tangle of pale green sheets, a heavy woven blanket, and another knitted afghan in a different shade of green.

"It's fine," she said. "And don't be sorry. In my book you get points for not assuming we'd make it to the bedroom." She paused. "Or you would if we were keeping score. Which we're not."

A corner of his mouth kicked up. "In this case, I'll take the points. Mostly because you haven't seen the bathroom yet."

"I can smell wet dog from here." And was touched that he'd made the effort, even if that hadn't included getting the water off the floor or the towels in the wash.

"I can fix that." Without warning, he scooped her off her feet once more, and as she laughed, he swung her around and kicked the bathroom door shut. "No more wet dog." Then he carried her to the bed and eased them both down, together.

The mattress and tangled bedclothes yielded beneath her, so much cooler than the banked heat of the man who held her, murmured to her, and kissed her softly. So softly.

Light spilling in from the hallway let her see the angle of his jaw, the intensity in his eyes. In some corner of her mind, she was aware of the differences between him and Patrick, who was her main source of comparison. Patrick had been thicker with gym-fed muscles, where Foster was lean. Her ex had liked to use his weight to pin and hold her, where Foster lay beside her, offering her places to put her hands, her legs, her mouth, and coaxing responses out of her that she hadn't known were in her to give. Then his strong hands moved over her, loosening her clothes and finding their way beneath, and a wash of heat raced through her.

Yes, she thought as he skimmed his palms up her torso to her breasts. *Yes, there.* And she stopped thinking, stopped comparing, and let herself feel. She felt the leashed strength in his body, the quiver of his muscles when she ran her hands over his back and down, then tugged his shirt open. The snaps gave with the sexy *pop-pop-pop* sound that she had imagined, and had her purring at the back of her throat.

"See?" he said, grinning down at her. "They give easily when they get hooked on something."

"Does that mean you're hooked on me?"

"Definitely." He rose over her and pulled off his shirt, baring his torso. His skin gleamed in the diffuse yellow light, sleek and hairless, and unmarked save for a long scar that streaked along his rib cage. When she made a soft sound and ran her fingers along the line, he said, "A bull got me with a bit of a love tap."

So will I, she thought, and reached up to kiss the spot, following it up along his body until he growled low in his throat and lowered himself to her. "It was a long time ago," he said. "This is now."

"Yes," she said, smiling up at him.

"Yes to what?"

"All of it." She wrapped her arms around his neck. "Show me what you've got, cowboy."

And he did. He undressed her gently, kissing each square inch of her skin as he revealed it, making her feel cherished, adored. He stripped and rose above her, caging her with his arms and making her feel protected rather than pinned. And then he made love to her—there was no other word for it, despite their agreement—overwhelming her, possessing her, and making her feel as if they were the only two people in the universe. They moved together, a languid give-and-take that sped quickly, inevitably toward an implosion that made her think of fireworks and thunderstorms, and left her helpless to do anything but hang on to him as the sensations raced through her.

Foster, she thought. *Oh, Foster*. She didn't say the words, though. They were too important, too intense and telling. So she clamped her lips on a moan and held the rest inside.

He didn't have the same reserve—he whispered her name in between the kisses he trailed over her body and rattled it on a groan when she wrapped her legs around to take him deeper. And then, when her pleasure flared to a climax and he followed her over the edge, he said it again. Her name, over and over again. Or maybe that was the thunder of blood in her veins, the pounding sound of her pulse as her body went places it hadn't been in . . . well, ever.

She closed her eyes and saw bursts of colors behind her lids, held on to him, and let the moment sweep her away. There was pleasure, huge and overwhelming; heat within and without, dampening her skin and making her feel safe and somehow elemental, as if she was closer to his world than she'd ever been. Then the climax ebbed, passing her by and leaving her feeling loose and boneless, and like she was exactly where she wanted to be.

He shifted off her, rolled to lie beside her, breathing hard. But he wasn't lost in his own moment—he stroked her arm, touched her cheek, brushed her dampened hair back behind her ear with a tenderness that almost overwhelmed her.

"Foster." She whispered it almost soundlessly against his throat, but she thought he heard her.

He tightened his arms around her, kissed her temple, and tucked her gently against his body. Part of her said that she should do something, say something. But the steady thud of his heart beneath her cheek and the rise and fall of his chest soothed her, told her that there wasn't any rush.

Some time later—probably no more than a few minutes, though it felt as if it had been longer—she stirred, thinking she should really say something . . . except that the only thing she could come up with was *Wow*. Wow, she hadn't known she could feel like this. Wow, she felt good. More, she felt *different*. And wow, she didn't know what came next between them. She didn't have any experience with this sort of thing, didn't know whether she should kiss him, compliment him, or get dressed and head back to her cabin.

Clearing her throat, she said, "I'm . . . ah . . . going to get a drink, if that's okay."

"Stay here. I'll get it." But the words were jumbled, and said into the pillow where he lay facedown, unmoving.

Okay. That answered the "should I get dressed and tiptoe out?" question. He wanted her to stay, at least for a bit. But he also didn't seem to be capable of moving. Which was kind of flattering, really.

"You're toast, pal." She patted his rear. "I'll be right back."

Even though he hadn't seemed in a rush for her to leave, she felt weird parading around his house buck naked. So she pulled on her clothes and carried her boots with her out to the kitchen. Still buzzing from what they had just done, she found tall glasses in a cabinet and ice in the freezer, and took a look around as she filled the glasses from the tap. The kitchen wasn't bad, she decided. The layout would be nice with some organizing, but the raw wood fit the style and the undoubtedly killer view that would show through the windows during daylight. Actually the whole place had some serious potential. It just needed some pops of color, some blinds, and—

Oh, heck, she thought as the ice water found its way into her veins. She was mentally decorating his home . . . in the middle of Nowhere, Wyoming.

She downed one of the glasses of water in three big swallows, then hissed at the ice-cube headache that followed. It was no worse than she deserved, though, and did a good job cutting through the post-orgasm fog. Because she might've gone into this with her eyes wide open, but somewhere along the way they had drifted shut. And now she was teetering on the edge of big trouble.

"Everything okay?" Foster padded in wearing his jeans and carrying his shirt.

His physique was drool-worthy, putting her hundred crunches a night to shame and making the well-loved part of her, the part that wasn't panicking, think, *Everything's just ducky*. But her head was backpedaling hard.

"I should go," she said, pretty sure she hadn't said those words in this context since college. "I'd like to look in on Lizzie and let her and Stace know I'm back, in case she'd rather sleep in the cabin tonight."

His expression shifted, and for a second she thought she had hurt his feelings. But she wasn't sure, and instead of debating, he pulled on his shirt. "I'll take you home."

"I drove myself."

"So I'll ride with you and walk home. It's only about half a mile if you cut across the ridge."

"I know the way. I'll be fine." She wasn't sure why she was arguing. It wasn't that she wanted to get away from him, just that she needed to get out of his house, out of the sense of domesticity she hadn't known she wanted. Maybe because she hadn't wanted it until just now.

She was happy with what she had back home, and she didn't want to leave here wishing for something else. *It's just the sex talking*, she told herself. *It'll pass.*

Maybe.

"I don't doubt for a second that you can make it home safe on your own, but my ma would twist my ear if she found out I didn't walk my lady right to her door at the end of the evening."

My lady. The words warmed her even through the nerves, and she exhaled. "We wouldn't want that, would we?"

"Exactly." He gave a low whistle. "Vader? Want to go for a ride?"

The border collie had looked like he was deeply asleep, but his head whipped up at the sound of his name, and at the word "ride" he scrambled to his feet and raced to the door, leaving a dog shadow of black and white hairs behind on his bed.

Foster had the sense to look a little embarrassed. "You okay with him coming? He's clean. Just, well, shedding. But the stuff that's falling off is clean."

She laughed helplessly, not quite sure how this had gone from a walk of shame to a family outing, but glad that it had. "Why not? The more the merrier."

So they pulled on their boots, piled in her Subaru, and made the short drive out to the main road, across the front of the ranch's spread, and down the long driveway to the main house and the cabins beyond. It was strange to see the blazing lights after a week of fires and lanterns, stranger still to have him sitting beside her in the little car, with Vader panting in the backseat.

"We're here," she said needlessly, and yanked too hard on the parking brake. She fumbled with her belt as Foster got out, then swung open her door, nearly nailing him with it. She flushed, realizing he'd come around to open it for her. "Sorry," she said. "I'm not used to . . . well, you know."

His quiet smile made things a little better. "At least let me get the cabin door."

"It's not locked."

He held her hand for the walk up the short flight of

stairs, and opened the door with a flourish. "My lady. Your chamber awaits you."

"Thank you, kind sir." She started to sail on through, but then stalled at the sight of the empty cabin, lit by only a night-light, with Lizzie's iPad charging in the corner and her pink sweatshirt tossed on the bed. After a week in a tent, it should've looked like heaven. Instead, the sight brought a spurt of panic.

"You okay?" He put a hand on her shoulder and squeezed.

She covered his hand with her own, but didn't answer. It wasn't his problem that it occurred to her at odd times that Lizzie wasn't always going to want to be with her. Mute or not, she would grow up, go to school, move on. And it wasn't his problem that she had started mentally decorating his kitchen, and freaked herself out.

"I'm just tired, that's all," she said, hoping he would let her get away with it.

He nodded. "I'll swing by the barn and check on the girls. You go on inside and get some rest. Vader? In you go." At his gesture, the dog came up the steps and padded through the open door.

"But—" She broke off the automatic protest, realizing that he had known. Somehow, he had known she needed company, and needed it to be uncomplicated. And, as usual, he had fixed the problem without fanfare.

"It'd make me feel better, knowing he was here with you," he said simply. Then he leaned in and kissed her, a light brush of lips that lingered and deepened, and brought a musky hint of their mingled flavors. Along with a buzz of the heat they had so recently made together, and an echo of *wow*. Voice low and sexy, he said, "Sleep well, Shelby-sweet, and dream of me. I know I'll be dreaming of you."

She didn't say anything, just lifted a hand and pressed it to her lips, overwhelmed. He seemed to understand, though, because he smiled crookedly, tipped his hat, and walked off, whistling into the darkness.

She watched him go, watched until the whistle faded away and she couldn't see his silhouette anymore in the distant lights of the barn. Then, suddenly feeling the chill through her thin shirt, she shivered a little and went into her cabin, which would've felt empty if it hadn't been for the black and white dog curled at the foot of her bed, cheerfully shedding on the wedding-ring quilt.

The following day was a more chaotic changeover Saturday than usual, which was surprising given that the guests were all veterans and knew the routine. But a lost wallet, an unexpected food allergy, and a lost EpiPen meant there wasn't a second for Shelby to get caught up in whatever she was feeling toward Foster. Which might have been for the best, since she didn't know whether that was well loved, awkward, or anywhere in between, and the inner Ping-Pong jangled her nerves. Finally, though, the airport shuttle pulled out, giving her a quiet moment to pause outside the kitchen's back door for a second and breathe.

Except that once she had the space to take a step

back and think about last night, she realized she didn't need the time or space, not really. First, because she'd been thinking about things on and off—mostly on—for the past twelve hours or so regardless of what was going on around her, and second, because despite her brief moment of panic, she didn't regret what she'd done. In fact, she was proud of taking something for herself for a change.

I have a lover, she thought, and found that the concept fit better than she would've expected. "I'm having a summer fling with an incredible man." She said it out loud this time, and the statement put a flutter in her belly and a smile in her heart.

"Well, somebody looks happy this morning." Krista let the kitchen door bang closed behind her as she came down the kitchen stairs.

"I . . . uh . . . hmm." Shelby didn't quite blush, but it was a close call. "I'm glad the shuttle got off okay, and grateful for a couple of hours of peace and quiet. It's such a pretty day, too. Not a cloud in the sky."

Krista rolled her eyes. "The weather. Right. Silly me, I thought the goofy grin and the cartoon tweety birds fluttering around your head might have something to do with Foster. Rumor has it you were kid free last night."

"Um . . ."

"I'm not angling for details. Just wanted to say that I'm happy for you both, and I'm here if you want to talk about it, or about anything. With or without brownie sundaes involved."

Shelby exhaled, only then realizing she'd been holding her breath. "Thanks. I mean it. Foster and I are . . . Well, I'm not sure what we are, but I know I'm happy about it, and I think he is, too." Unless he'd had second thoughts after she left last night?

"Trust me, he's happy. I heard him whistling this morning while he picked a bunch of burrs out of Justice's tail. And he *hates* picking burrs."

"Well, then." She was grinning like an idiot and didn't care.

"He and Lizzie are out by the corrals behind the barn," Krista said, with a thumb jerk in that direction. "They're giving Lucky his first baby leading lesson."

"Uh-oh. I hope she's not giving him any attitude."

Though there seemed to be less danger of that now. The foal watch had been a bust, with Princess hanging on to her baby for one more night, but Lizzie had shown up at breakfast with a big smile and a chorus of whistle chirps, conveying that she'd had fun and behaved herself, and wanted to do it again tonight. Whatever had been bothering her, it didn't seem to have been her mom's blossoming romance. And that was a huge relief.

"Go on." Krista nudged her in the direction of the barn. "You know you want to watch. Trust me, there's not much cuter than a kid and a cowboy working with a baby horse."

Yes, this was her life, Shelby thought. And that was her lover they were talking about. "I'm on my way. Catch you later?"

"Count on it. And, Shelby? Have fun."

"I will." *I am.* And wasn't that a wonderful thing?

She wasn't sure her feet hit the ground the whole way down to the barn, where Foster stood in Sassy's paddock near Lucky, running a lead through his hands while the foal watched with his ears flipped forward and an intrigued expression that seemed to say, "Is it good to eat? Is it a toy? What is it?" Lizzie, rapt, leaned on the railing outside the broodmare's paddock. Sassy stood nearby, content to let Foster work with her foal.

He seemed totally dialed into the little guy, but as Shelby came around the corner, his hat tipped up and his eyes went right to her, as if he'd been waiting for her. She missed a step, but kept coming, feeling like her goofy smile was suddenly lit from within. *Don't overdo it*, she told herself. This wasn't happily-ever-after territory, after all.

But it was happily—very happily—for now.

"Hey there," he said, but his eyes said way more than that. They said, *I was hoping you'd come. Are you okay?*

"Hey yourself." *I'm good. I'm great.*

"The bus leave?" *I'm glad you're here.*

"Finally." *I wanted to see you.* She included Lizzie in her smile and got a gap-toothed grin in response. "How's leading practice coming?"

"We're just getting started." The corner of his mouth kicked up. "Stay and watch?"

"I'd like that." It was that easy, she realized, that simple when new lovers were on the same page.

He nodded, satisfied, and he turned back to Lucky, in a move that Lizzie shadowed half a second behind him, putting a lump in Shelby's throat. There was such a contrast between his weathered confidence and her wide-eyed determination, between his battered black hat and her pink pony helmet, yet they were both utterly focused on the animals.

"Okay, here's what we're starting with," Foster said, crouching down by Lucky and scratching the itchy spot at the base of his mane, in a move that was pretty much guaranteed to get the little horse to stand still and crane his neck, wiggling his little nose in ecstasy. "He's been wearing his foal halter all along, so that shouldn't be an issue. And he's used to seeing his mom being led around while he follows loose. What we want to introduce now is the idea of him taking information from a lead rope clipped to his halter."

Lucky lost interest in getting scratched, craned around, and took a nip at Foster's sleeve. He got an "Ah-ah" in the cowboy's deep, warning growl, and subsided, looking suddenly angelic.

Shelby smothered a laugh. Foster shot her a wink. "He keeps this up and little Lucky Bugg is going to find himself nicknamed Bugger instead of Lucky." To Lizzie, he said, "We're going to use a butt rope to nudge him along." He demonstrated by clipping a long, soft cotton rope underneath Lucky's chin, looping it around his body and under his tail, and then back around, so Foster could pull on the lead and tail rope at the same time, urging the young horse to take a few steps with a rope push from behind. "Okay, here we go. But first, which way are we going to lead him?"

Lizzie hesitated, then pointed to Sassy.

"Yep, that's exactly right. We're going to lead him in

the direction he's going to want to go. That way, he's likely to do the right thing, and then we can praise him all over and back for being a good boy. Especially when we're starting off, we want to set him up to succeed."

Which, it turned out, was easier said than done. Foster's first attempt to lead Lucky went fine until he actually pulled on the butt rope, at which point the little guy squealed, humped his back, and went into a series of stiff-legged little bucks, just like the little wild foals had done.

Rather than standing back and waiting until he settled, though, Foster just guided the squiggles in the direction he wanted, while ignoring the goofiness. When they reached Sassy, he gave the foal a couple of pats. Then he looked at Lizzie. "Ready?"

To Shelby's surprise, her daughter slipped through the fence, grabbed Sassy's halter, and marched the mare to the other end of the paddock. Then she slipped back through the fence.

"Good job," Foster said, nodding as though he hadn't expected anything different. "Okay, let's try that again."

Good job? Shelby wanted to stand up and cheer, Snoopy-dance, heck, do the macarena, the robot, and the hokey pokey all at once, even though she'd be running the risk of spraining something. Instead, she grinned broadly and made herself stay put on her muck bucket as Foster and the foal wiggled their way to the other end of the paddock. Set yourself up for success, indeed. She wasn't sure if this was really the way he would normally have taught a foal, but by the fourth pass, Lizzie was staying in the paddock with Sassy, standing with a hand on the mare's shoulder. And Shelby had gotten over being all misty-eyed.

This was real. It was happening. The little girl who'd spent the first week hunkered in the corner of the kitchen with her hoodie pulled up, watching whisper-quiet movies on her iPad, had blossomed into a tan, pink-helmeted kid who made "come on, you can do it!" faces as Lucky came toward her.

Shelby's heart wobbled in her chest. And as man and child high-fived—gently, so as not to scare the horses—she let out a soft sigh. *Mine*, she thought, watching the two of them together. *They're mine*.

"That's good for today," Foster decided after the sixth pass, when Lucky marched from one end of the pen to the other like a pro. "We don't want him to start thinking this feels too much like work. So now we make it fun again. Come here. I'll show you."

Shelby held her breath as he coached Lizzie through unclipping the lead, bundling it up in her hands, and using it to rub the foal all over his body, getting him used to the feel, and then ending with a good scratch. Lucky, bless him, didn't move an inch. He just stood there, making joyful faces as she found his itchy spots.

"Finally, let's give Mama a treat"—Foster produced a small piece of carrot from a pocket—"and we'll call it a success."

"Does that mean you're ready for me?" Stace called from the barn.

Foster looked up in surprise. "Ready for what?"

Lizzie, though, straightened and blew a chirp on her

whistle. She gave Sassy the carrot and slipped back through the fence, then stood there for a moment, took a deep breath, and beckoned a "come on" to Stace, who was still standing just inside the barn.

Shelby sat up as Foster crossed to her. "Do you know what's going on?"

"At a guess, I'd say the girls cooked up something during foal watch." He crouched down beside her, rested on his heels, and leaned back against the barn wall beside her. "I wonder what they're—" He broke off as Stace led Peppermint out of the barn, fully tacked and ready to ride. "Well, I'll be darned."

"Oh," breathed Shelby. She caught his hand and squeezed tightly. "Oh, please." When Lizzie looked over at her, she summoned a calm, expectant expression that said *no biggie, you can totally handle this*. At least she hoped that was what it conveyed, because inwardly she was sending Peppermint a mantra of *please be good, please be good, please be good*.

Stace led the pony into the open space between the broodmare's paddock and the beginning of the fenced arena, then stopped and held out the reins. And, not hesitating for a second, Lizzie marched up to Peppermint with the same sort of determination Lucky had shown moments earlier heading for his dam. She took the reins, flipped them over his head, put a pink-booted foot in the stirrup, and climbed into the kid-size saddle like she'd done it a thousand times.

Peppermint stood like a champ, with one ear pointing at Stace and the other at Lizzie, as if he wasn't quite sure where his orders were going to be coming from.

But then Lizzie gathered her reins, looked straight ahead, and squeezed his furry little sides with her heels, and the pony flicked his ears and moved off smoothly at a careful walk.

"She's doing it." Shelby gripped Foster's hand so tightly that her fingers ached. "She's riding!" Joy burst through her and she stood, tugging him up with her. She pressed her face against his arm, then made a soft sound as it fell into place. "That's why she was so mad! It wasn't about you and me at all. She was frustrated by being on the roundup and not being able to ride!"

"And now she can."

"And now she can." There was a smile on her lips and in her heart. "I guess sometimes things need to build up to the point where you're ready to make a change."

He shifted but didn't say anything.

Stace kept pace with the pair as they walked slowly along. "Okay," she instructed, "now you're going to tell him to turn around. Lay your rein on his neck the way we talked about. Not too sharp. You don't want him to twist something and get hurt. That's right. Nice and easy."

Lizzie and Peppermint made a shaky U-turn and headed back. Lizzie's face was brilliant and alive, her hands steady on the reins as Stace coached her through some stops and turns, and then sent her out to ride a figure eight on her own.

Shelby's pulse thudded in her ears and she was tempted to say, "Wait, that's enough. Let's quit now while we're ahead." But she stayed quiet, held her breath, and watched as Lizzie guided the sturdy little gray pony through a lopsided Picasso of a figure eight, and then back over to halt squarely next to her instructor.

"Way to ride, kid!" Stace enthused. "Knuckle tap!"

Vision blurring, Shelby dug out her phone. "Wait. Let me take a picture!"

Lizzie rolled her eyes, but looked pleased.

"Foster, come on," Stace called, gesturing him in. "You're totally part of this!"

"I don't—"

"She's right." Shelby gave him a nudge. "Go on. None of this would be happening if it wasn't for you."

He got in the shot without further protest, but even through the tiny viewfinder, she could see that something was off. Maybe she'd gotten better at reading body language after being around the horses, or maybe it was more that she had started seeing through the quiet to the man beneath, but where before he'd been open and relaxed with Lizzie, now he was closed off, uncomfortable. Like a man who suddenly wanted to be someplace else.

Was it Stace? Seeing Lizzie astride? Regret that he hadn't been the one to get her there? *Doesn't matter*, she told herself. *This is Lizzie's moment*. His reluctance brought a pang, though.

Focusing on her daughter's face, she sang out, "Everybody say 'currycomb'!" She took the picture. "Got it! It looks great!"

Foster stepped away almost immediately and headed for the broodmare paddock to collect the lead rope and other gear. Shelby frowned after him but didn't say anything. More, she told herself to let it go. He hadn't said or done anything wrong, hadn't even hinted there was a problem. Maybe she was imagining the vibe.

"Hop down," Stace directed. "Oops, don't let go of the reins! We don't want Peppermint to get away and run wild all over the place, do we?"

And, glory of glories, Lizzie grinned at the thought and stepped in close to the pony, clutching the reins beneath his chin.

"You guys!" Shelby crossed to them, leaned in, and kissed her on the cheek. "What an awesome surprise! Did you plan this last night?"

Stace nodded. "We practiced in the tack room, with a saddle balanced on one of the saddle racks, and she said she was ready. So we went for it." She grinned at Lizzie. "And nailed it, thankyouverymuch. What do you say, kid? Want to go again tomorrow?"

Lizzie nodded emphatically.

"How about sixish, after the guest stuff winds down for the day?"

"It's a date," Shelby promised, squeezing Lizzie's shoulder. Going into auto-parent, she said, "Lizzie, what do you say to Stace?"

"Th-thank you."

The whisper stopped Shelby's heart.

Oh, my. It was all she could think, all she could come up with. *Oh. My.*

Stace went wide-eyed. "You're . . . um . . . you're very welcome, Lizzie. I'm very proud of you."

"Me, too." Shelby went down on her knees in the dirt and wrapped her arms around her sweaty, pony-smelling daughter. "Oh, I'm so proud of you, baby."

Always before, when she let herself imagine this moment, she had feared she would burst into tears and scare Lizzie back into silence. She had also imagined they would be alone, just the two of them in their condo, the safest of safe places. How strange to find safety around a bunch of thousand-pound animals, under the wide-open sky. And how wonderful to share it with friends.

"You're so brave," Shelby, still hanging on to her kid. "So brave."

Peppermint snorted as if agreeing, spraying them both with a cool, yucky mist.

Lizzie pulled away and swiped at her face, then wiped it on the pony's neck with a look of disgust that brought laughter bubbling up to choke Shelby. It tried to turn into a sob, but she didn't let it. Instead, she shared a huge grin with Stace, then turned to look at Foster.

He was gone.

15

"To Lizzie!" Gran lifted a glass.

"To Lizzie!" The small group assembled around the family dining table in the main house lifted their drinks, clinked haphazardly, and downed sparkling grape juice while the guest of honor, sitting at the head of the table and wearing a party-hat cone made out of a brochure, ducked her head and blushed. But despite being the center of attention, Lizzie wasn't anxious or blanked out.

Nope, she was looking pretty darn pleased with herself, as well she should.

Shelby sat right next to her, with Stace beside her on one side of the table, while Krista sat on the other, with two empty spots beside her. One belonged to Gran, who swept in from the kitchen bearing a pretty pink plate with a chocolate cake on it that got a chorus of "oohs" and "aahs." The perfectly round cake was spackled with a smooth layer of chocolate frosting and piped around the edges with white dots. The vertical was decorated with a flow of curves and lines that looked like the necks and backs of a galloping herd, and the top had triumphant script that read *We Love You, Lizzie!*

Most other cooks would've called it a masterpiece and taken pictures for their Web site. Gran just smiled. "Oh, it's just a little something for our girl."

Shelby couldn't speak. She could barely breathe. If this had been her family and she'd had something like this to celebrate, there would've been either a gift certificate and an unsigned Hallmark card or a party full of her father's drinking buddies and her mother wringing her hands, trying to anticipate every possible problem and head it off before it happened.

This, though . . . this was all about Lizzie, all about relative strangers being so happy for her that Shelby's eyes weren't the only ones leaking.

"Have cake." Krista put a plate in front of her. "You look like you could use it."

"Amen, sister." Shelby held out her fork to Lizzie. "Way to ride, kiddo." They high-forked, and both dug into their pieces of moist, rich cake. It was chocolate with an undertone of some sort of berry that Shelby didn't even try to identify, just let herself enjoy. "Mmmm. Wow. Gran, this is amazing."

Krista winked. "A step up from Twizzlers and Nutter Butters?"

"I don't have the faintest clue what you're talking about," she claimed. Inwardly, though, there was a pang because of that empty chair.

Foster hadn't come to the after-hours party. When Krista asked him, he'd said he was headed over to a neighboring ranch to help with a problem horse, but to pass on his congrats. Kind of like a tepid Hallmark. He didn't mean it like that, Shelby told herself. He had a life outside of her and Lizzie, people who depended on him. But the more she told herself not to be annoyed with him when he hadn't done anything wrong—and, more, he'd done plenty of other things right—the more it felt like she was making excuses, even to herself.

"You okay?" Krista asked in an undertone. "Want to meet up later for unauthorized ice cream?"

"After this?" She lifted her forkful of homemade sin. "I'm good on the sweets, at least for a day or so." Which wasn't really what Krista was asking, so she added, "I'm fine, really. Besides, I figure Lizzie and I are about due for a quiet night in the cabin."

But Lizzie tapped her plate once, then shook her head, looking suddenly worried.

"Uh-oh. Am I missing something?"

"Um," Stace said, suddenly shamefaced, "if it's okay with you, I invited her to sleep out with me again tonight."

Okay, so much for some quality time. "Right. Silly me. I won't have my kid back until after Princess has done her thing, will I?" But she said it with a laugh, and ruffled Lizzie's hair. "You sure you're not ready for a night in a real bed?"

She got a vigorous head shake and a cakey grin, and that was really what mattered, wasn't it? Lizzie hadn't spoken again since those two small words, but more would come. They would come.

After the impromptu party wound down, though, Shelby found herself hesitating again at the cabin door, acutely aware of the dog hairs on her bed and the lingering smell of Pert Plus. This morning, waking up with Foster's dog on her feet and the memory of his lovemaking, she would've bet her best client that she'd be spending tonight with him, too, or at least part of it. Now, though, she'd be surprised to see him, and not just because he'd said he had things to do.

He was running and she wasn't sure why, which left her thoughts racing, her stomach tight with worry. Maybe she should take Krista up on her offer of some roof time, after all.

"Don't be a wuss. You've spent plenty of nights alone." Except she hadn't really. Lizzie had almost always been nearby. "So get used to it." Pretty soon she'd be sleeping over at friends' houses, going to parties, dating . . . Shelby shuddered. "Okay, now you're freaking yourself out."

Not to mention talking to herself without an animal anywhere in sight. Even Mr. Pony was in the barn for the night. Worse, she wasn't sure who she was more annoyed with—Foster for not helping celebrate Lizzie's big breakthrough or herself for not being able to let it go. He didn't owe her. If anything, after all he'd done for them, she owed it to him to cut him some slack. And that wasn't her making excuses, it was her being a grown-up.

Right?

"Urgh!" Wishing she had snagged a beer on her way out of the party, she closed herself in the cabin, toed off her boots, and pulled her smaller suitcase out of the closet to rummage for a trio of books she'd kept tucked away. She took a detour back outside to give her quilt a vigorous shake, and with the dog hair factor decreased by at least half, she plopped down on the bed with the books: *Living with Selective Mutism*, *A Parents' Guide to SM* and *Silent Spring: Emerging from the Cocoon*.

She held them for a moment, irritation fading as she thought back to the last time she'd looked at them, right after Lizzie's fear-driven meltdown. Then, she'd agonized over her decisions, her plans, and eventually put the books away. Now, though, she had amazing new hope, given to her by two little words, a "thank you" whispered in a voice she had struggled to remember.

That was progress with a capital "P."

Cracking the *Parents' Guide*, she flipped through the well-worn early sections, stopping on the chapter entitled *Speaking Games, Mirroring, and Desensitization*.

Before, she hadn't had any foothold for the traditional therapies, which assumed the SM child would at least talk to family members at home. Now, though . . . that "thank you" had opened up a whole new world. She read for an hour, burning through three chapters and the last of the daylight, and storing up ideas on how to set Lizzie up for success in the days and weeks ahead. Maybe. Hopefully. She underlined and took notes, feeling like she was back in school, only the homework was so much more important now. Her blue pen died, and she headed back to the closet to dig out her purse—it felt weird to have it surface, dusty and somehow unfamiliar when it was usually such a day-to-day part of her life—and found a felt tip.

As she headed back across the room, a boot step crunched outside.

She froze, not in fear but in dismay, her palms dampening as those boots came up the stairs to her door, followed by a knock. After a short pause, Foster said, "Shelby, it's me. Open up, please."

For a weak, small moment, she was tempted to pretend she wasn't home. Back in the condo she sometimes did exactly that, knowing that there was a very good chance that the person on the other side of the door was trying to sell her something, convert her, or both. Here, though, it wasn't an option. For one, there were too many windows and she had her bedside light on. And for another, it was Foster.

"Give me a minute," she called, letting him think she was covering up, when really she was trying to pull her head together.

It was Foster. And he hadn't really done anything wrong.

Taking a deep breath, she found a smile and opened the door. "Hey."

He was wearing the same jeans and shirt he'd had on earlier, but wasn't wearing his hat, and looked tense and wary, like he was there to break bad news. "Shelby."

Her stomach sank. She hadn't been imagining things, after all. "What's wrong?"

"Will you come for a walk?"

She hesitated, wanting to tell him to just say it, get it over with, and let her close herself back up in her safe place. *Oh, Foster.* She wanted to pull the covers over her head and stay there until morning. Instead, she nodded and turned back to grab her fleece off the back of the desk chair. "Okay, we'll walk."

But as the cabin door shut behind her, their boots thudded off the porch and crunched on the gravel path, and the darkness closed around them, she couldn't help thinking of the other times they'd gone off together like this. She'd worn his hat, ridden his horse, and parked her boots under his bed. She hoped that she wouldn't look back one day and think that sleeping with him had been a big mistake.

He'd scared her, Foster knew, as he hooked his thumbs in his back pockets and led her up toward the ridgeline, toward the backcountry, where things always made more sense. He couldn't bring himself to hold her and tell her everything was going to be okay, though, because he didn't know that it would. So they marched in silence, with him wrestling with what he wanted to say—even though he'd gone through it in his head on the way over—and her . . . well, he didn't know what she was thinking, or how much she had picked up on earlier in the day, when one minute he was getting all *Horse Whisperer* with her kid, and the next, he was in full-on "Danger, Will Robinson" retreat.

"So . . . ," she said as they headed up the incline. "Are we going someplace in particular?"

"Not really. I just . . . I needed to be moving." He paused, then said, "I, ah, checked out on you today."

She hesitated, then nodded, the move just visible in the cloud-filtered moonlight. "Yeah, you did. What happened?"

The cheap, easy answer would've been "I don't know," but that would've been a lie. "I spooked and bolted."

"You what?"

"Like Brutus when he sees a shadow and thinks it's a monster."

Her voice went tight. "Who, exactly, is supposed to be the monster in this scenario?"

That was the problem with metaphors—sometimes a guy got trapped in them. The last thing he wanted to do was hurt her, which was part of what was making this so hard. "No monster. Just me not dealing with things like I should have."

"Like how things got pretty intense last night, you mean?" She sounded resigned.

"No, it wasn't that. Not in a million years." He scrubbed a hand across his face, feeling the smoothness where he'd shaved before coming over, like that would change anything. "Being with you was . . . it was incredible. Planets-shifting-on-their-axes amazing. And if that was all of it, I'd want to do it again and again and again. But then this morning . . . I don't know. One minute I was just fiddling around with Lizzie, showing her training stuff like I would any interested kid. Then the next, I'm in the middle of a family photo." And he hadn't known how to deal.

There was a pause before she said, "Stace was in the picture, too."

They had reached the top of the ridgeline, where things flattened out and a trio of boulders marked the high point, marking the edge of the homestead. He stopped there and turned to face her. "Look, I'm not trying to back away from either of you, honest. I want to be your lover and Lizzie's friend. But I also want to keep things separate and not have anyone get hurt at the end of the summer, when we go our separate ways." He braced for the inevitable "what if we stayed in touch?" Heck, he'd even thought it himself. But he knew better than to start a long-distance relationship, knowing what the outcome would have to be. Better to end it cleanly in September.

To his surprise, she balled up a fist and socked him in the shoulder. "Hello? Earth to McFly. That's what we already agreed to."

"But—"

"But nothing. I didn't change the rules. If you're feeling any pressure, you might want to step back and ask yourself where it's coming from. Because it's not me."

"It's just . . ." *Um. Well.*

She waited, then made a satisfied *hmph*. "Well, you get points for thinking about it, at least. Look, don't get me wrong, you're not the only one who adds two plus one and gets 'family' here. But just because the math makes sense doesn't mean the people do. You don't need to push me or Lizzie away to prove it."

He was silent a moment as surprise hummed through him—shock, really, along with shame and a huge, echoing relief—knocking off the rough edges he'd been fighting all day. He'd been expecting shouts, tears, and accusations, and he'd gotten put in his place, instead. Because she was right—he had talked himself into the spook, seeing imaginary monsters where there weren't any.

Maybe he should lay off Brutus some. Apparently, he wasn't any brighter.

"I've said it before and I'll probably say it again . . . you're not like other women, are you?"

She laughed softly. "Lizzie isn't the only one who's put in her therapy time. When Patrick left and I found out what had been going on, I didn't lose my marriage—that had been gone for longer than I'd realized—so much as I lost my faith in myself, in my own judgment. Between that and needing to be calm for Lizzie's sake, I've had my head shrunk plenty. If nothing else, I've got a decent toolbox when it comes to knowing what's going on in my head, and seeing when it doesn't line up with what's happening around me."

"You sure do."

"So . . . still friends?"

Suddenly, a day that had been seriously circling the drain got a whole lot better. He blew out a long, slow breath. "Friends and more, if you'll still have me."

"That depends. Got any Pixy Stix?"

"I might." He paused, his pulse thudding in his veins as his body started to catch on that things between them might be okay, after all. The relief was huge, the pressure in his chest back down to a throb of need. "So, what do you say, my sweet, smart, and oh, so forgiving Shelby? Will you come home with me and fool around by the glow of my light saber wall lamp?"

Her teeth flashed. "There's a metaphor there, and it's not a good one. And yes, I'll come home and fool around with you . . . but only if you promise not to freak yourself out again if the sex is transcendent tonight and my kid does something cute tomorrow." She sighed theatrically. "Those are our burdens to bear."

A few minutes ago, he would've said it'd be a long time before he laughed again. Now he proved that wrong. "From now on, I'll do my best not to channel Brutus on a grain high."

"I'd appreciate it. Right now, though, I'd appreciate it even more if you'd kiss me."

"I can do that." He wrapped his arms around her and brought his mouth down on hers in a kiss that was as much relief as passion, though there was plenty of that, too. Heat sparked and grew, and his body hardened almost instantly, recognizing hers as if they'd been lovers for months rather than just a day. "You amaze me," he said against her lips. "More and more each day."

When the kiss eased to an arms-intertwined embrace, she sighed against his shoulder and nestled close. "I didn't want this to be over. Not yet."

He kissed her hair and held her tight. "It isn't. It won't be, not until you want it to be." Or, rather, not until the end of the summer, when they both went back to their real lives.

The next morning, it was still pitch-black out when Shelby woke to the sound of the cabin door opening. Banishing sudden thoughts of grizzlies and coyotes—hello, door latch requiring opposable thumbs—she sat up in bed and reached for her flashlight. "Lizzie? Is that you?"

Before she could click on her light, another came to life with a double flash, then stayed on, showing her daughter's pink hoodie and camping-out sweats. Her ponytail had gone lopsided, and her eyes were wide.

Shelby sat all the way up and clicked on the bedside

light. "Hey, Dizzy Girl. You ready to spend a few hours in a real bed?"

But Lizzie came over and tugged on her arm, motioning *come on, come on, come on!*

Her head started to clear and her instincts did an *uh-oh.* "Is something wrong?"

"P-princess had her b-baby."

"Oh!" That was all she could get out, such an insignificant word that failed utterly to capture the upswelling rush of emotions.

"Come see. P-p-please?"

The last word had more than a bit of Roger Rabbit in it, but that wasn't what had Shelby choking up. "Oh, baby. You're really talking."

Lizzie sucked in a breath and her face went stricken. "Don't c-cry, Mommy. I wanted to b-b-before. I j-just couldn't." Tears flooded her eyes, and one drop tracked down. "I'm sorry."

Shelby's own tears cut loose, fat and scalding, and not willing to be held back any longer. She wasn't afraid of scaring Lizzie now, though. She was only afraid of not getting this right.

Pulling the little girl into her arms, she hugged her fiercely. "No, baby, don't be sorry," she said into the soft brown hair. "You didn't do anything wrong. You did everything right, you hear me? You're so brave. So, so brave."

"I'm s-s-s-s . . . I can't talk right."

Shelby's heart clutched at the ragged grief, the guilt and fear in those stumbling words. "Yes, you can. You just need some practice, that's all."

Lizzie hesitated. "I guess."

Realizing that she needed more than just "it'll be fine," especially when things hadn't been fine for a long time, Shelby eased back and waited until her daughter met her eyes. Then, channeling every shred of Zen calm she'd managed to come up with over the past few years, she said, "Elizabeth Michelle Brewster, you've beaten SM. Do you really think you can't deal with a tiny little stutter?"

It took a few seconds, but then the narrow shoulders straightened and the gleam came back into her eyes. "I c-can do it."

"Of course you can. You can do anything." The waterworks started up again—or maybe they hadn't really stopped—and her voice broke. "I'm so proud of you, sweetheart. And I love you so much."

"I love you, too, Mommy."

It had been years since she'd heard that, years since it had felt real. She wouldn't start bawling, she told herself. She just wouldn't.

Letting out a watery breath, she said, "Come on. Let's go see the foal, and you can tell me all about watching it be born."

She threw on a fleece and jeans while Lizzie waited impatiently, doing a little *hurry up, hurry up* dance that made Shelby's heart sing. "I'm hurrying!" she said, laughing, and jammed her feet in her boots. "Okay, let's go!"

"Whee!" The noise that came out of Lizzie as she bounced down the cabin steps sounded like one of the "I'm free!" squeals that Lucky liked to make when

he and Sassy were turned out into the bigger paddock to play. And, like the foal, Lizzie scampered off
away from her mother, then curved back around to
grab her hand and tug her toward the barn. "Come
on, come on. Sh-she's already n-n-nursing!"

Tightening her fingers and letting Lizzie pull her
into a jog, Shelby smiled so wide that her cheeks ached
and her heart sang a happy, happy song. Because no
matter what had happened in the past or would happen in the future, she had gotten this part right.

16

A few days later, Shelby watched the airport shuttle bump up the driveway, splashing a little in the winding down of a rain shower, and shook her head. "How is it Saturday already?"

The week had passed in a blur of cooking, word games, horses, and stealing time with Foster, and if she wasn't sure where the days had gone, she didn't mind. Not just because the guests—a group of execs from a big drug company who seemed to have missed the point of team building—had been particularly demanding, but because the weather looked like it was going to clear up after all, and it was time to ride.

When the bus finally disappeared, she glanced over at her daughter. "Hey, kiddo. Ready to— Lizzie?"

Her prodigal was already halfway to the barn, wearing the helmet cover that looked like a straw Stetson, and swaggering a little with her thumbs hooked in her front pockets.

"I'll take that as a yes." Grinning, Shelby followed.

Foster already had Brutus on the cross ties, slicking him over with a soft brush. He looked up when she came in, and gave her a long, slow grin. "Hey there, Mama Bear."

Her blood heated and her pulse kicked up a notch, but she gave back as good as she got, letting her eyes run over him and linger until his gaze went smoky. "Hey."

Things had been great between them since the prior Saturday's near flameout. He'd made time to show Lizzie how to work with Lucky on halter training and basic skills like picking up his feet on command and keeping his teeth to himself, while also arranging things so he and Shelby could be together for some adult fun. Today, though, he'd surprised her by suggesting that the three of them ride out together.

"Is Loco ready?" she asked archly.

"You wish." He flicked her hat down over her eyes. "Groom your own critter, lady."

Lizzie's giggle was music to her ears.

Shelby moved down the aisle and laughed to discover that Loco was already brushed smooth, his tack neatly organized by his stall door. "I was kidding."

Foster shrugged good-naturedly. "It's my day off."

She looked in on Princess and her filly, a petite redhead who was utterly gorgeous and knew it. "How's our little girl doing?"

"A-plus. As for the gremlin . . ." He rolled his eyes in the direction of Sassy's paddock, where Lucky was snoozing in a patch of sunlight, looking deceivingly angelic. "He figured out how to dump out his mama's water buckets last night. Oh, joy."

They traded quips and comments as they finished

getting the three horses—or, rather, two horses and one small gray pony with a Napoleon complex—ready for the ride. Foster ran a last check of all the tack, just in case, and nodded his approval. "Let's mount up and move on. Last one out is a rotten egg."

As Lizzie hustled Peppermint out, Foster used Brutus's body as a blockade so he'd be second in line. Shelby groaned in mock protest and called, "You two seem to be forgetting which one of us has lunch in her saddlebags!"

They mounted up and set off, and she filled her lungs as they broke free of the buildings and started up the gentle incline leading to the main trail. The rain had quit, leaving the ground wet but the air crystal clear. The horse's hooves made sucking noises in the soft soil, counterpointed by the creak of leather and the jingle of their bits. In the distance, a rainbow arched from one mountain to the next, its colors deep and vivid against the whitening clouds.

Shelby stood in her stirrups, wanting to get that much closer to the spectacle. "Lizzie, look! A rainbow!"

Her daughter's face split in a wide smile, and she held up two fingers of her free hand.

Sure enough a second rainbow echoed the first, fainter, but uninterrupted.

Foster rode close so his knee bumped against Shelby's. "I'd say that's a sign of good things to come."

"I like your thinking." Gesturing to Peppermint, who was striding out in a nearly running walk that had him well in front of the horses, she said, "Are they okay?"

"He won't get much farther ahead than that. If she's not worried, then I'm not. And honestly, she's probably safer in front of Brutus than behind him."

And Lizzie didn't seem worried at all. She sat straight and tall in the saddle, craning from side to side as if afraid she was going to miss something. The over-size straw hat made her look a bit like a satellite dish, but Shelby kept that one to herself. She was getting to know her daughter all over again, and had learned to watch the teasing.

Switching her attention to her mount, she said, "What do you think, Loco? You happy to be out of the arena?" She patted his neck and got a soft snort in return.

Brutus, on the other hand, was tossing his head and jigging in quick, mincing steps that were designed to jar his rider as much as possible. Foster just rolled his eyes. "And here I thought he could use a light day after working hard all week to keep the dysfunctional drug execs in line. Clearly, I should've run some of the oats out of him before doing the family trail ride thing."

Shelby grinned. "Watch out or you'll lose your bachelor cred. Family trail ride, indeed."

"Okay, how about 'trail ride with my two favorite ladies'?"

"That'll work." She liked that they could joke about it, liked that it hadn't stayed a sore spot, liked . . . Okay, fine. She liked just about everything about him, which added a sparkling magic to being at Mustang Ridge with Lizzie.

In so many ways, she had made the right choice, coming here.

Peppermint reached the flat section at the top of the ridge, stopped, and turned back to wait for them without any obvious input from Lizzie, who was still in radar mode. Brutus gave a little crow hop and shook his head, annoyed at being beaten by the little squirt, but he settled when Foster reined him in beside the pony. Shelby pulled up on the other side of Lizzie, far enough away so Peppermint wouldn't feel hemmed in, and they stood for a moment, looking out across the wide bowls that fell away on either side of the ridge.

The rainbows were gone and the clouds overhead were breaking up and letting dusty rays of sun shine through, turning the fields into patchworks of dark and light.

Shelby let out a happy sigh. "It's gorgeous."

Foster met her eyes, and his voice dropped a notch when he said, "It sure is."

Brutus laid back his ears and faked a nip in Peppermint's direction, and the pony made a face and squealed without moving his feet an inch.

Shelby laughed. "I think that's our cue to stop gawking and get moving."

"That, or run Brutus here up and down the hill a dozen times and get out some of the ya-yas," Foster said drily.

"I vote we all take a run down the hill—or at least a decent jog. So . . . where to, trail boss?"

"That's up to Lizzie. What do you say, kid? You want to ride into the backcountry and have lunch at this really cool lake where you can sometimes see wild mustangs, or do you want to head to the next ranch over and check out their buffalo and ostriches? Which, by the way, are also really cool."

The big straw hat ducked a little, but then she looked up at him and said, "The l-lake, please. I'd l-like to see the mustangs."

Shelby had more or less stopped tearing up at the sound of her daughter's voice, but she didn't try to stop the grin, or the warmth that ran through her when Foster met her eyes over Lizzie's head. He'd been the one to point out that it was time to stop with the yes-no copouts and start asking questions that required actual answers.

Progress.

"Then the lake it is. I can't promise you mustangs, but thanks to Gran and your mom, we'll get a rocking picnic either way." He reined Brutus around and pointed to a narrow trail that snaked down the ridge. "That's the one. You and Peppermint can lead on."

With the sun beaming down on Shelby, her cowboy at her side and her kid leading the way astride a fat gray pony, she could only let her head fall back and laugh.

"What's so funny?" Foster asked.

"I'm happy, that's all. Really, really happy."

He nudged Brutus over, leaned in, and kissed her, quickly but thoroughly. "Me, too." Then he straightened up in his saddle and gave Loco a playful slap on his rump. "Okay, you two, stop dawdling. Let's ride!"

They rode for most of the day, going slowly to account for Lizzie's inexperience and Peppermint's height challenge, but still covering a good amount of ground out to the lake. There weren't any mustangs at the watering hole, but they saw a pair of eagles and a rangy coyote while they ate thick turkey, bacon, and sourdough sandwiches with homemade half-sour pickles. On the way back, they saw the dust trail of a distant band of mustangs, rounding out Lizzie's day. It was a long one, though, and by the time the three-boulder landmark came into sight, her straw radar dish was bobbing tiredly in time with Peppermint's steps.

The horses had all been lagging for a bit—even Brutus had gone flat-footed—but they picked it up as they started down the hill for home. As the ranch came into view, though, Shelby frowned at an unusual commotion in the parking area. "What's going on down there?"

Foster tipped back his hat and frowned. "Please tell me we don't have a bachelor party booked for this week."

"No, it's the NeverEver package, all newbies, four big families, and some couples. Why a bachelor party?"

"Because it looks like somebody brought a party bus."

"Is that what that is?"

"Or maybe an RV. Something . . . Uh-oh." Brutus's head came up, as if his rider had just clamped on, and Foster's voice dropped an octave. "Dang it, I think that's the *Rambling Rose*."

When they reached the barn, Foster waved Shelby off toward the main house. "Lizzie and I can see to the horses if you want to go make sure Gran is okay and Krista isn't homicidal yet."

Gratitude washed through her. "I owe you one."

"Just doing what I can to help out without getting in the line of fire."

"You're not making me feel any better."

"Sorry. Rose is a bit on the scary side."

This coming from a guy who called an eight-inch scar a love tap. "Oh, great."

"You can take her. And Gran could probably use the backup. Krista does her best, but . . ."

"Rose is her mom."

"Bingo." He pulled her in for a quick kiss. "Go get 'em, Mama Bear."

Out in the parking area, the huge RV dwarfed Krista's big dually truck. The size of school bus plus a little, it was a deep, sparkling bronze color with white and purple waves streaking the sides. And, sure enough, RAMBLING ROSE was painted above the waves. The open cargo hold was half-full of big pink plastic bins and several more were stacked outside, along with a few pieces of matched luggage, suggesting that Krista's parents had started unpacking, but then stalled.

Shelby wasn't sure if that was a good thing or not.

Telling herself to give Rose the benefit of the doubt despite the stories she'd heard, she headed up the stairs and through the front door. She hadn't gotten more than two steps down the hallway leading to the kitchen when she heard raised voices.

"Well, for goodness' sake, Barbara," said a woman in an "I'm trying to be reasonable" tone. "This is how they do it in Paris."

"Oh, poosh. You've never been outside North America." That was Gran's voice, clipped. "And my way is fine."

"Is that what you're going for here? Just 'fine'? No, of course not. Let me show you again. You just—"

"Mom, you must be exhausted." That was Krista, sounding harried. "How about we—"

"Oh, no," Rose trilled. "Eddie drove the last leg so I'd be all rested and ready to hit the ground running!"

Shelby hesitated and gave serious thought to hiding out in the barn, instead, but then took a big breath and stepped into the kitchen doorway. Her stomach dropped at the sight of two plastic bins in the far corner, one of them open to reveal expensive copper pans. Gran and Krista stood on one side of the butcher-block counter, facing off against a formidable, steel-haired woman who looked like the Nurse Ratched version of Krista, with a little Julia Child thrown in around the edges. A couple of inches taller and wider than her daughter, Rose was wearing a red-edged white apron and a matching toque that made her tower over the other two. And it didn't take a body-language expert to see that if there wasn't already a problem, there would be soon.

Here goes nothing. Stepping through the door, Shelby said brightly, "Hey, guys, I'm back. Want me to get started on the cookies for tonight?"

Rose looked over, then blinked in confusion. "I'm sorry. Who are you?"

"The sous chef."

She took an obvious glance down. "I thought you were due any day."

Moving to stand right next to Gran, Shelby said, "That's Bertie. I'm her fill-in, Shelby."

"You can't be."

"Excuse me?"

Rose turned on Krista. "You didn't tell me you'd hired another cook."

"Um. Yeah, I did."

"Don't be silly. Well, anyway. I'm sure it's a pleasure to meet you, Sherry."

"Shelby. And thanks." *Sort of.*

"You're just in time. I was just about to show Krissie and Barbara how to make the most amazing Béchamel sauce, just like they do at the Cordon Bleu. That's in France, you know. It's a cooking school."

Krista moved around the counter to touch Rose's arm. "Mom, why don't we—" A clatter from the hallway interrupted, and a big bear of a man in denim and plaid came through carrying two of the plastic bins. He had hair that was more salt than pepper, a goatee a couple of shades darker, and a pencil stub stuck behind one ear.

Peering around the bins, he navigated the counter without missing a beat. "Rosie, these are from the pasta class you took in Dubuque."

Rose beamed. "Thank you, sweetie. Just put it wherever there's room. We'll get things organized around here later."

"Dad—" Krista began.

He ducked his head to plant a kiss on her cheek. "Sorry, sweetheart. I already tried. If I had my way, we'd be touring the Hoover Dam right now." With a wink at Shelby, he headed for the door.

"Oh, you. Such a tease." Rose waved him out, calling after him, "I also need the green pans and the box with the hand mixers in it."

"Mom—"

"Now, where were we? Hollandaise, right?"

"*Mom!*" Krista's bellow cut through the kitchen and left a ringing silence behind. When she finally had Rose's attention, she said firmly, "You can't just come in here and take over. We have guests, and we've got a good system in place."

Rose blinked. "I'm not taking over, sweetie. It's just a demonstration. Then I was thinking we could make these darling little Napoleons I learned in pastry class."

Shelby couldn't tell if she was manipulative or oblivious, or some mix of the two, but the whole "give her the benefit of the doubt" theory had lasted less than five minutes. She was firmly in Camp Gran on this one. "With all due respect," she said, "we need to get started soon on dinner service for the new guests."

"Oh, Sherry, don't be silly. There's plenty of time. That's the beauty of Barbara's plain cooking."

Gran exhaled a *poosh* under her breath, and pushed away from the counter. "I've got things that need doing. I'll be back at four." The side door slammed behind her.

Shelby winced and started to go after her, but Krista caught her arm. "Wait. Hang on a sec." She hustled her into the hallway, stopping near the menu board, which didn't say anything about hollandaise or Napoleons. "I need a favor."

"I'll talk to her."

"Not Gran. I want you to stay here and keep Mom occupied. Let her teach you something if you can stand it, but keep her away from dinner. And for the love of God, don't let her touch Herman."

Darned if the thought didn't bring a surge of dread. "Of course. You'll make sure Gran is okay?"

"Yep. Then I'm going to track down my father and find out what's really going on here."

"You didn't know they were coming?"

"Last I checked they were on their way to see the World's Biggest Donut or something." Krista shook her head. "No, there wasn't a hint, and I don't know if this is a three-day whirlwind visit, or something more. Don't get me wrong, I love her. Of course I do—she's my mom. It's just . . ."

"It's okay." Shelby pulled her into a quick hug. "It'll be okay. Go. Do what you need to do. I'll take care of things here."

Brave words, but she had a feeling that was going to be easier said than done. And, sure enough, when she came back into the kitchen, Rose narrowed her eyes. "Where's Krista?"

"One of the guests needed her." Shelby waved toward the cabins. "Something about a clogged toilet, a missing toy, and a minor tsunami. She'll be back as soon as she can." It wasn't exactly a lie, though the clog in question had been a few weeks ago and the renegade rubber dinosaur had long since been rescued, sterilized, and returned to its owner.

"Oh." Rose gave her an up-and-down, then shrugged. "Well, then, we'll just have to put together something that will surprise the boots off her when she gets here, won't we? Grab your apron, and let's get started."

"I, uh . . . sure. Right." Remembering that she was fresh from the barn, she donned one of Gran's aprons and headed to the sink to wash up, saying over her shoulder, "So, Chef. What's the plan? I'm all yours." At least until four, when dinner service needed to get cranking.

Come on, Krista. You can do it. Hopefully she would be able to calm down Gran and get her father on board with some sort of a plan to contain her mom's enthusiasm. From everything Shelby had heard about the rambling duo, Ed was mellow in the extreme, but pretty unstoppable once he'd made a decision.

Mollified, Rose dug into her plastic bins and started pulling out books and little jars of spices. "So, Shelly. I think I remember Krista telling me about you. You're the one with the deaf daughter, right? Or not deaf . . . what was it? There was something wrong with her."

Oh, this was going to be a couple of very long hours. Tamping down the knee-jerk mama bear "rwor!" she said, "It's Shelby, and there's absolutely nothing wrong with my daughter." And she knew darn well Krista hadn't put it that way.

"Didn't she tell me you and Foster are dating? Or was that someone else?"

"Yes, Foster and I are dating." She couldn't really deny that one, and didn't really want to. Even saying it to this stranger—and a strange stranger, at that, no matter who she was related to—gave her a buzz, especially on the heels of their family trail ride.

Okay, now she was calling it a family deal. Note to self: don't let the boundaries blur.

Rose unplugged Gran's commercial mixer and shoved it aside to plug in a Salad Shooter straight off the Home Shopping Channel, or maybe the "As seen on TV" aisle at Walmart. With a sidelong look at Shelby, she said, "I was surprised to hear about the two of you, actually. It always seemed to me like he just shut down that part of his life." She smiled brightly. "I think it's wonderful that you were able to get through to him. He's such a dear man."

She seemed genuine, suggesting that she wasn't malicious so much as self-absorbed to the point of oblivious, so Shelby made herself return the smile, along with a noncommittal "That's nice of you to say. And I agree, he's a very good man."

"But such a loner. I always thought that was a shame, though of course he has good reason not to trust women. You know, what with the divorce and all."

Shelby, who had been about to change the subject before things got weird, froze with the water running in the sink and her hands sudsed up. Because things had suddenly gotten very weird. "Divorce?"

Busy measuring flour into a big bowl, Rose didn't seem to notice the edge in her voice. "It's only natural for him to be wary after the way her lawyers cleaned him out. Took the family farm, the stock, everything except his horse and his saddle." She nodded to herself. "A thing like that is going to change a man."

"I don't . . ." Shelby couldn't finish, couldn't breathe. *I don't want to hear this.* But maybe she should, because it put a whole new spin on things. And, clearly, it wasn't something he'd been planning on telling her himself.

Five weeks. They had known each other for five weeks, almost six, and had been lovers for two of them. Yet he'd never mentioned being married, or that he'd lost the Double-Bar H in the divorce.

"How's he doing with the negotiations, anyway?" Rose had her nose stuck in the refrigerator, rummaging through stores that were intended to get them through a week of guests. "Last I knew, he was saving every penny up so he could buy his old place back, regain the family honor, that sort of thing."

"You'll . . . you'll have to ask him yourself." The ache inside her was more bewilderment than anger, and a creeping sense of dread. *Don't freak,* she told herself. *You both agreed this was just for fun, just a casual thing.*

But, oh, it hurt.

"You're right, we shouldn't gossip." Rose glanced over at her, brows furrowing when she realized Shelby had been washing her hands for a good five minutes, maybe longer. "This isn't surgery, you know. You ready to get to work? I'm thinking we'll do this darling squash soup I know."

Don't throw up. Don't throw up. She owed it to Krista

to buy her the time she needed, owed it to Gran to protect Herman and their dinner fixings. She didn't have the option of losing it, not now.

She so badly wanted to, though. *Divorced*. It didn't compute with the man she knew, but why would Rose lie? *Maybe she's confused.* That brought a spurt of hope, but it died quickly when it lined up too well—a loner with a horse and a saddle, who lived a stripped-down life because he was saving every penny he could to buy back the Double-Bar H. Oh, God. She wanted to press the back of her hand to her mouth and hold in a sob, wanted to block out the creeping dread that said she had badly misjudged him, and what was going on between them.

But her hands were clean, and she had a job to do. *You can do this.* More, she would *have* to do it. She owed Krista and Gran better than a meltdown right now.

She was shaking as she shut off the water, but she straightened and found a wobbly smile as she turned to Rose. "Where do you want me to start?"

Shelby made it through two hours of the Mustang Ridge version of *Hell's Kitchen*, nearly wept with relief when Krista and her father showed up at four to kidnap Rose for a welcome-home dinner in town, and did her best to make the dinner service as easy as she could on a very subdued Gran. All the while, though, she roller-coastered her way from "he should've told me" to "ohmigod, what now?" to "get a grip, he hasn't really done anything wrong," with too-frequent detours down "well, at least there's chocolate." Lots of chocolate. Enough chocolate that by the time Tipper and Topper headed out with dessert, she had a stomachache and the smell of sugar made her want to hurl.

So much for all that "I've got my head on straight, lots of therapy, self-aware, blah, blah" she'd been spouting the other day. Because by the time she pulled up in front of Foster's place near sunset, she was a mess.

After killing the engine, she sat for a moment, staring at the bunkhouse. It didn't look any different, with its rough-out exterior, zero landscaping, and trio of tired rockers on the porch. It was the first time she'd come on the spur of the moment, though, and the first time she hesitated before getting out of the car.

Maybe she should leave, drive around some, and come back when she was more settled, when she knew what she wanted to say.

But then the door opened, and there he was, looking so damn happy to see her that her heart hurt. He lifted a hand and called, "Shelby, hey. How're things in Kitchen Land?"

"Momentarily quiet." She walked toward him, but stalled on the top step. "I, um, know we didn't have plans."

"You don't need an invitation." He caught her hand and leaned in to kiss her, then hesitated and drew back. "Unless you do?" He searched her face. "What's wrong?"

"I. Um . . ."

"Come in." He drew her inside and shut the door. "Do you want something? Soda? Wine? Intravenous Nutter Butter drip?"

Stop being so sweet! It made her feel worse. "Nothing, thanks."

He pulled her into his arms and wrapped her in a warm embrace that didn't make her feel nearly so safe as it had done earlier in the day. "Was Rose so awful?"

She tried not to snuggle in, but even just being there—being with him—smoothed out some of the rough edges she was feeling, made her wonder if she was overreacting. They hadn't promised each other anything more than good times, really. Still, it hurt that he hadn't confided in her. "She, um, said some things that bothered me."

"About Lizzie?" His voice rumbled against her, warm and soothing.

"About you, actually." She made herself push away, but couldn't look at him. Instead, she went to the window and stared out at the sunset, which had turned the sky a delicate peach that bled down to red where it met the dark mountain silhouettes. "She said you were married."

And, just like that, the vibe changed.

There was a long pause before he said, "Once upon a time, yeah. I was." His voice was inflectionless, and when she looked back at him, she could've been looking at the man she'd met in the barn that first day, cool and closed-off.

The fading sunset was easier to watch. "She said you lost the Double-Bar H in the divorce, that your ex-wife cleaned you out down to Loco and your saddle."

"I got the truck, too, and it was her father's lawyers, not Jill herself. I think she would've been okay with less, but she'd always been daddy's little girl, and old man Winslow couldn't stand the thought of it being no-fault. Which meant it had to be my fault." He paused, then said carefully, "What happened to not doing the high school gossip thing?"

"I didn't mean to." Her gut knotted. He wasn't apologizing, wasn't agreeing that yeah, he should've told her once things started getting more serious between them. She drew in a shuddering breath. *Don't lose it. Just don't.*

He crossed the room to stand right behind her, then touched her shoulder. "Shelby, look at me."

She turned around and leaned back against the windowsill, hating that he'd gone back to looking quiet and withdrawn. But at the same time, while she might hide her emotions for Lizzie's sake, she knew better than to ignore them when it came to a man. Been there, done that, had the wool pulled over her eyes. "I know this isn't fair. I know we said—*I* said—that we're just having a good time, carpe diem and all that."

"What happened between me and Jill is ancient history."

"It just . . . it seems like the sort of thing you mention to a lover."

"Not if it doesn't have any impact on today. A good horseman takes the lessons and leaves the bad memories behind."

"You told me once that a key to training greenies is making sure that the lesson they're learning is the one you're trying to teach."

"What I did at twenty-two and regretted like hell at twenty-six doesn't have much bearing on the guy I am now. And, by the way, you've been getting along with that guy just fine up to now." He paused, voice roughening. "What changed, Shelby? Why is this suddenly a big deal?"

They were the same questions she'd been asking herself most of the afternoon. "You know about Patrick."

"Because you told me. And if you wanted to know more about me, you could've asked."

"Would you have answered?"

"We'll never know, will we?" The words carried a bite, but then he muttered a curse, scrubbed a hand over his face, and dropped down to the couch. "I don't want to fight about this."

"Me, neither. But it hurts knowing you didn't trust me enough to tell me."

"It wasn't . . ." He scrubbed both hands over his face. "Hell. I hate that I lost the Double-Bar H, hate knowing how disappointed Grandpa would've been. I don't like talking about it, even thinking about it."

"How close are you to buying it back?" At least he'd told her that much, although he'd made it sound like a pipe dream, where Rose seemed to think he was closer than that.

Exhaling, he met her eyes and said, "I made a new offer right before I left for the roundup. Old Winslow always has six different projects going at any one time, and one of these days, he's going to need the money more than the revenge."

"A few days ago . . . and you didn't tell me." That shouldn't have hurt as much as it did.

"Honestly? I thought about it, but I just figured

that's not what we're about. It's not like you want to stay out here in the middle of nowhere, and I'm sure as heck not moving to the city. So why throw that into the mix when we're having a good time?" He paused, expression shifting to regret. "Look, I'm sorry you found out about all this from Rose, and I'm sorry it upset you. That's the last thing I want to do."

No, the last thing you want to do is get involved for real with me and Lizzie.

And there it was, crashing down on her like a piano dropped from high above, making so much noise and mess that it took her a second to figure out what had really happened, what it meant. She actually backpedaled a couple of steps and stared at him in such horror that he stood and came toward her, hands outstretched.

"I'm serious," he said. "What do we need to do to get past this? Do you want me to tell you all the gory details about me and Jill and the Double-Bar H? I will, if that's what you want."

"No, no. It's not that." Not anymore. It was far, far worse.

"Then what?"

"I . . . I should go. I'm sorry. I need to go." She darted across the room and fumbled with the doorknob.

He was right on her heels, and slapped a hand on the door to keep her from opening it. His voice gained an edge. "Shelby, come on. What's wrong?"

"It's not your problem. It's mine." *Mine, mine, all mine.* Just as she had thought when she watched him and Lizzie together, seeing them as a unit. A family.

"So tell me. Maybe I can help."

"Don't push me, Foster."

He caught her arm. "Damn it, Shelby, talk to me!"

"Fine!" She yanked away, but then spun on him, full of miserable fury. "You want to know what's going on? I screwed up, that's what!"

"Screwed up how?"

"By falling for you." It hurt to say it, hurt even more to see his face go utterly blank.

"Falling . . . in *love*?"

"Not love. Not yet, I don't think." She pressed the back of her hand to her mouth. "Maybe. I don't know. It's close, I think." The awful roller coaster feeling in her stomach wasn't anything she'd ever experienced before. It wasn't the buzzing flush of a high school crush or the happy confidence she'd had going into her wedding, convinced she was doing the right thing with the right guy, only to have it go very wrong. Now it was even worse, because she wasn't confident, wasn't convinced of anything.

He had gone pale. "I didn't want . . ."

"I know," she said quickly. "And I don't blame you." At least she was trying not to. "We had an agreement. I just . . ." Her throat locked tight, and she had to force the words. "I didn't even realize it was happening. But now . . . I'm sorry. I . . ." As hard as she fought them, sudden tears broke free, trailing down her cheeks in wet trickles that made her even sadder.

"Shelby, don't. Please." He reached for her, but didn't make contact. "Tell me what you want."

"I don't know." But she did, really. "I want more times like this morning, with you, me, and Lizzie out together. And I want . . . I want this to be real. Not just a summer fling, but a relationship. Something we're working on, trying to see if there's a future."

"How can there be?" His eyes darkened. "My life is here. Yours and Lizzie's are in Boston." He paused. "Unless you were thinking of staying."

"Of course not, no. I haven't . . . Of course not." She wished he had let her escape, wished she could've had some time to work this out in her head. But maybe it was better this way. She didn't have time to talk herself out of anything, just had to go with her gut. "We could do something long distance. I could visit . . ."

He was already shaking his head. "I think we both know that wouldn't work. We're just, I don't know, wired differently. When two people are this far apart, trying to find a compromise is impossible, and it'd just drive us both crazy. In the end, things would get ugly. I don't want that."

A flicker in his eyes—desperation, maybe, or guilt— spurred her to ask, "Are you talking about you and me, or you and your ex?"

"Okay, point to you."

The pressure in her chest turned to pain. "I'm not keeping score."

"I know, and it pisses me off that suddenly I am." He scrubbed a hand through his hair, leaving it standing on end. "I wish I could say what the heck, let's give it a try."

"But you can't." She said it dully, already seeing the answer in his eyes.

"I've got a life here, plans here. My family took a big hit when I lost the Double-Bar H."

"And when you get it back?" She hated that she sounded desperate, felt desperate.

His eyes went very sad. "Even then, I don't think I'm the guy you're looking for, Shelby. Maybe you're right. Maybe things with Jill changed me more than I want to admit. I guess when things fell apart with her, I lost the fire. I just want to be a cowboy, not a father or a husband."

He hadn't ever pretended any different.

She nodded, swiped at her face, and swallowed back the tears she didn't want to shed in front of him. This wasn't his fault, wasn't anybody's fault. It just wasn't meant to be.

And if she kept telling herself that, she might believe it one of these days. A month or two from now, maybe longer. Much longer.

Taking a deep breath, she said the death-blow words that, a few hours ago when they'd been picnicking by the watering hole and watching hawks soar high above, she never would've expected to be saying. "I can't do this if we're not headed in the same direction. I wish I could, but I can't."

She braced herself for anger. Instead, he caught her close, and wrapped her in a warm, tight embrace. "I'm sorry," he said into her hair. "I'm so sorry."

The feel of his arms around her and the pained rasp in his voice said this was real, it was really happening. Choking back a sob, she hugged him back. "Not your fault. But I need to go. I'll . . ." She swallowed and forced a smile. "I'll see you around, cowboy."

And then she bolted out the door.

He didn't try to stop her. Maybe he said her name just as the door closed. But the word was full of grief and regret, and it wasn't loud enough to call her back.

Out in the Subaru, she sat for a few seconds with her forehead pressed to the steering wheel and her heart pounding a sick, shuddering rhythm in her chest. He didn't come after her, and she didn't blame him. Because she hadn't just broken Rule Twelve, she had also shattered the unstated corollary, good old not-so-lucky number thirteen: *if you have a summer fling with a cowboy, for God's sake, don't fall for him.*

17

This isn't just any old heartburn.
It's a MegaFizz heartburn!

Foster watched her brake lights disappear while he tried like heck to catch his breath and put his head back on straight. Which wasn't easy when all the oxygen had gotten vacu-sucked out of the room, like he was standing in an air lock that'd just been vented, and any minute the outer doors would open up and *whoosh*, out he'd go, into outer space with all the other garbage.

Okay, maybe not. But that was about how it felt, or as if his insides had been removed, leaving his chest aching and hollow.

"It was the right thing to do," he told Vader. "Better to end things now than let it go on and blow up later."

The dog didn't give him a "whuff" or a tail wag, just looked at him with a doggy expression that was either accusation or mild indigestion.

Restless, Foster prowled the downstairs, moving things that didn't need to be moved, like the broken headstall hanging over the back of a chair and his white straw hat, which had found its way to the table next to the door, though not yet onto his head. It wasn't until he had shuffled through a couple of catalogs that had come in since the Great Purge and rearranged the afghan twice that he admitted he was looking for his phone, that he needed to talk to the one person he trusted to make absolute sense, except sometimes when it came to her kids.

Ten minutes, three dust bunnies, and the can of whipped cream he and Shelby had emptied a couple of nights ago later, he found the phone under his nightstand.

He powered it up, mildly surprised that the battery still had a charge, and took a minute to remember how the menus worked.

Tish answered on the third ring, with a cheery "Hey, little brother. What's cooking?"

"Ah . . ." He hesitated, suddenly not sure he was ready to talk about it, even with her. "Nothing much. What's up with you guys?"

"Oh, you know. Summer leagues, barbecues, pool parties, episode number four hundred and two in the ongoing saga of 'no, you can't have your own phones at the ages of seven, six, and four' . . . In other words, business as usual." She laughed. "Which probably makes the single thing sound pretty good right about now, huh?"

Before, that would've gotten a "You know it." Now, though, it brought a pang. "I guess."

Her voice shifted. "Are you okay?"

No, he wasn't okay. He was torn up over losing

what had seemed like the perfect relationship, and hated knowing that Shelby was hurting, too. And worse, that he'd been the one who'd done the hurting. Part of him wished that he could've felt elation rather than panic when she dropped the "I'm falling for you" bomb. He wasn't that guy, though, couldn't be that guy.

Problem was, if he told Tish the whole story, she would march up one side of him and down the other, and demand that he make it up to Shelby and ask her to give him another chance. So instead, he said, "I'm fine. Just wanted to say hi, check in on the spawn, that sort of thing."

She wasn't buying it. "Seriously, Foster. What's wrong?"

"I sent Old Winslow another offer the other day, and for a change he didn't tell me to go pound sand right off the bat. Told me to give him a week or two to think about it, and he'd get back to me."

"That's great news! I'll keep my fingers crossed for you."

"Keep 'em crossed for all of us, not just me. This is a family thing. It's going to need a little work, of course." Okay, lots of work, but he was up for it. "You and the kids could come out, and Mom and Dad. It'll be like old times. All of us back where we belong."

"Whoa there, Sparky. No offense, but I've said it before and I'll say it again . . . You need to be doing this for you, not the rest of us."

"I know, but—"

"But nothing. Like it or not, you're the only cowboy

in the family. Mom and Dad are happy being condo dwellers, and I've got myself a white picket fence here in the burbs. Don't get me wrong—I respect what you're doing, but please tell me you're doing it because you want the Double-Bar H for yourself, not because you're trying to make something up to the rest of us, or Grandpa's memory or something."

Had the air suddenly gotten thinner all of a sudden? "It's the right thing to do. I'm the one who lost the family's ranch, so I'm the one who needs to get it back."

"Family isn't a piece of land. It's family."

"I know that, but the Double-Bar H is important, too. I don't want us to lose those memories."

"They're memories. They stick with us wherever we go."

"Ugh. Have you always been this annoying?" He kept his tone light, but something had gone shaky inside him.

"You only call me annoying when I'm telling you stuff you don't want to hear."

"Which is often. Admit it, you dig playing devil's advocate."

"Maybe, but only because I want what's best for you." Her tone went serious. "It's because I love you, Foster, and I want you to be happy."

"I . . ." He stalled out, not because he didn't usually say it back, or because he was mad at her, but because the idea had suddenly gotten complicated. "Thanks, Tish, and right back at you. For now, though, I think I'm going to beat a retreat from this conversation. I'll talk to you later, okay?"

"Sure thing. Better yet, come visit." She paused. "And, Foster?"

"Yeah?"

"Call me when you're ready to talk about what's really bothering you, okay?"

His chuckle felt rusty. "I will." But after he disconnected, he stared at the phone for a long time, replaying the conversation, aware that while she had told him before not to buy back the Double-Bar H just because he thought he owed it to the family, this was the first time it had resonated a little.

But if he didn't buy the ranch, what else would he do with himself?

He scowled around the bunkhouse, which was nice enough but hadn't ever been intended as his final stop, and then out to his truck, which sat in the drive with its nose pointed down the road, as if saying *let's go*.

"Heck with it." He told Vader to stay put and headed for the truck, but not because he was hitting the road. No, he was headed for the barn. Horses made sense, even when nothing else did.

When he flipped on the barn lights, he got a chorus of hopeful whickers from the stalled horses, and felt, for the first time since Shelby came up on his porch and he got a look at her face, like he could breathe. Bypassing Brutus, he made straight for Loco's stall. "Hey there, partner. You up for a ride?"

Shelby got Lizzie settled for the night, which wasn't easy given that she was overtired, wired from the trail ride and too many cookies, and really wanted to sleep in the barn even though there weren't any more foals due. On the plus side, though, Lizzie was worked up enough that she didn't notice that her mother was on another planet, and not a happy, green-and-blue one. Something more like Mars—bleak, windy, and a weird color.

It was past eleven by the time Lizzie finally conked out. But even though Shelby's body was exhausted, her head was far from ready to quit for the night. Her thoughts spun and her chest ached, and if removing her heart and setting it aside for a little while had been an option, she totally would've gone for it.

Unfortunately, she was stuck with her heart, and the ache that came with it. How had she let this happen? She didn't want to be in almost-love, and if she did, she would've done it with someone who made more sense.

Right?

Finally giving up on the idea of sleep, she found her flip-flops and headed for the kitchen. Maybe she could eat herself into a sugar coma or, failing that, at least reorganize things for breakfast in the wake of Hurricane Rose and the Kitchen Gadgets of Doom.

Hey, that was almost a slogan. Or how about *Welcome to Mustang Ridge, where strangers are family and some of the family members are strange*?

She managed a tired chuckle as she came up the back stairs to the kitchen, but it was interrupted by a jaw-cracking yawn. "This is stupid," she told herself. "You should be in bed."

"Amen, sister." Krista lifted a fork. "Join the midnight snack club." Seated at the butcher block counter, she had a messy plate in front of her and a glass of milk off to one side.

Shelby missed a step in surprise, but then gave a big sigh of relief as some of the terrible tightness loosened in her chest. "Bring it on. What've you got?"

"It's one of Mom's Napoleons. Don't tell Gran."

"Tell her what? As far as I see, you're just getting rid of something that'll upset her." Snagging a fork from the drying rack, Shelby took the chair opposite her. "Make that *we're* getting rid of it." She dug in, feeling like she could finally breathe again after far too long. The first couple of forkfuls were just a chocolate binge, but eventually the taste worked its way past her misery. "Hey, this doesn't suck."

"Decent, huh? It's no Herman, granted, but it's got some texture."

"Herman." Shelby took a guilty look over her shoulder at the cold room. "Shoot. I need to feed him. Can't believe I almost forgot." Actually, she could.

"Gran didn't do it?"

"She was pretty distracted this afternoon." They both were.

"Yeah." Krista grimaced. "This just in . . . they're staying."

It took Shelby a moment to reorient, but in a way she was grateful to focus on something other than the part of her that was labeled "Foster" and kept saying *I can't believe I fell for him, I can't believe I told him, I can't believe I broke up with him.* "Your parents?"

"No, the cartoon chipmunks. Of course my parents." She made a face. "Sorry for sniping. I'm in a mood, obviously. Anyway, it turns out that my mom has been wanting to come back for a while to—ahem—*share* her new culinary expertise with the guests, and she decided that now was the perfect time, what with Bertie going on maternity leave." She paused. "And I'll admit that after you and I talked about Gran, I mentioned to my dad that it's getting to the point where she can't do all of it on her own, even with a stellar assistant. But this wasn't what I was thinking. No way, no how, and certainly not as a drop-in 'Hi, we're here, where should we put our six tons of luggage and kitchen crap?' kind of thing!"

Shelby hesitated. "What did your dad say?"

"Not much. He's happy to be back in his workshop and hanging out with Gramps, and isn't going to go to war over this. Which means, yippee, I've got my parents back, indefinitely."

"Um . . . congratulations?"

"Yeah. Not so much." Krista sighed. "Don't get me wrong. My dad is great in his own, nonconfrontational way, and I do love my mom. She was the first one on board with the dude ranch idea, and she helped me bring the others around. But when we actually sold off most of the stock and started building the cabins, she just . . . I don't know. Decompressed or something. It doesn't bother my dad—he's just happy he's got time to fiddle with his gadgets now—but even he admits that she's changed. She used to be in charge of the books, while Gran did most of the cooking. Now she doesn't want anything to do with the paperwork. She wants to be Emeril."

"It can't have been easy, being the daughter-in-law most of her life."

"You're right. And Gran . . . well, she has her ways. I sympathize with my mom, I really do. But that doesn't change the fact that Gran's an awesome ranch cook and she's got a great system that works for the guests. Even Herman adds a little je ne sais quoi to things."

"Yes. Yes, he does"

"Meanwhile, Mom . . ." Krista regarded a forkful of Napoleon. "She has flashes of brilliance in the kitchen, I'll admit it. But she also has plenty of 'what the hell is this?' moments and routine flake-outs that weren't a big deal when it was just us, but became a big problem when people started paying us to feed them at regular intervals."

"I take it you can't ban her from the kitchen?"

"Nope. She and Dad have equal shares in the ranch, along with my grandparents, Jenny, and me." She grimaced. "And honestly? I don't want to tell her she can't be in the kitchen. She's my mom, and she really loves cooking. I know, I know, this is business and I have to protect Gran. But still. I'm hoping we can come up with some sort of middle ground. Maybe Mom could do family meals and Gran can handle the guests . . . though that's assuming they can find a way to share the same air."

Shelby took a pointed look around at the pink plastic bins stacked haphazardly in the corner near the freezers, the as-seen-on-TV appliances that crowded out Gran's enameled mixers and blenders, and the various jars and bottles, not all of them labeled, that had appeared on the storage shelves. "It's not going to be easy."

"Probably not." Krista sighed. "I won't ask you to run interference."

"You don't have to. It's in my job description."

"Not the way I remember it."

"Please. You and Gran have done more than Lizzie and I can ever repay. You took us both in, gave her all the time and space she needed. Then you did the same for me when I didn't even know I needed it, and . . . Darn it." Shelby hung her head as her eyes filled. "Sorry. I . . . Shoot. I thought I had it under control. Sorry, ignore me, please."

"Hey, now. What's this?" Krista reached across and grabbed her wrist. "Oh, heck. You didn't come for an update, did you? You needed a binge of your own. What's wrong? Is it Lizzie? Foster?"

Shelby nodded miserably, throat locking on the words she didn't want to say.

"Which one?"

"Both. Neither. It's me. Darn it." She got up, grabbed a couple of paper towels, and gave her nose a noisy blow. "Sexy."

"I'll use my sleeve as a napkin if it'll make you feel better."

"The sign of a true friend."

"I am. So tell me what's wrong."

Shelby sighed, feeling the tears drain to exhaustion and a dragging pain inside her, the kind that said something awful had happened, reminding her over and over again even when she was trying hard to forget about it, at least for a few minutes. "Foster and I broke up," she said finally.

Krista's eyes widened with shock, then darkened with pain and sympathy. "Oh, sweetie." She was on her feet in a flash and rounded the counter to catch Shelby in a hug. "That rat! What did he do?"

Shelby was surprised to find that she could still laugh. "It wasn't his fault."

"Of course it was. He's the guy, and this is the girls-only midnight snack zone."

"It's okay. I'm okay." Shelby straightened, sniffling. "I thought I could keep things casual, but it didn't work. I didn't realize it until today. I was getting on his case for not telling me about his divorce, and realized I was upset because that meant he used to want a family but doesn't anymore, at least not with me and Lizzie . . . And then I figured out that the only reason it was a problem was that I was starting to see the three of us that way."

"See? I told you it was his fault."

"It's really not. But thanks for being on my side."

Krista hugged her harder. "Always. What can I do to make it better?"

"You just did." The heartbreak that remained wasn't going to go away in a night—far from it—but between the sugar and the sympathy, Shelby could feel herself winding down, thought she might be able to sleep now. Pushing away from the counter, she said, "Thanks for the pastry therapy, and the ear. I think I'm going to pack it in."

"I'm going to call it a night, too." Krista shot a bleak

look around the kitchen. "Tomorrow's going to be a long day."

"I'll be in early to make sure breakfast goes smoothly." And it wasn't like she was going to be able to sleep in. Already, nerves were coiling in her belly at the knowledge that she was going to have to see Foster tomorrow, and the day after that, and the day after that . . .

With a final hug, Krista dumped the plate and silverware in the sink to soak and headed for the far hallway, which led up to her quarters. Turning back at the door, she said, "We're all going to be okay, Shelby. We care about each other, and that means that we'll do our best to work things out with the least damage possible. We might not all get what we want—probably won't—but we'll do our best."

Her throat closed. "That's not how things work where I come from."

"Well, it's how it works here." Krista smiled tiredly. "Get some sleep. Tomorrow is a new day."

As Krista's footsteps faded, Shelby ducked into the cold room to do her final kitchen chore for the day. Suddenly so exhausted that her head spun and her eyes felt dry and gluey, she left the door open and the lights off, and made quick work of giving Herman his dose of flour, water, flat beer, and a slug of Gran's secret concoction out of the hidden bottle.

Inhaling the faint, chilled scent of yeast and feeling her breath hitch on leftover tears, she said, "You know what, Herman? I think you've got the right idea. Asexual reproduction may be the way to go."

It wouldn't be nearly as much fun, granted. But it would take away a whole lot of heartache.

Foster didn't know how long he'd been riding. Long enough that his head had finally quieted down and he didn't want to escape his own skin anymore. Granted, there was still a hurting hollow inside him. He hadn't been looking for a woman he could care about, but he'd found one. She was fiercely loyal, sexy, sensual, and funny as heck. And, most of all, she got the geeky stuff, the junk food, and the silliness that he adored, and had a good touch with the horses. In some ways, she was perfect for him. It was too bad they were completely wrong for each other. It was too bad . . . well, it was just too bad.

Tish's comments were eating at him, more now than ever before. He didn't know if it was because it felt like he was finally getting close to making a deal with Old Winslow, or if it was just easier for him to fixate on that. Or maybe it was that a big part of him still wanted to tell his sister about Shelby. Problem was, he knew what she would say: that he might have to give way on some things if he didn't want to spend the rest of his life solo save for his horse and his dog, and that just because he'd picked the wrong woman before didn't mean he was more likely to make another mistake. Exactly the opposite, in fact.

Or was that was what he was starting to think?

But that was the thing, wasn't it? When it came down to it, there were telling similarities between Shelby and Jill, numero uno being that they both lived a faster, flashier life than he did. And as much as he told himself that Shelby was caring, consistent, and giving, how much did he know about her, really? He had thought he knew Jill well enough, that their chemistry would see them through any rough patches, and he'd been dead wrong. And this time he wasn't talking about a fellow horsewoman, a rodeo queen who knew what it meant to have a ranch.

Thing was, knowing that didn't stop his heart from hurting, didn't stop a large part of him from wanting to ride back down to Mustang Ridge, bang on Shelby's door, and tell her that he wanted to give it a go and see if they could find some middle ground.

But what kind of middle ground was there? He didn't want anything long distance, didn't want to move, and she had already said she wasn't planning on sticking around. More, he had to think about Lizzie, too. His heart gave an uncomfortable lurch at the reminder that Shelby and her daughter were a package deal. He didn't know if he could step into the daddy role at this point in his life, or if that would do either of them any good. Sure, he got along fine with the kid when it came to the horses, and he'd been able to help some with the SM, but those were small, isolated things. Like when he was hired to work with a problem horse at another ranch, coming in a couple of hours a day, but knowing he could leave when he was done.

Day to day, though, he didn't know if he was ready to try, especially when failing would mean hurting not just himself but two other people he cared about deeply. He needed to know he could do it, needed to know they wouldn't ruin things if they tried. But life didn't come with guarantees, did it? And . . . His brain logjammed, making his fingers tighten on the reins, to the point that Loco shook his head and craned back to shoot Foster a look of *What gives?*

He needed a reality check, that was what gave. But when he reined in at a high spot where he thought he might get reception, and pulled out his phone to call Tish and catch an earful for waking her up, he didn't get even a ghost of a bar on his cell. Maybe the sparse cloud cover was enough to kill the signal, or maybe the satellites were out of range, who knew? Either way, his reach-out was foiled.

But as he started to put his phone away, an icon caught his attention. Apparently, he had mail. And given that he'd only given the address to a few people, he had a pretty good idea who it was from.

Winslow. And hello, irony.

Pulse kicking up a notch, like his system was getting ready to fight words on the screen, he clicked over to his e-mail program. And yep, sure enough, it was from his ex-father-in-law. The subject line said *Re: ranch*, as though there would've been any other reason for the old bastard to get in touch. Should've said *Re: the ranch I made sure my daughter got, only to have it sit empty for the past decade because she's got the attention span of a dummy foal*.

Bracing for the worst, Foster opened the message. "What now? Time to up the price another twenty just for kicks?" He skimmed it.

Stopped. Read it again as his pulse thudded.

The words blurred, and not because the phone was dusty, but because there was no way the message really said *Your last offer is acceptable. Let's make the deal.*

Except that was exactly what it said. The old goat was finally ready to move on, or else he had another deal in the works and needed the money. Or the house had burned down and Foster was about to pay way too much for land. He didn't care, though. He stared at the message a moment longer while his pulse leveled off and his stomach roiled at the realization that this was it.

He was really going to do it. Finally, after all these years, he was going to get the old place back. And not just so the family could visit or to appease his guilt. That was part of it, sure, but he also flat-out wanted the Double-Bar H to be his again, and for the rest of his life. He wanted to run a few cattle, but mostly turn over mustangs, taking likely prospects from the gathers and putting a good start on them, making them into solid citizens that would suit the amateur riders who made up the bulk of the horse trade these days. He wanted to wake up in the main bedroom, with its creaky third board and sticky window, and he wanted to knock back his first cup of sludge-black coffee sitting on the porch. And yeah, maybe he wasn't alone in the hazy images—dreams, fantasies, whatever. Maybe in the far-off future he saw himself with a wife, a few kids—that was what a rancher did, after all. He had his family, made his legacy. But no matter how hard he tried, he couldn't plug Shelby and Lizzie into the mental pictures.

He had tried to make it fit before, and had spent the

past eight years digging himself out from underneath the mistake. This, though, wasn't a mistake. It was what he'd been working toward for so long, and he needed to remember that, and not let himself get derailed.

Moments later, he had fired off an e-mail of a single word: *Agreed.*

Message failed. Do you want to save and resend later?

"Sure. Whatever." He closed the program, dropped the phone back in his pocket, and breathed the night air, waiting for it to hit him that he was getting the old place back. It was everything he'd wanted, everything he'd been working toward. Except as Loco shifted beneath him, mouthing his bit, and the cool night made its way through his jacket, Foster had to admit that he wasn't excited, wasn't particularly happy. He was just . . . tired. Let down. Something.

And that something had brown hair and laughing eyes, and had told him she was falling for him.

18

The next morning, Shelby dragged herself out of bed feeling like she'd been on the wrong end of a roundup. Like underneath it. Her eyes were scratchy, her head hurt, and her throat was sore, and if she'd been at home, she totally would've called in dead to work. She couldn't leave Gran in the lurch, though, especially not with Rose in the picture.

Needing the comfort, she pulled on black pants and her old chunky boots and headed for the kitchen. She went in through the front door, then paused, sniffing, as a cold weight settled in her stomach, an unease separate from heartache.

There was nothing warm and yummy in the air. No yeast, no sugar, no cinnamon . . . no nothing.

Her pulse kicked as she headed down the hall, calling, "Gran?"

"I'm . . . I'm in here," came the wobbly answer from the kitchen, almost inaudible.

Had she fallen? Had a heart attack? The scenarios whipped through Shelby as she hurried into the kitchen. "What's wrong? What—" She broke off at the sight of the older woman standing at the main counter, hunched over Herman's bowl. His towel was off and the room smelled stale.

Gran's face was ravaged and gray, her eyes stark. "He's dead."

Shelby's stomach plummeted and she hurried to Gran's side. "What . . . How . . ."

"She killed him."

"Rose? No." Shelby couldn't believe it. There was a difference between being oblivious and being outright cruel.

"We've always argued, but I never thought . . ." Gran pulled the bowl closer, wrapped it in her arms. "How could she?"

A split second later, every fiber of Shelby went *Oh, no!* and her stomach plunged toward her toes as she realized something awful. Really, truly horrible. And having to do with an unmarked bottle that hadn't looked exactly right. She had been too caught up in her own misery, too exhausted to see it last night . . . but now she did.

What had she done?

"Um . . . ," she began, then faltered.

"I knew Rose wanted the kitchen, but I never thought she would sink to this. He's our Herman." Snapping upright, Gran shoved away from the counter and, fists balled, headed for the back hallway and the stairs leading up. "I'm going to go up there right now and—"

"Wait—"

"No, don't try and stop me. I gave her my son and

put up with her garbage, but this is too much. I'm going to—"

"*It was me!*" Shelby's shout echoed in the kitchen, and then she covered her mouth with both hands, stifling a sob as the other woman—her boss and friend—froze and then, slowly, turned back.

"Shelby?" It wasn't accusatory so much as baffled.

"It was an accident. Last night . . . the bottles . . . I thought you'd just put the secret sauce in a new container, and I dumped it in. I'm sorry." It came out as a whisper. "It must've been something Rose brought in. The bottles must've gotten mixed up on the shelf."

Gran's eyes flooded anew. "I . . . I thought she did it on purpose. We've played tricks on each other off and on through the years, but this . . ."

"I know. I'm sorry. I'm so sorry." Shelby peered into the bowl and cringed at the sight of a slick, liquid gray mass. "Are you sure he's . . ."

"Gone." Gran came back over, retrieved the towel, and draped it over the bowl, smoothing down the edges so they hung neatly. "He's gone." She looked small and tired, making Shelby's heart hurt. She wanted to apologize, but she couldn't undo what she had done.

How had she been so careless? She was supposed to be protecting Gran's back, not stabbing it.

"Gran," she said softly. "I think you should take the morning off. I'll manage breakfast."

"But the baking . . ." She trailed off, stricken, because there wouldn't be any baking. At least not the way there normally was.

"I'll have Tipper clean out the bakery in town. We'll make do."

"No, don't use store-bought. There are . . ." Gran's voice broke. "There are some of those nasty yellow yeast packets in the back of the pantry, behind the extra bottles of vanilla. You can use those for today."

"I will." Shelby wanted to hug her but didn't know how. Not after what she had done. "Go home. Take a few hours." Hopefully her Arthur hadn't yet left for the day. Either way, Shelby would go tell Krista. If anyone could help, it'd be her.

"Okay." Gran hefted the bowl, held it wrapped in her arms. "But I want you to promise me something."

"Anything."

"Don't tell anyone about Herman. Not a soul, got it? I don't . . . I need some time."

"But Krista—"

"No," Gran said, her wobbly voice gaining some volume. "Nobody can know. Not Krista, not Lizzie, not even Foster."

That brought a pang. But Shelby nodded. "Whatever you want. And, Gran . . . I'm sorry. So sorry."

There was no "poosh" or casual wave. Just a tired nod. "It was an accident. You didn't mean it."

No, but she had done it all the same. She'd gotten so wrapped up in things with Foster that she hadn't paid enough attention. Herman's demise was bad enough. What if it had been even worse? What if she'd hurt an actual person, or one of the animals, or burned the place down? Her thoughts raced as Gran shut the door gently behind her, making her feel ill.

This was a disaster. *She* was a disaster, and she had taken down Herman and Gran with her, right when the kitchen needed to be at its strongest to withstand a semihostile takeover. Which was probably why Gran didn't want anyone to know what had happened. Shelby didn't know how delaying things would make a difference, but if that was what Gran wanted, she would get it. Which meant she needed to turn out a fabulous breakfast and pull together a day's worth of bread without a starter.

She took a deep breath. "Focus," she told herself. "You can do this." She warmed up the ovens, found the venerable *Joy of Cooking* that Gran sometimes used to prop open the side door, and dug out the yeast packets from the back of beyond. All the while, her stomach churned and tears leaked from her eyes while she fought to hold it together like never before.

This time yesterday, she'd been teasing Gran about her apron, which had *Kiss the Cook* embroidered on it in six different languages, and had been a gift from Jenny. And she'd been looking forward to riding out with Foster and Lizzie, having a picnic, having fun. *Family* fun, darn it. And now . . .

Now nothing. Just bake.

By the time Tipper and Topper arrived to start setting up, Shelby had bread under way. It wouldn't be up to the ranch's usual standards, but the new guests wouldn't know and the regulars wouldn't say anything once they found out Gran had gone back to bed. Well, Rose would probably say something, but that would've happened anyway. The idea of facing her—of facing any of them, really—made Shelby want to set off across the backcountry barefoot, but she cowboyed up and got breakfast on the table, assuring Krista and the others in the family dining room that Gran was fine, nothing to see here, move along. She pulled it off, too, even earning a stiff nod of approval from Rose for the quick berry sauce she'd whipped up to top the buckwheat pancakes that had been a Hail Mary when a whole batch of muffins failed to rise.

Shelby was just about to escape when Krista scooted back her chair and snagged her arm, tugging her down. "Hang on. I need to give you the heads-up on something."

"Uh-oh. What?" *Please, don't let there be biscuit complaints.*

"My dad was waxing the RV last night around midnight—don't ask—and met up with Foster and Loco coming back in from a ride."

Aw, darn it. Loco. It hurt more than she would've thought, even after everything that had already happened in the past twelve or so hours. "It's his horse."

"That's not the part I wanted to tell you." She paused. "He told my dad that his ex's father finally accepted his offer. It looks like Foster will be getting his old place back sooner rather than later."

"He . . ." Shelby swallowed hard. "Oh. Well, congratulations. To him, I mean. I know it's something he's been working toward for a long time." Sort of, and only because she'd dragged it out of him. And, darn it, she wasn't going to cry again, not in front of everybody.

"I just . . . I wanted you to know." Krista's eyes were

full of sympathy. The old Shelby might've done the "don't pity me" thing, but now she wanted to lean on her friend like there was no tomorrow.

There was always a tomorrow, though.

"Thanks. I . . . thanks." Shelby gave her a one-armed hug and stood. "I'll see you all later," she said, louder. "Fried chicken for lunch. Be there or be square." She left on the heels of an appreciative rumble from the small crowd, but the hallway blurred around her. *Don't cry,* she warned herself. *Don't you dare cry. You're tougher than that.* She had made it through a divorce and handled life with an SM child. She could deal with this, too.

A last few straggling guests were headed along the gravel path to the dining hall as she came down the main stairs. Determined to be professional, she found a smile for the harried-looking parents and trio of hopped-up little boys, and called, "Enjoy your breakfast!"

The woman blinked at her, blurry-eyed. "Please tell me there's coffee."

"Absolutely," Shelby reassured her. "I recommend the local blend—it's called 'Mud in a Cup,' but don't let the name fool you. As far as I'm concerned, it's better than the best that Starbucks ever poured." Thanks in part to a couple of adjustments she had made to the brew, thank-youverymuch.

One of the boys—eleven or so, wearing braces, a buzz cut, and an *American Idol Live* T-shirt—piped up, "What about the horses?"

"They get their own breakfasts," she told him. "The dining hall is just for people."

He gave her a "duh" eye roll. "I know that. But when do we get to ride?"

"After breakfast," the dad said. "Just like the last ten times you asked."

Shelby's smile got closer to being real. "You'll have a blast. The horses are very well trained, and the wranglers are top-notch." To the parents she said, "Stace is great with the kids, and Foster . . . he's, um, the trail boss, and knows the backcountry like nobody else. He'll make sure you have some fabulous rides."

The dad grinned. "Friends of ours came last year and couldn't stop talking about it. We can't wait to get started."

The mom just said, plaintively, "Coffee?"

"Go." Shelby waved them on their way. "The caffeine is on the right as you walk in. Do not pass go, do not collect."

As they moved off, she realized it actually made her feel worse that she'd enjoyed the exchange, as if she was finally hitting her stride just as things were falling down around her.

What was she supposed to do now?

She had to go talk to Gran, she knew, and see if there was any way she could make amends. But on the way, needing a moment to herself, she diverted into the barn, coming to a halt outside Loco's stall.

The glossy bay didn't give her his usual "what have you got for me?" whicker. Instead, he stayed at the back of his stall with one hind foot cocked and his eyes at half-mast.

"You're tired, huh, buddy?" Yesterday's trail ride

had been slow and easy, but there was no telling how hard and far Foster had ridden by moonlight.

Pressing her forehead to the bars of the stall door, she sighed. "Oh, Loco. What am I going to do now? I don't know if I can handle another whole month here, not like this." She didn't want to see Foster every day, knowing she wouldn't be with him every night, and she didn't want to make things worse in the kitchen. She'd been hired on to help Gran, but it was starting to feel like too many cooks, especially if Rose would be taking some of the load off. "I don't know. Maybe we should just leave."

"Leave?" The word was a plaintive little sound, stopping her heart. Seconds later, a nearby stall door rolled open and Lizzie stepped out, eyes wide and unhappy. "Why?"

For the first time, instead of *ohmigod, she's talking!* Shelby's only thought was *oh, crap.* She opened her mouth to say that she didn't mean it, she was just blowing off some steam . . . but that would have been a lie. Because suddenly, the idea of hitting the road sounded awfully good. She could go back to work, back to her life, and Lizzie would get the therapy she needed now that she was talking again. Gertie would be delighted to see her, and thrilled with the progress she'd made. There wouldn't be any awkwardness with Foster, and Rose and Gran would be forced to work something out, taking the pressure off of Krista and—whether or not she wanted to admit it—Gran herself.

Swallowing the grief that lumped in her throat at the thought of leaving Mustang Ridge, she said, "Krista's mother is here now, baby. They don't need another cook."

"So? Y-you can help F-Foster with the b-barn."

"It's not that easy, Dizzy Girl."

Her little brows furrowed. "Krista's making you l-leave?"

"No, it's—"

"Is it because of m-me?"

"Of course not." But she'd hesitated a split second too long.

Lizzie's already chalky face headed toward crumpling and her eyes brightened with tears. "It is. It's because I'm t-t-t—"

Heart plummeting all over again, Shelby dropped to her knees. "No! Sweetie, no. I'm so proud of how brave you've gotten, how much you're talking, all of it. So proud. But I'll be just as proud of you back home. Don't you want to see your friends and show them how far you've come?"

Her lower lip poked out. "I want to stay with L-Lucky."

We don't always get what we want, kiddo. Trust me on that one. "He belongs to Krista."

"I don't care." The tears welled up, broke free. "Foster says—"

"Don't cry, baby."

"I'm not a baby!" The shout surprised them both. Shelby rocked back on her heels as a suddenly red-faced Lizzie advanced, hands balled into fists. "Stop ordering m-me around!"

"I didn't mean—"

"Yes, you d-did! You're always telling me what to do, or d-dragging me around!"

Something went *snap* inside Shelby. "I wouldn't order you around if you'd talk to me, Lizzie! Tell me what you want, what you need, and I'll do my best."

"I want us to stay here forever!" This shout was louder than the last, with the stutter gone.

"Well, we can't!" Shelby yelled back.

Lizzie sucked in a breath to retort, but Shelby held up a hand and used her Mom voice. "Hold it right there. I think we both need a time-out." God forgive her, she was telling her kid to shut up. But she needed the moment. After a ten-count, she exhaled and said, "Look, I haven't made up my mind. I have to talk to Krista and Gran." And Foster, though that would be the hardest conversation of all. She needed him to know it wasn't his fault, any of it. He'd been honest all along. She was the one who forgot to listen. "And you and I can talk about it before I decide." She might even get Gertie on the phone. She didn't want to mess up their progress, but she also didn't want to give in just because Lizzie was on the verge of a tantrum. For a change, she wanted to do what worked for her, not anybody else.

Maybe this was what the others had meant when they said she needed to do some things for herself. Or maybe not. Her head was spinning, and she wasn't going to get it any clearer like this, with the familiar barn smells surrounding her, and her darling daughter glaring at her like she'd just fondued a puppy.

"I'm going for a walk. Do you want to come?" she

asked after a brief hesitation, losing Mom points for hoping her kid said no.

Lizzie scowled and shook her head.

"Are you hungry?" Shelby didn't even know if Lizzie had made it to breakfast. Another couple of demerits to go along with the giant yelling penalty.

Lizzie turned away. With her shoulders hunched, she looked too much like her old self. But her face was flushed and angry, even the tear streaks better than blankness.

Guilt echoed through Shelby, but she couldn't undo any of what had happened—not getting in too deep with Foster, not poisoning Herman, and not upsetting her kid. Leaving was starting to feel like the most sensible answer. They were only supposed to be there a few more weeks, anyway. Maybe it would be better to make the break sooner than later.

"Okay. I'll be back in the kitchen in an hour. Mind your manners and remember the rules." That got Shelby a bad-tempered shrug, but she was feeling pretty bad-tempered herself, so let it go and headed out of the barn.

Her heart tugged, though, and she turned back at the door. "I'm sorry, Lizzie. I don't want to fight with you." She faltered, remembering how Foster had said the same thing last night. "We'll talk later, I promise."

Silence.

As Foster headed for the barn, he was dreading the day ahead. Over the years, he had built up his defenses against Sunday mornings, with the new greenhorns coming in and him having to deal with the inevitable battle to keep the puffed-up "I rode once on a vacation in St. Croix and know everything" dudes from committing suicide by annoyed equine, while not scaring the "I rode once on a vacation in St. Croix and got run away with" wimps to the point that they refused to throw a leg over.

Today, though, his defenses were seriously low. He was running on, like, three hours of sleep, too much junk food, and a skunked beer he'd found in the back of the fridge, left over from New Year's, maybe. "Some celebration," he muttered. But it'd been impossible to celebrate getting the ranch back given the way things had gone with Shelby.

Yeah, maybe he'd said what he needed to say for a change, and yeah, maybe he was doing what was best for both of them. All three of them. But he sure as heck didn't feel good about it. He wanted to see her, wanted to talk to her, wanted to tell her . . . Hell, he didn't know what. All he knew was that he didn't want to leave it like this.

She wasn't in her cabin or the kitchen, though, so he headed for the barn, hoping that they could have a few minutes of privacy before breakfast ended and the dudes descended.

Ducking through the door, into the welcome shadows of the main barn, he called, "Shelby?"

There was a scuffle in one of the back stalls, a muffled sob.

"Aw, heck." He covered the distance in four long strides. "Shelby-sweet, don't . . ." He trailed off, staring into Sassy's stall. "Lizzie? What are you doing?"

Dumb question. The kid-size saddle that Lizzie used on Peppermint was perched on the broodmare's broad back, stirrups sticking out on either side, so it looked like a flattened leather spider. Meanwhile, Lizzie had her head buried in Sassy's side, red-faced and puffing as she struggled to get her pony-size cinch around the huge belly. Nearby, Lucky was tugging at an overturned muck bucket, which Lizzie had no doubt used as a booster to get the saddle onto the mare's back. The foal looked devilishly entertained and Sassy, bless her, was ignoring the proceedings much as she ignored her foal's antics. But Foster's blood went cold as the what-ifs ran through his mind.

What if she fell under the mare and got trampled? What if Lucky had put a foot through the rope handles of the muck bucket and yanked it out from underneath her? What if she had overbalanced and hit her head on the wall or, worse, the corner feeder? He saw each scenario in his mind's eye, thanks to a lifetime of being around horses and witnessing the freak accidents they could cause and suffer. But for the first time, each image hit home, making him want to rub his eyes and scrub them away while his pulse rate shot into the stratosphere.

She's fine, he told himself. *She didn't get hurt*.

Which was good, because he was going to kill her.

"Lizzie," he said sharply. "Stop what you're doing and come out of the stall this minute!"

The set of her shoulders and the tilt of her head said she knew he was there, but she kept fighting with the girth, not seeming to realize that there was a good foot of flabby chestnut belly between the end of the cinch and the bottom of the leathers, and it wasn't going to happen.

Lucky for him, she hadn't thought to go back into the tack room for a longer girth.

He strode into the stall and caught one of her arms. "Young lady—"

The moment his fingers made contact, she spun and launched herself at him. Lucky scattered behind his dam as Foster raised his hands to grab the little girl, hoping to keep her from punching him where it hurt. He caught her arms, held her tight . . . and then froze when she wrapped herself around him and clung, shaking.

She wasn't attacking him. She was hugging him as if her life depended on it.

Something shifted deep inside him, and he looked quickly around for whatever had scared her so badly, though he knew there wasn't anything there. Just the barn and a half-tacked broodmare who hadn't been ridden in months.

"Lizzie, what is it? Are you hurt?" She didn't seem it. He didn't see any blood, and she'd been just fine a few seconds ago. "Okay, now. You're okay. Ah . . ." He looked around, realizing he had a potential mess on his hands. She was stronger than she looked, making it impossible for him to peel her off without hurting her. Meanwhile, Lucky was pulling on the free end of the cinch, making the saddle tip across Sassy's broad back. Any second now, it was going to come down on him.

But the little devil had already survived worse, and Lizzie needed Foster's attention right now.

"Come on. Out we go." He swung her up in his arms and perched her on his hip like a little kid. And even though her legs dangled down past his knees, she wrapped them around him, buried her head under his chin, and hung on tight, the way Tish's kids did, only different, because here he wasn't Uncle Foster, and something was very wrong. Which left him standing there, cuddling Lizzie and using his spooky greenie mantra on her. "Whoa there, easy. Settle down. Nobody's gonna hurt you. You're okay now. We'll work this through, and everything's gonna be fine." He hoped. Had Shelby told her they'd broken up? Was that what this was about? Heart tugging, he rubbed her back. "Shhh, little one. I've got you."

"Hey, Foster," Stace sang out as she came into the barn. "Ready for a new group of—" She broke off, eyes widening. "What's wrong?"

"I don't know."

"Want me to get Shelby?"

That was the obvious answer. She would know how to handle a meltdown—she'd done it before, would undoubtedly do it again. This was part of being a parent, and he wasn't. But there was something about having those skinny little arms wrapped around his neck, something about that utter trust, that had him turning away from Stace.

"I got her. Can you untack Sassy and take care of things in there?"

"Untack?" She looked in the stall, and her eyes widened. "Sure. Of course."

While she set about rescuing the saddle from Lucky

and vice versa, Foster juggled Lizzie enough to ease the choke hold she'd gotten around his neck, and peel her back a little. "Come on, now. You know I'm not as good as your mom at the guessing games, so you're going to have to talk to me."

Her eyes were wet, her face miserable.

"Are you mad at me?"

Nothing. Then, slowly, a faint head shake.

His relief that she hadn't backslid all the way warred with concern. "Then what is it? Come on, you know you can talk to me."

"I—I—I . . ." She buried her face in his neck.

The soft stutter tore at him. "Easy there. Take a deep breath and try again."

She just hung on tighter, soaking his shirt with silent tears.

"You're fine. It's gonna be fine. But if I'm going to fix it, you need to tell me what's going on."

Slow down. Think. "Why were you saddling Sassy?"

Nothing. Then, softly, "S-so we could ride to the w-waterfall and live there."

Uh-oh. "Uh, why would you want to live at the waterfall?"

"Because L-Lucky needs me. I c-can't leave him."

The heartburn intensified, searing down to his gut and flooding him with the sudden urge to slap a couple of saddles on the nearest horses and head off to the grotto with Lizzie and her mother both. Which didn't make any sense . . . but neither did what he was hearing. "You're not leaving for another month."

"Mom said." The two words came out sulky, angry, agonized.

"She said you were leaving now?"

"Yes!" Her eyes filled anew and spilled over, and she sucked in a shuddering sob. "But I don't want to go. L-Lucky needs me!"

"I . . ." His throat locked up as the knowledge of what he should do warred with what he wanted to do. He knew damn well he should take Lizzie to her mom and let the two of them figure things out while he stepped back, putting distance between himself and a family unit that didn't fit into his life. Not now, and not into the new-old life he was in the process of building for himself. But what he wanted to do was whatever it took to make sure they didn't leave, not now. Not ever.

Lizzie's lower lip poked out mutinously. "You said you could fix it. You promised."

Aware of Stace's eyes on him, he eased the little girl down and knelt in front of her, holding her arms partly to keep her from taking off on him, partly because he wasn't ready to let her go. "I'll talk to her."

"Wh-what are you going to say?"

That was the question, wasn't it? "I don't know, Lizzie. But I'll think of something good."

19

Shelby's head hurt. More, her heart hurt, worse than it ever had before, even during the worst of things during her divorce. Maybe that was because by then, she had already mourned the dreams she'd had for her family. And with Lizzie's gradual slide into silence, Shelby hadn't been heartbroken so much as guilty and afraid.

This, though . . . this was heartbreak.

If she left Mustang Ridge, she wouldn't just be saying good-bye to the people and horses she'd come to love—she would also be leaving behind the woman she'd become here, the one who wore pointy boots and butt-hugging jeans, who galloped across moonlit fields and kissed a cowboy. She couldn't stay that person, though. She had already proven that by messing things up with Foster, with Gran, even with Lizzie.

But she could try to fix at least one of those relationships, starting now.

Even though she should've been cried dry by now, tears stung her eyes as she slipped through the side door into the kitchen and breathed in the lingering breakfast scents. The scent of yeast—even from the evil yellow packets—had her breath hitching, and her voice wobbled when she called, "Gran?"

There was no answer, but Gran's cottage had been empty, and Krista had reported seeing her headed this way, carrying Herman's bowl.

On her way through the kitchen, Shelby swiped at a few crumbs that Tipper and Topper had missed in their cleanup, trying not to think about doing her last dinner service, taking her last ride, saying good-bye.

Never seeing Foster or the others ever again.

Her vision blurred as she headed for the back stairs leading up to the family quarters, thinking maybe Gran had gone to talk to Rose or—more likely—Ed. She was nearly there when she heard a soft bumping sound coming from the pantry.

Her pulse kicked, because that wasn't a noise she'd heard before, wasn't one she recognized. And she'd be darned if she walked past it on a day like today. She had to be able to do *something* right. Hoping it wasn't a mouse, and then revising that to hope it was a mouse instead of another snake, she grabbed a big wooden spoon, stopped and exchanged it for a broom, and then tiptoed over to the pantry.

The latch was sprung, the door cracked open, which was no doubt how the little health code violation had gotten in.

Shelby ripped it open, broom raised. "Aha!"

"Aiee!" Gran reeled back and banged into a shelving unit, which dumped a box of graham crackers onto her head.

"Ohmigod!" Shelby dropped the broom and backed away. *Tell me I didn't just do that.*

The older woman clapped a hand to her chest. "Are you *trying* to kill me?"

"I'm sorry." Shelby got a hand over her mouth before a bubble of horrified laughter could erupt. "Oh, Gran. I'm sorry. I'm a train wreck today. Someone should just put me out of my misery."

"Oh, stuff and nonsense. Come in and close the door before anyone else sees." As if the whole broom thing hadn't happened, she turned back to her commercial mixer, which was inexplicably parked on a folding chair in the middle of the pantry.

That wasn't what struck Shelby the most, though. It was more the realization that Gran looked fine. Maybe a little strained around the edges, but her color was good, her face was bright and happy . . . and the familiar blue-and-white bowl was sitting on the shelf beside her, glistening and clean, with a new checkered towel—this one a cheery yellow and white—sitting folded beside it.

"Um, Gran? What are you doing?"

"Why, resurrecting Herman, of course." She gestured to the mixer bowl, which held a floury white slime that smelled like a combination of yeast and feet.

"But he's—"

"Dead. Yes. But you and I are the only people who know that." Her brows drew together and her tone went downright menacing. "Right?"

"Right! Um, yes. I mean no, I didn't tell anyone what

happened. But, Gran. He'd been alive for more than two hundred years."

"Closer to forty, actually."

Shelby shook her head, feeling a little like the first time she met Herman, when she wasn't sure if she was being *Punk'd*, and if not, how she had lost control of the conversation so thoroughly. "I thought Mary Skye started him in eighteen whatever."

Gran nodded. "That's right. And then I left him out in the sun in 'seventy-three when Eddie compound-fractured his arm falling off that pig-eyed sorrel of his. By the time I got back from the doctor, he was toast. Herman, I mean, not Eddie. Eddie was fine."

"You mean . . ." Shelby scrambled to catch up. "So I actually killed Herman the Second?"

"I wouldn't bet on it. When I was stressing about the 'seventy-three incident, Arthur mentioned there being a huge fuss in the kitchen one time when he was a teenager, and that it was something about Herman. I'm betting I'm not the first of the Skye women to do a quick 'now you don't see it, now you do' on the family starter. For all we know, this is Herman the Fourteenth." She patted the mixing bowl. "In fact, I think that's what I'll call him in my head. . . . But we'll just call him Herman for short, okay?" She looked at Shelby like it was a real question, like there was any possibility that she wasn't going to go along with it.

"You never told Rose?"

"I'm telling you," Gran said, as though that made perfect sense.

But I'm leaving. She tried to say it, but couldn't make the words come out, as if she'd gone selectively mute all of a sudden. Apparently, the tree didn't fall far from the apple.

Not seeming to notice the silence—or considering it an answer in itself—Gran added a little more milk, gave it a quick mixer burst, and then tested the slime between her fingers, beaming like she'd been panning for gold and had finally found a few little flakes. "He's ready." She unhooked the mixer bowl and held it over the blue-and-white Herman bowl. "Drumroll please." Without waiting for a response, she poured.

Shelby watched dubiously. "Is it supposed to look the same?"

"It will. It just needs to mature into a sustainable culture. It'll take a few days to establish it, a few weeks for it to really be useful as a starter, and a year or two for the flavors to take hold. We'll run into town and get some good yeast to use for the next couple of weeks, and make the breads really early, just like you did today. With a little luck and a few white lies, nobody ever needs to know there was a little hiccup in our Herman."

Which just made Shelby feel worse about her decision. "I'm not going to be—"

"There," Gran said, interrupting as usual, and letting the mixer bowl clatter onto a nearby shelf. "All better." She turned her attention to Shelby, seeming to see her tear-reddened eyes for the first time. "Oh, honey, please don't look at me like that. It was a sourdough starter, and it was an accident."

"But this morning, I thought . . . You looked heart-broken."

Oh, right. That was me.

"I was. I still am, a little." Gran's lips tightened. "It's still a big deal, losing a Herman. And part of it was the whole Rose thing. You were the one who used the bottle, but she was the one who put it there. Don't worry, though. I'll get her back for it."

"Um—"

"Don't tell Krista. She gets tense when Rose and I fight."

So did Shelby, but that wasn't what mattered right now. What mattered was that she was being given a Get Out of Jail Free card when and where she least expected it, and wasn't sure she deserved it. Not to mention that she was struggling to wrap her head around the idea of Herman the Second, or the Fourteenth, or whatever.

Gran's expression softened. "Not everything is as it seems, Shelby, even when you think you know what's going on. And sometimes the things worth having are worth fighting for. That counts for both kitchen space and men."

Her heart shuddered. "You know. About Foster, I mean. Krista told you."

"She thought you might need to talk . . . or make a change sooner than you had planned."

There went the tears again, not just because it was out there, but because Gran's eyes held only kind compassion. No judgment, no blame. "I don't know what to say," Shelby whispered.

"You don't have to say anything right now, dearie. You just need to take the time you need to make the decision that works best for you and Lizzie. We love you, and we'll support you no matter what."

Her throat closed. "It seems like I've been waiting my whole life to hear someone say that."

"Well, there it is." Gran held out her hands. "I'd hug you, but then you'd get Herman all over you."

Shelby laughed through the tears, and hugged her anyway. "Thank you," she said fiercely. "Thank you so much."

"For what?"

"For everything. For forgiving me, for teaching me, for giving me room to figure some things out on my own . . . for all of it. Most of all, for being you."

"Poosh, go on with you. Who else would I be?" But when Gran stepped back, her eyes were bright and kind, and she patted Shelby's cheek. "It's fine. We're fine. And no matter what you decide, Krista and I will always be here for you."

A safe place, Shelby thought, and felt some of the knots inside her loosen up.

Not all of them, though. Not the ones labeled "Foster." She needed to talk to him, needed to . . . she didn't know. "I hate the idea of leaving." The pang was actual pain. But that didn't mean it'd be the wrong answer.

"We'd hate seeing you go."

"It feels so selfish." She almost whispered it. "Lizzie loves it here, and she's gotten so much better. And leaving you with Rose—"

"Don't. You can't live for everyone else, or you'll

make yourself crazy. Lizzie will adjust, as will we. So I guess the question is . . . what do you want? What would make you happy?"

Another thing nobody had said to her in . . . how long? "I want to say that I can see him every day without it tearing me up, to think we could go back to being friends or something, but I can't. It'd . . ." She hated how choked up she was getting, even though she'd gone in with her eyes wide open. "I . . . darn it, I want to be a grown-up about this!"

But Gran shook her head. "This isn't about whether or not you're a grown-up, dearie. It's about whether or not you're in love."

"I'm not—" For a change, Gran wasn't the one to interrupt. Instead, Shelby interrupted herself. "At least I don't think I am. . . ." But the roller coaster was still there and the crazy feelings hadn't subsided. She wanted to see him, talk to him, be with him, *stay* with him. She pressed a hand to her stomach. "Oh, damn. I can't be. I'm—"

A shrill whistle split the air, thin with distance but unmistakable.

Shelby spun. "*Lizzie!*"

20

When Shelby came charging into the barn, Foster's heart lurched in his chest and he had to stop himself from immediately reaching for her. She was in full-on mama bear mode, eyes flashing and face set in "I can deal with any crisis" lines, reminding him of the first time he saw her. Then he'd thought her lovely, fancy, and a little dangerous. Now he saw the unhappiness beneath, felt it in himself . . . and hoped he was about to make it better, not worse.

He knew the moment her eyes adjusted to the darkness, because her choppy strides faltered and her eyes went from Lizzie to him, and then to the crowd behind him—not just Stace, Ty, and the other staffers, but nearly a dozen early-bird guests who had wanted to get a jump on the horse stuff and were getting a show, instead.

Shelby slowed and stopped, looking at her daughter. "Lizzie? What's wrong?"

The little girl glanced back at Foster, and he nodded encouragement. *Go on,* he urged silently. *You can do it.* And, bless her, she squared her narrow shoulders and faced her mother, tuning out their audience so she could get through this. He hoped.

"I'm s-sorry," Lizzie said in a small voice. "I shouldn't have said those things to you. And I shouldn't have t-t-tried to ride Sassy to the w-waterfall."

Shelby blanched. *"What?"*

He held up both hands in an *it's okay* gesture behind Lizzie's back, and saw Shelby fight to marshal her emotions. He could practically see her counting to ten, twice. And he didn't blame her. If what he'd felt when he saw Lizzie trying to saddle Sassy was even a fraction of what she was used to dealing with . . . well, he had a feeling that being a parent might be an even harder job than he'd originally thought, when it had just been a concept, not a real kid. Back then, he had thought he had a whole bunch of other things to get lined up first, before he took any sort of a run at having a family of his own. Now, though, he was starting to think that he needed to be more flexible, like the horse trainer he was supposed to be. No two greenies came along exactly the same way, at exactly the same speed. Maybe his life was coming along at Brutus speed— slow at first, and with some scuffling and fighting, but then gaining momentum once he was on the right track.

Maybe it had been sleeping on it, or at least what little sleep he'd gotten. Or maybe it had been there for longer than just last night, worming through his subconscious in a series of what-ifs that had come together the moment Lizzie wrapped herself around him and told him to fix things. Right then, he'd felt like a Jedi, a superhero, like he could do anything, possibly even fix his own problems, along with hers. Yeah, it would mean giving up some stuff, making some changes, and he could hear Tish's imaginary "I told you so" in his head. But the thing was, he didn't care. He wanted what he wanted, and he was willing to admit that what he wanted had changed. Maybe on fast-forward, and maybe enough to make him nervous as hell, but still.

It would be worth the risk, though, even knowing that there weren't any guarantees. Not with horses, and not with life.

"I wanted to stay with her and L-Lucky, but they need to l-live here." Lizzie paused, twining her fingers together behind her back. "And I need to be with you, no matter w-what." She added in a small, rebellious voice, "I'd like to s-stay here, though."

Shelby coughed, maybe to hide a disbelieving laugh. "Was that an apology?"

Lizzie nodded, contrite. "I'm sorry, Mama. I'll go back to Boston if that's w-what you w-want."

The statement dug in, tightening Foster's chest, but that was nothing next to the pressure that came when Shelby went down on her knees in front of her daughter and drew her into a bear hug. Her face, visible over Lizzie's shoulder, was luminous. All of the tension was gone, all of the questions and regrets erased in a perfect moment.

Unconditional love, that was what he was seeing. It was the kind of love that changed lives, bound families together, made a man bigger than himself. The kind of love he'd never had before, never wanted, maybe hadn't even recognized. He recognized it now, though, wanted it now.

Wanted them. More than anything, he wanted a life with them.

"I'm sorry," Lizzie said, clutching around her mother's neck. "I didn't mean to be bad."

"You aren't, you weren't." Shelby drew back, then grinned mistily. "Okay, maybe a little. But there've been lots of changes lately. I think we can cut each other a little slack, especially when you're being so brave. Because this, dear kiddo, is pretty brave."

Lizzie looked back over her shoulder at the others, and smiled shyly at Foster.

That put Shelby's attention on him. She steeled herself, stood, and came over to him. "Thank you for doing . . . well, whatever you did here. And I owe you an apology."

His heart twisted, trying to hog-tie itself in his chest. "You don't owe me a damn thing."

"We had an agreement—"

"Yeah, we did. And now I want to renegotiate it." Feeling shaky, he was almost tempted to go down on his knees as she had done with Lizzie, but knew that would just freak them both out. So instead, he took her hands and held on tight, the way he would the lead rope of a wrangly mustang he didn't quite trust to stay put. Then, hoping he would get this right, he said, "I'm sorry I didn't tell you I was married. She was a daddy's girl rodeo queen who took my breath away. We were crazy about each other, and we figured that'd be enough, but it wasn't. I assumed she understood ranching life, she assumed we would keep rodeoing indefinitely, and we were both wrong. We split up, she told her daddy a couple of whoppers, and he took me down. That's the short version. You can have the longer version any time, ask any questions you want. And again, I'm sorry I didn't tell you sooner. Because you were right—that's the sort of thing a man should tell his woman, especially if it's one of the things that's making him head shy when it comes to getting in deeper."

Color had flooded her face as he was talking. Now she blew out a long, shuddering breath. "You don't have anything to apologize for, and you don't owe me an explanation. That's not the kind of relationship we had."

He wanted to spin and bolt like the barn was on fire. Instead, he charged into the blaze. "Maybe. But it's the kind of relationship I want with you. I want to be with you for real, Shelby. You, me, and Lizzie. I want to make it work." Suddenly, he couldn't read her—was that shock or panic? His heart tightened painfully in his chest, feeling like Brutus had just stepped on it. "So . . ." He moistened his suddenly dry mouth. "What do you say?"

Shelby couldn't breathe. This wasn't happening, couldn't be happening. There was no way he was talking about their relationship in front of all these people—an audience for a man who kept himself so very private and closed off. But there was nothing private about this, and nothing closed off about the man standing opposite her. His face was set in its usual calm lines, with a hint of the familiar wariness. But his body was in motion—a shift of balance, a squeeze of her hands, a shrug to shift his collar half an inch on his neck.

He's nervous, she thought, and on the heels of that realization came another, even more astounding one: *this is real.* "But last night—" she began.

"I spooked," he said bluntly. "Instincts, old habits, whatever. I didn't stop to ask myself whether they still applied. I just saw a garden hose move in the bushes, thought 'snake!' and stampeded."

A bubble of laughter came out of nowhere. "Am I the snake or the garden hose here?" she asked, just as Stace muttered behind her, "Really, Foster?"

He colored a little. "I, ah . . . I believe I mentioned that I suck at this. But that's the thing—you get that. You get *me.* And at the same time, I think I get you, too. And there's nothing I want more in this world than to keep learning about you, and being with you and Lizzie. So please, give me another chance. Let's try again, this time for real. Nothing casual, no time limits, just the two of us. The three of us."

Shelby looked down at Lizzie as the ground shifted beneath her, making her feel as if one wrong move would send everything crashing down like a life-size game of Jenga, with pieces falling down around her, taking all her hard-won points with them. But this wasn't about points. It was so much more important than that.

"It wouldn't work," she said, voice wobbling. "You know the person I am here, but she's not real. Back home, I'm always going a million miles an hour, racing from home to work and back again, always hurry-hurry-hurry except when I'm with Lizzie. Even when I am, my brain is still going, keeping score and seeing slogans wherever I look. And half the time they're not even good slogans!" The last came with a clutch of nerves as she realized that her inner advertiser had gone silent. Now she saw the sunset for its beauty, not its potential to sell eye shadow, and she didn't know if that was a good sign or a bad one. She hadn't even come up with a decent blurb for Mustang Ridge.

The lines deepened at the corners of his eyes. "Now who's spooking at garden hoses?"

"I don't . . . I won't . . ." Babble. She took a deep breath. "Krista said you got your family's ranch back." Saying it twisted something inside her. "Congratulations."

"Thanks, but you know what? It's been waiting for me a long time now, and it can keep on waiting if it needs to. What matters is that the potential is there."

"But your family—"

"Never blamed me for what happened as much as I blamed myself. My mom and dad love Flagstaff, and Tish is just as happy to visit me here as there." He paused, voice dropping. "Or wherever I wind up. That's not set in stone, Shelby. The only thing that's set in my head right now is that I want a chance to be with you for real, and see if what we've started here has got a forever future."

Forever. She tried to whisper it, but couldn't. The word stayed locked inside her.

Lizzie gave her a two-handed push toward Foster. "Go on, Mom. You know you w-want to."

When had her kid gotten so smart? Shelby looked down, going misty. "Oh, baby." But this wasn't about what Lizzie wanted, or even about what made sense. It was—at least it could be—about the future.

"I think . . ." She paused, trying to find the words for the fear and excitement that came rocketing through her. That was the great thing about Foster, though. She didn't always need the words. So she gave a little cry and launched herself at him.

He caught her and spun her in a big circle, his laughter rumbling against her as he held her tight and buried his face in her neck. "Does this mean you'll stay until September and give it a chance?" He held her away a little, his face going serious. "You don't have to. You can go back now if you want, and I'll come out when the season is over. Spend the winter. I've got a few old rodeo contacts I can lean on for a job. Or—"

She put a hand over his mouth. "Stop." Then she put her lips where her fingers had been, and kissed him. "We'll figure something out."

"Yippee!" Lizzie danced away to Sassy's stall. "Lucky, did you hear that?"

A huge smile split Foster's face as he looked down at Shelby. His arms tightened around her, bringing her body flush with his. "Yippee, indeed."

And then he kissed her for real, long and deep and bending her back, much to the amusement of their audience. The Shelby who'd come to Mustang Ridge might have pushed away, blushing. This wasn't professional, wasn't the kind of thing that happened in public back home—at least once you were over the age of eighteen or so, and got a clue. The woman she'd become here on the ranch, though, wrapped her arms around her cowboy and gave back as good as she got.

Ty hooted in approval and Stace clapped, grabbed Lizzie, and spun her until she threw her head back and laughed. The sound soared up and echoed in the barn, warming Shelby's heart as much as the rumble of Foster's chuckle heated her body.

This, she thought. This was her safe haven. Not the people or the place, but the knowledge that she could handle whatever came next.

"Shelby? You in there?" The half-panicked cry came from outside the barn.

She turned in Foster's arms. "Topper?"

The younger man skidded at the barn door. Not catching on that something big was happening, he waved furiously. "Come on! Hurry! Something bad is happening in the kitchen!"

Shelby hurried into the main house, thinking how quickly things could change. The last time she'd come up the porch stairs, she'd been miserable, convinced that everything she cared about had suddenly unraveled on her like a cheap sweater with its tag pulled off. And now she had Foster and Lizzie right behind her, and a whole new set of possibilities opening up in front of her.

It was incredible. Wonderful. Unbelievable.

Hers.

Then she swung through the door, and heard the yelling, loud and clear.

"You ruined my apple tarts!" Rose shrieked. "A whole batch of them, gone. Oh, my babies."

"Dra-ma," Foster sang softly behind Shelby as they double-timed it down the hallway. Near the end, he caught her arm, planted a quick kiss on her cheek, and said, "Lizzie and I will stay here, in case a quick get-away is needed."

In other words, in case the grown-ups stopped acting like grown-ups or Lizzie got worried, and he needed to beat a quick retreat.

She shot him a grateful glance. "Thanks."

As she stepped into the kitchen, Gran said, "You promised Krista that you'd leave the baking to me." Her voice was calmer and quieter but held a thread of steel.

The combatants were squared off over the butcher block counter, glaring at each other while Krista hovered in the background. Looking super relieved to see Shelby, she mouthed a silent *Help!*

Rose glanced over and narrowed her eyes. "Oh, great. Reinforcements. Have you come to gloat?" She looked nine feet tall in her toque, and like she could kick Shelby's butt if she decided to.

Deciding not to be intimidated, Shelby came around beside Gran, wrinkling her nose at the weird aroma coming from the cooling rack, which was full to overflowing with pastries that smelled more like enchiladas than apple anything. "That depends. What happened that's gloat-worthy?"

Rose flushed. "This . . . You . . . Urgh!"

Krista came up next to Shelby and said in a low voice, "Mom's cinnamon got switched out for ground ghost pepper."

"Oh," Shelby said, with a longer thought of *Ohh*. "That would explain the smell." Ghosts were the hottest peppers on record, and the powder most certainly wasn't intended to take the place of cinnamon.

"If you'd been sticking to the deal, you wouldn't have needed your cinnamon, would you?" Gran said in her "well, there you have it" voice.

"I could've been making pork chops with apple chutney!"

"Well, you weren't, were you? You were trying to show me up with your Food-Channel-of-the-week special."

"How dare you!"

Gran leaned in, eyes narrowed dangerously. "You think I don't know you tried to poison Herman?"

"Mom!" Krista gasped. "You didn't!"

"She did," Gran insisted. "If Shelby hadn't caught that she switched out the jars, we'd be having a very different conversation right now."

Shelby didn't notice it, she thought, *and this isn't a conversation. It's one step away from a kitchen cage fight.* But even the tension wasn't enough to bring down her mood. Not when she saw Foster and Lizzie peer around the edge of the hallway arch and give her a double thumbs-up. Giddy heat bubbled in her veins, and she was one step away from a Snoopy dance that would probably send Rose over the edge.

For the first time, though, Krista's mother looked uncertain, maybe even a little guilty. "I . . . I didn't. I just wanted—"

"You wanted him dead," Gran hissed, looking like she was enjoying herself now.

"No! I didn't. I just—"

"Ladies, ladies!" Foster strode into the room with Lizzie on his heels. "Let's not let this go further than you intend. You know what they say: it's all fun and games until somebody loses a pie."

The combatants turned to glare at him while Krista smothered a half-hysterical giggle. Shelby snagged Lizzie and tucked her near the wall so she was out of the line of fire if this boiled over and things turned physical—salad tongs at ten paces, maybe, or flying biscuits. Then she stepped up beside Foster and said, "He's right. What's more, you're family, which means you're going to have to find a way to deal with each other. So, as someone who's spent some time in the kitchen recently, I have a proposal." It had been percolating since her conversation with Krista last night, and might not be perfect, but it was a start.

Rose hesitated, but then nodded stiffly. "Go ahead, Shelly."

Shelby squelched the eye roll. "I vote that you institute blue tape and a schedule. The tape cuts the storage areas into three parts—Gran's, Rose's, and shared—and you two agree not to mess with each other's stuff. The schedule divides the kitchen hours into blocks—blue for Gran and red for Rose, or whatever you want. My first instinct is to say that Gran does the baking and sweets and Rose handles the savories. Or you alternate days. Whatever. The point is that you cross paths as little as possible."

"Shelby." Gran's voice wobbled with dismay. "My kitchen!"

"I know." She caught the older woman's hands and squeezed. "I know you want to do it all, but think about it. You keep telling me to do things for myself, but when was the last time you did the same thing?"

"But I don't—"

"Well, you should. Take an afternoon in town. Go riding with Arthur. Catch up with some friends. Be with the people you love."

"Go riding?" The concept seemed foreign.

To her surprise, it was Rose who said, "You know . . . it could work." She paused. "If you're willing to try it, Barbara, I'd be on board."

Gran wavered, but it was obvious she was thinking about it. "I don't know."

"Let's give it a shot," Krista urged, wrapping an arm around her shoulders. "Just a week, maybe two, and see how it goes."

Gran took a shuddering breath. "Okay. I guess . . . okay. We can try." But then her head came up and she locked on Shelby. "I'm going to need an assistant."

She didn't even hesitate. "You've got one."

"Really?"

"Yeah, really." Her grin felt like it lit her up from the inside out. "I'm staying—we're staying—another month to be with Foster . . . to be with all of you." She couldn't imagine leaving now, didn't want to. She wanted to stay right there at Mustang Ridge, with her daughter and the people who had become her family. Maybe she would even reach out and try again with her own family. If Gran, Krista, and Rose could make it work, maybe she and Mercy weren't that far off.

For now, though, this was her safe place. And, most of all, staying there with the people she loved would give her the time and room she and Foster needed to figure out if they were meant to be.

21

Mustang Ridge: Where family comes together.

One month later

"It's not much to look at." Foster's nerves jumped as the turnoff came into view, and he nearly hit the gas and kept going.

"Don't you dare drive by it again," Shelby warned from the other side of the truck. "I let you get away with it last week, but enough is enough." Her voice softened. "It'll be fine, cowboy. Lizzie and I can see past some bad paint and falling-down fences."

If that was what she was expecting, she was in for a big disappointment. "Well, there were a couple of leaks before the old—um, before Winslow had the plumbing shut off and the system drained out. And, well, there's some mold." Lots of mold. "A few spiders." Armies of them, actually, along with a platoon of mice. *Should've set out those traps last week.*

He'd subbed out the critical stuff, and had been working on getting the place fixed up in his off hours, but he hadn't wanted to sacrifice his time with Shelby when things were still up in the air. Which was part of the nerves, really.

"If you don't take us to your ranch today, we'll just come out here by ourselves when you're busy," Lizzie warned.

Shelby winced. "Way to keep a state secret, kid."

"Oops. Sorry."

"No, we're going." Foster eased up on the gas and turned down the drive. "We're going." Fingers crossed. Things had been great between him and Shelby, and in the him-Shelby-Lizzie department, but nothing was settled, really. Which had him sweating as the familiar landscape rolled by. The fencing was tired, but he'd shored up the wire and boards and trimmed down the worst of the verge. At the time, it'd felt like a huge improvement. Now, though, it felt like he hadn't done a damn thing.

You've gotta start somewhere, he reminded himself, as he'd been doing off and on for the past four weeks.

Vader whined as they crested the last hill, and Foster slowed way down. "Go on, Vader." The dog jumped down and ran ahead of them, barking his fool head off as they rounded the turn and the house came into view. It was gray and patched, and the roof had a decent sag, but the porch was wide and welcoming, and the barn behind it was in good shape. And there were good memories everywhere, at least for him.

Shelby reached across and touched his hand. "It's lovely."

"It's in the middle of nowhere."

"Mustang Ridge isn't that far."

"Forty minutes, maybe an hour."

"That's a short commute in Boston." She squeezed his fingers. "Besides, that's not what's important here. What's important is that it's lovely . . . and your grandpa would be proud of you."

His throat closed, but that was okay. He didn't need to say what she already understood. But at the same time, as he pulled up in front of the house, he was strung as tight as a greenie being trailered for the first time. He cleared his throat. "Welcome to the Double-Bar H, ladies."

"Yippee!" Lizzie was the first one out, dancing across the parking area with Vader bouncing beside her and then running on ahead, up the porch steps.

"Wait for us, Lizzie-kin," Shelby called. "Remember, you're not to go on or in any structure without Foster's permission. He knows what's safe around here and what isn't."

He slipped an arm around her waist. "What rule number is that?"

"I've lost count, but it might come under the umbrella 'don't be dumb' policy otherwise known as the Anti–Darwin Award Act."

"Ah. One of my favorites."

She grinned up at him. "Mine, too. It's just that sometimes it's so darn hard to figure out the difference between a really brilliant idea and a really dumb one."

"Which way are you leaning when it comes to me?"

"Brilliant." She reached up on her tiptoes to brush her lips across his, making his body tighten with need, even though they'd slipped away together not twelve hours earlier. He'd be counting the hours—as usual—until they could do it again.

"Come on, come on!" Lizzie bounced on her toes at the bottom of the porch stairs. "Vader's already gone inside!"

"He must not have heard the rule." Foster led the way up the steps and opened the door. "Ladies first."

Lizzie scooted in, but Shelby stopped just inside, turned back, and tugged him inside with her. "Hey, cowboy, stop stressing. How many times do I have to tell you that I'm tougher than I look? A leaky roof isn't going to scare me off."

"It's not the roof I'm worried about."

"Oh?"

Hell with it. He'd planned on waiting until she had seen the whole house, maybe even after their picnic lunch, giving her a chance to get over the "ohmigod, it needs so much work" and come back around to "it's lovely." But, really, it didn't matter what she thought of the Double-Bar H. That wouldn't change how he felt.

So, standing a couple of feet inside the front room of his falling-down family ranch, with its stained ceiling and cracked plaster, he just said it. "Shelby, I'm in love with you." It came out easier than he'd expected, feeling right. So he grinned and said it again, louder. "I love you."

Her eyes widened, then filled. They hadn't said it yet, holding off by some unspoken consent, or maybe because she was waiting for him to say it first. He hoped. Because as she stared at him, speechless, the nerves headed toward panic that she'd changed her mind about him, about them.

"Oh." She lifted a hand to her heart. "I love you, too. So very much."

The panic subsided, but the nerves remained. "Wait. I'm not done yet." Aware that Lizzie had circled back with Vader, that they were both watching with wide, interested eyes, he went down on one knee and pulled out the worn leather box he'd gotten out of safe-deposit a few days ago.

Grandpa, wish me luck.

Working the latch, he opened the box to reveal a square-cut diamond, brilliant in a simple setting that was worked with the Double-Bar H logo on either side.

She gaped. "*Foster.*"

"It was my grandma's. Now it's yours, if you'll wear it . . . and if you'll take me." He had thought of how he wanted to say this, how to tell her that he knew it was quick, that they still had things to work out, but that he was committed to her, to Lizzie, to the family they would make together. In the end, though, he was a simple guy with simple words. So he said, "Shelby, I love you like crazy. Will you marry me?"

Shelby stared at the ring, feeling the sturdy floorboards go unsteady beneath her feet, not because the house was coming down around them—though that was certainly a solid possibility—but because the pieces of her world were finally all falling into place, though not in any sort of pattern she would've expected at the beginning of the summer, when all she had been looking for was a place to sort things out with her daughter.

"Foster . . ." She couldn't breathe, couldn't find the words.

"Please say yes." He didn't look wary anymore, didn't look closed off. He looked like a man entirely in his element, as he did when he was working with the horses. Only he was here with her. And he loved her.

Suddenly, she could breathe again. The air rushed out of her, along with a word: "Yes."

His face lit. "Yes?"

"Absolutely, yes!" Her pulse hammered in her ears and the blood sang a happy chorus in her veins.

"Thank God." He rose and caught her against him in a whirling kiss.

"Woo-hoo!" Lizzie surged up to wrap her arms around them both, turning it into a family hug.

Embracing her tightly, he whispered, "Oh, sweetheart. You had me scared there for a minute."

"But not enough to spook and bolt?"

"Never." He slipped the ring on her finger, where it snugged into place like it had been made for her. "I'm well and truly gentled, darling. No more stampedes from me. I'm a family man now."

Easing away, he pulled out another, newer box and went down on both knees in front of Lizzie. "What do you say? Can I marry your mom?"

She grinned at him. "Duh."

"Excellent." He held out the box, then flipped it open. "This is yours."

Inside it gleamed a replica of the heirloom ring, threaded with a silvery chain. Lizzie's mouth opened in an *ooh*, and she said, "Is it mine?"

"All yours, if you'll let me be part of your family for good."

"Put it on me!"

Shelby couldn't stop grinning, didn't even try, as Foster draped the chain around Lizzie's throat and fumbled with the clasp. Her heart tugged as she thought of him doing that for her prom, her wedding . . . A shared future. And what a future it was, with him there with her, every step of the way.

He rose and cleared his throat. "Welcome to the Double-Bar H family, ladies. Because no matter where we live or what we do, we'll always be a part of this place."

Shelby saw the shadows in his eyes, though, the moment he braced himself for the bad news.

"About that." Heart singing, she pulled out a small cardboard box and held it out to him. "I've got something for you, too. It's not as shiny, but I think you'll like it."

"I'll love it." He took the box and shook it. "Light saber?"

"Maybe for Christmas, if you're a good boy."

"Deal." He popped open the box and frowned down at the business cards. She saw the moment he got it, the moment he saw.

The cards read *SB Advertising. Whether you're looking for talking lizards, a new jingle for your singing hot dogs, or the perfect pun to launch your new campaign, we're here to make you look good, and have fun doing it.* The address was the one they were standing in.

His eyes came up to hers. "You mean it?" His voice was thick with emotion.

"Hey, I bought business cards, didn't I?" She smiled. "Yes. I mean it. This is your home, and Lizzie and I are going to make it ours, too. We love it here in Wyoming . . . and we love you."

He caught her in a triumphant embrace and kissed her long and deep, while Lizzie and Vader spun in dizzying circles and made joyous noise. And when things finally quieted down, he said, "For the record, that ring is a binding contract. No bolting off after you get a good look at this place. It's like me—we both need some work."

She laughed. "I promise. No takesies backsies. Come on . . . show me our new home." And, hand in hand, they walked through the falling-down house, seeing the possibilities.

GRAN'S GREEN RANCH CHILI

(The Easy, Do-at-Home-with-
Grocery-Store-Ingredients Version)

Takes ~ 8-10 hours, but most of the time you're ignor-
ing it in the Crock-Pot. I like to cook the meat the night
before and then throw things together sometime before
lunch, for a fabulous chili dinner.

SERVES 6–8 PORTIONS, MAKES GREAT LEFTOVERS.

INGREDIENTS:

pork loin, beef pot roast, or similar meat, ~ 3–4 lbs.
two cloves of garlic, skinned and crushed
one packet of chili seasoning
one yellow onion, diced
1 Tbsp. butter or oil
2–4 Tbsp. flour
two 4-oz. cans of chopped fire-roasted chili peppers
one 7-oz. can of chopped jalapenos (use more chilis instead
for a milder flavor)
salt
Crock-Pot

REPARATION:

1. Place the meat in a pot, cover it liberally with water,

add garlic and $\frac{1}{3}$ of the chili packet to the water, and bring it to a boil. Reduce the heat until the water is just barely boiling. Let the meat simmer for ~ 1 hour. (Don't let the water boil off!)

2. Let the meat sit until it's cool enough to handle. One easy way is to put it in the fridge overnight. Alternatively, take the meat out of the liquid (called "stock liquid" below) and put it in the fridge for 30 minutes. (Save the stock liquid, though.)

3. Cook the diced onion in the butter/oil on medium heat until the onion pieces turn clear. On low heat, mix in ~$\frac{1}{4}$ cup of the stock liquid, then slowly stir in the flour until the mixture thickens. Remove the pan from the heat, add the chili peppers and jalapenos, and mix it all together. Put the mixture in the Crock-Pot.

4. Shred the meat with your fingers or a fork. Discard the fat, and mix the shredded meat with the onions and peppers in the Crock-Pot. Add more of the stock liquid if you want to adjust the consistency. Season it to taste with salt, pepper, or more of the chili packet (remember, you can always add more seasoning but you can't take it away, so be a little cautious!)

5. Set the Crock-Pot on low and cook for at least 5 hours.

6. Ring the dinner bell!

Serving suggestions:

Layer the chili in a bowl with shredded cheese and refried beans, top it with cilantro, scoop it up with nacho chips.

Roll the chili into a corn or flour tortilla with shredded cheese, shredded lettuce, diced tomatoes, sour cream, beans, and the sides of your choice for a whopping burrito.

And above all . . . have fun with it!

Now that you've enjoyed summer
at Mustang Ridge Ranch,
turn the page for a peek at the
next book in the series,

WINTER AT
MUSTANG RIDGE

Coming from Signet Eclipse in
January 2014.

With his assistant gone for the day and no overnight guests of the small- or large-animal variety,
the veterinary clinic was quiet by six. After a quick
phone call to his father—their usual "Yep it's cold. Nope
the fish aren't biting. How's the clinic?" routine—Nick
focused on banging out the last of the day's paperwork.

"Want some?" He broke a corner off the pizza slice
he'd been working on, and held it out to Cheesepuff.

The fat orange tabby gave the offering a suspicious
sniff, then turned away with a sidelong look that said,
Hypocrite.

Okay, so maybe he'd given Ted Dwyer a lecture on
feeding his hunting dogs table scraps not an hour ago.
And, yeah, the Puffmeister wasn't exactly svelte. But
still.

"What's a little pizza between friends? No? Your
loss, and more for me." Nick downed the last of the
day-old DiGiorno, washed it down with some root

beer, and let out a satisfied sigh. "I think that does it for today. Don't you? Want to roll upstairs?"

The cat flicked one ear back, then yawned.

"Your call. I'm heading up." Sure, another guy might be worried about getting caught talking to his cat, but a vet could get away with stuff like that without losing his man card.

After three-pointing the soda can in the recycling bin, Nick shucked off his "I'm in the office being all official" lab coat and headed across the office to hang it up. He was halfway across the room when the buzzer rang, letting him know someone was coming down the long driveway. A moment later, headlights crested the hill and lit the picture window out front.

"Guess I spoke too soon, huh?" But, hey, at least he was still downstairs and not in the shower wearing nothing but soap. Been there, done that. And besides, this was part of the deal when you ran a one-vet clinic and lived in the apartment upstairs. "Let's see what we have."

He pulled the coat back on, got it buttoned, and headed out into the reception area just as snow boots thudded on the front porch and the door swung open. A blast of frigid air swept in, haloing a bundled figure as sparkling ice crystals caught the light. The furry pink boots and five-foot-something height said female, possibly young, but the rest of the details got swallowed up in a huge pink parka, a blue wool hat, and a striped scarf.

But more important was the sight of the big, blanket-wrapped dog in her arms and the smears of blood on her coat.

Never a good sign.

Adrenaline kicked in. "Come in, come in. You can go straight back to Exam One."

Instead, she spun back at the sound of his voice, her bright blue eyes widening in the gap between hat and scarf. "You're not Doc!"

Maybe it was the adrenaline coming from the near miss with the truck plus a too-fast drive to the clinic, or the relief of getting there in one piece with the stray dog still breathing, but Jenny's mind blanked at the sight of the stranger standing in Doc's office.

Brain freeze. Did not compute.

He looked like a young Harrison Ford, with tousled brown hair, a square jaw, and sparkling hazel eyes. He was wearing jeans, a lab coat, and worn hiking boots. Okay, so maybe he didn't look all that much like Indy—there was no leather, fedora, or bullwhip in sight. But there was something about him that rooted her in place. And she wasn't one to grow roots.

Slightly uneven teeth flashed behind a charmingly crooked smile. "Doc Lopes retired and handed the practice over to me about six months ago. I'm Nick Masterson." Nodding to the blanket-wrapped bundle, he added, "Who do we have there?"

The question kicked her brain back into gear, bringing a flush and sidelining her surprise that Doc wasn't Doc anymore, and the new guy was hot.

"I don't know. He was up by our driveway. I was trying to get him, almost had him, but"—her voice cracked—"he got away from me and wound up under an eighteen-wheeler. I don't know how bad he was hit."

His eyes sharpened on her. "Are you okay?"

She shook her head no, then changed it to a nod. "I'm okay. But the dog—"

"I'll take him back and see what we've got." He held out broad, competent-looking hands to take the blanket-wrapped bundle. "Do you want to come with us?"

Swallowing a hard lump of emotion, she shook her head. "No. I'll . . . ah . . . I'll wait out here. Unless you need help?"

"Not for the initial look-see." He took the dog gently in his arms, showing none of the strain she had felt at lugging the fifty-some pounds of deadweight. "I'll be a few minutes."

He disappeared into one of the exam rooms, leaving her alone in the waiting area, surrounded by empty chairs, well-thumbed animal magazines, and posters that alternated between cutesy propaganda for adoption and menacing blowups of the life cycles of fleas.

Gravitating to the fleas, which looked like something out of *Aliens*, she stuck her hands in her pockets and read up on third-stage larvae. When she was done with the short paragraph, she couldn't have repeated any of it—her mind was stuck on the *varoom* of the truck and the way things had gone to hell in a split second.

If she had just held on to the dog, they'd be back at Mustang Ridge, sitting next to the woodstove right now. Or maybe tucking into Gran's chicken and biscuits.

"Hang in there, buddy," she said softly.

Part of her wished she had followed them into the

back room, but it wasn't like her being there would have helped. Besides, she needed a minute to regroup. She'd driven up here expecting old Doc Lopes, and instead got a guy who looked like he'd be right at home in her world.

Flea eggs take two to fourteen days to hatch. Hatching occurs only when the environmental conditions are exactly right for their survival.

"No problem there." Jenny sighed. "Winter in Wyoming isn't right for anything except making daiquiris." Not that she would want a frozen drink right now. She was only just beginning to thaw out in the clinic's warmth.

When conditions are hot and humid, the flea egg hatches and the larva emerges.

"They'd like Belize," she commented.

"Never been there."

"Oh!" She spun, flushing inside her layers when she found the vet standing behind her, looking amused.

"I talk to the cat all the time. Never tried the posters before." Taking pity on her, he continued. "I've had a look at the dog, and wanted to talk to you before we go any further."

The flush cooled. "Is it bad?"

"He's actually in pretty decent shape. It doesn't look like the truck wheel rolled over him, which is good, but I won't know how good until I take some X-rays and run a few blood tests. Beyond that, he's got a healing wire cut on a front paw and he's skinny as heck. I'd say it's been a while since he saw any love, though he's friendly enough that he must've had a family at some point."

Jenny's chest tightened. "Poor old guy."

"He's actually not that old. I'd say three or four years, which is going to be in his favor for recovery."

"Good." Relief came out of her in a whooshing breath. "That's good. Do what you can for him. I'll cover the bill and give him a home." Granted, she was making a promise that Krista and the rest of her family at the ranch would be keeping when she left, but any of them would've said the same thing.

The vet hesitated. "It could get expensive if the damage is worse than it looks."

"I'm good for it. X-rays, tests, surgery, whatever he needs."

"Is there someone you should check with first?"

"Are you trying to talk me out of it?" *Or fishing for info on whether I'm taken?* He wasn't wearing a ring, but she didn't think that was where it was coming from. Either way, the conversation was starting to feel out of sync, like she was missing something.

"I'm just making sure you know what you're getting into."

That was when she realized what was so strange. He wasn't treating her like she was an extension of Mustang Ridge, wasn't assuming that she knew as much as a lot of vet techs by virtue of being ranch born and bred.

Wow. Weird. And kind of nice, actually. "I can handle the dog and the bill. Run a tab, Doc, and let's get this party started."

A crooked smile crossed his face, making her think of Indy again. "Yes, ma'am." He turned away and headed for the reception desk. "I'm going to need you to fill out some paperwork. You can leave it on the desk, along with a number where I can reach you with an update."

"Can I wait here until the X-rays are done?" She didn't know where the impulse came from, but it felt right.

"It'll take some time."

A glance out the window warned that the snow was still falling, but the Jeep had four-wheel drive and there was no rush getting back. "Like you said, it's been a while since anybody cared about him. I'd like to wait."

He handed over a clipboard with a pen stuck at the top. "Make yourself comfortable. I'll be out with updates as warranted." With a half wave that wasn't quite a salute, he disappeared into the exam room.

Not letting herself glance back over at the fleas— Gawd, had he really caught her talking to a *poster*?— Jenny dropped into a chair and fumbled for the pen. It wasn't until her gloves got in the way that she realized she was boiling, and not just from embarrassment.

How had she not noticed that she was overheating inside her marshmallow of a coat and six-mile-long scarf? *Because for the past three days, you've spent way more time shivering than sweating*, she thought, and shucked off her vest, hat, and hoodie, piling them off to the side. Which left her sitting there in jeans and a clingy turquoise thermal that had come out of the high school section of her closet.

Suddenly feeling like something out of some fashion-intervention show—*next, we perform a fashion intervention on a twenty-seven-year-old videographer who still dresses like she's a teenager*—she dragged her fingers through her hair, like that was going to fix anything. She had asked for Audrey Hepburn, and with a little work she could come close to that mark. Add in some hat head, though, and she was more Sonic the Hedgehog than Hepburn.

And she was primping. Which was ridiculous.

Okay, so Nick Masterson was seriously yummy and he seemed like a nice guy, but she was back home at Mustang Ridge to work, not play. And he was a local.

"So not going there," she said, and got busy filling out the forms.